BLOOD TRAIL

WRITTEN IN STONE BOOK 2

DAVID RHODES

SEVERED PRESS
HOBART TASMANIA

BLOOD TRAIL

ISBN: 978-1-925840-77-3

ACKNOWLEDGEMENTS

Thanks to Linda for all of her encouragement.

Thanks to Tristy for her encouragement and some very good suggestions.

Thanks to Indiana University Professor, Earth and Atmospheric Sciences, P. David Polly for meeting with me and providing some very important information.

And special thanks to my wife Sarah for all of her support and understanding.

CHAPTER ONE
THE MENU

Skate looked up slowly and met the eyes that were staring at him. He didn't move. He didn't want to let him know what he was thinking, what he was about to do. Then he took a slow breath and moved his hand down as he spread the cards on the table. "Three tens," he said confidently. The others threw their cards down as he knew they would, but not Brownie. He got that look in his eyes and then he smiled, and Skate knew he had been suckered in again.

"Sorry, Skate," Brownie laughed as he threw his cards down. "Full boat, three aces and two eights, Bud. Looks like I win again."

As Brownie raked in the scattered dollars and candy bars, Hood slapped the table and complained, "That's five hands in a row, Brownie. If we weren't passing the deal, I'd think you were cheating."

Brownie just laughed again and replied, "Actually Hoodie that's eight in a row and about seventeen out of twenty. Sorry guys, I'm just on a lucky streak. You know you'll get a chance to win it all back and probably will. But today, I am king of the cards." He held up the deck as he riffed the cards and asked, "Another hand?"

Everyone was quiet for a second then Hood sniffed and said, "Yeah. Why not? What else are we going to do, and I need my money back to buy Christmas presents."

TexMex shook his head and told everyone, "I don't know amigos, I've lost too much money and I'm bored with this game. Brownie is too lucky today."

Skate dropped his head and bit his lip as he thought, "amigos"? From the day they met he had decided that TexMex wasn't as much Texas or Mexico as he liked to let on. But that was okay, none of them were what they wanted everyone to think they were. Brownie never talked about himself but sometimes when he drank too much it was obvious that he had been dodging someone, the law or a gang, before he was recruited. He had two tear drops tattooed at the corner of his right eye and though Skate knew the tattoo had different meanings, he never asked Brownie what they meant to him.

Brownie had also been a Walker the longest and sometimes his talk wasn't about moving around and staying low, it was about the "bad old days". He had seen a lot of people die when things first started, and he could describe every grisly and stomach-turning death in minute detail. That was good, it kept everyone from making mistakes. It had been over six months since a person died...so they joked about putting up a sign: 180 Days Without A Chomp.

Hood talked a lot about himself which made everyone else figure that he was lying. Some days he was from Louisiana and on others from somewhere in Maine. He had either been a car salesman, computer hacker or he was an out of work actor. Take your pick among those and another dozen possibilities. There was only one thing everyone agreed on about Hood, he always had money to lose, and it was always someone else's.

Though he didn't talk about death as much as Brownie did, he had seen a few. He seemed to take some pride in the fact that some of his modification suggestions for the shells and bubbles had been used. And he always told everyone before a Walk that this was his last one. At least he had been saying it for the three months that Skate and been on board. But it was just talk.

And Skate knew that no one actually knew that much about him either. Son of a wealthy businessman who was always working, he doubted if anyone on the outside was even concerned about his disappearance. It had been almost three years since he had just left. Of course, he had taken a lot of money when he disappeared, but he had wasted all of it. Then life got rough. But that didn't seem to matter now that he was a Walker. They were tight and where else could you get the adrenaline rush they did?

So, if Brownie had his secrets, they all did. Were they all square pegs driven into the same round hole...or was it the other way around? It didn't really matter, it was always the same; do your job, stay alive, get the rush, collect your money and then wait for the next call. It wasn't too bad.

Of course, he hadn't seen anyone die yet.

Skate watched closely as Hood dealt the cards but really didn't know what to look for even if someone was cheating. As the last card settled in front of him he picked up his hand and almost shouted. Four jacks. He took a slow breath and did his best not to give away his hand. As he looked up Brownie was looking at him and asked, "How many?"

Skate was quiet for a moment then shook his head and replied, "Just one I guess."

Everyone laughed as Hood threw him a card and Brownie said, "Never try for an inside straight, Skate, never."

"Well, you got to try sometime don't you?" Skate asked, and everyone just shook their heads.

As Skate started thinking about how he was going to bet the hand, Paycheck came over the intercom, "Alright guys, we're almost ready. Start getting dressed and I'll brief you in a minute. Let's get this *Rex* bite then go home."

Skate folded his cards as Brownie said, "Leave your cards where they are boys, when we get back something tells me I'm going to win again."

"Maybe I got that straight," Skate said. He smiled as everyone laughed loudly and Brownie slapped him on the back.

They quickly pulled on what Skate called their long underwear. Thin stretchy material that kept them a little cooler when the bubble went up and that was all that counted. As Skate stretched his underwear into place, TexMex snorted, "Hood, why don't you lose some weight. The rest of us make this stuff look good, I mean we could be underwear models, but man you have one bad body." Hood just snorted as everyone else said, "he's right".

It only took a second to slide the earpiece in which was all they needed for hearing and speaking. Worked on some type of bone vibration or conduction or something like that. Then the helmet with the cameras, the utility belt and finally the thick-soled hiking boots. There was only one more piece of equipment then, the DOPE. Skate was always amazed by it. The DOPE just looked like a piece of thin, clear plastic that was as wide as your back. It ran from the waist up to just above the neck. Its real name was Dorsal Protection Equipment, so of course it was called DOPE by everyone.

Skate looked around at Hood, Brownie and TexMex, and wondered what they were thinking about as they put on their DOPE. The *Rex* that was supposed to be out there? If they were coming back? Or how silly four men looked when the DOPE deployed, and it looked like they were hiding inside a piece of bubble gum?

Brownie started in on Hood again but before Hood could reply, Paycheck entered the room and asked, "Everybody doing okay?"

Everyone liked Paycheck and quickly answered "Yeah". Brownie added, "I'm feeling lucky today, man, tell me this is going to be good."

"Well, it's good and bad."

"How's that?" Brownie asked. "Tell us the bad first."

Paycheck quickly replied, "Well, like we told everyone earlier, there's a big *Rex* out there floating in and out of tracking range. We haven't had an attack by a *Rex* yet so we're hoping it keeps coming this way. We did a drone check and it's about two hundred yards away and if it starts to turn away we're going to make some noise to lure it in. So, one of you is going to get chomped by a *Rex*. That's got to be bad somehow."

Everyone became silent as they slowly checked and then rechecked how tight the straps of their DOPE was. Paycheck looked from one to the other then said, "Guys, it will be okay. A *Rex* can't get through your DOPE."

"How big is it?" Hood asked.

"About sixteen feet tall, maybe forty feet or so long."

TexMex whistled and said nervously, "That's big, man, that's big. Nothing smaller to warm up with?"

"Guys, it's going to be okay. Really. We know its bite strength and your DOPE has it covered."

"You left out the good part," Hood told Paycheck.

"I talked with my brother and whoever takes the attack gets a bonus. We know it's tough on you physically and mentally too. That's good isn't it?"

Brownie snapped his fingers and said, "Then let's get this done. I've been lucky all day and I know it's not going to stop now. Bring it on."

Paycheck smiled and said, "Go get him," and walked upstairs. Skate stuck some candy bars in his utility belt and as they started down the ramp that led to the outside Hood suddenly stopped and asked, "Wait a minute. Brownie. What did you win that last hand with?"

"Full house," Brownie replied.

"I know that, but what were your cards?"

"Three aces and two eights."

TexMex quietly said, "The dead man's hand."

Hood shook his head as he looked at Brownie and agreed, "Dead man's hand, aces and eights. Brownie you need to stay inside."

Brownie told them, "I see what's going on. And let you take the bonus? Not today, Hoodie, not today."

Hood shook his head and replied, "It's on you. Dead man's hand, that's all I'm saying."

Paycheck cut in through the earpiece, "Gentlemen, if you are finished discussing Wild Bill Hickok's last card game, let's move out. There's a *Rex* out there waiting for lunch and one of you is on the menu."

Hood laughed and replied, "You know, I like that. The Menu. Instead of Walkers call us 'The Menu' from now on."

"We'll get called something else if we don't get out there," TexMex said. "Come on, let's go."

As they continued down the ramp an opening appeared in the grey wall in front of them. Not a door or a gate, part of the wall just disappeared. Paycheck called the wall a curtain and it was the bubble that encased the Unit and kept them safe. It didn't have to be grey though; it could be any color or even clear. It was just like a giant DOPE and just one more thing that Skate always marveled at. But he didn't marvel much now, there was a *Rex* out there and it was getting closer. And they weren't running away from it, they were going to walk right up to it and see which one of them took the bite.

Skate was always nervous just before they walked through the wall. He thought about the candy bars he was carrying for a second and realized he wasn't hungry anymore. Then just before he stepped through the opening he paused and took a deep breath. He always thought about the first time three months ago, when he still couldn't quite believe they were going to time travel and face off against dinosaurs. Didn't take long before he found out it was true.

He could still see the teeth, the size of the mouth, how unbelievably fast it was. But it hadn't gotten through the shell. The DOPE didn't look like a bubble back then; it was more like a turtle shell. None of the '*saurs* had ever gotten through the turtle shell. Sure, there had been a few bumps and bruises but nothing he couldn't live with. Plus, he had joined the club that day. The 'I survived a dinosaur attack' club. But still, he always worried. It was a small club and not a lot of members were still alive. Only four.

Brownie had all those stories about the beginning of the testing, when it really was "let's just see what happens". The turtle shells hadn't stopped the teeth in the beginning. And when they got that part right, someone tried on an *Ankylosaurus* and that clubbed tail. The big ones were the problem. They couldn't break through the shells with their strikes but anyone inside had their internal organs turned to jelly as the shock wave passed through them. And someone had been in a shell when one of the big ones with the long necks had laid down on top of him. Hood said it had weighed a hundred tons and there was nothing left of the shell or the guy that had been in it. Skate didn't quite believe that, but you never knew.

That was a long time ago though, before he was hired. Everything worked the way it was supposed to now. No problems. Still, before stepping through the wall he paused, this was the moment that he always had to get past, that first step outside the safety of the Unit. Into the open and whatever lay in front of them. After all, it wasn't *if* they got attacked, it was *when*. He got his breath under control and kept up with the others.

He knew they paused at the wall too. He kept telling himself, "No problems".

Well, there was one problem, the heat. As he walked outside it swept over him like lava was being poured on him. Today they were in a jungle and it was hot. Very hot. Or maybe it was the humidity. He was already sweating uncontrollably. Better than not sweating though, then you had to worry about heat stroke. And the DOPE was worse. They needed some airflow in the bubbles and he heard they were working on it, some type of ventilation or something, but the system wasn't ready yet. But how would you do that without giving the 'saurs something to get a good bite on? He decided he'd rather be hot and sweaty.

Paycheck came across loudly, "Okay, move forward and keep a look out. We'll tell you when the Rex is close, but it might decide to come in fast. Remember, once you anchor down you'll be okay, but if you are slow and it gets to you before you're in the ground…well, we'll need some new Walkers won't we? Or a new Menu." There was a short chuckle then the radio went silent as they fought their way through a tangle of giant leaves.

Skate thought it had to be worse than anything in Africa. He couldn't see three feet in front of him. And sometimes the sound was deafening. Not roaring or growling from animals, it was the insects and the little chirps and yelps from all the smaller saurs that you couldn't see. He liked to see them, at least he knew where they were and what they looked like then.

The only good part was he knew the area was being scanned and if there was anything close by, Paycheck would let them know. Nothing was going to ambush them. He paused for a second to look at a giant red flower and got caught on a thorn. By the time he pulled himself free the others were several yards ahead. Brownie was in front followed by TexMex and Hood.

Paycheck came over the radio and said, "Keep up with them, Skate. All of you, keep close. You're almost to the target area."

Of course, that set everyone loose. "Yeah, c'mon Skate, quit hanging back," Hood said. "You have to earn your money here, not get it from Daddy. It's not Christmas yet either."

"It's not Christmas anywhere around here," TexMex chimed in as he swatted at the thick heavy leaves they were walking through. "And Santa couldn't get through here."

"Santa and his reindeer would all get eaten," Brownie laughed nervously.

"Better them than us," Hood cut in. "How much farther, Paycheck? Will it be Paradise this time?"

"You tell me," Paycheck answered. "You're there. Keep a sharp lookout."

Skate guessed they had walked about a hundred feet from the Unit when they broke through some taller brush and short trees and moved into an open space. It wasn't Paradise. In front of them was a small, dirty beach which was about as long as a football field and maybe one hundred feet wide. There was a dark forest surrounding it on three sides and everyone wondered which part the big *Rex* was in. And, if it liked to check the beach. That was probably where everything came to get a drink and Skate had seen enough wildlife specials to know what that meant.

Skate looked to his left at the water and wondered why any animal would come to this spot. It was just a little inlet off of a nice-looking lake, or was it an ocean, with blue water he could see farther down the beach. But the water here was black with dark brown swirls and was covered in places with some type of greenish mossy looking stuff. The water was kept in constant shade by the long heavily leafed branches of some surrounding tall trees. There were insects flying and crawling everywhere and the whole place smelled bad, rotten. This was not where Skate would have come for a swim. It wasn't Paradise.

Then Skate had a thought, why would the *Rex* or any other animal come here? If this was an ocean it was salt water and dinosaurs didn't drink salt water. Then he paused and wondered if they did.

He looked up and the sky was blue and there were a few clouds floating slowly across it. He could have been back home but the *Pteranodons* flying overhead told him he wasn't. *Pteranodons*, not *Pterodactyls* like they saw last time. And though there were birds, they didn't look like the birds Skate was used to looking at.

Then Paycheck was back in their ears and he sounded excited, "I think our *Rex* is about to come through the trees, maybe a hundred feet to the right of you."

"I got some movement in the trees right in front of me," Brownie said excitedly a few seconds later and everyone immediately fanned out. You didn't need to have anyone bumping into you while you were trying to set your DOPE. Skate looked down and made sure it was dirt or sand he was on. The DOPE would not drive into rock.

Then there it was and they all froze for a moment as it came out of the tree line. Each of them thought it was the biggest thing they had ever seen. "Look at the size of its head," Hood said quietly. Skate thought it looked just like he imagined, mean and hungry.

No one moved, and the *Rex* didn't pay any attention to them as it looked from side to side. Its mosaic patterned skin was mostly brown and tan but on both sides of its jaw and running down its back there was a red and green splotchy pattern. Slowly it started to turn back into the forest.

"Someone better move," Paycheck called out and Brownie started running forward. The *Rex* spun around and took one step forward then stopped.

Brownie started moving from side to side like a crab and Hood came over the radio with, "Brownie, no way your DOPE is going to fit over you."

"Why is that?" Brownie asked.

"Because your balls are too big my friend. You can have all of *that*."

Brownie laughed and said, "Paycheck, get that bonus ready". As he walked forward again he called out, "Come on big boy, come and get some of this."

The *Rex* launched forward at an amazing speed, but Brownie dropped to the ground and the DOPE covered him in an instant. Three feet of protection all around him but it was the anchors that really made the DOPE work. Eight long, curved, hardened-plastic spikes that shot deep into the ground to hold the DOPE in place.

Paycheck called out, "Brownie, stay low and tight." Like Paycheck had to say that to any of them, Skate thought. Don't tell us something we already know. We know the drill, stay low and if you get killed you don't get paid. Brownie answered back, "Yeah, yeah, I know, I know. It can chew all it wants."

The *Rex* tore into the DOPE with a fury but because the bubble dampened outside sound they could all hear Brownie clearly calling out excitedly through their ear pieces, "This is wild, I mean wild. Unbelievable. Its teeth are driving into the bubble but it's not breaking. They're huge, but they're not breaking through. I'm completely safe. I'm not even getting knocked around much. Fantastic."

"Then it looks like we have a winner," Paycheck said. "When it gets done you come in while everyone else hangs out for a while and we'll see what we can get to -" In the background, they all heard a shrill alarm and Paycheck asking himself, "What are *they* doing?"

Then the *Rex* suddenly stopped its attack and turned its head toward the jungle and in an instant it ran from the clearing. "What's up?" Brownie asked.

Paycheck was on quickly, "Well, I'm not sure why the big *Rex* left, but there are three smaller *'saurs* coming toward you. I wouldn't think the big *Rex* would -" Then one of the new animals walked onto the beach.

"Multiple *'saurs*?*"*, Skate thought. That had never happened before and instinctively he knew this was bad. He hoped the smart people that were upgrading the DOPEs had already thought about something like this.

"Is that another *Rex*?" Hood asked. "I thought you said it was little."

"I think it is a *Rex*," Paycheck said. "But it's only about twelve feet tall, a juvenile I think. See, it has feathers on its arms and legs."

"But aren't there two more?" Skate asked.

"And what does that mean?" Brownie asked.

Before there was an answer the new *Rex* was on Brownie who just asked, "What's this one think it can do that its big brother couldn't? Get lost, junior, I want to go in and collect my bonus."

Then the other two came into the clearing and Paycheck said, "Looks like three juvenile *Rexes*. The others still have some feathers too. And, since there are three of them, maybe two more of you will get attacked."

"And all get bonuses?" TexMex asked.

"Juvenile ones," Paycheck replied.

But one of the other *Rexes,* slightly bigger than the others, took an interest in Brownie's DOPE too and tried to pull it away from the first one. As they twisted the DOPE back and forth Brownie started screaming, "It's starting to tear, it's starting to rip." Suddenly it did and the two *Rexes* staggered backwards with pieces of the bubble flapping in their mouths. Brownie flipped out of the DOPE and landed on his head and shoulders and was still for a moment. Then he slowly staggered to his feet. He stood there, dazed and swaying slowly from side to side.

Hood started screaming, "Brownie, run for the Unit. Run, run." But Brownie didn't appear to hear him and as he slowly raised his hand to his head the larger *Rex* ran over to him and bit down on him all the way to the waist. As it picked Brownie up it shook its head and one of Brownie's legs dropped down to the ground. As the big *Rex* tilted its head back and swallowed, one of the other *Rexes* ran over and scooped up the leg.

As the *Rexes* turned their heads toward Hood, TexMex and Skate, all of them dropped down and activated their DOPEs. Skate could hear the heavy breathing...the panicked breathing...the 'I'm about to die' breathing. No one moved as one *Rex* jumped on TexMex and then the other two tore into his bubble also. TexMex started screaming, "No, no. Please. Someone draw them away from me." He seemed to have better luck for a few seconds longer as he shouted, "It's holding," Then his bubble suddenly split open and TexMex tumbled out. But he hadn't landed on his head and as he jumped up he knew he couldn't make it back to the Unit. He tried to run into the jungle instead but that didn't work either as all three of the *Rexes* moved in for the kill.

Hood shouted, "Let's go while they have their backs to us," and jumped up and started running. It should have worked since the *Rexes* were busy with TexMex. Should have. But just as Skate was thinking of running too he saw the dark, dirty water suddenly boil near the shoreline and out of it came the biggest, ugliest alligator he had ever seen. Fifty feet at least with a head that was the size of a small car. Bigger than the head of the adult *Rex*. Then all Skate could see were rows of gleaming teeth as the animal snapped down on Hood. Skate expected it to grab Hood's DOPE and chew on it for a while but instead the bubble immediately popped and collapsed with one loud snap of the giant jaws. The DOPE and Hood disappeared inside the jaws in the blink of an eye and the monster backed up and disappeared into the water.

Skate blew the DOPE spikes out of the ground and ran. It seemed like forever and he kept thinking he heard something behind him, something was after him. But nothing got him. He tripped on something but stayed on his feet. Then he was through the opening and he knew he was safe inside the Unit. He dropped to his knees, shaking and sobbing as he tried to catch his breath.

A second later Paycheck was in his ear saying, "You're okay, Skate. Take some deep breaths and get yourself under control. Take it easy." Skate slowly stood up, his legs were weak and wobbly, but he was still alive. He started walking toward the Unit but Steve said, "Hang on Skate, you left something behind."

"What?" Skate asked, he was confused.

"Look behind you." Skate turned around and at first he didn't see it, then there it was. One of his boots about twenty feet outside the barrier. He looked down at his feet, he had run right out of one of his boots when he tripped. "Hang on," Steve said quietly, "let me check something." A few seconds later he continued, "Okay Skate, nothing on the screen within two hundred yards except those *Rexes* and they're starting to move away. Grab it quick and get back inside."

Skate knew there wasn't any reason to argue, you did what Steve said, he was the boss. Still, he paused at the wall, took a deep breath, and then moved out as quickly as he could. He picked up the boot and when he turned around the Unit was just a shimmering blur. Then it was gone and there was nothing left but jungle where it had been. He stood completely still, it had to be a joke. Steve and Paycheck wouldn't leave him like that.

He put on his boot and stared at the empty space for several more minutes trying to will the Unit to return. Then he moved into the jungle and crouched down under some broad leaves. As more time ticked by, he knew it wasn't a joke. They weren't coming back for him.

He started shaking but this time he knew it wasn't just from the adrenaline of watching the attacks. He had just seen his friends horribly killed but it was knowing there was no way he could live for more than a few days in this terrible place that started him shaking. Then, as a small dinosaur ran across in front of him he suddenly thought he could catch food, he could build a fire, he could survive.

Then just as quickly he realized he couldn't. He didn't have any weapons. How could he live when he would never know what was going to suddenly appear from some dark shadowy place to rip him apart? He couldn't even get water, there were monsters there too. And he was all alone.

Behind him he heard a roar and decided he needed to move away from the sound and try and find some place to hide. He wasn't ready to die just yet. As he moved out from under the leaves he turned away from the beach area, he knew he couldn't go that way.

He picked his way through the thick brush and though he scared up a *'saur* every once in a while, everything was small and quickly moved away from him. Slowly the trees and vegetation thinned out and the walking became easier. He realized though that he was more exposed, and he suddenly felt like something was watching him. He walked quicker and had to stop himself from breaking into a run. He wasn't faster than anything that might be behind him and all it would do was tire him out.

Skate was looking back over his shoulder when he stumbled and pitched forward. He stayed on his feet but realized he was now looking over a cliff at a drop of about fifty feet. He stepped back and knelt down as he caught his breath. He turned his head around quickly, had he heard something or not? It was open space behind him and there was nothing there.

He took a deep breath then moved closer to the edge of the cliff and looked down. No way to climb down the rocky wall, he would have to walk along the rim, but that would not leave him any way to escape if he was attacked. Then he saw something. Just a few feet to his left, part of the wall jutted out creating a two-foot wide ledge, maybe down a drop of eight feet from the top of the cliff. And there was some type of indentation there, it looked like the opening of a cave or at least something deep enough to hide in. The way the rocks looked between the rim and the ledge, Skate thought he could climb down to the ledge and back up easily.

He took a deep breath then climbed quickly down to the ledge and then back up again. No problem. He walked carefully along the ledge and looked inside the opening and found it was the smallest cave he had ever seen. It was only about five feet deep and four feet high, but he hoped it would keep him out of the sight of anything that was looking for something to eat. He didn't see any signs that an animal lived in the cave or at least nothing had for a while. As he started to sit down he realized the deflated DOPE was still attached to his back and the now deflated plastic bubble had been hanging behind him, dragging on the ground. It would have slowed him down if he had tried to run. He unstrapped the DOPE and set it down in the cave opening, just in case something did want to get in.

Then he took off the utility belt and emptied all of the pouches and laid everything he had on the rocky floor. There were the two candy bars he had picked up after the poker game and two protein bars that he always kept in the utility belt. There was a small knife in case he had to cut his way out of the bubble, a flashlight, four cans of water, and a small green tank of oxygen to open and bleed O^2 into the bubble in case they were trapped for a long time.

In other words, he thought, nothing. Food for a couple of days and you couldn't call the knife any type of weapon, not when everything that wanted to eat you had claws and teeth that were longer than the blade. The cans could be refilled which meant he could get water, but that meant getting close to a pond or river to fill them, and that wasn't anything he wanted to do at the moment. And the oxygen? He cracked the valve open for a second and thought it made the cave smell better. At least it was oxygen from his time.

There was a roll of thunder outside and he was glad he had found some shelter. In a few minutes it was raining hard, but the cave stayed dry. The temperature dropped, and Skate started feeling cool, so he wrapped the plastic around him as he ate one of the candy bars. It was soft from melting in the heat, but he didn't care about that, he only cared that now he had less food. He was going to have to think of a way to hunt or scavenge. As night came he could hear the unseen animals moving and all the sounds they made. Some of those sounds ended suddenly. He leaned back against the cave wall and dropped into a fitful sleep.

Skate didn't leave the cave for two days then was finally driven out by hunger and thirst. He crawled over the rim of the gorge slowly and moved inland. He found a small stream and carefully drank the water. It had an odd taste, but he didn't care. He drank until he couldn't drink any more then filled the cans. Downstream he saw some small animals moving about and approached them by crawling through some thick brush. They didn't seem to notice as he reached out cautiously and stole five fairly large eggs from a nest. He placed them in the pouches on the utility belt and made his way back to the cave.

Again, he stayed inside for two more days. The raw eggs didn't taste bad, but he hated the texture, runny and slippery. But you can't gag on the only food you have. He moved out again when he was too hungry and thirsty to stay inside. He knew that every second he was outside the cave he was in danger, but he had to have food and water. He thought for a moment about walking toward the sea but decided it would be too much of a risk to walk that far from his shelter.

Skate returned to the small stream and as he was drinking he was surprised when he realized there were several animals less than a hundred feet downstream from him. They had just suddenly appeared and were quiet as they moved through the water. He recognized them as duckbills and he knew they were herbivores. They didn't seem to be paying any attention to him, and when they suddenly snapped their heads up and looked around, Skate quickly moved back into the brush.

He didn't know what they were, but he was glad he had hidden. The two animals that concerned the duckbills were about five feet tall and mostly gray with green tiger-like stripes. They circled the duckbills for a few seconds, but they weren't big enough to take on the much larger duckbills, so they disappeared across the stream and into the jungle.

Skate waited for several minutes then continued to the nesting area and stole four more eggs before one of the nesting animals saw him. It was faster than he thought it would be and bit savagely into his hand with its beak-like mouth. He cried out and as other animals ran toward him he stood and ran for the cave. It took him a few minutes before he realized he was making a lot of noise. He slowed down and as he caught his breath there was a noise behind him that suddenly stopped. It was quiet. Were the small animals still after him? No. Something had spotted him but as he looked behind him he couldn't see anything. Still, he knew.

Skate thought for a moment, he was about two hundred feet from the cave. Too far. He started forward and when he came to a small clearing he stopped beside a tree and put down two of the eggs, maybe that would interest whatever was after him. Near him was a long branch that had fallen to the ground.

He picked it up then started walking and then, as fear started filling him, he started to trot. After about fifty feet Skate heard growling and fighting behind him and he turned again to look. The noise stopped and then the animals stepped out into the open. There were three of them, about three feet tall and standing on two legs with long, curved claws for toes. Their sharp teeth glittered in the sunlight as they chittered back and forth. Multiple 'saurs. The beach flashed through his mind and he shook his head to clear his thoughts. But he kept thinking, 'this isn't good'.

As Skate tried to slowly move away from them they all swung their heads toward him and started forward. He pulled the last eggs from his pack and set them down then turned and ran. He looked back and watched as the animals ran past the eggs without stopping, they were closing on him and he knew he had to stop and fight.

He turned suddenly and swung the branch. Though it surprised the animals, only the closest one was hit and that was only a glancing blow as it veered away. He got the branch back in front of him just in time to partially deflect another animal that had jumped toward his chest. The force of the attack broke the branch in half and almost knocked Skate down. Before he could recover the third animal sunk its teeth into his leg and began shaking its head violently side to side. Skate brought both halves of the branch down on the animal's head and it fell away from him and didn't move.

There was a hiss behind him and Skate turned to see one animal still ready to attack and another with an arm hanging limply by its side. Skate thought for a second and then began beating the animal that was lying on the ground with the two parts of the branch. Then he turned toward the other two and struck the ground in front of them several times. The injured animal turned and ran and after a final hiss, so did the uninjured one.

Skate dropped to a knee catching his breath and closed his eyes trying to control himself. After a couple of deep breaths, he looked down and was startled by the blood he saw on the ground. And then he realized it was his blood. He was bleeding from a deep gash in his chest but what alarmed him the most was the blood spurting from his right lower leg. The 'saur he killed had ripped open an artery. He tore off his shirt and tied it tightly around the upper half of his calf muscle; the blood stopped spurting but didn't stop seeping from the wound. He could also plainly see that there were three tears in his right side and that two of them exposed ribs.

His first thought was to get back to the cave and see how he could take care of the wounds but after just two steps he knew that wasn't the answer. Too much pain and now the leg was bleeding faster. It only took him another second to realize that he only had a few minutes left to live. Then just as quickly he thought there was one hope left, maybe Steve and Paycheck would return. It was his only hope. Without thinking, he slowly started walking back to where he had been left behind. Back to the Unit, to the only possibility of life.

With every step though it began getting darker and he soon started stumbling and falling. As darkness replaced his sight he fell one last time and couldn't get up. He propped himself up on an elbow and hoarsely shouted, "Help", but there was no answer. Instead, as he collapsed back to the ground, all he saw was a dark shape moving toward him.

CHAPTER TWO
IT'S A HISTORY BOOK

Steve waited for his brother to come up the stairs. Ben was going to be mad. He was always mad when Steve did something he didn't like so he knew this would be no exception. Ben stepped quickly into the room and sat down and didn't say anything for a full minute. Finally, he slapped a hand on the table and asked, "Steve, why did you just leave him behind like that? The others were dead, actually gone, so I can understand why we didn't waste time with them. But Skate was alive, we didn't have to leave him behind like that."

Steve waited for a few seconds to let Ben cool down then replied, "First, he was probably toasted after that. He saw three people horribly killed. How long would it be before we could use him again? And, we didn't need him telling anyone else what happened. The next team is ready, they've been out a few times already and they make these guys look like what they were, amateurs.

"Next, every Walker we've had has died. Every one. He just got lucky today, in fact all of them had been lucky. Can you believe it had been six months and not even a scratch? Today was just a long time coming, and don't fool yourself, it was coming soon enough." He paused and looked at the lights flashing on a holographic screen then continued, "Besides, Skate's been dead now for over thirty million years, so who cares."

Ben shook his head and started, "I just think – "

Steve cut in, "That's right, you think. You think you're supposed to be nice. You're "Paycheck", you think you should be one of them. You think things could be different. They can't. We take people that life has passed by and give them some type of life for a few days or even months. We feed them and give them some place to stay. Then we tell them about the adventure they're going to have and all the money they are going to make. Everyone's dream. They take a few Walks and die like they were supposed to, not homeless in some alley."

Ben snorted and said, "I guarantee you none of them have thought about how great it was they were being ripped apart by some 'saur instead of dying from an alcohol binge. They all died screaming."

Now Steve was getting mad, "You knew what we were going to do right from the start. *You* have helped plan every step. No Walker comes back. That's what I said, and you didn't disagree. Then we *both* agreed we would be spending less money if they didn't come back and more importantly, we wouldn't have to wonder about anyone talking. Now you do still agree with all of that, *don't you?"*

Something about how Steve spoke the last sentence caught Ben's attention. He could almost see the Unit disappearing as it left him behind in some deadly prehistoric land. Quickly he replied, "No, no, I understand what we have to do. I just don't think we should be the ones to do the killing. Leave it to the animals."

"Brother Ben, we do let the animals kill them. We bring them and then we have them take the Walk. We just don't stick around and watch it happen every time. But, if you are wanting to split hairs, I'll go along with you, I won't leave anyone behind again. Okay?"

"Yeah, okay," Ben agreed.

"Besides," Steve continued, "the new team is ready like I said. The Team, not Walkers. They are well organized and professional. They do things right and soon they will have the equipment they need. Think about that and your Walkers, you didn't even have them going out with the newest protection. How were you rationalizing that? They were dead when they stepped outside today and it doesn't matter how they died. Are we good now?"

"Yeah, we're good."

"Data," Steve said and immediately there was a list of numbers floating in the air in front of them. "Look at that," Steve continued. "The shells stood up to the first *Rex* and even for a few seconds when two were clamping down. Couldn't take the shearing force though as they twisted and pulled all at the same time in different directions."

Ben leaned forward and nodded, "Look at the numbers spike. Otto didn't think of that, did he?"

"Why would he?" Steve asked. "What was the information that we had on the *T-Rex*? Solitary hunters. Loners. Territorial and would fight to keep other *Rexes* out. We suddenly had three of them appear and not only were they not fighting each other, they actually joined together to get their prey just like a pack of lions or wolves. They were cooperating and seemed to be social, if we can apply human values to them based on the short period of time that we observed them."

"And that's not the information we had," Ben agreed. "Otto will need all this new data and it will take him some time to get new specs out and into a finished working product. How is he doing with our last information?"

"Good, he loves the challenge. Better airflow and communication in the shells. He's about to send out work orders so I'll have him wait until he figures this out too. Let's get it all out at once, not piecemeal."

Ben nodded and said, "Tell him to work on the assumption that the shear force will be higher, a lot higher. Those *Rexes* looked small, we need to plan for fully grown animals chewing on the same shell."

Steve replied, "I agree and that brings up the second animal, the one that came out of the water. Look at this bite force chart."

"It's unbelievable," Ben said. "Over 20,000 pounds before the readings stopped. That's almost twice as much as a *Rex* bite. Now I understand why it snapped through that shell like it wasn't there. Do you know what it was?"

"Not yet," Steve told him. "But now we know not to just scan the land anymore. Next time we need to look everywhere, what's in the sea doesn't stay in the sea."

"But it wasn't a fish."

"No, and I'm not sure what it was. Looked like a croc."

Ben nodded and said, "We need help. I've said it all along. We're just making things up as we go along. If we had someone with the right information from the beginning, we'd already be signing those military contracts. We needed help with the shells, so we got Otto. What we need now is someone who knows dinosaurs."

"You're right and I know just who to get. Did you read the book I gave you?"

"What?"

"*Written in Stone*, did you read it?"

"Sure. It took me a while with all of the work we have to do," Ben said. "What does that have to do with anything? Why was it important that I read the book?"

"Because it's a true story."

Ben stared at Steve for a moment then asked, "What exactly do you mean?"

"The author, Danny Jameston, is a police officer for Buckland College. It's a small school out west but it has a very reputable paleontology department headed by Dr. Ron Fontana. He has a daughter, Lauren, who is also a paleontologist of some renown herself."

"Okay, what am I missing?"

"Now you know who three of the characters in that book are; Danny is Don, Ron is Roy and Lauren is Laura."

"So, you're saying they traveled in time?"

"Most definitely. Them, and everyone else in the book actually made those three Walks, I mean jumps, Charles Dawson called them jumps."

"Charles Dawson is…?"

"Charles Dawson is Carlton in the book. He developed their time machine. From what I have learned he has taken a lot of jumps to a lot of different times. He recorded all of them, has an extensive library of almost every major event since 1950 and a few before then."

Ben nodded and said, "So it's a history book. No wonder I liked it."

Steve thought for a second and replied, "Yes, exactly. History. Or science-fact. In whatever way you want to think of it, it's a true story."

"So, all of those people survived dinosaur attacks and even the asteroid? Hard to believe."

"But us time traveling isn't?"

"Okay, you have me there" Ben agreed.

"Listen, the scientists knew the animals, knew what to watch for. Jameston and one of the bad guys shot *T-Rexes* and all of them fought different *'saurs* when they jumped. They seemed to know what they were doing at least most of the time. And, they came back."

"Not all of them?"

"Right, not all of them. Some of them didn't make it back. But we only want to speak to the smart ones. The winners."

Ben leaned back in his chair and asked, "How do you know all this?"

"Do you remember a scientist, Dr. Gary Taggit, used to stop by the house?"

"Maybe, if I saw him."

"I met him at some function or other and he took a liking to me, or at least to my money. He was a paleontologist and was always needing financing for various expeditions as he called them. Digging up bones, trying to find something new and interesting. Can't say it was a complete waste of money, he did give me several interesting fossils.

"Then one day he just stopped coming around. I heard he was onto something important and I did a little checking, I wanted to make sure he wasn't holding out on me, that I was getting all I should for my investments. I found out he had hooked up with some local small-time operators and was working on a big dig out west. Seemed to me he was conning someone, and I wanted to make sure I wasn't next. So, I just kept watch for him to see what he came back with. Like I said, some of it might have been owed to me.

"But he never came back. He just fell off the face of the Earth. Now I was really curious. What was so big that he didn't need my help anymore? He wasn't hiding from me, no one had seen him for months. There wasn't anyone at his home so of course I let myself in, several times. And what I found in his notes and on his computer was startling and unbelievable. He had found proof of time travel, fossilized words in rock that was written millions of years ago, and he was going back in time with some time traveler."

"Carlton, I mean Charles Dawson?" Ben said.

"Yes."

Ben paused for a moment then said, "Taggit, Gattig, wait…I got it now. So, the book is an actual account of their time travel and all the things that really happened. What happened to all of their records and samples?"

"Gone," Steve replied. "Taggit tried to leave them behind but he failed. Got killed for it actually. But, I told you, with Taggit out of the way I found out a lot of things from his work. From there I turned to Dawson and that's where the real treasure came from. He didn't even have anyone watching his house or any type of alarm system. His idea of security was so poor I just walked right in and looked at anything I needed to. The same thing Lauren Fontana did in the book. I couldn't believe it."

"What if you had gotten caught? You should have just had someone hack him."

"Couldn't happen. I didn't just show up at his house without a plan. I had information, I knew when he wasn't going to be there and for how long. After all, I already knew from the book that there was no security. I got the information without needing to bring someone else into our plan. Then, I turned the information into reality for us and set about upgrading everything with Otto."

"Aren't you afraid that Otto will get some plans of his own?"

"As you know I put things I need out to different companies, so no one can ever connect the dots. Otto only knows small parts of what I am doing. We are the only ones who know exactly what is going on and that it will make us rich."

"It will," Ben smiled. "It will. But back to the book?"

"You said we need someone who knows dinosaurs. I agree with you. But I think we need someone who knows the animals and time travel."

"Dawson?"

"No, he's just a scientist and though a remarkable one, he doesn't have the expertise we need. We need a paleontologist, we want Dr. Ron Fontana."

Ben leaned forward and asked, "How are we going to get him?"

"I think if I just talk to him, one on one, I can get him interested in what we are doing. You know he was the first one to want to go out after Taggit kidnapped them. He's excitable and a little unpredictable. He wants to know things, things you can only get from being in the field."

"What about his daughter?"

Steve replied, "We don't need her anywhere around when we talk to Ron Fontana. She seems to be too pragmatic, too much of a 'there's only one way of doing things' type of person. And, she didn't seem to be too thrilled with time travel. She is hooked up with Dawson now though."

"Did Dawson stop travel?" Ben asked.

"No, but he has slowed down considerably. Doesn't do much."

"How do you know that?"

"You know I have my source that keeps me informed of things."

"Now he's someone you need to watch out for. He's only interested in what you will do for him."

Steve nodded, "I know, I know. But he's in Dawson's house several times a week and no one suspects a thing."

"I think we should try to get Dawson too," Ben suggested.

Steve scoffed, "I don't think so. I think I can safely say I know more about time travel now than he does or will. I'm not interested in him at all."

"What about the author, that Danny guy. You said he killed a *Rex*, must be a tough guy."

"I'm not sure about him. Yes, Danny shot a *Rex* and didn't back down from anything. But, if the book he wrote is completely truthful then he's all about right and wrong. That wouldn't make him a good fit for us since we, uh, cut corners here and there."

"Like leaving Skate behind," Ben said. As Steve clenched his jaw, Ben added quickly, "I'm not bringing it up again, I'm just saying that's an example of what he might not like." Quickly he changed the subject, "What about the locals Taggit used? Can we get them?"

Steve looked hard at Ben for a moment then said, "Going back to Danny for a second, Taggit got the drop on him in the end so I'm not sure he is as smart as we need him to be. And the locals didn't make it back, remember? Pete and some girl and a couple of other guys. So, I want to speak with Ron Fontana alone. Make him understand we just need his expertise, hopefully get him excited and we'll have our information. In and out and we drop him off at his front door."

"Will we?" Ben asked.

"Of course," Steve replied. "We might need him again. Deep down I think he wants to know what dinosaurs were really like. He liked the jumps, he liked it all. If we can get him alone then we may be able to use him more than once."

"I'll read the book again," Ben said as he stood up and walked to a work station. But he wasn't sure he believed anything Steve had just said about not leaving anyone behind. Still, things were working out just like Steve had said they would. They had a lot of money. A lot. All thanks to Steve going back in time and making some lucrative investments in all the right stocks at all the right times. Of course, it took a lot of money to fund what they were doing. Otto's experiments were very costly, but he did come up with some unbelievable inventions.

But now they were adding an extra expense with the mercenaries. The Team. He agreed with Steve, they were good, but how much could they keep to themselves? What if they talked or did something stupid? He paused for a moment as he realized that apparently that was what Gattig, or Taggit, or whatever, did. He hoped Steve had thought about that. Then he laughed to himself, Steve always thought about everything.

Ever since they were kids Steve had been the smart one. While Ben was out baling hay or chopping wood, Steve would be thinking. And he always came up with some plan that required little effort on his part but usually made him more money than Ben made. There wasn't any jealousy though. Ben just accepted things, even when Steve, who was four years younger, joined him in the same high school classes. He still remembered the day Steve told a teacher he was wrong about some math problem and the teacher had sarcastically told him to prove it. Steve just walked up and did. He corrected the teacher's equation then said, "And I've been thinking about..." and just started writing numbers and symbols. He wrote for a long time and then Steve was taken from the class and was put in a college, all for free.

Ben lost contact with Steve for a while and when he graduated high school he couldn't afford to go to college. But he was tough from years of hard work and knew how to stay focused and get things done. He started a home repair company that was successful, and he was well liked by his customers and employees.

Then one day Steve came back. As they shook hands, Ben saw he was still the big brother in height but Steve out-weighed him now. "Too much sitting around," Ben had told him, and Steve just smiled and said, "I have a present for you." It was a brand-new car and Ben didn't know what to say so Steve did all the talking. He told Ben how he was rich and how he wanted Ben to run his company for him. That part was too much work and it wasn't what Steve was interested in. "We'll be rich together," Steve told him.

And he was right. From the beginning Steve knew what direction to take and Ben knew how to get the most out of the workers. All types of projects which eventually led to their business, EXENCO. They all made money. Then one day Steve had called him in for a talk. The talk. At first Ben thought that Steve had gone crazy. He was talking about time travel and how he was ready to do a test. Ben had agreed to go just so he could then convince Steve he had been working too hard and he needed a rest.

Steve drove to a remote area on some land that Ben remembered they had purchased over his objections. What would they ever need it for? In a matter of minutes, he knew. It had been fantastic, unbelievable, something that even now he had a hard time accepting. But it was true, Steve had devised a way to travel through time.

With this new information, they worked even harder. Ben didn't see Steve for weeks as they each worked on their own projects. Then they would meet and compare notes and sometimes test what Steve had invented and what Ben had built. But soon Ben couldn't keep up, couldn't understand what was needed. He hadn't argued when Otto was brought in to help. Otto was a genius, right next to his brother, the two smartest people Ben had ever known.

Things began moving at a breakneck pace, as projects got bigger and better and then they needed a team of field operators. "Walkers," Steve called them. It was the hardest part for Ben to accept. Using street people, the unemployed, to take the walks, many times to what Ben knew was their certain death. But Steve had convinced him, or maybe the money did, that it was okay. The people they chose were on their last legs anyway. They had actually given them a better life, even if it was just for a few weeks, before they met their inevitable death.

But then Steve needed better "Walkers". People who could think a little and weren't afraid to take chances. A new breed of unemployed person. They weren't as hard to find as Ben thought they would be. When Steve started to leave them behind though Ben had balked. There were long arguments which Steve finally won, to a degree. Part of the reason was they were still doing the "Walkers" a favor, giving them more than they had. But Ben knew some of them could have made something better for themselves with the money that they were promised. So, in the end, it was the money that convinced Ben and he knew that made him as bad as Steve.

And now there was the military unit. Well, not exactly military. The unit was made up of ex-military men and women who knew how to get things done and if needed, blow things up that got too close. They were professional and seemed loyal to Steve. "The Team". Ben wondered if that would change if they knew what happened to the other "Walkers". Ben knew that Steve was only loyal to him.

Steve watched Ben walk away and as he absent-mindedly started working on something, he wondered if it was time for Ben to go. He had outlived his usefulness a long time ago. He had needed Ben at first, he was great at organizing and motivating anyone. But Steve was the smart one, the important one. He had received scholarships to prestigious universities, won awards, graduated with top honors and had been pursued by companies for his intellect.

But he had known that was not what he wanted, he needed to be his own boss. He had better ideas than anyone else and had made a lot of money. There was one problem though, no one that worked with him liked him because he was too much of a snob and too distant. Steve had to agree with that and so he had reached out to Ben and Steve had to admit the move helped them both.

Then he had met Taggit or met him again. Taggit said they had met a few times in college, but Steve didn't remember and decided he was lying. But he had taken some paleontology classes and enjoyed what Taggit told him about his research. He had funded a few things then really got curious when he searched Taggit's home...and then Dawson's.

Dawson's research was unparalleled and at first left him stunned. But what if it was all just smoke and mirrors? How could anyone travel through time? As he read Danny's book though he realized everything was real and copied everything Dawson had done. Within a month he was experimenting with his own time travel machine built to Dawson's plans – then he gave them some much-needed updates.

Poor Ben couldn't keep up. Steve had known the day would come, but he quickly found Otto, Dr. Otto Witted. No one else but Otto could create exactly what Steve asked for. He was a genius. Not to his own level of course, but a genius none the less.

But with genius comes expense and now the Team needed money for training, weapons and a host of other things that only Ben seemed to understand. He shook his head, he laughed at the Team behind their backs. They were good, very good, but so smug and conceited. He thought it was funny that they referred to themselves as *the* Team because they had been out a few times and survived. They hadn't really done anything yet, a few short walks and a couple of DOPE bites. But they would see more soon. A lot more.

The bell sounded, and he realized they were back in Florida in real time. As he walked out of the Unit, Ben caught up with him and asked, "What's the schedule?"

"A few Walks over the next few days and then I'm going to contact Dr. Fontana. We might be doing something major soon, within six months I hope. So, stay ready."

"When haven't I been?" Ben asked as he slapped Steve on the shoulder. "Are you coming by on Christmas?"

Steve seemed surprised and asked, "What? Christmas?"

"Yeah, Christmas. I know there's no snow on the ground but it's that time of year. You really didn't know?"

Steve laughed and replied, "No, I really didn't know. I'll see you at Christmas."

"Okay," Ben answered and then he was out the door.

Steve turned and walked through a small office where he found Otto and quickly briefed him on what had happened. He finished with, "Otto, now you know what I know, and I'll have all the stats waiting for you. I need the DOPEs to be tougher, a lot tougher, and resistant to shear force you haven't thought of yet. And we still don't know what it was that came out of the water, but I need to know if we can test its bite without getting someone killed."

"Yes, sir," Otto replied. "I've also been thinking about a design change for our military friends. With your permission, sir, I would like to -"

"You have my permission, Otto. You know what I need, and you have never let me down yet. Give it a shot, jump onto it with both feet. I want to have a time frame for when it will be completed. Order whatever you need."

As Otto walked out of the room he said, "Thank you, sir, will do."

Steve continued on and as he opened a door to the warehouse, he was surprised to find Otto standing in front of him in the darkened room. "Didn't you just go the other way?" Steve asked.

"Yes, I did, sir. But, I hope you don't mind, I jumped onto what you wanted with both feet. Let me tell you what I did, and I guess then you can tell me if I shouldn't have."

"Okay," Steve replied slowly.

"Today was the first time you ever asked me to provide a time frame for a project, so I knew it was important. The instructions and field data you provided me took me in some different directions altogether. I worked non-stop for the next two weeks at home on new equipment designs to meet your needs. Then I wrote up the orders for everything and when I heard Ben was going back a year or so for some personal reasons I asked him to mail some packets for me. These packets were to various manufacturers with detailed instructions to create the items you needed.

"Ben mailed the packets and this morning all of it was delivered to me. I mean, this me, not the one that is already on the way home for the next two weeks."

"I think I understand," Steve said slowly. "So, what have you done?"

Otto turned on the storage room light and Steve was surprised to see it was half-filled with boxes and tarp-covered objects. "Show me," he said. Otto pulled a tarp away and Steve was surprised to see what looked like a small rocket. "What is that?"

"It will get our satellite up quicker and is easier to control."

"Okay," Steve said. As he pulled back another tarp he said, "These drones look different."

"You know the problem you told me about, the *Pterodactyls* attacking the drones? This can take the cameras to a height that the *Pterodactyls* don't fly. These new drones are heavier and can carry larger cameras. Better video and a better warning system for approaching dinosaurs. The new cameras have infrared capabilities too, so they will be useful at night."

Otto opened a crate and continued, "The new DOPEs are tougher than anything we had before and anything you're going to run into. And I mean anything, including whatever it was that came out of the water. Plus, the new ventilation I told you I was working on and a better ear piece sound system. The new DOPEs are smaller and lighter too, fit closer to whoever has one on. But they are tough, a new fiber I came up with. Oh, and they have some camouflage capability just like the Unit. Not as long lasting, but if they can't see you they can't eat you.

"I updated the DOPE's defense capabilities too. Wait until you see what they can do, but here is what they look like." Otto opened up a crate and pulled out a flat piece of plastic that looked like a DOPE but was definitely different. There were pieces of plastic dangling from it.

"Is it broken?" Steve asked.

"Watch," Otto replied and shook the DOPE hard and threw it out in front of him. When it landed it had taken the shape of a DOPE but there were six, foot-long spikes, sticking out of the top of it.

"That's different," Steve said. "Those look sharp."

"Sharp? Yes, but that's not all. They pack a punch with an electrical shocking capability that should get any attacking dinosaur's attention."

Steve touched the end of a spike and said, "I bet I don't want to feel that, do I?"

Otto nodded and replied, "No, sir. It's made to stop a *Rex*, I'm not sure what it would do to you."

"Probably kill me."

"There's a ton of other stuff too sir, well, more like three tons. Food, fluid replacement, weapons, ammunition, and the new tactical uniforms work with the DOPEs, the Team doesn't have to wear special clothing. I've updated the drones and bots so that when they are linked they set up a perimeter alarm also. You and Ben should be able to track anything that is within 300-yard radius on land, or in the water. The higher you take the drones allows you to track animals outside of 500 yards and of course watch them approach or move away.

"Sir, I know how important this Walk is to you. It could be what gets you the military contract. I hope I didn't go too far."

"Too far?" Steve asked. "This is unbelievable, amazing. A few minutes ago, I was hoping you could have all this done in six months, but realistically a year. And now it's already done and...and just amazing. Does Major Donald know about this yet?"

"No sir.

Steve pulled out his phone, put it on speaker, and in a second was asking, "Major, what are you and the Team doing tomorrow?"

"Training sir. Another day in paradise."

Steve nodded his head and said, "I see. I just wanted to let you know that I'm standing here with Otto and he has some new toys for you, a lot of new toys. It's the equipment you've been asking for. No, that's incorrect, isn't it, Otto. It's *more* than just the equipment the Major has been asking for."

"*Really!*" was the quick reply. "Otto, did I get most of the things I asked for?"

Otto smiled and said, "No, you got *all* of the things you asked for, plus more. A lot more. And I don't mind bragging a little and saying that you'll be pleased with what you now have."

"Otto, I have never known you to brag so I can only believe I will be amazed."

"I'll see you early tomorrow?" Otto asked.

"Yes, sir," Major Donald snapped and hung up.

Steve put his phone away and said, "Otto, you have outdone yourself. You did not go too far, and I'll bet Major Donald and the Team will be extremely pleased. I'll bet she's contacting all of them right now."

Otto smiled again and started to say something else then dropped his head and turned away quickly.

"What's on your mind, Otto?" Steve asked. He smiled and continued, "If it's a raise, I think you'll get it."

"No, it's not that. You treat me better than I could have ever hoped for. No, I was..." Otto started then paused. He took a deep breath and continued, "I was wondering, I mean you can say no of course, but I was wondering if I could go with you next time, or one of these times? Back in time." He looked down at the floor and continued, "I didn't used to be that interested in what you did, but now I would like to see how my inventions actually work in the field. I'd like to go back in time and see first-hand what needs updating or discarding. I'd be able to form better ideas about what is needed. Plus, it seems exciting."

Steve put a hand on Otto's shoulder and told him, "Of course you can go. You're a member of my team. Think how valuable you are to me, to the Team, you're even more valuable than Ben and that's saying a lot. If you want to go and watch what we do then just be ready, it could be any time." He looked at all the new equipment again and added, "Maybe just a few days."

"Thank you. Thank you, sir," Otto said. Then his phone buzzed, and he nodded his head as he looked at the screen. "It's Major Donald. I bet she wants to know how soon they can start." As he answered his phone, Steve saw Otto was smiling.

Steve smiled too and walked quickly through the warehouse and offices out to his car. He looked up at the blue sky and felt the heat of the day. Was it almost Christmas? Ben was right, it just didn't seem like it.

His phone buzzed, and he answered quickly and asked, "Something new?" He listened for a moment then said, "I understand, I want to look at everything you have." He glanced at his phone and said, "Okay, I got the photos and will check them later. I'll transfer your pay and a bonus to your account in just a few minutes. I'll check back with you soon."

Steve hung up and smiled; maybe it would be a merry Christmas.

CHAPTER THREE
NORMAL REACTIONS

She stopped. To move another inch, to even blink an eye, could mean a sudden, horrible death. She breathed slowly, trying not to make any noise, but for some reason it was hard to take a breath. She didn't know why, and she started to gasp. But she knew she shouldn't, she had to be quiet.

She listened for noises but they all seemed muffled now and she couldn't tell what was far away or what was too close. She fought to keep the fear down and for a moment she was able to control herself, then she felt it building up. Panic. She tried taking deep breaths but only gasped harder and louder. She was making too much noise. Then she heard the sound she dreaded, footsteps running…toward her. She jumped up but got caught in a tangle of vines and leaves. She tried to push through them, but she couldn't, they were everywhere, tightening around her arms and legs.

Then she heard the hiss behind her and there it was. Glowing red eyes and glinting white teeth tipped with blood. It moved toward her slowly and opened its mouth wider and wider until she could see nothing else as she struggled to get away. She thrashed wildly at the vines and thrust her arm toward the gaping mouth, trying to push it away. She tried to scream as her arm disappeared inside of the mouth. With a lunge she pulled away…and woke up.

Lauren found herself on her hands and knees in the middle of the bed, the covers wrapped tightly around her. As she tore them away from her she began crying and couldn't stop. She was used to the dreams, but they were getting more violent and terribly real lately. She sat on the edge of the bed and took deep breaths as she slowly got herself under control. Why was this happening? It was the holidays and Dad and Lisa were flying in. Danny was already here, and he and Charles were…and then she knew what was wrong.

Charles was spending more and more time jumping and if he wasn't jumping he was in the workshop. And sometimes she didn't know where he was. Their time together was disappearing, it was almost gone completely now. She knew he still loved her, but things had changed. In the beginning she had still gone on jumps with him and she thought it was exciting. But little by little her concerns about accidentally changing the timeline had taken over. Finally, she told him she didn't want to jump anymore and asked him to stop too. They talked it out and she finally agreed that he could jump a few more times because he still had some projects he needed to complete.

But that was two years ago and there was no sign that Charles was slowing down. How was taking Danny to a baseball game working on a project? And Lauren had found out he was renting a condo just a couple of miles away. Why? Was there someone living in it? Was there someone else? She had put things off for too long, had been too afraid of what she might find out. She took another deep breath; after Christmas they would have to talk again. She just couldn't keep going on like this.

Lauren dressed and went downstairs. The tree looked great with all the decorations and the presents stacked around it, but she didn't feel any holiday cheer. She hoped she could keep it from the others. Then Aria came in smiling and singing and when she saw Lauren she asked, "How are you today, Lauren? Just five days until Christmas, isn't that wonderful?"

Lauren couldn't help smiling as she replied, "It is wonderful, Aria, it is. And the house looks beautiful, thank you so much."

"It is my job and my pleasure, Lauren. I love this house so much I would almost take care of it for free." Then she laughed and continued, "But only almost."

"I wouldn't want you and Tony to take care of it for free. You do too much for us, cleaning, driving us around, keeping us on time for things and so much more. That's why one of your Christmas presents is a raise."

"Thank you, Lauren, but – "

"Sorry," Lauren cut in, "no buts. I know you are trying to get back into college and I want to help out as much as I can. You won't accept a loan, so I'll give you a raise instead."

"I don't know what to say, you are so kind."

Lauren picked up a box from under the Christmas tree and said, "Here is your real present, do you want to open it now?"

"No, I like to wait until Christmas to open presents. I'm a traditional kind of girl I guess."

"Then please take it home with you. Where is Tony? I want to give him his present too."

"You know how he is, everything has to be just right. He'll be along in a moment."

Tony was moving very quietly downstairs and he couldn't help looking over his shoulder as he paused outside the door. He listened for a few seconds, but he didn't hear any voices from inside the room. He was nervous, this was the first time he had gone into the room when there was someone else in the house. As he pulled the item out of his pocket he almost dropped it but just managed to hold on. It looked like a small flashlight, two inches long, and it fit easily into the palm of his hand. He held it about an inch in front of the retinal scanner and pressed a small button on the end of the device. Tony was surprised, instead of a beam of light coming out like he had expected, five small, different colored beams came out. He held the beams steady in the center of the scanner lens and watched as they started spinning and changing colors. It only took a few seconds and the door opened.

Tony put the device back in his pocket and quickly entered. The room lights automatically came on, so he had no problem walking to a large table in the center and finding what he was looking for. He had no idea what it was, but it was something new, so he had been asked to take some photos of it. He took out his cell phone and took several shots from different angles and also a short video. If it looked interesting enough he knew he would be asked to scan it later. When he was done he glanced around quickly to see if there was anything else new but there wasn't. Then he saw the box of scrap metal Charles had accidentally set in front of the surveillance camera. He moved the box out of the way and pushed the camera further back under some shelves. Couldn't be too careful.

As always, he paused for a second to look at the corner of the room, at the open space with its exposed twisted beams and missing bricks. Tony always wondered what had gone wrong there and Boss had actually come to the house once just to look at the wreckage. He shook his head and wondered if maybe Boss had some bricks missing too, then he walked out of the room pulling the door shut behind him. Too easy.

Tony walked up the stairs and as he got closer to the main room he heard Lauren ask, "What are you doing for Christmas?"

Aria answered, "I'll be at home with the family. Tony has a girlfriend, Paula, and he'll be at her apartment some of the time, but he'll be home a lot too."

As Tony walked into the room Lauren said, "Tony, I hear you have a girlfriend. When did this happen?"

"A couple of months ago, Lauren."

"And I'm just now hearing about it? Please bring her over sometime."

"Well, maybe."

"We'll all be here on New Year's Eve. Why don't you stop by just for a few minutes that afternoon? You too, Aria. I know you probably have plans for that night but if you have time we'd love to have you stop by."

Tony hung his head slightly and replied, "We'll do that, ma'am, I mean Lauren. We'll bring Mom with us too."

"That's wonderful," Lauren told him. Then she handed him a small wrapped package and continued, "Now here's your present and I'll let Aria tell you about your raise. Other than New Year's Eve I don't want to see either one of you back here for two weeks. Have a great time off."

"We will," Aria said as they walked out the door and toward their cars. "Isn't Lauren wonderful?" she asked Tony. "I want to be like her, so kind and understanding."

Tony paused by his car and looked down at the present for a second then tossed it into the back seat. He looked up and said, "Mom, we're just workers to people like her. What you think is kind and understanding, I think is condescending. You think she likes us, that we're special. We're not. We just happen to work for her but think about it, it could have been anyone. We were just lucky."

Aria sniffed and said, "You know that's not true. We both know what is condescending and what isn't. She's not, and neither is Charles. They are nice people. And so are all of their friends. I like all of them."

"Whatever."

"Pick me up on New Year's Eve okay? I do want to visit. And if you aren't going to come over, then let me know."

"Yeah, okay."

"How is Paula?"

Tony smiled and said, "She's great."

"There's my big boy," Aria said. "See you at the house." Tony nodded and couldn't help smiling again as Aria drove away.

Charles leaned forward and watched intently. He was surprised to find he was so interested in the outcome. He felt the heat on the back of his neck, so he tilted his head slightly, so the brim of his hat kept the sun off it. He glanced to his right at Danny and heard him pleading under his breath, "Come on, Pops, come on."

Charles smiled and stared back out at the field as the batter dug in. The pitcher checked the runner on second then threw toward home and the umpire called, "Ball one". Danny nodded his head and clenched his fists. The batter swung at the next pitch but didn't get all of it and he popped it foul along the first base side. "Hang it there, hang in," Danny said louder. Then he shouted, "Straighten one out, come on." That fired the sparse crowd up and everyone joined in shouting encouragement.

The batter nodded his head and dug in again and slowly swung the bat over the plate a couple of times. The pitcher checked the runner again and then delivered the pitch. The crack of the bat let everyone know the ball had been hit hard and as it bounced in the outfield grass and rolled quickly between the outfielders, the runner on second scored easily. The crowd applauded and as some of them moved out onto the field Charles and Danny stood up and started to turn away. Then Danny took one last look at the players, took a deep breath, then they walked toward the pasture where the car was parked just beyond the left field fence.

As they got in the car Charles noticed Danny had a tear running down his cheek. Charles put a hand on his shoulder and said, "Your dad really came through. That was a great game."

"It was," Danny agreed as he drove out of the field. "But..." Charles let the silence go until Danny continued, "But it's almost the end of the Negro Leagues. Did you see the crowd? Just a handful of people, almost none. Dad's too old now for a look from the majors and he's about to move to Clear View and start working as a janitor at Buckland University. What if...?"

"Well you never would have met the Fontanas and then we would never have met. You wouldn't have gone on the jumps with us and you wouldn't have written your book. We wouldn't be here watching your dad play ball and –"

"And seeing Grandad again," Danny cut in. "He was sitting behind the plate. I wanted to walk over to him and say something to him, just one more conversation. You know he died suddenly, a surprise. Just one more talk." Danny smiled and continued, "But at least I did get to see him and hey, Dad got the big hit and won the game. You're right, I have to keep remembering, the past has to be what it is, or was. I'll be okay, Charles."

"I know you will be and remember, I set the camera down next to me, so you'll have the whole game on video."

Danny smiled and said, "That's true, I will. Thanks, Charles. I'm feeling better already." Charles smiled back, but he wasn't sure Danny was telling the truth.

Lauren watched as the golf cart drove slowly down the drive toward the house from the building where the time machine was. As it got closer she opened the door and waved and as they parked and walked up she asked, "How was the game, Danny?"

"Great," he replied. "Dad got the winning hit in the bottom of the ninth."

"Wow, I wish I would have been there." Then she saw the look that Charles gave her and wished she hadn't said that. You shouldn't say you wanted to time travel when you didn't.

"When do Ron and Lisa get here?" Danny asked. "I've been so excited about going to the game I almost forgot we were all getting together today."

"They're getting here about dinner time," Lauren said. "They'll be in and out during the next week or so but basically they will be here until after New Year's, just like you. It's going to be the longest we've all been together since, well, the jumps. The longest time together in years."

Danny nodded and said, "Sounds great, it really does. I think I'll go to my room and take a shower and a nap. I'll be back down in a little while."

As Danny went upstairs, Charles said, "It'll be good to have everyone here. How long has it been?"

"We've only seen Dad and Lisa once since last Christmas. It was June, and they were supposed to come back for the 4th but didn't make it." Lauren sighed, "I wish they'd settle down, maybe buy a house close by."

"They like their privacy."

"I know but Dad's getting older and I worry about him…and I miss him."

Charles put a hand on her shoulder and said, "I know. We'll talk to them some this week, no pressure, just see if we can get them to at least think about it. You know, there are several houses not far from here that I bet they would like."

"Yes, let's sneak up on them and make them think it's their idea."

"Sounds like a plan."

"Good. Now I think I'm going to take a nap too," Lauren said with a yawn.

"I'll be up to join you in a few minutes," Charles told her.

Lauren stopped and asked, "You're not going to jump again are you?"

"No, I just need to finish up a couple of things in the basement then I'll be up."

"Promise?"

"Promise."

As Tony drove away from his mom, he said loudly, "Call Steve's cell."

The call was answered quickly by a man who asked, "Something new?"

"Yes. Sending you photos now," Tony said as he hit a button on his phone.

There was a pause and he was told, "Okay, I got the photos and will check them later. I'll transfer your pay and a bonus to your account in just a few minutes. I'll check back with you soon."

"Okay, I'm –," but the man disconnected the call before Tony could say anything else.

Lauren woke and saw that Charles had come and laid down just like he said he would. He was sleeping but still looked tired. What was wrong with them? They were always tired. As she got up Charles woke and said, "I'll be down in just a minute."

As Lauren walked downstairs she heard a noise and ran to the back door. "They're here," Lauren called out as she opened the door. Then she rushed forward and shouted, "Dad," as she gave him a long hug.

Ron hugged her back and said, "It's good to see you, how are you Lauren?"

"Great," Lauren told him as she kissed his cheek. "What about you?"

"We've been great too," Ron said.

Lisa stepped up beside Ron and said, "We have, and we've been so busy." She hugged Lauren and said, "We've missed you, we're sorry it's been so long."

Lauren took Lisa's hand and said, "We've missed you too. But get inside, Charles and Danny are waiting for you." There were more hugs and kisses and Lauren helped Ron bring in some presents from the car and put them under the tree. Then she called out, "Dinner will be served in just a few minutes, go sit at the table and I'll be right out with the chicken."

"I'll help," Lisa and Danny both said, and they disappeared into the kitchen as Ron and Charles sat down.

"You look tired," Ron said.

Charles smiled and replied, "I am a little tired. Maybe a lot. I'm…I'm catching up on things and some other things have come up now and, well…well there are just not enough hours in the day so sometimes I have to make them."

Ron nodded and said, "I understand, I truly do. But I've been able to cut back some and with Lisa I've had more fun since, since we, you know, we…"

"Jumped."

"Yes, since we jumped. I'm still working and going into the field, but every day is an adventure with Lisa and I'm looking at things differently than I used to. You should try it."

Charles nodded his head but before he could say anything the food was being placed on the table and Lauren was giggling as she asked, "My father did what?"

"I admit it," Ron said. "Whatever Lisa said, I did it."

"I don't doubt it," Lauren said. "But really, a nudist camp?"

"That's all she's mentioned? Well then really, a nudist camp. A liberating experience."

"What else is there to talk about?" Danny asked.

"Nothing nude, I mean new," Ron replied, and everyone laughed.

As they ate Lisa remarked, "You know every time I visit here, I'm always amazed at how big this house is."

"Can you believe," Lauren answered, "that when Dad and I first came here Charles lived in this house all by himself? Most of the rooms were shut off and he just opened them every once in a while. When he thought of it anyway. He didn't even have any help. No security system either."

"It's true," Charles agreed. "But I never thought about burglars and certainly not about anyone breaking in. My world was time traveling. I always knew there was a chance I would have someone confront me about time travel, but that's all. Who'd want to break into this old house?"

"You just lived in your own little world," Danny said.

"It's true," Charles agreed.

"It took me a year to convince him to finally get alarms and cameras," Lauren said. "And it was another six months before he finally quit accidentally setting things off. And getting him to agree to hire Aria and Tony was like pulling teeth."

"Again, true," Charles said. "But I do feel safer now and the house is cleaner and I'm not always hunting for something to eat."

Everyone laughed and then for at least a minute it was quiet as everyone picked at their food. Then Lisa suddenly said, "I'm still afraid to be here." Everyone paused and looked at Lisa as Ron put a hand on her shoulder.

"What do you mean?" Lauren asked.

"I'm sorry," Lisa said. "I'm sorry. I didn't mean that. I'm just tired, that's all. Excuse me."

As Lisa started to stand up Lauren said, "No, Lisa, please tell me what you mean."

Ron pulled Lisa back into her chair and said, "She means the dreams. She's had more than a few and I have too. Dreams about the jumps and what happened. Vivid, disturbing dreams that happen at random times but when we talk about visiting here they become more frequent and more horrific."

"I'm sorry," Lisa said. "Ron hasn't had that many, it's me who is weak. I just –"

"You're wrong," Lauren said quietly. "You're not weak. I have dreams too. Nightmares I guess. Intense and unforgettable and I have had more lately too. Maybe subconsciously it has been because all of us were going to be here." She tried to smile but couldn't as she continued, "Or, we were just reading each other's minds."

Danny spoke up, "This is the longest time we'll be together since the jumps. Maybe we are thinking about it."

"You've had these dreams too?" Ron asked.

Danny nodded, "Yes, and fortunately I've had some training about this type of reaction."

"What kind of training?" Lisa asked.

"First," Danny asked, "we've all had some dreams?" Everyone nodded, including Charles. "Well, when I was a police officer I was taught early on that I was going to be involved in situations that would be terrible, that would affect me emotionally. That if I wasn't careful, they would influence me so much that they could change my personality. I'm talking about accidents, shootings, suicides, anything that took me outside the realm of my normal life.

"And I had some of them." He paused as he glanced at Ron and thought of how he was the one to tell him his wife had been killed in a car accident. "Calls to things that I had to step back from and take a deep breath and then just focus on doing my job. To tell the truth it actually seemed easy to do. For a while I thought I wasn't affected. Then a wise sergeant grabbed me one day and said he was making an appointment for me with the departmental psychiatrist. I told him I didn't need to go, even got a little upset about it.

"Then he asked me, 'What did you do last night?' and I told him I sat around and watched the game. Then he kept going back further and further and suddenly I realized that's all I had been doing. He reminded me that I used to go out with the guys two or three nights a month and actually play some softball and basketball. Not just sit around. Then he asked me about my grade in a night class I was taking. I actually couldn't tell him what it was, I had forgotten about the class.

"Finally, he reminded me about all the mental health training I had and asked if I recognized anything. I had to admit I did. I was still coming into work, but I didn't really want to. I wasn't producing. I had cut myself off from everyone and was living in my own little world. From that point on I couldn't wait to go in and talk to someone about things. It was a great session and I was honest about everything with the mental health professional but more importantly with myself.

"Afterwards I proposed a policy that an officer had to attend a mental health evaluation session after any traumatic event. No waiting to see if they were slowly spiraling out of control. There was a little push back at first from a few officers but now everyone would think the department didn't care about them if they took the sessions away. It's good stuff."

"PTSD," Charles said. "You know, I think we all have heard of it and know what it does, but I never connected it to myself or Lauren. I mean, we're not police officers or firemen or soldiers."

"That's just it," Danny replied, "it can happen to anyone."

"What was the best thing you learned?" Lisa asked.

"That you will have normal reactions to abnormal situations. Normal reactions including 'I wish I hadn't seen or done what I just did'."

Danny paused as he took a drink of water then continued, "It took me a while to piece things together after the jumps. Basically, because I did see a mental health evaluator for being shot by Taggit. Like I said, for me and the department that was just the normal policy. I was healing from my wounds and writing the book, so the opinion was that of course I might think of things from time to time." Danny hung his head for a moment then continued, "But my being shot wasn't what was causing the problems. We lost some…well, friends. They didn't start out that way but that's the way they ended up. Even Jimmy. And I still see them. Smiling, talking, alive. And then they turn to gray statues and crumble into dust."

Danny sighed and continued, "And don't forget, I shot the *T-rex*. So, I *was* involved in a shooting along with all the other abnormal things we did. I had been terrified but too busy to think about it. We all were. Took me a while to sort everything out, but I finally did and all of you will too. But, you need to talk about it with someone, professional or not. Talk to someone. Put it out there and let it go."

There was more silence then Lisa said, "I still see Marilyn, or what was left of her. I should have stopped her from leaving the tree and I ask myself why I didn't. I should have but I didn't. In my dreams I try but…" and she trailed off.

Danny shook his head and said, "You couldn't have stopped Marilyn. She was headstrong and didn't listen to anyone. Well, she would have listened to Pete. You didn't kill her, and you didn't cause her to die. Everyone has to remember; it all goes back to Taggit."

"That's right," Ron agreed. "We didn't want to go on any jumps to begin with, and even though we eventually got caught up in the excitement of them, everyone was okay until he left us behind to die. No one here is to blame for anything. We were forced into a living nightmare and I think Danny is putting us on the right track. Normal responses to abnormal situations. We weren't meant to do what we did and definitely not see what we did."

"I understand everyone blaming Taggit," Charles said. "But I know you have to blame me too for what happened. It was my invention that caused all of this. That's what I have wrestled with. I have an addiction to time travel. I guess I had to, or I wouldn't have been able to focus on my work like I did and actually achieve my dream. But now I have doubts. So, I have cut back on the jumps and I try and calculate the impact of the jump. Something Lauren tried to get me to think about when Ron and her broke into my house."

"Broke into your house?" Lauren laughed. Then she took his hand and said, "We don't blame you. If you're in a car wreck you don't blame some guy on the assembly line. Taggit did this to us. No one else. We just have to figure out how to get to the other side of things."

"Follow Danny," Lisa said. "He seems to have some sort of handle on things."

Danny shrugged and replied, "Well, 'some sort' would be the correct term. I think for the most part I'm doing okay, better than I was. But I still have the occasional dream and sometimes I panic if I hear an odd or unexpected noise behind me. But if we talk about things together, and if you can talk about things with a professional, you will all get better too."

"How did you explain things to your professional?" Lauren asked. "You couldn't just start talking about time travel and dinosaurs."

"I told her that writing my book was giving me nightmares and odd dreams and we went from there. In the end I think she just blamed it all on police work and I let her go with that."

"That book of yours brings up a sore point with me," Charles said. "Danny, you changed your name to Don. Lauren became Laura, Ron is Roy, and Lisa was changed to Lois, but I am Carlton. Couldn't my name have been Chuck or even Carl? I mean Carlton just doesn't sound like me."

"I think it does," Ron quickly said.

"Oh yes, definitely," Lisa added.

Everyone looked at Lauren who shrugged her shoulders and said, "His vanity license plate does have Carlton on it."

As everyone laughed Charles shook his head and said, "I hate all of you, I really do. Now who needs some dessert?"

As everyone started to move around, Lisa said, "You know, I told Ron we should probably leave after Christmas and then come back before New Year's. Spend less time here. But now...now I think we should stay. I know I'm still going to have nightmares but our talking about things just now has made me feel better. I'd like to keep it up."

"I couldn't agree more," Ron smiled.

Lauren hugged them both and said, "All of us, every day, we get together and talk. We'll get through this together."

Lauren opened the door and hugged Ron as she said, "Where have you two been? It's late and Christmas Eve, I thought you would get back earlier. I was worried."

"Sorry, sorry," he told her. "We've been doing a lot of talking like Danny said to do. I know we've been talking a lot with all of you, but it did us some good to talk alone too. Oh, and we had to buy more presents too. You know you could have called?"

"I know, didn't want to be the nagging daughter and I've been just fine. Charles and Danny have been going out for a few hours each day, so I've been going to some yoga classes. Also, ordering food and making sure everything is just right for tomorrow."

"Yoga," Lisa said as she hugged Lauren. "Tell me all about it. Remember, that's what I was doing when Ron first saw me."

"I promise I can't forget that," Lauren replied. "Anyway, it's a great yoga class, well it would be if that is what I was using it for. After you guys took off, Danny and I continued to talk about things, so I use the class time to sort things out. Not what I'm supposed to be doing, but the class is quiet and more importantly it's not here. Not in this house. I think it's helping, no bad dreams in a while."

"Where's Charles been?" Ron asked.

"What?"

"You said you and Danny have been talking. What about Charles?"

Lauren frowned as she replied, "Charles has been busy, very busy. But he says things are winding down. There haven't been very many jumps lately and he's about to pull the plug."

"Do you believe him?" Lisa asked.

"I have to," Lauren said quietly then quickly changed the subject. "But enough about me, how about a hand setting the table? They should be back any minute with all the food."

Just as the last plate was set out, Danny and Charles walked in carrying sacks and boxes of food. "Hey, everyone's here," Danny shouted as he hugged Lisa.

Charles set his food down and said, "I've got to bring in a few more things, be right back."

"Danny, you are looking thinner every time I see you," Ron said. "Slow down on your diet. How are you doing so well?"

"Just counting calories," Danny said. "But don't worry, I'll probably gain everything back over the next two days. Lauren, I can't believe all the food you ordered for tonight. I thought we were just picking up some burgers."

"What do we have?" Ron asked.

Danny took a carton from one of the sacks and said, "Chicken, fried and barbecued, potato salad, green beans, salad, potatoes to bake, pies, cookies, some sort of stew, turkey, mac and cheese, biscuits, muffins, more veggies and…lots of other stuff."

"Did the other stuff include mashed potatoes?" Lauren asked. "I didn't hear you say mashed potatoes."

"Yes, my dear, it does," Charles said as he came back in. "I knew that Christmas Eve or not, if there were no mashed potatoes I'd be going back out to find some." He was carefully balancing five shoe boxes as he walked past everyone into the front room and left them by the Christmas tree.

"Elf shoes?" Ron asked.

"You'll find out later," Charles said.

"Okay," Lauren said. "Now about this food, it's for tonight, tomorrow and probably the day after," Lauren told everyone. "So, don't eat it all tonight. You might explode."

"Yes, Mom," Lisa said as everyone laughed.

"Can we eat now?" Ron asked.

"We can," Lauren told him.

After they finished, Danny said, "Okay, I actually can't move. I may have to sleep right here at the table."

"So, you can't eat that last little piece of cherry pie on your plate?" Lisa asked as she reached for it.

Danny looked down slowly then picked it up and ate it. "Cherry pie, my one weakness." Then he grimaced and said, "I shouldn't have done that because now I really can't move and may actually explode like Lauren said."

CHAPTER FOUR
STEGOSAURUS

The restaurant wasn't very crowded as Ron and Lisa were seated. Lisa started laughing and said, "I still can't believe I ran down to Danny's door without any clothes on. We may have to cut back on those nudist camp visits."

"Speak for yourself," Ron replied. "I happen to like the nudist camps. Wish I would have started going sooner."

"But it was so embarrassing."

"*You* were embarrassed?"

"Not me, silly, Danny."

"He may have been, but I noticed he didn't complain any."

Lisa giggled and said, "No, I guess he didn't. You should have seen the look on his face."

Ron replied, "He's been smiling for days so I've seen the look on his face."

Lisa slapped his arm and asked, "Aren't you jealous?"

"Well, I wouldn't want you making a habit out of it, but we have all done something embarrassing in our lives. And if I remember right, you were nude the first time I saw you."

"And I apologized for it."

"And I've been smiling ever since."

Lisa leaned over and kissed Ron and said, "That was the right thing to say. But now I'm wondering if you like the nudist camps because of all the other women."

"There's other women there?" Ron asked.

Lisa kissed him again as she said, "You are two for two Mr. Ron."

They ordered lunch and as they ate Ron asked, "I don't think you have had any dreams lately have you?"

"I think we are all having fewer dreams," Lisa replied. "Lauren says our talks are really making a difference. We've all talked a lot, well, not everyone. Charles is not around and he is hard to speak with." She paused and asked, "You don't think they are having problems, do you?"

Ron looked surprised as he paused, then said, "No. I don't think they talk like we do, but they still love each other. All of us will get through this and come out on the other side even stronger. We will."

"I know," Lisa said then looked up at a man who had just stopped by their table. He was carrying a briefcase and as Ron looked up, the man smiled and said, "I am sorry to bother both of you, I waited until I thought you were finished eating. Professor Fontana, could I speak with you for just a moment?"

"I'm sorry, do I know you?"

The man sat down and replied, "I'm sorry, no you don't." He reached forward and continued, "I am Steve Weston." Ron shook his hand and as Steve shook Lisa's hand he said, "And I know you are Lisa. Both of you are incredible people and I am honored to meet you."

"I'm not sure why," Ron said.

Steve nodded his head and replied, "Well, we have a few things in common."

"Like what?" Lisa asked.

"Well, I am a scientist, a rather brilliant one if I'm to be honest here. And, well, there is no easy way to say this, like you - I have traveled in time and seen dinosaurs."

Ron opened his mouth to speak and found he couldn't. Lisa spoke in a whisper as she asked, "What do you mean? Why would you think we traveled in time?"

Ron jumped in with, "I'm afraid he must be teasing us, Lisa."

Steve shook his head and said, "Well, no, Dr. Fontana I'm not. I read Danny's rather informative book and –"

Ron laughed nervously and said, "I'm sorry, that was just a science fiction book. None of it was real." Then he stood up and said, "I think you are confusing reality with fantasy. I'm sorry, we really have to go."

"Just a moment," Steve said as he opened his briefcase. He turned it, so Ron could look inside of it and as he did, Ron went white then red. "This is reality, not fantasy, and I was wondering if you knew exactly what this is?"

As Ron slowly sat back down, Lisa looked in the case and saw what she thought was a dark brown and splotchy yellow animal horn or tusk. It was about two feet long; a little over four inches across at its base and it tapered to a narrow point with thin spiral rings that looped around it from top to bottom. She looked at Ron who was staring into the briefcase, so she sat back down too. She held her breath as Ron slowly reached forward and took the object out of the briefcase and pulled it toward him. When he didn't move for several seconds she asked, "Ron, what is it?"

He laid the bone on the table and looked up at Steve and asked, "Where...where did you get this?"

"Do you know what it is?" Steve asked.

Ron picked the bone up quickly this time and replied, "Well, let's decide what it isn't first. Without being able to do a detailed comparison with examples I may not get it right, but…" he paused then took a deep breath. "It's obviously not a tooth which would be solid and not contain living tissue inside of it. A tooth would also have an enamel covering, not keratin like this." Ron looked closely at it and added, "Probably β-keratin."

He turned it slowly in his hands and looked closely at the wider base and continued, "I would also say that it is not a horn, the keratin covering is not thick enough. It's a bone, a bone with an appropriate cortical structure including vascular tissue. But…"

"But what?" Steve asked.

"But it also has thick external vascular grooves."

"That makes me think that it's probably a spike, an animal spike."

"Does any animal living today have a spike like this?"

Ron shook his head and said, "No…I mean, I don't know for sure. I study dinosaurs, not modern animals."

"So, you're saying it could be a Narwhale spike for instance, or from a gazelle?"

"No, no I'm not saying that."

"But you aren't saying what you believe, what you know. It's from a dinosaur, isn't it?"

Ron didn't speak, he found he couldn't. Then Lisa answered, "Yes, it's from a dinosaur. Ron just doesn't want to tell you. This is upsetting both of us."

Steve reached out to take the bone from Ron as he said, "That is not what I wanted to do. Far from it. I'll put it back and –"

But Ron pulled it away from Steve and said quietly, "It's the hind spike of a *Stegosaurus*. An older animal I believe."

Steve smiled and asked, "Tell me, how do you know?"

"Well, it's two feet long so it's not going to be a tooth or claw. It's cone shaped, so that makes it a spike. There were other dinosaurs with spikes, *Triceratops*, *Ankylosaurus*, and *Sauropelta* to name a few, but all their spikes are different. The *Stegosaurus* hind spikes had their own distinct shape."

"How do you know they belonged to an old animal?" Lisa asked.

Steve smiled and sat back as Ron told her, "There's not much pitting on the spike, not as much as you would see on a younger animal. Also, the vascular grooves are more pronounced. On a spike from a younger example they wouldn't be." He ran his hand over the tip of the bone and added, "And this spike has been broken and then it has healed many times. It has been around for a while."

Steve nodded toward the spike and asked, "What's the main thing you notice about it?"

Ron took a breath and laid the spike down on the table and then looked up at Steve, "That it's not a fossil."

Steve smiled and continued, "You're right, it's not a fossil. I told you, I have traveled just as you did." He nodded his head and continued, "And you're right about it being from an older *Stegosaurus*. My team found one that did not appear to have died from any wounds. There were no other animals around, so it seems to have died from old age."

"Not every dinosaur died violently," Ron said.

"No, but it usually didn't take long for the scavengers to do their work. That and the heat and humidity. The team cut the tail off the animal and we brought it back. I was hoping to preserve it as it was in real life, but I couldn't figure out a way to keep the spikes upright. So, I had them removed and, well – here's one of them. A hind one as you said."

Ron tapped the table a couple of times and said, "I wish I would have been there." He picked the spike up and held it with the point straight up, "The Thagomizer didn't look like this." He moved the spike, so it was parallel to the table and continued, "It was like this. The spikes were out sideways from the tail, not up."

"Thagomizer?" Steve asked.

"I can't remember the exact name," Ron started, "but Gary Larsen drew a Far Side cartoon where a caveman named Thag something or other had been killed by a *Stegosaurus*. The cavemen called the spike part of the tail the Thagomizer."

Steve leaned forward and told Ron, "I wish you had been there too. You have the knowledge and answers that we don't. I can use you on my team, Ron. There are still too many things we don't know."

"We don't want to go back anymore," Lisa said. "We aren't over the first time yet."

Steve looked at her for a moment and then said, "I know what you mean. We have lost some men, good men, because we thought we had the answers. I still see them…and hear them. But I'm not asking either of you to Walk with us."

"Walk?"

"Sorry, that's what we call going out from our time machine, our Unit. Again, I would not ask you to do that." He turned to Ron, "I just want to show you some video. You might find the *Stegosaurus* interesting. And I want to know about an animal I have not been able to find anywhere in dinosaur records or descriptions. A real monster from the sea. There are other things too. Ron, I just need your knowledge. That's all."

"What about Charles?" Lisa asked Ron.

"I would like to meet with Charles also," Steve replied. "Compare notes and thoughts. He's been doing this longer than I have and would be a valuable source of information."

"Actually, I don't think he would," Lisa admitted. "He's cutting back on his jumps and is getting ready to stop them altogether."

"I think he realizes Lauren was right," Ron added.

"Yes," Steve said. "If I remember right, Lauren doesn't like going back in time and disrupting things. Let me assure you that is not what we do. On one of the first Walks, my team came across a mammoth and there was talk of shooting it. I stopped them immediately. We're talking mammals and we weren't that far back in time. I decided right then that all Walks would only be when dinosaurs were the dominant species so that millions of years and several different global disasters would stop any chance of disturbing our timeline."

Ron didn't say anything as he looked down at the spike. As he touched it again Lisa said, "Ron, I think we should leave."

Steve picked up the spike and put it back in the briefcase and said, "I understand. I'll leave you my card and also this, you don't have to travel back in time with us. But I would like you to stop by my facility and look at some video and answer just a few questions. Like I said, some of my team have been injured or killed because we thought we knew what to expect and it turned out we didn't. I need help and I'll pay both of you for whatever information you can provide."

"Why would you pay to talk to me?" Lisa asked.

Steve turned to her and said, "Because you were there. You saw it and felt it. You know things my team doesn't. You lived through an experience that others didn't." As Lisa bit her lip, he continued, "I'm sorry I put it that way, but it's true. And I don't want what happened to your friends to happen to my team."

Lisa quickly thought of Marilyn and dropped her head. Then she turned to Ron and said, "Maybe we could go for a few minutes. I don't want anyone else getting hurt."

"We'll do what we can," Ron told Steve.

"When would you like to come by?" Steve asked.

"Now," Lisa answered. "Can we come by now?"

Steve smiled and replied, "Of course. I have a car outside if you'd like a ride or you can follow me."

"We'll follow you," Ron said. "Let me pay the bill first and –"

"Professor Fontana, please let me get it. I'm honored you both will be joining us."

As they walked out of the restaurant, Ron asked, "Us?"

"Yes, my brother Ben will want to be there also. He actually will have most of the questions." He pointed to a car and told them, "I'm in the small blue car there. I'll have my driver make sure we don't lose you." He shook both of their hands and said, "I can't tell you how excited I am about this."

As Ron drove, Lisa asked him, "We're doing the right thing, aren't we?"

Ron paused and said, "I think so. I really do. This Steve is just another time traveler, like Charles. He wants to keep his team safe, that's all."

"But what if he is a time traveler like Taggit? What if he really doesn't care?"

"Have you changed your mind?"

"No, he seems genuinely concerned, but Taggit fooled us, all of us. I just don't want it to happen again." She trailed off with, "Not again."

"I agree," Ron told her. "I think we need to go slow and see just what this is all about. He's smart, he not only time travels but he was able to piece everything together just from reading Danny's book. Let's just see."

As they turned through a gate beside a sign that read EXENCO Experimental Energy Consultants, they saw a large complex of buildings spread out over several acres. All the buildings had solar panels on top of them and in the distance behind the buildings they saw wind turbines. As they parked Steve came up and said, "Welcome to my business. As you can see, my company practices what it preaches. We are concerned with the state of the environment and are constantly looking for new ways to provide quality energy to the world without damaging it."

"This is stunning," Ron said. "Is time travel just a hobby then?"

Steve thought for a moment then replied, "I guess you could say that, but not really. It is a passion of mine, visiting prehistoric eras and seeing the animals that lived then. I mean, it really has no use. I agree with all of you that animals cannot be brought back to the present and I'm not a publicity seeker. I'm not going to show my videos to anyone else but you and hopefully the other time travelers. So, maybe you are right, just an expensive hobby."

"What powers your time travel unit?" Lisa asked.

"Excellent question. When we stop we immediately deploy windmills and the solar panels are part of the Unit design. There are other sources we try to tap into also, like the heat of the ground we are resting on, strictly in the experimental stage I assure you, but promising. Of course, there are other methods but like Charles asked during your jumps, would you understand if I told you? If so, I would love to discuss it with you. Maybe get a new perspective on things. But now, let's go in and meet my brother."

They quickly walked through a few offices until they found Ben at a console surrounded by large screens. Steve told them, "I'm going to leave you in my brother's capable hands. I will be back soon though." Then he asked, "Ben, can you take over?"

Ben jumped up and smiled as he shook their hands. "How nice of you to stop by," he told them. "I have a lot of questions for you if you don't mind."

"It's why we are here," Ron said.

"I don't know if I will be much help," Lisa told him. "I don't know a lot about dinosaurs."

"We don't either," Ben replied. "But that's not all I'm interested in, I'm sure you'll have some interesting perspectives and ideas."

"She will," Ron agreed. "She's one of the smartest people I've ever met. If she needs to say something, she will."

"Great," Ben said. "But I almost forgot, would you like a tour of the facilities first? See everything we do?"

"Maybe later," Ron replied. "Steve said something about a video of an animal you couldn't identify?"

Ben turned around and a holograph panel appeared. As he moved his hands, Lisa looked at Ron, it all seemed too familiar for her. But he was looking intently at the screens, so she just took a deep breath and didn't say anything. Then she gasped as the screens were filled with the image of an open beach area with two figures wearing odd suits running toward them. She shouted, "No," as the animal burst from the water and its mouth snapped shut on Hood and disappeared back into the water.

Ron turned to her and took her hand and said, "It's okay, it's just a video."

"But that man just died."

"He did," Ben agreed. "I'm sorry, I thought you knew what we were going to see. I thought Steve had told you. It's what we're trying to stop. Why we need answers."

"Just give me a minute," Lisa said. "Steve didn't exactly tell us what we were going to see but he did mention people had died. I guess I should have known."

"Just tell me when."

As Ron smiled at her, she told Ben, "Go ahead, I'm ready now, but what happened to the second man we saw?"

Ben paused just for a moment then smiled and told her, "He made it back to the Unit just fine."

"Okay, go ahead then."

The video jumped back to the people running and then slowed down as the animal came out of the water. They watched it three more times and then Ron asked, "Will the video go any slower?"

"Yes," Ben said, and the animal came out of the water one frame at a time.

Ron leaned forward and watched without blinking. As the mouth closed, he told Ben, "Stop right there. The animal is almost completely out of the water, we can see everything we need to, and it's unbelievable. At first, I thought it would be *Lemmysuchus* or *Deinosuchus* but now I see it isn't. Let me think on this for a moment."

"So, all of those would be different than a sea crocodile? That's what we thought would come out of the sea."

"Yes, yes, much different than your standard sea crocodile. It's not a *Leldraan*." Ron stared at the screen for a few more seconds then said, "You know, it could be, it looks like it, but bigger. It's got the snout, but there haven't been..."

As he trailed off Lisa asked, "What do you think?"

"Well, again, no fossils have been found in the U.S. but of course that doesn't mean a lot when you remember the small percentage of fossils we have actually uncovered. But, I think I may be right."

"Okay, but what do you think it is?" she asked.

"A *Sarcosuchus*, well, a *Sarcosuchus* on steroids and in the wrong place."

"What do you mean?" Ben asked.

"*Sarcosuchus*, and I mean *Sarcosuchus imperator*, is found in Africa. It's a huge animal, though smaller than this one, but they have the same snout. But some teeth belonging to *Sarcosuchus hartti* were found in Brazil so that places the animal in South America. Still, there is nothing to link these animals, but..."

"But you have a theory, right?"

"Well, *Sarcosuchus* could have migrated to the Inland Sea. And, being in the area we see here, a beach or shore, that is where they would be. They lived in sea and freshwater. What other animals were in the area?"

"There were some *Rexes*."

"So, that would be the late Cretaceous and *Sarcosuchus* has been dated from early to late Cretaceous so..."

"So, it's a *Sarcosuchus*?" Ben asked.

Ron shook his head and answered, "Well, maybe. *Sarcosuchus*-like is a better way of saying it. The length of the animal is right, forty or fifty feet or so it looks like, but the body is bigger, bulkier, especially the head. This could just be the North American version of it after a few million years of evolution."

Ron looked at the screen for another moment and asked, "The pack the man was wearing, was it to protect him?"

"Yes," Ben answered. "It stood up to a *Rex* bite, so we thought –"

"So, you thought it would stand up to the bite of a sea crocodile if you ran into one."

"To tell you the truth, we didn't really think about it that much. We concentrated on land animals."

"Well, there is a lot of conjecture about the bite force of all dinosaurs and also crocodilians. The *T-rex* is thought to have had the largest bite force of any land animal, but crocs have enormous bite forces. This animal is larger than any crocodile or crocodilian than we have encountered before. No wonder you misjudged it."

Ben nodded his head and told Ron, "I wish you had been in on the planning stages. You could have given us vital information instead of us learning through trial and error." He looked at the screen, "We wouldn't have lost these men."

"Men?" Lisa asked.

"Yes, men. Some others lost their lives just before this incident when three juvenile *Rexes* attacked. We thought *Rexes* hunted alone."

Ron leaned forward and said, "Only recently has it been theorized that *Rexes*, especially young ones, may have pack hunted. Can you show me?"

Steve walked in just then and said, "Professor Fontana, you've been here for over an hour. I know you are in a hurry, but I would like to show you a few other things before you go, perhaps you can come back soon?"

Ron smiled and replied, "Yes, I can come back. I think I can help you."

Steve clasped his hands together and told them, "I'm so happy to hear you say that. That puts my mind at ease."

"Mine too," Ben added.

"We don't want to see anyone else killed though," Lisa told them.

"Of course not," Steve said. "Ben, why don't you come with us? I was going to show them the Unit."

"Great," Ben said as he turned off the screens and joined them.

"Follow me," Steve said and led the way down a long hallway to a large room the size of a football field. Inside, Ron and Lisa were amazed to find what appeared to be a two-story building. It looked like it was made out of some lightweight metal and though there were windows they couldn't see any sign of a door.

Well, here it is," Steve told them. "It's how we travel. I know from reading Danny's book it's different to what Charles Dawson built, and it is definitely different on the inside."

"Can we see?" Lisa asked.

"Of course," Steve said.

As they approached the Unit, a door appeared in the middle of it and they stepped through. Screens activated, and holographic images of controls and number readouts appeared. "I can show you more later," Steve said, "but to keep things simple, right now we're in the Viewing Room. We're just outside the Conference Room, upstairs there is a Control Center and, work stations, and to the sides are Team areas and different storage compartments." As he sat down he asked, "Do either of you have any questions?"

Ron shook his head and said, "Well, no, I guess not. Not yet anyway."

Lisa smiled and said, "He wants to see the Stegosaurus. But he knows I don't want to, that I'm still afraid of what happened. I'm sorry."

Steve nodded and asked, "Would both of you sit down for a moment in the Conference Room?" As they both found chairs around a table, Steve continued, "I understand completely. But I might be able to take both of you for a…a jump if you will, to satisfy Ron's curiosity, and Lisa, calm your fears. It seemed limiting to me to have a stationary launch pad for the Unit so to speak. Think of how you didn't have to worry about appearing in the same building, at the same time as Taggit when you returned in the Unit that was kept in the elevator shaft. Charles Dawson was brilliant in that regard. It gave me the idea.

"As you saw when we entered this building it is large, very large. I designed it that way, so the Unit could be moved. One reason was in case there was ever any trouble, but the other reason was to go back and watch what happened during a Walk, troubleshoot to use Ben's language."

"You can go to the same site twice?" Ron asked.

"Or more if necessary," Ben said. "We don't do it often, but we do have the ability to drop back into the same time. Just not the same space of course."

"But doesn't the first Unit see the second?" Lisa asked.

Steve shook his head and replied, "Remember the camouflage Charles Dawson had? The holographs on the outside of his Unit? Ours is similar but I modified it some. Because you are right, we wouldn't want the first set of Walkers to know they were being watched."

"So, what are you trying to say?" Lisa asked.

"That if we go back to see the *Stegosaurus* I can guarantee your safety. The first set of Walkers deployed all safety devices, so we knew, and that's *knew* one hundred percent, that there were no large, dangerous animals within a half-mile of us. They didn't even need to put on their shells, the protection they wear on their backs against attacks."

"We saw it earlier," Ron said. "In the video of the possible *Sarcosuchus* attack."

"Oh, so you thought you recognized a dinosaur? Which one was it, Ron?"

"On the beach, right after the *Rexes*."

Steve smiled and said, "Thank you for watching the video Professor, knowing what the animal was will help us design better protection for the Team."

"I could only guess at what it was."

"I'm betting your guess is better than what we *think* we know." Steve looked at Lisa and added, "And thank you, Lisa. I know it was probably hard for you, especially since there was a death involved."

"At first it was, but the more we watched I suddenly knew that Ron could help. Maybe I could too in some small way. I don't know how, but I don't want anyone else to die."

"I'm happy to hear you say that. I'm sure -"

"So, I think we should go back right now, if that's possible," Lisa suddenly said. "It's safe, nothing happens. Statistically it won't get any better than right now to visit the *Stegosaurus* site."

"I'm surprised," Ron said. "Are you sure?"

Lisa took a deep breath and quickly said, "Yes, I'm sure. I can deal with this and I can tell this is important to you. Plus, it might help with getting rid of my dreams."

Steve put a hand on Lisa's shoulder and said, "At any time you change your mind just say the word and we'll immediately return."

"Thank you."

Steve turned, and as he started talking, holographic images appeared. As he began manipulating them Ron leaned over to Lisa and asked, "Are you sure?"

Lisa smiled and said, "Yes."

Ron turned to Steve and told him, "Looks like we are good to go whenever you'd like."

Steve smiled and replied, "That's good because we're about forty million years out already."

Ron looked up and then he laughed and said, "Sorry, looking for the haze from our previous jumps. I forgot we were inside a building. I don't have the sensation that we're doing anything."

"Do you think that's better?" Ben asked.

Ron thought for a moment then answered, "Yes, I think it is. I don't know why, maybe less distraction."

"Yes," Lisa agreed, "less distraction. I'm nervous, especially now that I know it's really happening again, but with no visual cues I'm staying under control."

"That's an understatement," Ben said. "I'm monitoring both of you and first, it appears both of you are in exceptional shape. Lisa your resting heart rate is 48. You say you are nervous, but it still is only up to 60, which is 10 below Ron's 70 which is excellent considering what we are doing. Ron, what's your secret?"

"I watch what I eat and do lots of yoga," Ron said quickly. "I have my whole life." Then he smiled as he shook his head and continued, "Well, let's just say since I met Lisa, she has me on track."

"I'll say," Lisa said as she swatted Ron. "Before me he thought good food was hot dogs and beans and yoga was a catcher for the Yankees."

Everyone laughed as Steve turned and said, "I'm glad we're having a good time. But let's step back into the Viewing Room, we have arrived." As they entered the room they were surprised to see that the two windows they had seen earlier had disappeared and the whole wall seemed to now be a window. Outside was an open space that ran about fifty yards to a dark green jungle. Tall trees waved in an unfelt breeze as they towered above smaller trees with shorter ferns hugging the ground under them.

"Okay," Ron said, "this is impressive. What are we looking through?"

Steve smiled and told them, "It's a fabric that I invented. Certain electric currents make it see-through, or it can be opaque. It's also how we camouflage the Unit. When the Team arrives in a few moments we'll have to camo up, but we'll still be able to watch what is going on."

"Great," Ron replied.

"It's strange without any noise," Lisa said.

"Ben, some sound," Steve commanded and immediately they could hear the wind blowing, animal calls and insect noise rising and falling. In the distance, a roar was heard, and Lisa covered her ears and asked, "Can you turn it off now?"

"Mute," Ben said, and it was quiet again. Then he said "Camouflage," and though the wall still looked the same, Steve advised,

"The Team will not be able to tell we are here now." About a minute later, seemingly out of nowhere, the *Stegosaurus* appeared slowly walking from left to right about twenty-five yards away from them.

"I forgot how big they were," Lisa whispered.

Steve stood up and said, "This one is old, like you thought Professor Fontana. So, it's big, about fourteen feet to the top of its plates and if I remember correctly it was measured at 37 feet 2 inches in length. Our scans estimated its weight at about 5,000 pounds, maybe a little more."

"That sounds right," Ron said. "It looks thin."

"Thin?" Ben asked.

"Yes, it should be well over 6,000 pounds, closer to 7,000."

"What else do you see, Professor?"

"Well, do you see its mouth, the beak? It looks deformed, like it has been injured. That would certainly mean death for a *Stegosaurus*. See how low the head is to the ground? All it ate was vegetation and it had to find it at the right height. There's been speculation that they could rear up on their hind legs but seeing the size of this animal I would guess that only juveniles might be able to do it before they grew too large."

"What else?"

"The plates. They're not staggered and not exactly mirror images along its back. That could just be for the *ungulates* like this one though. But the main thing I see is that some of the plates are redder than the others, full of blood for cooling is what the best guess is they were for."

"It's 115 degrees out there with about 80 percent humidity," Ben noted.

Ron nodded and said, "But not all of the plates are full, and I think that, as we already know, it indicates the animal is in distress. Things aren't working the way they should. And though it has also been surmised that the plates were carried both up and down at different times, the plates on this animal seem to be drooping. It's losing control of body functions."

"Anything surprising?" Steve asked.

"Just seeing it in real life. How tall the back legs are compared to the front. Like I said the low carried head and how the body arches up to the top of the plates and then that tail. Look at those spikes. Three feet for the front spikes and the hind ones are two feet long but compared to the rest of its body they look like toothpicks."

"And they're more parallel to the ground like you mentioned," Steve added.

Suddenly the animal stumbled and dropped to its front knees. Its mouth was open and as Steve had the sound come back on they could hear its plaintiff cries. Then it toppled over on its side with its belly toward them and took several large breaths, and then the animal's sides stopped moving.

"Watch the area just beyond its tail," Steve said and a few seconds later the Unit appeared. Two drones lifted up from it as what appeared to be small versions of a lunar land rover shot out and disappeared into the vegetation around the *Stegosaurus*. Two minutes went by without any movement, then eight people in light green camouflage uniforms walked out of the Unit toward the dead animal.

"Come on, people," a woman in front called back. "I know the readings say there's nothing around but let's not waste any time. Get to it. I want pictures, video, measurements, scans and samples right now and do it right. You know the drill. Let's go."

Five of the people moved quickly past her and there was a flurry of activity around the fallen *Stegosaurus*. Two others took positions at the head and tail of the animal and had their rifles up as they scanned the jungle around them. One of the plates was removed from its back, as were teeth and skin samples and impressions. Lisa flinched as a deep incision was cut into the stomach and a large container was used to collect some of its contents.

After about fifteen minutes the woman shouted, "Okay, let's get back in," followed immediately by, "Wait!" She paused as if listening to something then everyone gathered by the spikes on the *Stegosaurus* tail. The woman then said, "I know you said just one, but it would probably be easier to just cut part of the tail off, and then you would have four spikes."

A man in the group stepped forward and pulled what looked like a small circular saw from a bag on his side. The blade began to spin silently, and it took less than a minute for him to cut the tail section away. The woman and three others quickly picked it up and one of them said, "This is heavier than what I thought."

The woman replied, "If you worked out once in a while it wouldn't be. Paycheck, can we leave this slacker behind?" Laughter came from the group and then they disappeared back into their Unit. The drones and land rovers returned and a few seconds later it vanished.

"That was impressive," Ron said. "Real teamwork."

"Thank you," Ben replied, "but I almost messed it up."

"How?"

"I'm Paycheck. I started to answer just now."

"What did you say to her then?" Lisa asked. "They all thought it was funny."

Ben looked down for a moment and replied, "Let's just say I suggested the Team stuff him into some part of the *Stegosaurus* and leave it at that."

Everyone laughed as Steve told them, "Well, we are on our way back. As promised, no injuries to the Team or to any of us. I know you're thinking it is because we already knew what was going to happen, but we always *do* know what is going to happen. We launched drones and bots and Ben and I personally watch for any animals in the area on video and infrared. I don't want to sound like I'm boasting, but we have the best detection equipment available. The only time the Team comes in contact with an animal is because I want them to. When we have to get certain information."

"And the drones and bots cover everything?" Ron asked.

"No," Ben answered. "Those are the scouts. If they see something, or when we stop and feel it is necessary, we send up high altitude cameras. We can cover a huge area that way and then see any trouble or animals of interest."

"How do you get those back?" Lisa asked.

"We don't."

"What about the possibility that a fossil of it, or impression or something, could be found later?"

"Great question," Steve cut in. "All the materials used on the drones, bots, cameras, everything, is a bio-degradable resin. Once in the elements it has a three-day life then it just decomposes. Believe me when I say no one associated with our business ever wants to leave anything behind that could compromise our endeavors. That's one of the things I want to get across to everyone on your team."

Then the door opened, and Ron and Lisa saw they were back in the warehouse. "Professor Fontana…" Steve started but Ron stopped him.

"Please, Steve, I'm Ron and this is Lisa. I think Lisa and I need to talk and then we will speak to Charles and Lauren. I will give you a call sometime after the holidays."

Steve and Ben smiled as they all shook hands and Steve told them, "Ron, Lisa, I look forward to your call."

Then Ben escorted them back to their car and as they drove away Lisa said, "It was all like a dream."

CHAPTER FIVE
SECRETS

"But what did you think of it?" Ron asked. "What do you think of Steve and Ben?"

Lisa thought for a few moments then said, "I didn't know what to think at first. I wanted to stay quiet, I mean I'm not any kind of expert. But I let my feelings show and I usually can't stop myself from saying something. But both of them seemed to like I was talking, contributing. I hope you didn't mind."

"Not at all," Ron assured her. "I was surprised you wanted to jump again."

"I was wanting to support you but afraid of actually going. But we were kind of swept up in things and when Steve said we were traveling I just decided to go along and hope for the best. And, this was completely different than last time. We weren't being kidnapped, and it obviously was much more relaxed. But still, it was a little surreal and I half believed that it wasn't happening. Or maybe I hoped it wasn't.

"When I looked out of the window though and saw the jungle, well, there it was so we really had jumped again. I could feel my anxiety level rising but I kept reminding myself we already knew what was going to happen. It was okay, no one was going to die."

Lisa paused then continued, "Then the *Stegosaurus* came out of the jungle and I couldn't help but focus on the animal. It was huge and, this will sound funny, it was majestic. I could see the muscles ripple as it walked, hear it breathing and feel its life. When it paused, and I knew why, I became sad and actually wanted to go out to it. I wanted to help it in some way. Maybe save it. But when it stopped breathing I knew it had died and in reality, had been dead for millions of years. I couldn't help it, I could only watch.

"Then the Team came out and I found myself trying to watch each person to see what they were doing. I found that part fascinating though a little gruesome also. Each of them knew exactly what to do and they moved like clockwork. I have to admit I was impressed by that. They were getting whatever was needed to help further their efforts to help military men and women. You know, there are times when we may not agree with a decision that is made that sends our military into harm's way, but you can't turn your back on the individuals who make things happen. Those who do the work. So, I started looking at the whole thing differently."

"How?" Ron asked.

"That *Stegosaurus* dying would have meant nothing. Just a meal for other dinosaurs and then turning into dust. Now I understand all that still happened but before it did, information that might be used was obtained. It just seemed...seemed right to me somehow. I know it sounds funny, but that's what I think."

Ron nodded and said, "I wanted to go outside too, I wanted to help them with whatever it was they were doing. You know I still love the field work. And, I agree with most of what you said. The animal wasn't killed for scientific purposes, they didn't unnecessarily kill an animal for research. And I can understand taking some of the body parts. I guess Steve may want to study them, he likes dinosaurs, but I wasn't sure about the blood and tissue samples. I'm still trying to figure that out."

"What bad reason could he want them for?"

"Cloning. That's what I'm worried about." Then he shrugged his shoulders and said, "You only have to watch a few movies to know that's a bad thing." Then he continued, "It's something we need to ask about when we see them again."

"So, you are thinking about helping them?"

"Yes. Like you said, it seems for a worthwhile purpose and we need to stop them from blundering around and getting people killed. But that brings up again, what did you think about Steve and Ben? You didn't answer that question."

"Sorry, I thought saying I started liking what was happening did answer it. To the point though, I think they are being honest with us. Ben especially. He seems very personable and I thought he really wanted to help us. He seemed to have a great amount of respect for you. Steve was, well he seemed the science type. Like you used to be and still can be sometimes. Focused on his work and though he does okay talking with people he is a little awkward with some social skills. He was trying though, and I feel like he really wants your help."

Lisa put a hand on Ron's shoulder and said, "You know if he wants you to be a consultant he will probably pay you a lot of money. I know you love the field, the digging excites you, but more than once I've heard you complain about the cold and the heat and the rain and the heat and the dust and the heat and the sand and the heat and..."

Ron laughed and said, "Okay, okay, I get it. I have to admit I have been thinking about transitioning from full-time paleontologist for the university to a consulting position. There is a lot of new blood waiting to move up. Now if I had two consulting jobs I could cut out some of the field work and yes, stay cool since apparently I complain about the heat all the time. And I just remembered, you'll be getting paid as a consultant too."

"Well, I'm not sure about that but I was thinking you'd be around more."

"More yoga?"

"More yoga."

Steve congratulated himself and then shook his head. They had bought it, hook, line and sinker. He could see Ron was barely able to contain himself as he brought out the spike. *The* spike. As soon as he opened the briefcase it was all Ron could see, all he wanted to touch. But Steve knew he had to go slow, reel Ron in a little at a time. Answer all his questions, and Lisa's questions too. He had to win them both over and he had done it.

There were some surprises too. He had not thought for a moment that they would want to come to his facility and to see what he was doing. What had he said that made them want to come? He couldn't remember half of what he told them, just kept trying to say the right things to them. The things they wanted to hear. He must have succeeded because they didn't hesitate. What had Lisa said? "*Maybe we could go for a few minutes. I don't want anyone else getting hurt.*" Yes, that was it. Ron wanted to go and then Lisa gave him the green light. A sad story did it, he'd have to think of some more. You needed to know what motivated people.

Then he didn't have time to clue Ben in, but it didn't matter. Ben was Ben and he was being totally honest about everything in his own personable way. It couldn't have been scripted any better. A sad story, then tie in the military, and the next thing he knew they were actually asking to get in the Unit and go see the *Stegosaurus*. Unbelievable. Whatever fear Lisa had seemed to disappear, and Steve thought Ron was going to jump through the window to get at the *Stegosaurus*.

Beautiful. He was sure they would want to help, and they would be a great help. Well, at least Ron would be. He wasn't sure about Lisa but if she kept Ron on the Team then that's all that would matter. Ron had known everything about the *Stegosaurus* just from looking at the spike. Yes, they needed him and his knowledge.

Then Steve remembered he had talked about Charles Dawson too. Why had he said he wanted to meet him when he didn't? Charles might notice that a few things looked familiar, like he might have invented them instead of Steve. But it had already been said and who knew, maybe his wanting to meet Dawson had helped Ron and Lisa decide to visit the facility and then travel. Maybe it was okay, Dawson probably wouldn't want to come anyway. After all, Lauren Fontana wasn't a big fan of traveling and supposedly Dawson was getting ready to quit.

But then he realized they all had to come. It was the only way. As Steve turned around there was Ben standing in the doorway to his office. "What are you thinking about?" Ben asked.

Steve had the feeling he knew exactly what he was thinking about, but he brushed it off with, "About how you are the best brother anyone could ever want."

"How's that?" Ben asked.

"The way you spoke with them, getting them emotionally involved, how you kept them interested. I couldn't have done that, and you did it as if you had rehearsed what you were going to say."

"So, you were watching? I wondered where you went to."

"I visited Tiny for a few minutes, but I wanted to watch you and see how you handled them."

"Just being myself, that's all. Honesty is the best way to go with people who can figure out things."

"I can't believe they were ready to travel so quickly."

Ben smiled, "I have to admit that surprised me too. But we have to be honest with them and do the right thing by them."

"Just what do you mean by that?"

"We can't leave them behind somewhere. We can use them, pay them, and then let them go on their own way. They won't talk about anything they did or saw. They haven't so far, and they won't in the future unless –"

"Unless?"

"Unless they suspect we're not being honest with them. They will see right through us and that will only lead to problems we don't need. Whatever you are thinking about doing, let's keep it straight all the way. We'll still get our money in the end."

Steve smiled and told Ben, "That's exactly what I was just thinking. Really, it was. We need Ron and Lisa and they will provide us with the information we need to be successful. Plus, they are friendly and who wants to harm their friends?"

Ben smiled back at Steve and said, "I'm glad we're thinking along the same lines. Now let's get out of here and don't forget you are coming over for Christmas."

"I'll be there," Steve replied as Ben turned away. Then he shook his head and thought, "Weak, he is too weak." Then he walked out of his office and down the hallway and used the retinal scanner to open a sliding door. The lights came on in the room automatically and he gazed down into a room that was twenty feet below where he was standing. It was empty except for a large metal table in the center of it and one metal chair. The feeding room.

Steve pressed a button and a loud bell rang one time as a door slid open in the feeding room. It entered quickly as it always did, a green and yellow blur of activity as it stalked around the room. "You're not weak though, are you?" Steve said quietly. Then he pressed another button and a large chunk of meat dropped down onto the table. Steve smiled as the creature savagely attacked it. "Merry Christmas, Tiny."

"Well, I can't move again," Charles said as he pushed himself away from the table. "Ron and Lisa, you didn't eat much. Did you eat earlier and what did you do over the last few days? We haven't seen much of you and we've missed you."

"That's nice," Lisa replied.

"It is, it really is," Ron added. "You see we had to take care of several things and to let you in on a secret, we were house shopping. We're thinking about moving to Florida."

Lauren jumped up and hugged both of them and as she sat down she said, "Charles and I were just trying to decide how to suggest that to you. Where are you looking?"

"Within twenty or thirty miles of you guys," Lisa said. "We looked at some nice places."

"What brought this on, Dad?" Lauren asked.

"Well, I've been thinking about stepping down at Buckland, maybe do some consulting and some occasional field work. It's getting a little harder each time I go out and there are others who I know will do a fine job replacing me. It just seems like the right time. Plus, there is something else that has come up."

"If Lauren and I moved out, would you want to live here?" Charles asked.

The room immediately got quiet as everyone turned toward him. Lisa spoke up, "Well, no, probably not. It's too big of a house for us and, well, everything that happened here."

"I understand."

"Well, I don't," Lauren said. "Am I missing something? Are we moving?"

Charles paused then said, "I'm not sure. This is a big house, I've come to realize it over the last few years. I felt I had to live here since it was my family's but that is not the case anymore. Plus, I think there are too many bad memories here for both of us." He paused and smiled at everyone else and continued, "Not to mention people we want to have visit us. Maybe it's just time to move on."

As Lauren kissed Charles, Lisa said, "How sweet. So, we're all looking for a new house. What about you, Danny? When you are officially retired don't you think you should move to Florida?"

Danny smiled and told them, "You know, I have been thinking the same thing. But I want to use my work insurance for a last round of medical checkups and things like that before I take the big step. That stuff is expensive, and I'd like to have someone else help pay for it."

"That's great," Lauren said. "Let's look at some houses after Christmas. Who knows, maybe we'll all find something before the new year."

As they got up from the table to move into the living room, Danny asked, "We don't all have to live in the same house, do we? I mean I love you all but –"

"But you don't want to see Lisa walking down the hallway naked again," Ron cut in.

"No, I was afraid it would be you next time," Danny replied, and everyone laughed.

They talked the rest of the evening about new houses and even the jumps they had made. They drank a toast to Pete, Marilyn, Mitch and Jimmy, then everyone went to their rooms. As they got in bed Lauren told Charles, "I hope you really want to move out of your house."

He nodded his head and replied, "I do, really. You see, it is just a house now, not a home anymore. We need a new start to put the past behind us. I know I keep saying it, but I am close to shutting things down. The start of the new year will also see my stopping all my time travel. It's time to stay home and concentrate on other things."

"Like?"

He pulled her close and said, "Well, like you for one thing. You don't complain a lot, but I know there are other things you would like to do. Make a list and let's do some of them. And, I want to put my knowledge to work on other projects. I've learned a lot in my life, not just for time travel, but for other things as well. We can put our heads together and come up with something. I have a lot of money, maybe I can fund some charities or create some scholarships. Time to give back. But I'll need your help."

She hugged him and said, "You'll get all the help you need. From all of us. We can keep busy just trying to stay up with Dad and Lisa." She lay back on the bed and then suddenly sat up and said, "Dad said there was something else too. Another reason for wanting to move to Florida but he never said what it was."

"Maybe Lisa is pregnant," Charles said.

As she fell backwards all Lauren could say was, "Oh, my God."

Lisa looked at Ron and asked, "When are you going to tell them?"

"Well, I was thinking about tonight, but I agree with you, now is not the time. Maybe tomorrow night, I don't think I can wait another whole day. We just have to figure out how to do it."

"That's the easy part."

"It is?"

"Yes. The hard part will be explaining why we did it and why we think it is a good idea to work for Steve. "

"Who will give us the hardest time?"

"Lauren," Lisa said, and Ron just nodded his head.

Danny was staring at the ceiling like he had every night for the last year. He wasn't seeing anything; just staring…and thinking. Life and death, death and life. Then he smiled and thought about all the friends he was with and decided tonight was not the night for more worrying. He smiled and closed his eyes.

The next day was fun with lots of food and presents. As they gathered in the front room afterwards Danny looked at the stack of boxes Charles had brought in and said, "We didn't open these presents yet, Charles."

"Those are for later," he replied. "They're special."

"I like special," Danny said.

"I've eaten too much," Ron told everyone. "I think I might take a nap."

"Oh, no you don't," Lauren told him. "Last night you said you had something else to tell us. So, besides looking for a new house, what is so important?"

The room became quiet as neither Ron or Lisa said anything. As Ron fidgeted in his chair it was clear that it was something he didn't actually want to talk about. He started to speak and then he stopped and looked at Lisa who said, "We time travelled a few days ago. We saw a *Stegosaurus*."

Lauren started to laugh but saw the somber look on her Dad's face. She quickly looked at Charles who shrugged his shoulders and shook his head. "What do you mean?" she asked.

Ron leaned forward in his chair and said, "That we got into another time machine, built by another person, and traveled back in time again. It seemed the right thing to do then and it still does. It's the reason we are moving to Florida, I'm going to consult for them."

"*Them*? Who is *them*?" Lauren shouted.

Lisa flinched, and Ron took her hand and told Lauren, "There's no reason to shout. I will tell you who they are, but I want to talk about this, not argue. Let me explain things so you can understand how we have reached this decision."

As Lauren sat back in her chair with a "Hmph" Ron looked at Charles and said, "I feel like we cheated on you. I know that sounds strange, but it was a spur of the moment thing and we didn't think to call you."

Charles smiled and said, "Ron, neither one of you need my permission to do anything. But I am interested to know who this fellow time traveler is and how he travels."

"He wants to meet you too."

"Back to the point," Lauren said. "Who is this person and come to think of it, why did he talk to you if he knows about Charles?"

"The person is Steve Weston. He and his brother Ben own EXENCO."

"I know the name Steve Weston," Charles said. "I have read about him. Very intelligent. Very."

Lauren frowned at Charles and motioned with her hand toward Ron as she instructed him, "Keep going."

"Well, he knew to talk to me because he knew Taggit and had read Danny's book. He –"

"He read my book?" Danny asked. "Did he like it?"

"I didn't ask him. I'll –"

"Focus. Focus, Dad," Lauren cut in.

"Oh, yes. Sorry. Well he simply put two and two together and realized the book was a true story. Taggit, Gattig, I guess you should have made up completely different names, Danny." Before Danny could say anything, Lauren motioned again, and Ron kept going.

"He has a passion for dinosaurs, sort of a boyhood type of thing I gathered. But more importantly, he wants to create new types of protective equipment for military personnel. His thought is that if their gear protects their Team, the EXENCO Team, from attacking dinosaurs it should withstand a lot of things in this era. Probably a valid point."

"Would you be going in the field with this? Did you test something when you jumped?" Lauren asked.

"No, no," Lisa said. "Listen, you know that I hated jumping to begin with. Though I got carried away with some things I was terrified the entire time. Time has not dulled that fear. But there have been some casualties with the EXENCO program, people have died because they can engineer creative solutions to problems, but they don't always know what those problems are. That's why they contacted Ron. He answered several questions for them during our meeting and they were very impressed with his knowledge.

"We actually jumped because it was a controlled setting. We went back and watched them take samples from a dead *Stegosaurus* during a previous jump or Walk as they call it. There was no danger and it went as they explained it would. I was still terrified, and I don't ever want to repeat the experience, but these men seemed to know what they were doing."

Lauren shook her head and said, "I just don't believe this. You didn't go back to a baseball game with Charles and Danny, you went back to them. To the dinosaurs. I haven't even gone out into the field since all of that to find a fossil and I definitely wouldn't go back to see a live dinosaur. And I didn't think either of you would either."

"You're right," Ron said. "And if you told me you had gone back to see them before our meeting with Steve I would have thought you had gone crazy. But you haven't talked with them or seen their operation. And they do want to talk to you. They view both of you, and Danny and Lisa, as experts. They want your thoughts and ideas about how to make sure no one else dies during their product testing. They are willing to pay –"

"I don't want their money," Lauren said curtly. "And I know how to make sure no one else dies; don't go back and experiment with animals you don't understand."

"But they're going to," Lisa said quietly. "They want to protect our service men and women. So, I feel we need to help them."

The room was quiet for a few moments then Danny spoke up, "As you know, I was in the Army. If it helps to develop something that will save a military casualty then yeah, I'll talk to someone. I don't want pay though and like Lauren, I'm not going back."

Everyone looked at Charles who started off slowly, "You're probably all thinking I want to go meet the new time traveler, to find out how he does things, so I can modify my machine. I don't. As I have told you and as I have promised Lauren, I don't want to jump anymore. I can see in this room, and remember vividly, just exactly what my jumps have cost. But I would like to meet him, so I can explain that to him. And suggest he stop now before it is too late. But, I'm sure I can't stop him, it will have to be his own conscience that does that."

Lauren stood up and walked into the kitchen. Charles followed her and put his arm around her as she nibbled on a cookie. "What do you want me to do?" he asked.

"Part of me wants you to stay as far away from this man as possible. I'm afraid he'll have something new and innovative and you'll want to start jumping again. Going to a few places with Danny scares me enough. Why would Dad and Lisa go back again? Over 100 million years. Dinosaurs? What possessed them to do that?"

"Probably your Dad."

"Dad?"

"He loves dinosaurs. He still goes into the field even with the memories of all that happened. Lisa supports your dad, wants him to be happy. Plus, she is her own woman. She cares about people and it seems like this company cares for the people in our military. That would resonate with her, a lot. I wouldn't be surprised if your dad jumped again, but I don't think Lisa will. So, I don't think Ron will either. He loves and respects Lisa very much."

Lauren put the cookie down and hugged Charles, "Okay, I'm getting a perspective on this now. I don't like it, but there it is. As long as you don't get involved –"

"You have my word."

"And Dad and Lisa and Danny keep their bodies in the present then I guess I don't really have anything to worry about. Except Dad, like you said."

"As long as there are no nudist camps a hundred million years ago I think you'll be alright," Charles said.

Lauren smiled and replied, "That's not the argument I would have used but you're probably right. My Dad, the nudist. Let's go back in."

Danny, Ron and Lisa were talking when they walked back in and Lauren said, "Guys, I want to apologize. Sorry I went over the top but, well, we've been talking about this and I never would have thought it would come up again. Never. And I want to meet this Steve too. I have to feel it's right."

Lisa walked over to Lauren and hugged her as she said, "I understand. I'm still not exactly sure how I became okay with everything, but I did. And I think you will too."

"We'll see, but don't expect me to become involved."

"Well, I will say this," Lisa went on. "I haven't had any dreams since we jumped. I haven't woken up with my heart beating so hard I thought it was going to jump out of me. I'm not saying it cured me, but maybe it has helped me put things into perspective."

"That's interesting," Danny said. "You always hear if you fall off the horse you got to get back on."

"But I've never heard if you stick your head in a lion's mouth and they bite it off you have to do it again," Lauren replied.

"Agreed," Danny said. "But we didn't get our heads bit off, just messed up. I'm not saying I'd jump to sleep better, but I might."

"How did they jump to the same place and time?" Charles asked. "How did they know it was going to be safe?"

Ron came in from the kitchen carrying a piece of pie and said, "Their machine, or Unit they called it, is in a huge warehouse type building. They simply moved the Unit from one side to another, about a hundred feet, and appeared in a different spot at the same time. They have similar camouflage to what you had, they were invisible to the first Unit, or the same Unit, or whatever you want to call it. Since there had been no problems with the first jump and we were in the same place at the same time they knew it would be safe."

Charles nodded and just said, "Interesting."

Ron looked at Lauren and asked, "By the way, what did you think we were going to surprise you with? You seemed like you had an idea."

"Well, I didn't have a clue, but Charles thought Lisa might be pregnant and well, I started thinking about it and got excited. You know, after I got over the image of you drooling along with the baby."

Ron shook his head as he said, "Sorry, Lisa isn't pregnant."

Lisa put her hand on Ron's shoulder and said, "Not yet anyway."

"I would have rather heard you were pregnant than you jumped again," Lauren said.

"But now it's in the past, literally," Ron said. "We're keeping things in perspective now, remember?"

"I remember," Lauren told him. "No baby, no jumping. Got it."

"Yet," Lisa interjected.

Ron winked at Danny and Charles and told Lisa, "I have decided I need to be with you as much as possible. This makes it easy to retire and start working for Steve. I'll be home every day and night and family and friends will be close...until the first dirty diaper."

"You said it," Danny agreed.

"Amen, Brother," Charles nodded.

"Men," Lauren and Lisa said in unison and everyone laughed.

"Dad, call this Steve tomorrow and set up a time for all of us to go talk to him. Then let's get out and find you a house. A home. The perfect home."

"I'll call Steve right now and leave a message for him to call me."

Ron pulled his phone out of a pocket but when he called, Steve answered, "Hello, Ron, and Merry Christmas."

"Steve, I'm so sorry to bother you today. I thought this was your business phone and I was just going to leave a message."

"Ron, this is my business phone. I always have it with me because I'm always working. How can I help you?"

"I was wondering when we could meet?"

"Well, if you're not busy I could meet you and Lisa for lunch or dinner tomorrow."

"Actually, I want you to meet all of us."

"All?"

"Yes, Lisa, Lauren, Charles and Danny. We would all like to meet with you."

"How soon and where? The same restaurant?"

"Is a restaurant okay?" Ron asked everyone.

"No," Lauren replied quickly. "I'd like to see his business. Can we get a tour?"

"Lauren would like –"

"I heard," Steve said. "It would be our pleasure to show you anything you want to see. What day works best for you?"

Everyone looked at Lauren and she thought for a moment then said loudly, "How about the afternoon of New Year's Eve? Say one or two? We'll be busy this week. Does that work?"

"It certainly does. I'm looking forward to meeting all of you. Should I send a car for you?"

"We'll meet you there, sir," Charles said.

"That's fantastic. I'll see you then and please, my name is Steve. Goodbye, Ron and Lisa."

"See, that was easy," Ron said.

Steve disconnected the call and smiled as he said, "That was easy."

Then he called Ben who answered, "Steve, you never made it over today."

"Sorry, but I have some good news."

"What's that?"

"Ron has everyone coming to see things on the 31st."

"But that's -"

"I know, New Year's Eve, don't worry. They will be here early enough you can make it home in time for whatever you have planned."

"Okay. Well then, this is good, right? Fantastic."

"Fantastic," Steve agreed. He disconnected the call and leaned back in his chair and started thinking.

CHAPTER SIX
THE TEAM

Everyone was on edge before they started for EXENCO. Though they had kept busy all week with errands and talking about the past jumps, Lauren had constantly reminded them they needed to be careful when they met Steve. "He's traveling in time and he wants to make money. Two things that we know don't go together. I know he says he's doing it for the military and he seems to be a good guy, but we have to watch him."

Finally, Danny had told her, "Lauren, we agree with you that we have to be careful. We all know what happened last time and we don't want it to happen again. But let's give the man a chance. Ron and Lisa seem to think he's okay."

After that Lauren seemed to think it was her against everyone else and though she was friendly she seemed distant. She didn't speak up during any of the sessions with Danny and would sometimes just walk out of a room. Charles spoke with her the night before the meeting and asked, "What do you plan on saying to these people?"

"I'm not sure."

"You seem angry. Is it about the meeting? Danny thinks you are mad at him."

"What? No, I'm not mad at Danny or anyone else, I just...they are traveling in time. You know I don't like that, I feel it's wrong. But I don't know what they do or are going to do. All we'll have is what they tell us and somehow, we're going to have to judge whether it is true or not. But, we don't know them. I just have a bad feeling about all of it. But I'm not mad at Danny or anyone else."

"He'll be glad to hear that," Charles said as he gave Lauren a hug. "Don't worry about tomorrow. If anything seems wrong I'll back you and we'll walk. Of course, we have to convince Ron."

"Dad," Lauren muttered. "Sometimes I don't know about him."

"Lisa is pretty smart."

Lauren nodded and said, "You're right. She's smarter than a lot of us realize. But anyone can get fooled."

"Hopefully, not all of us."

The next morning Lauren stood up at the kitchen table and announced, "I'm sorry everyone. I haven't made the past few days very fun for any of us. I just wanted to make sure we were all thinking right about this and not getting ahead of ourselves. With that said, I'm ready to hear whoever and whatever with an open mind. I will say I'm not going on any jumps." She looked at Ron and Lisa and continued, "But if anyone else wants to, I understand. Just think about it, that's all I'm asking."

"We will," Ron told her. "I know sometimes I jump before I look but we're not doing that here."

"Then let's go before I change my mind," Lauren said.

"That's like a four-second window," Charles said. As Lauren smacked him on the shoulder he laughed and continued, "Too late." Everyone else laughed also and as they drove to EXENCO they talked about the New Year and finding a house for Ron and Lisa.

Lauren stopped talking as they pulled into the EXENCO parking lot then said, "You know, I've driven past these buildings a million times and they've always interested me. Windmills all around and solar panels across the roofs, it all seemed progressive and…and…"

"And something you would support?" Charles asked.

"Yes, but –"

"But now that you know about the time travel you aren't sure."

Lauren nodded and replied, "Yes, that's right. In my world those two somehow don't go together." She took a deep breath and continued, "But they aren't really connected."

"Like paleontology and nude yoga," Ron suggested.

Lauren shook her head and said, "Not the image I want before this meeting. Let's go before someone else thinks of something."

"I already did," Lisa said. "You and Charles should join our yoga class."

"Ahhh," Lauren mock-screamed as they got out of the car. "Not what I want to hear. Not what I want at all."

As they approached the main doors, Steve and Ben came out to meet them. "Ron and Lisa," Steve said, "good to see you again." He shook hands with them then turned to Charles and paused for a moment, then said, "Mr. Dawson, this is indeed a great pleasure. It's an honor to meet you, sir."

Charles shook his hand and said, "Sir, the honor is mine. I can't believe there is another time traveler, another who has figured out how to do it. Perhaps we took the same path, we should compare notes. And Steve, please, call me Charles."

Steve smiled and said, "Charles, that would be great. We might be able to combine our ideas and create something even better."

Charles shook his head as he replied, "If you come up with something better, good for you. My interest is strictly academic now, I'm just about finished with jumping. I want to spend more time with Lauren and my friends."

Steve turned to Lauren and as he shook her hand he said, "I understand if you are upset with all of this. None of you have to travel, no one at all. We just want to talk to you about your experiences to gain knowledge that we don't have. Unlike Taggit, we aren't going to kidnap anyone. Just talk."

"That sounds…reasonable," Lauren replied slowly. "I don't want to offend you but yes, I am uncomfortable being here."

Steve smiled as he said, "Just let me know what I can do to help."

Then he turned to Danny and as they shook hands Danny said, "Steve, I hear you have great taste in books."

Steve smiled and said, "Danny, your book unlocked a lot of things for me. It put me in touch with Ron and Lisa of course but your narrative on the perils of time travel kept me from making some simple mistakes that I know I would have. Like going back without adequate preparation. If that had happened I may not have been as resourceful as Charles and saved myself. Plus, your bravery," he paused and looked at everyone, "all of your bravery, was very inspirational and motivating."

Steve stepped back and continued, "But it's actually 'we', my brother Ben is the person who gets things done around here. Without him I'd probably still be spinning on square one or like I said, taken a trip by myself and gotten into some kind of trouble. This is Ben."

"Hello," Ben said. "Let me echo what Steve has said to you, what an honor this is. Very exciting too. Ron and Lisa helped us so much the other day that I just can't imagine what we will learn by speaking to the rest of you." He quickly turned to Lauren and said, "That is, if you want to. I understand if anyone does not want to discuss anything with me."

Lauren just nodded, and Steve said, "Let's go inside and talk. I know you just ate breakfast, but we have some juice and pastry just in case."

"That sounds great," Lisa said. "I am hungry again." Ron took her arm as Charles, Lauren and Danny smiled. Steve led the way along a hallway that was lined with photos of EXENCO products. Lauren looked carefully at each one as they passed but didn't say anything.

Ben opened a door to a small conference room and as they sat down Steve said, "We'll keep this brief. I don't gloss over things or beat around the bush. I'm direct and Ben likes to tell me that sometimes I'm too blunt. But that's me. I'm trying to devise ways to reduce injuries and deaths in our service men and women. There are some things right now, and I emphasize right now, that are beyond our capabilities to stop. But as we take these small first steps we may be able to conquer them soon.

"Like many people I have had a life-long fascination with dinosaurs. They were the dominant species on Earth for hundreds of millions of years, defeated in the end by circumstances they couldn't control. Their speed, weight, strength and defensive capabilities were far above what our bodies can defend against. It stood to reason then that if we could create the means to keep us safe from them we could keep our fighting forces safer. Imagine ultra-light but ultra-strong body armor that a soldier could wear."

"Law enforcement would be interested in that also," Danny pointed out.

"Yes, they would," Steve agreed. "We are developing a line of products for them also. But Danny, you were in the military weren't you?"

"Yes, sir."

"Danny, what if you could enclose a foxhole, trench or even an entire camp inside of a shell that would stop bullets and rockets? What if there were smaller units that you could wear on your back that allowed you to drop down and an enemy tank could run over you without harm? What if these personalized units were equipped with communication, weapons and even camouflage capabilities that would make a soldier, an airplane, or even a ship at sea invisible?"

Steve spread his hands and said, "We have this and more in new weapons and recognition pattern capabilities. We –"

"You have this already?" Danny asked.

"Yes," Steve said. "Through trial and error, where unfortunately some of our team lost their lives, we believe we have in-the-field equipment ready. We just need a few more tests and we'll be ready to approach the Pentagon with our proposals." Steve stood up and continued, "That is why we would like your help. Again, you do not have to take Walks or even go back in time. You can watch video and you will have access to all of our information generated by the Walks. All of it."

"This would be fantastic even if only some of what you are trying to achieve happens" Danny said. "It would be world changing."

"Yes, it would," Steve agreed.

"I have a few questions," Lauren said quietly.

"I was hoping you would," Steve said. "Please, be direct."

"Why did people have to die? Couldn't you have used robots or some other mechanical device?"

Steve nodded to Ben who started, "We tried, but were unsuccessful. If a lot of animals were around, their bodies would block signals and equipment would not function correctly. They couldn't get close enough to the 'saurs. If there was a successful test it was sometimes hard to get the device back. There were times they couldn't return on their own or were carried away.

"But we needed tests involving people. The Walkers could get as close as we needed, they could deploy the spikes like they were supposed to. When the 'saurs left they were able to simply return to the Unit."

"If they lived."

"Yes, if they lived," Steve agreed. "Being a Walker was a dangerous job. The men knew what they were getting into and just like an astronaut or a test pilot, they did the job to the best of their ability. They weren't just lab rats, we supplied them with the best technology available at that point in time. It's why we wish we knew about you sooner, maybe some of them wouldn't have died."

"You said being a Walker "was" a dangerous job."

"Yes, *was*. Perhaps Ron and Lisa told you we have a team of professionals now. They, and the technology we use, has taken much of the risk out of our interactions with the animals. We have had zero injuries in the field."

"How much money do you expect to make on this venture?" Lauren asked.

"We hope to cover recent costs plus twenty percent."

"Recent costs?"

"Just the last year's costs," Ben told her. "We're eating the rest."

"How much are you eating?"

"500 million or so."

"And last year's?"

"Close to 100 million, but that's a drop in the bucket compared to the 600 billion the Department of Defense spends in a year."

Lisa half raised her hand and then asked, "But don't most businesses use a markup of 50 percent?"

Ben nodded his head and replied, "That's true. But we have two separate plans in work here. First, we want our equipment in the hands of the military as soon as possible. Exceptional equipment at an exceptional price. This EXECON 'saur project is being funded by our endeavors in creating new energy resources. The wind, the sea, rivers of all sizes and other areas I am not at liberty to discuss just yet. We make a lot of money on the energy side of things, a lot, so if we can have the government take over the military side of things then, well, then we can reduce energy costs too. Other companies will be forced to follow our example and suddenly cheaper energy will be available for everyone."

Steve broke in with, "Before you think we're a bunch of saints, we do hope for some considerations for tax breaks." He looked at Lauren and said, "Because we are after all, businessmen."

Lauren nodded and said, "I do have one more question. What do you expect us to do with all of this important scientific data you will be supplying us? I mean after we provide information to you to make your equipment better?"

"Whatever you want to," Steve answered. "Do you want to publish photos and papers with real information? You didn't before but maybe you do now. It would mean letting everyone know about time travel but, well, that would be up to you.

"Perhaps you just want to write papers with your information disguised as logical conclusions and then sit back and receive praise for your insightfulness as you are proven right. Or, just sit back and continue to watch as your fellow paleontologists continue to fumble around for answers. In short, you may do with it whatever you would like. It is part of the price we are willing to pay for your services. Along with money or jobs, whatever you want.

"We pride ourselves in having the best when it comes to employees and consultants. We consider you the best. All of you would be valuable members of our team along with Ron and Lisa. I know you don't think so, but we do."

The room was silent as Steve stood up and told them, "Well, that's my speech. I hope it didn't bore you and I hope you understand what we are about. If you would like a tour of the facility, Ben will be more than happy to give you one. I imagine you will also want to return home and talk among yourselves." He shook hands with each of them again then left the room.

Ron was smiling as he asked, "What did you think?"

"Very interesting," Charles said. "I especially like the part about costs being reasonable."

"Yes," Danny agreed. "Can you imagine cheaper energy? It would go global."

"Lauren, what did you think?" Lisa asked.

"I think I would like Ben to give us a tour and then talk about things at home."

"Great," Ben said. "Let's go." He led them straight to a large room and told them, "I will take you anyplace else you want to go, but I imagine this is high on your list." He pointed to the time travel Unit and said, "This is what we travel in. It's -"

"It's so different," Charles interrupted. "Mine was just a cage, something to get there and back. It had a few work stations but this...this looks like it could do much more."

"It can," Ben agreed. "But Steve's first Units were small also. This is an end product of probably something similar to what you started with. I'm sure Steve will be glad to -"

"No," Charles shook his head. "No. I did what I did and if time travel has passed on to someone else then so be it. I don't need to know anything, I'm not traveling anymore."

"I understand," Ben said. "Does anyone else want to go inside?"

After a moment of silence Danny spoke up, "Not really. Even if I went inside I wouldn't understand what I was looking at. If Charles thinks it looks impressive, that's enough for me."

Ben looked at Lauren for a moment then shrugged his shoulders and said, "Okay, there is more to see." As they started down a hallway they passed a door and could hear loud shouting and laughing. "The Team," Ben told them.

"What team?" Lauren asked.

"The group that replaced the Walkers. The men and women who test the equipment for us."

Lauren stopped and asked, "Can we meet them?"

Surprised Ben said, "Sure, well I think. Let me check with Major Donald." He was back in the hallway in about a minute and smiled and told them, "Come right in."

They filed into a large locker room and saw men and women dressed in light green and gray uniforms. They were joking with each other but when they noticed Ben and his group they quieted down. A woman stepped from the group and commanded, "Team, *atten-hut!*" The men and women immediately snapped to attention and the woman continued, "Team, this is the group I told you about. The other group of time travelers who defended themselves against the *dinos* with rifles, smoke grenades and even an electronic stun device. They were up close and personal with them and have the scars and lost team members to prove it." She turned back and said, "I'm Major Donald and we are honored you are here."

Danny stepped forward and said, "Major Donald, I'm –"

"Sergeant Daniel Jameston," the Major interrupted. "The recipient of two purple hearts and many other commendations." She saluted him and then shook his hand. Then she continued talking to the Team, "This is Charles Dawson, the original time traveler and his wife Lauren and her father, Dr. Ron Fontana. Lauren and Ron are accomplished paleontologists and Ron may become a member of EXECON. And this is Lisa who is, and yes, I'm including you Sinewave," the Major said loudly, "the smartest person in the room. She may become a part of EXECON too."

"She's smarter than me?" one of the men asked.

"Prettier too," someone added.

"You know us," Danny said. "So, who are all of you?"

Major Donald turned to the group and as she said their name each one nodded. "The men are Ricardo, Cat, Whitey, Stork, Ammo, Sinewave, Blonk and Chesky. The women are Junk, Maybe, Rover, Stoney and Lost. We are The Team. We have better equipment than you did and more firepower, but just like you, we walk up to the *dinos* and take the bite."

"We didn't exactly walk up to them," Lauren said. "But I understand what you're saying. How many times?"

"Twenty walks, ma'am," Major Donald replied.

"Are you training today?" Danny asked.

"Yes, sir. We're walking tomorrow so we wanted to get one last time in today with some new equipment."

"Can we watch?" Lauren asked. As Ron and Charles looked at her she added, "I want to see what they do."

"Yes, ma'am, you can watch," Major Donald told her. "Team gear up and let's go."

Immediately Ben said, "Come with me." They followed him out and he quickly took them through a large room filled with various crates and tarp covered objects. Then he led them up a staircase and into a long, rectangular room with a large window facing out over an open space, about 50 yards wide and 25 yards deep. The space was thickly filled with various long grasses, ferns and trees. It looked like a jungle and there was a small stream winding near the far edge. They could hear various animal and insect noises and when they looked up they could see flying shapes that appeared to be high in a blue sky.

There was a man sitting in front of a holographic control board who nodded toward them and said, "Welcome, I'm Otto."

"What is this?" Lauren asked.

"It's our training simulator," Otto said. "Let's see how The Team handles my new problem."

They crowded toward the window and watched as The Team slowly made their way into the jungle and through the vegetation. All of them were wearing helmets, backpacks, vests and carrying an odd shaped rifle. Otto moved a hand and a loud roar was heard. Major Donald's voice could be heard saying, "Drop and stop," as The Team knelt down and stayed still as a realistic looking *Tyrannosaurus Rex* suddenly materialized and crossed in front of them until it disappeared into the thick vegetation.

"One and three," Major Donald barked, and some team members started forward and were followed closely by everyone else. As they approached the stream they fanned out and as some chirping sounds were heard their rifles came up. A voice said, "We got something in front of us," then another voice added, "Looks like 'carny's'" and Major Donald followed with, "Get ready."

Suddenly seven shapes appeared in front of The Team and started toward them. The shapes were some type of thin hard material which depicted a dinosaur that walked on two legs and had elongated heads, small forearms and long tails. Their green and grey color made them hard to follow even though the animals were about ten feet long. A few seconds later five more of the animals appeared and started following the first seven. A few barely audible clicking noises were heard which quickly became a hundred clicks in about five seconds. Each of the moving shapes stopped at different spots and then a horn sounded three short tones. The Team stood up and high-fived each other then started back.

Lauren looked at Danny and shook her head and as he nodded he asked, "Why couldn't we hear their shots?" Danny asked.

"Those are air rifles," Ben said. "Let's go down and take a look. Otto, could you ask them to stand by their targets?"

Ben led them out into the training area and to the dinosaur targets. They found the targets were thick pieces of some type of polymer and that they were suspended from overhead arms with stabilizing cables. Each target had been shot many times and Danny told them, "That was good shooting. When Ben said they were air rifles I thought they might be underpowered. What kind of ammunition do you use?"

"Nothing that's on the market," Major Donald told him. She held out what looked like a plastic bullet that was about three inches long. It was a half inch in diameter at its round base and quickly tapered to a point. Danny took it and whistled, "That is a mean looking round. Built for maximum penetration. Does it flatten out and stop or keep on going?"

"Penetration is about two feet, we don't want them going through an animal and possibly striking a member of The Team." She turned to a short, stocky man and said, "Ammo, hold up one of the red rounds." He did, and they could see the entire bullet was red and its tip was a little rounder and thicker. "That's an explosive round," she explained. "It won't matter how far it penetrated when it goes off."

"Got it," Danny told her.

"How did you like the training?" Whitey asked.

Before Danny could answer, Lauren asked, "Why not holographic targets?"

"Because these targets keep moving toward you if they are not hit. When one of these run into you you're flat on your back and sore the next day. Made everyone a better shot."

Lauren shook her head and said, "Well, it was a great show but all of you just got killed."

"What?" Whitey asked hotly. "That was perfect. We –"

"Just got killed," Danny finished for him.

There was some low grumbling among the team members until Major Donald held up a hand and asked, "What did we do wrong?"

Danny looked at her for a moment then asked, "Let me show you." Then he turned to Ben and asked, "Can I talk to Otto?"

"Of course."

"Okay, then I want everyone else to return to your starting point," Danny told them. "I'll let you know when you can go."

There was still some low comments from The Team as Danny, Ron, Lisa, Charles and Lauren returned to the control room. Danny and Lauren talked with Otto for several minutes before he smiled and started moving some holographic images around in front of him. "We had to do it," Lauren told Danny.

Lisa heard her and asked, "No one will get hurt, will they?"

"Just their egos," Danny replied. He picked up the microphone in front of Otto and said, "Team, you're on again."

As the Team started moving Steve walked up to Ben and asked, "How are things going?"

"I'm not sure," Ben said. "Danny and Lauren seem to think we are doing something wrong."

"What?" Steve asked.

Ron nodded toward the window and said, "Watch."

The Team started forward just as it did earlier and as the *Rex* appeared Major Donald said, "Stop and drop", and everyone did. But this time the *Rex* swung toward them and took two steps forward before stopping. It raised its snout into the air and sniffed loudly twice then took another step. Someone asked, "Is it going to charge?" and the *Rex* launched itself forward at the Team and then quickly faded away.

"What was that all about?" another voice asked and was quickly answered by the major, "It was about us failing. Apparently, we forgot these things can hear. Stay quiet and move out." They started forward and at the edge of the stream a voice whispered, "There's movement ahead of us."

"Get ready," Major Donald advised again.

Three shadows moved and just stopped. Other shapes could be seen moving quickly right and left through the trees on the other side of the stream and a second later a voice shouted, "We're flanked on the right. I need –" Four of the moving targets exploded into the right side of the group knocking three team members down before all the targets stopped.

The left side of The Team moved to face the threat as Major Donald shouted, "No, no. Stay where you are and –", but it was too late as five targets came in from the left side, behind the turned team members. As they penetrated the team's position the three original targets moved across the stream and into them. All the targets stopped after another five yards then were immediately taken up and out of the scene. The horn sounded three times. This time there were no high fives as only a few of the team stood up.

"Anyone hurt?" Otto asked.

"I think Ricardo and Junk are out cold, and at least three of us are still kneeling down," someone said.

"Stork, here. I may have a broken ankle."

Ben looked at Otto and pointed down to the training area and Otto quickly advised, "We're coming down."

It only took a few seconds for everyone to get to the Team and Sinewave jumped up from the ground and shouted, "What the hell was that all about?"

Danny surprised everyone by shouting back, "What was that all about? That was reality, son. What do think the 'saurs are going to do? A frontal attack with drums and fifes playing? These were pack hunters and they know how to dissect a herd and kill whatever they can. Do you think they are going to walk up to you? Even the speed I asked Otto to move them at wasn't fast enough. If you aren't shooting before they move, you don't stand a chance. They divided you, flanked you, cut you up and had you for lunch. That's what the hell that was all about."

Danny stepped back and quietly asked Major Donald, "How many casualties do you have? I didn't mean for anyone to get hurt."

"Rover, how many?" Major Donald snapped.

A woman stepped from the back and told her, "Ricardo and Junk were out but are back with us though they may have a headache for a while. I didn't see any signs of a concussion. Cat and Ammo had the wind knocked out of them but are okay now. Stork's ankle is swelling up, but my guess is it is sprained and not broken. The rest of us are banged up with bruises and scrapes but we'll live."

Major Donald turned to Danny and was quiet for a moment then said, "Thank you." Then she paused and continued, "I think."

"I hated to do it, but I didn't think just telling you would have made a difference."

"You were right," Sinewave said. "I'm sorry I sounded off. I –"

"Have nothing to be sorry for," Lauren told him. Then she looked at Major Donald and continued, "As long as you learn from it. You should already know not to move when a Rex comes along. When they hear you, they aren't going to take a second to decide if they should do something, they'll just do it. You would have had to handle the *Rex* before you even got to the other *'saurs*. And from them, expect attacks from all sides, at all times."

Major Donald turned to the Team and asked, "Anyone ready to go home? We have a New Year's walk tomorrow, remember?"

As everyone shouted, "No", she told them, "Then let's get this right." As they moved back to the starting area she asked Doc, "Is Stork going to make the Walk?"

"Sorry, Major. Like I said, I don't think it's broken but he can't put any weight on it. It's bad enough to take him out of tomorrow."

"I could try," Stork told her.

"Next time," Major Donald said and walked away.

"Stork, I need to escort everyone back to their car," Ben said. "But then I'll come right back for you."

"Nonsense," Steve said. "Stork can you walk or hop on that to the loading dock?"

"I think so."

"Excellent. Ben, take your time and I'll take care of Stork. Ron and Lisa, always a pleasure, and Charles, Lauren and Danny, I hope to see you soon."

"Maybe tomorrow," Danny said. "Ben, when do you leave?"

"About one."

"Okay," Danny said. "Let's get back to the car, I need to think...and talk. I might want to go with you."

As Ben led them out of the training area Steve told Stork, "Lean on me, young man. I'll get you out of here."

"Thank you, sir. I hate to be a bother."

"A bother? You're no bother. You're part of the Team. All of you are helping our research project move successfully forward. You're no bother at all."

"Thank you, sir. I'll be ready for the next Walk."

"I know you will, but you seem to be slowing down. Starting to hurt more?"

"Yes."

"I know Rover said it might not be broken but I'm going to have a driver take you to the hospital first for x-rays. If it's not broken, well, you're still on the clock, aren't you?" Steve asked as he slapped Stork on the shoulder. "Might as well get paid for doing nothing for a while."

"Sir, I don't mind just going home. I don't want to waste your time or money."

"Nonsense. We take care of all our employees. If it's just sprained, so be it. If there is a break though, it's better to get it taken care of immediately. What will you tell them at the hospital?"

"We know the drill, sir. Fell down some stairs."

Steve agreed, "That was some fall."

"Woke us up," Stork said. "It will take our training to a different level."

"I agree. And now I have a suggestion, sit in here for a moment while I go get a golf cart. I don't know why I didn't think of it sooner."

"Will do, sir," Stork said as he walked through the door Steve had opened and sat down at a table. "Feels good to get off my feet."

"Be right back."

Stork sat with his eyes closed for a few minutes as he fought down the pain. It felt like it was broken but he hoped it wasn't. He opened his eyes and realized he was in a room he had never seen before. It looked like everything, the chair, table, walls, even the floor, was lined with aluminum. It gleamed. As the door opened behind him he turned to ask about the room when he froze. It wasn't the door to the hallway that had opened, it was a sliding door and stepping through it was Tiny.

The pain in his ankle was forgotten as he jumped up and backed away from the animal. He couldn't remember what it was, but he knew that it was a carnivore and despite the fact it wasn't even four feet tall, he had seen it rip a cow to pieces. It was Steve's favorite show and tell piece when it came to the dangers of dinosaurs.

The animal walked slowly into the room, looking side to side with its claws tapping the metallic floor. Stork saw a chance and started moving toward the open door when it suddenly slid shut. The animal barked and turned toward Stork who shouted, "Steve...Steve? Mr. Weston? Tiny has gotten loose. He's in the room with me." Then he turned toward the door he entered the room through and pulled on the handle. It was locked. He started beating on it then he turned around slowly. Tiny was crouching down and looked like he was about to attack. Stork dropped to the floor to try and crawl under the table, but it was too late. A crushing weight drove him down and there was unbearable pain in his back. He began screaming.

High above the room Steve looked down with satisfaction. He was always amazed at what Tiny could do. Not just with the surgical precision of the teeth and claws, but how his body turned at just the right angle at just the right moment to rip flesh, muscle and crack bones. Efficient. He waited a few more minutes then opened the sliding door and Tiny ran back through it dragging Stork's body. Then the drains opened, and the water cascaded over every inch of the room until it gleamed again.

CHAPTER SEVEN
DECISIONS

The car was silent on the return ride as everyone contemplated what they had seen and what Danny had said. When they returned to the kitchen there was still silence until Danny said, "Okay, everyone. Let me tell you what I'm thinking. First, I know Lauren saw it and I think the rest of you did too. They were training wrong, not considering the reality of a live dinosaur attacking them. But they listened to us and I'll bet right now they are training harder than ever. I feel pretty good about that.

"Next, I found it exhilarating just to be looking down on that training area. Almost too real. And when the *Rex* walked through, well, it was amazing. Now I don't want to go out with them, I don't need that again, but they stress safety and I think I would be safe in their Unit. I could help Ron do something, whatever he wanted me to do. I mean you all know the terrible thing that happened to me back in time, so I wouldn't want that again."

Everyone looked at each other for a moment until Charles asked, "What terrible thing happened to you? You got shot in the present and I know you shot a *Rex*, and there was one near you in the creek…what am I forgetting?"

"You don't remember? I tore my pants!" He looked at the blank faces then said, "My good pants. Torn. Remember?" Then he couldn't help himself and he burst out laughing. "Sorry guys, I had to cut the tension somehow."

Everyone smiled, and Lisa said, "Danny, I'm glad you're going to help Ron. I'm going to go too if he is. I don't know what I'll do but I'll try."

"But Lisa," Ron protested, "you don't really want to go and –"

"And don't worry," Lisa finished for him. "I'm with Danny. I felt safe in their Unit the first time we jumped, and I think I will again. I don't want to Walk either, but maybe I will see something that will help them. I really hope I can help."

"I hope you can too," Ron said. "I agree their Team could use some direction, a dose of reality, but they all seemed driven to succeed, just like Steve and Ben. I didn't see anything today that would make me rethink my position on things."

Everyone looked at Lauren who started, "I'll admit that EXECON seems wonderful. Almost too wonderful. I actually use some of their products. But, can a company really do all that Steve told us or were we just hearing empty promises? Taggit made a lot of promises if you remember." As Ron started to say something she held up her hand and said, "I'm not done yet."

As Ron sat back she continued, "I'm not comparing EXECON to Taggit...yet. You want to know what I think so I'm telling you. Things might just be too good to be true. But two things we do know, what about all of the bullets that they fired? There were hundreds of them. That increases the possibility one will become a fossil."

"Actually, all of their equipment is biodegradable," Ron told her. "It disappears after two days."

"Okay but think of a find featuring a dinosaur whose skeleton looks like Swiss cheese. How's that going to be explained?"

Lauren then continued "Okay, so equipment being left behind is not a problem but what about footprints? And that rover thing that was on treads. I hope I'm not asked someday what kind of animal left that trackway. What precautions are they taking to minimize these risks?

"Apparently they have had a lot of people killed during their jumps. The more deaths the more likely human bones will be found too many millions of years ago to make sense. That's another awkward question.

"And that brings up all of these findings and information Steve is coming up with. And he's just going to give it to us? Give it to us out of the kindness of his heart? So, we can guide paleontology along the correct path? Behind the scenes of course, or no, wait, we can lead the way with our vast knowledge as everyone bows before us." Lauren grimaced and said, "Okay, a little over the top but there you go. I like their talk to a degree...but I still need proof of their intentions. That's where I'm at."

"I liked that," Lisa said. "You still have questions and concerns, but it sounds like you are keeping an open mind. I think that's all Steve and Ben want. See for yourself and then act as you feel you should."

Lauren thought for a second and said, "I guess you're right. Still, I hope I'm worrying about nothing, but afraid I'm not."

Lisa looked at Charles and asked, "What about you?"

Charles smiled and said, "I have to admit I was impressed with everything I saw and heard. Steve, Ben, and the team atmosphere all struck a nice chord with me. I did like the part about cheaper energy and our military being able to better take care of themselves. I also liked how Steve, the boss, helped...what bird was he?"

"Stork," everyone said in unison.

Charles smiled as he said, "Yes, Stork. There didn't seem to be a big divide between upper management and lower personnel so to speak. He seemed like he really wanted to help Stork. But I also share the same concerns Lauren does. I'm starting to think more like she does. How will you explain a human fossil inside of a *Rex*? You'd be forced to admit to time travel and that would open a whole new load of problems for you. All of you. Everything in the past that seemed suspicious, or ever went wrong in history, would be linked to you. Your time would be spent defending yourself against accusations and possibly even fighting off lawsuits.

"Then there is me. All paths would lead back to me, the one person who has always tried to fly under the radar. My life would be a constant stream of people wanting to travel with me, or they would want me to bring them things, artifacts, live specimens. I don't want to sound self-centered, but I have always been a private person. A few years ago, there would never have been this many people in my house. I didn't have that many friends and didn't want them. I had my work and that's all I needed.

"So, if Danny goes along tomorrow I think I'll go too. Not," he said to Lauren, "for the thrill of a jump. I just want to see how they handle things. I want to know if they mean what they say. I'll keep an open mind also."

Ron smiled and said, "This is great. We'll go with them and you can see for yourself. We can talk later and if you have any reservations you will let us know so we'll keep an open mind also."

"That's right," Lisa said.

"Well, okay," Lauren said. "I guess we're all going to keep an open mind."

"Is anyone hungry?" Ron asked. "Lisa and I will run out and get something, okay? Maybe Mexican."

"Sounds good," Danny told him. Everyone else agreed and as Ron and Lisa left Danny told Charles and Lauren, "I think I'm going to take a nap."

"Sounds like a plan," Charles said. "Let me…" then he paused and didn't say anything else.

"Charles, is there something wrong?" Lauren asked.

"No, I wanted to make sure they were gone and that any listening devices in this room were compromised."

"What are you saying?"

"That I need to talk to both of you without Ron and Lisa around, and without Steve listening to us."

"What?"

Charles stuck his hand in his pocket and as he picked up a glass of water he answered, "Because I wasn't quite truthful just a minute ago. My main reservation is that Steve is a liar."

"Okay, you're way ahead of us here," Lauren told him. "Slow down and tell us what you are talking about."

"Steve, and probably, Ben, are liars."

"What do you base this on?"

"This," Charles told them as he pulled a small object from his pocket that looked like a garage door opener.

"And that is…?" Danny asked.

"It measures certain types of energy readings. I turned it on at different times today at EXENCO and found something very surprising."

"Or not," Lauren said. "Considering you had it with you in the first place."

Charles nodded toward Lauren and said, "That's why I married you. Smart, very smart. I'll cover that in a moment, but I found my equipment energy signature in several places in EXENCO."

"That does sound strange," Danny agreed. "But should all energy signatures be different? I mean, it all relates to time travel, right?"

"It wouldn't matter if we were talking about opening a can. What I make, I can differentiate from what someone else creates. Steve is using my technology."

"How did he get it?"

"Well, unfortunately it wouldn't have been hard. Remember, I didn't have any type of safety for the house. Once he figured out things he would have gotten what he needed about me from Taggit's records. He probably watched me and came in whenever he wanted to. It wouldn't have taken him long to find what he was looking for."

"So, he just rebuilt all of your equipment and claimed credit for it? What did he take?"

"I'm not sure, I didn't see any of the equipment itself. It probably looks different. I was trying to get into the computers but couldn't."

"I don't understand," Danny told him. "How do you know it was yours then?"

"I read the firewall configurations. Different setups in different places. Remember, we were in his office, the room where the time travel unit was and in the training area control room. All different, but all protected by me. Interesting."

"So, why did you think something was wrong in the first place?" Lauren asked.

"I think he still has a way into the house. Things in my workshop have been moved around."

"He's been in the house recently?" Lauren asked.

Charles paused then answered, "Maybe. Or, he has a way of knowing what's going on. That's why I activated my bug jammer before we started talking."

"Well, that's creepy. You mean he could be watching our every move?"

Charles shook his head, "No, I don't think he cares about what *we* do. He wants to know what *I* do, what I'm working on. I found a camera in the workshop a few weeks ago so I put a box in front of it so whoever put it there couldn't watch. Now I believe that it is probably Steve and Ben."

"I'm going to punch him in the head," Lauren muttered.

"No, we can't do that. Remember, the reason I'm going tomorrow is to see what I can find out. I may even have to become an employee. Whatever it takes. If he is creating weapons and new defenses for the military, what better way to fund what you are really doing than have the government helping you out."

"And you're certain –" Danny started.

"I'm only certain that he is a liar...and probably a burglar. I doubt that he has changed his ways just because he wants to create cheaper energy. He's a criminal."

"Why didn't you want Dad and Lisa here? They would have believed you," Lauren said.

"Because I don't doubt that Steve knows by now I tried to get past his firewalls. I doubt if he realizes I know they were mine, but he will know I was poking around. He'll expect me and you to still be skeptical. Danny is a detective, so he'll even expect a little reluctance to accept things from him, even if he does the jump tomorrow. But let's face it, if Ron and Lisa suspected anything, they couldn't hide it. They are naturally outgoing, and he would immediately notice any change in their demeanor toward him. They can't know. It's that simple."

Danny nodded and said, "I agree. But just because you're poking around doesn't mean it just wasn't professional curiosity. He can't know for sure you're actually on to him."

"That's true, but he'll be suspicious. And, I'm sure he's thought about at least one other thing that I have."

"Which is?" Lauren asked.

"Right now, there could be another five, ten, who knows how many, time travelers in the world. They could be in New York, Paris, Canada, Japan, anywhere. But you have to wonder, how could two different people, from different backgrounds and educations invent time travel...and they live in the same city? Not five miles from each other?"

Danny and Lauren didn't answer so Charles said, "Danny, start talking about your retirement and how you would like to work for EXENCO. I'm going to turn off the jammer at some point, so it will seem like there was a problem with the bug and it just came back on." As Danny started they heard Ron and Lisa coming up the drive.

Steve watched the Team from the control room for a while and was glad to see they were responding to Danny's scenario changes. Immediately they started reacting and functioning differently. Good. If Danny came on board he would put him in charge of them. Team Director. He couldn't make up his mind about Charles and Lauren though. They could go either way, but that wouldn't matter. He felt Ron and Lisa would stay and if Danny decided not to join, well, things would still be okay.

He left the Team and as soon as he walked into his office Steve saw the message on his screen and clenched his jaw. It only took him a few seconds to locate the attempted security breaches and to figure out who it had been: Charles. What did he suspect? Steve looked closer at the attempts and decided it wasn't anything to worry about. Four times in his office, three times by the unit but just once in the control room. Not the same number of times in each room and not repetitive, not a hundred times in one minute. And in each room, there were fewer attempts. Trial and error. Charles had just been fishing, trying to see what he could find out. Annoying and not very professional.

He activated the camera and was surprised that it wasn't working. Before he could touch anything though the kitchen appeared on the screen and he heard Danny saying, "...what I saw today. If tomorrow goes well I'm on board." To Steve's surprise Charles answered, "I have to admit I liked a lot of what I saw today. I think I'll go too, I'd like to see how things are handled and talk to Steve a little more." Lauren started, "Well, if you..." then Ron and Lisa walked in carrying plastic bags of food. Lauren switched to, "Let's eat", and they all walked out of view.

Steve sat back in his chair and shook his head, something was wrong. Why had the camera not been working correctly to begin with? It was the second camera that had problems within two weeks and the other one was in...the workroom. Tony. It had to have been Tony. How had he been found out? It didn't matter, he had been, and Charles was trying to put things together. Would he tell the others?

Steve thought about turning on the dining room camera but then decided not to. It sounded like they were thinking about things and even leaning toward going with him tomorrow. Good. A few seconds of conversation when they arrived, and he would know who knew what. He turned off the computer.

As Aria picked up Tony he asked, "Mom, can you run me by EXENCO? Boss said he wanted to talk to me for a minute."

"Should we pick up Paula first?"

"No, let's go see Boss first and then maybe I'll have some good news for the New Year."

"Like what?"

"Who knows. A raise or maybe a better job."

"Moving up in the world. Good for you."

"You should work there too. I mean it."

"Maybe."

"And thanks again for driving us around tonight."

"Remember I don't want to be out too late. We're going to Lauren's and wherever Paula's family party is and then home by one."

"No problem. We won't keep you up too late," Tony laughed. "Hey, stop right here and I'll be right back. No, wait. Come in and meet Boss. Let him know you're interested in a job."

"Do you think it will be okay?"

"Sure. Come on."

As they walked into EXENCO, Steve was waiting at the main entrance. He seemed surprised for a second then asked, "Tony, who is this?"

"This is my Mom, Aria."

"Nice to meet you, Aria," Steve said. "Please follow me to my office. Tony, I want to talk to you about your future with EXENCO."

Tony smiled and glanced at his mother as he replied, "Thank you, Boss. Mom might be interested in a future here also."

Steve looked at them both and smiled as he said, "I think I can take care of both of you."

As everyone met in the dining room the next morning Charles said, "Happy New Year again everyone." Then he added, "Lauren has decided to jump too."

"That's great," Ron said. "What changed your mind?"

"I want to see what EXENCO is up to and this seems the best way. A controlled jump and what they promise is a no risk field operation, what more could I ask for?"

Lisa smiled and told Lauren, "You'll see, they are different, it will be different."

"Well, it's already different," Charles said as he pointed at Danny. "Not going to tear your best pants this time, are you?"

"No, I'm not," Danny agreed as he patted his khakis. "These will hold up, maybe better than me this morning."

"What do you mean?" Lauren asked.

"I'm not feeling very well," Danny said. "A little touch of something I guess."

"Do you want to stay here?" Charles asked.

"No, I'll be okay…I think."

"In that case," Charles said, "I have something for everyone." He stepped out of the kitchen and was back in a few seconds with the five boxes he had brought in on Christmas Eve.

"I've been wondering about those," Lauren said.

"Well, I had been meaning to surprise everyone with a vacation trip to Hawaii. Thought we could use these to hike around some of the volcanoes." He pulled a tan pair of hiking boots from a box and told the others, "But, we can break them in on the jump and then head for the volcanoes later."

They quickly put their boots on and Lisa said, "These are really comfortable. Very nice. Thanks, Charles."

"And thanks for the trip to Hawaii too," Danny told him.

"Everyone just has to call me Boss Man while we're there," Charles said. "Does that work for everyone?"

"It does until we get there Charles," Lauren said. "I mean Boss Man."

Everyone laughed as they climbed into the SUV and the ride wasn't as quiet as the previous day. They discussed where they might be going, and Ron and Lisa described their thought and feelings again about all they saw and heard on their last jump. But as they talked, Lauren and Charles exchanged looks and more than once she squeezed his hand.

Steve met them again at EXECON with "I'm so happy to see all of you."

Ron and Lisa greeted him warmly, but Charles told him as they shook hands, "Steve, I like a lot of what you said yesterday and I'm going to jump today to evaluate things. I'm sorry I can't do better than that."

Steve replied, "I completely understand, Charles. If you have any questions, or doubts, about what we are doing bring them up immediately. Please, don't hesitate. I want everything to be transparent to you."

Lauren said, "I'm afraid I'm in the same boat, Steve. I want to believe but after…well, after our last experience with –"

"Taggit," Steve finished for her. "Again, I understand. Don't hesitate to call us out on anything. And I mean anything. We will be an open book for you."

Steve then turned to Danny who held up his palms and told him, "Steve, I like what you are doing, but I'm not sure I am going with you. I really don't feel that well. I may drive back and see if I can come and pick everyone up later."

Ben had come up while Danny was talking, and he said, "Well, it actually won't be that long. We'll be traveling in about 30 minutes and no matter how long the Walk is I'll still come back just a few seconds later in this time."

Danny shook his head and replied, "I forgot about that. A week for you could still be just a second here."

"Plus," Ben continued, "the air in the Unit has various medicinal, uh, vapors floating through it. We don't want anyone taking whatever to the past or bringing it to the future."

Charles shook his head and said, "I didn't think about that before any of my jumps. Sounds interesting, I hope you can fill me in a little about it."

"Of course," Ben said. "Anything you want."

As they walked into EXECON Steve fell behind them to think. Lisa and Ron seemed normal and as outgoing as ever. Though Danny was ill he did not seem different and neither did Lauren. In fact, even Charles seemed exactly the same. Maybe Charles was just curious about his time travel ability and was just snooping around. Still, very unprofessional. And suspicious. He'd keep an eye on all of them just the same.

As they walked into the locker room they were greeted with a lot of kidding from the Team. "There they are, the ones who made us work until midnight," Ricardo called out. "We missed New Year's."

"And I got knocked down two more times," Cat said which was answered by several members shouting, "Five more times."

"But, seriously, you made us better," Major Donald said to Danny.

Several people nodded as Ammo added, "A lot better."

Then Stoney asked, "Where did you get those boots? They are *sooo* cute."

Everyone laughed, and Charles turned red as he said, "It's my fault, I got them because we are going to hike some volcanoes. Sorry they aren't like yours."

"Paycheck, can Otto get them some real boots like these?"

"Not today." Ben replied as he looked at the boots. "And, maybe never. Let's just think about what we're going to accomplish today."

"Hey, can we call Stork before we go?" Ricardo asked. "Might as well poke him a little bit."

"I'll call him in a little while," Steve said. "Right now, though, I'll be in the Unit like usual. Ron, you and Lisa will be with me. I think you will like this."

"I think you will too," Ben agreed. "We're going back 66 million years ago to where we lost four good men. First, we're going to look for that sea monster for Ron and Lauren and then I want the Team to try and coax either the big *Rex* or the juvenile *Rexes* back…but they may have to walk to get to them. I doubt if we'll be lucky enough that they will visit the beach again."

"We'll get it done," Major Donald said quickly. "We want to use the equipment for real. We're excited."

"Aren't you afraid?" Lauren asked.

The Major paused then replied, "Of course there is fear. It's the unknown. Going up against giants makes us all contemplate our own mortality. But where others run, we go forward willingly and with our eyes open. Just like all of you did."

"But we had to."

Major Donald smiled and said, "So do we. It's in our DNA."

Ben brought up a holographic map of the beach area showing where all of the animals first appeared and where they were last seen. He discussed drone and bot deployment with Steve and asked Major Donald about equipment and personal needs. When he was satisfied he looked at Major Donald and nodded.

She turned to the Team and asked, "Well, what are we waiting for? Let's get this done." Everyone moved quickly for the door to the hallway and then sprinted toward the Unit.

"I think we'll walk," Lauren said, and Ron, Lisa, Charles and Danny quickly agreed with her.

As Steve saw Otto join them he asked, "Are you ready?"

"Yes, sir," Otto replied. "And thank you again for bringing me along this time. I am looking forward to this."

Steve just nodded as they stepped inside the Unit. He looked closely at Danny who was sweating profusely and said, "Danny, you don't look well but I think you will start feeling better soon enough. We have a first aid room with a couple of cots, you're more than welcome to lay down."

"I will take you up on that in a few minutes," Danny said. "I'd like to ask the Team some questions about their equipment first."

"Be my guest," Steve said. "What about everyone else?"

"I think I'll go with Danny," Lauren said.

"We're just going to sit here," Lisa said as she took Ron's arm.

"Charles?" Steve asked.

"Well…"

"Why don't you come up to the control room with us?" Steve asked. "I think you'll find it interesting."

Charles smiled and said, "I'm on my way."

Danny and Lauren followed the Team into another room and Ammo asked, "What do you want to know?"

"Has anyone given any thought to shooting a lot of these special bullets and then someone finding some of them in the future? Are you sure they are biodegradable?" Lauren immediately asked.

"Blonk, can you explain this?" Ammo asked. "He's better at it than I am."

Blonk stepped up holding some of the bullets and told Lauren, "These are made out of a synthetic polymer that immediately begins breaking down when it is exposed to air. In the factory after they are shaped they are immediately placed in vacuumed sealed pouches that keep the air from coming into contact with the polymer. When the bullet is removed from the package the countdown to the bullet turning to dust begins. They hold their shape and density for about two days then just dissolve. Just like everything else we have."

"Everything else?" Danny asked.

"Sure," Blonk replied. "What if we left a rifle behind? Not good. *Everything* disappears. Bullets, guns, knives–"

"Clothes?" Danny asked.

"No way," Maybe said. "The guys would always want to go out for a week. They're not going to see what's under this uniform."

"I got pictures," Whitey said.

"We all do," Junk said as everyone laughed.

"So, the clothes are just normal?" Lauren asked.

"Sure, clothing material doesn't last long in all of the heat and humidity," Ammo said.

Lauren took one of the bullets and asked, "What type of material is it?"

"You'll have to ask Otto about that. All we know is that it works and don't take it out of its special container until you're ready to use it. Like I said, the countdown to needing to replace something begins as soon as you do."

"What about the explosive bullets?" Danny asked.

"Same thing. I mean you have to have explosive elements of course, but they are still inside of a casing that will just dissolve. If it explodes first your hard shrapnel does its job and then it all just –"

"Then it all just goes away," Danny continued for him. "Pretty amazing."

"Hey," Ricardo said. "Sarge, you're going out with us, aren't you?"

"I hope to," Danny said. "I wasn't feeling too good earlier but I'm getting better now. I still might lay down for a few minutes."

"Okay, but let's get you hooked up. Cat, grab the Sarge a vest, gun, some ammo and oh, you'll need a couple of these on your belt."

"What are they?"

"Grenades. Still made from the same material as everything else, still do the job." As Cat and the others led Danny away to show him some other gear Ricardo asked Lauren, "What else do you want to see? Do you have some knowledge about guns?"

"Yes, and I used one when we walked. But I don't want to use one this time," Lauren told him. "But tell me about those backpacks."

"The DOPE, Dorsal Protection Equipment. They are also biodegradable, but they are strong, very strong." Ricardo looked around for a moment then said, "Junk, put the holo-dope on and come over here."

One of the women said, "Sure," and walked over to a wall mounted workstation. "Holo-trainer, DOPE specs, Junk." A holographic pack appeared to float in front of her and Junk turned around and seemingly put it on.

"Okay, Junk, drop down and give Lauren a run through of what you can do."

Junk dropped down onto all fours and instantly the DOPE spread out over her as six sharp spikes stretched out from the top of the pack. "No commands?" Lauren asked.

"No," Junk answered. "It senses when you have dropped into this head down, knees on the ground, elbows tucked in, position. You may not have time to shout a command or in a stressful situation even remember to do so. I think it was influenced by the invisible bike helmet design."

"The what?"

"Out of Sweden if I remember right, look it up. Now, once I am down I am perfectly safe. No amount of ripping, tearing or twisting will break through the DOPE. And, the spikes will either keep things away to begin with or give them a stick if they feel the need to bite. If they are persistent though, you can also juice them." To emphasize the point Junk touched part of the DOPE and an electrical charge jumped briefly between two of the spikes.

"The DOPE will withstand an external pressure of about 12,000 pounds which covers a lot of dinos but of course not the big ones if it decides to sit on you. We have communications, fresh air and we carry a small amount of food and water with us just in case a dino won't leave for a while." As Junk stood up the holograph disappeared. She smiled and said, "I hope that answers some of your questions."

"It did," Lauren agreed. "Thanks." She turned to Ricardo and told him, "And thanks to you too. Looks like Danny is keeping busy so I'm going to find Charles."

"Anytime, ma'am," Ricardo said and walked over to Danny and asked, "Doing better?"

"Yes and no," Danny replied. "Everyone has been great, and I do feel better because it has taken my mind off things. But I still think I'll lay down for a while."

"Understood," Ricardo said. "Follow me." Ricardo led him to a small room with two cots, a stainless-steel table and cabinets filled with first aid equipment. "We'll get you when we arrive."

"Thanks. I don't want to miss anything."

Lauren sat down beside Charles who was intently studying some holographic readouts. "Having fun?" she asked.

"Yes, actually I am. Very interesting data."

"When do we leave?"

Steve and Ben laughed, and Ben answered, "About 15 minutes ago."

CHAPTER EIGHT
THE WESTERN INLAND SEA

"What?" Lauren said as she glanced up at the ceiling of the Unit.

Charles quickly told her, "I had the same reaction, looking up for the sun and moon lines. We're totally enclosed. Some type of interesting polymer I'm learning about."

"I can change it, so we can see through the top," Ben volunteered.

"No, I think I actually like it this way better," Lauren told him. "I was still getting used to the fact that we were going to jump, now I have to get used to the fact we already are."

"Well, just like you did with Charles, we are traveling slow," Ben told her. "We always do. It gives everyone a chance to check all of their equipment and to get ready physically and mentally."

"They can't get ready enough," Lauren told him.

"You're right," Steve said. "But they get ready enough that when they walk they handle their jobs quickly and efficiently. Will you be walking?"

"No, I think I will stay inside with Charles."

"Great," Ben said. "If you would like, I can show you how to operate a station."

Lauren paused, it was too much like the last time. "Maybe I'll just watch for a while." Ben nodded and went back to what he had been doing.

"What are you working on?" she asked Charles.

"Something amazing," he replied. "You're going to have to see it to believe it. Watch." He activated a screen with his holocontrols and she saw a *Stegosaurus* on it. Charles moved his hand and immediately points of light flashed on the animal's body. Then some of its plates lit up and part of its tail and spikes. Across the image she read;

Animal: *Stegosaurus ungulatus*   Probability: 99.9%

"What is this?"

"It's like facial recognition," Charles told her. "The Unit's computer has parameters in its database for many animal features like horns, skull shape, plates, spikes and many others. It compares these specifically selected landmark features to identify it."

"I can see it's a *Stegosaur*," Lauren scoffed.

"I'm sure you can, but what if you didn't know what time period you were in and you saw a much smaller *Stegosaur*? Would you know which one it was? Immediately? If the database has the animal then you would know."

"And if it doesn't?"

"Then EXECON needs help with identifying animals and placing the information in the database. No walking, just lab work."

As Lauren looked back at the screen Ben said, "And just like with facial recognition, if we had named this guy Fred it would have told us it was Fred the *Stegosaurus*. Pretty amazing." As a door opened Ben continued, "And you can thank Otto here for the technology. He just updated the Unit's computers a few days ago. Otto, say hello to everyone."

Otto looked at Lauren and Charles and smiled as he said, "Hello. I am so happy that you have joined us today and that you like the technology."

"Can you tell me how you came up with it?" Charles asked.

"Well, facial technology is being used more and more, even with animals. You can get close to tame animals of course, but not to wild ones. They run or attack, and of course dinosaurs have their own set of problems. But with the drones we use we can take the correct type of photos, you know, from different angles. Though the side shots are the hardest."

"Why is that?" Lauren asked.

"Dinosaurs react to stimulus, ready to eat it or defend themselves against it. They don't hear or see something and casually look at it, they look to see what they need to do. Tame animals will look away from a camera or wander around, but dinosaurs will stare and then you have to be ready for the possibility of a charge. If they have seen our camera they turn and follow its every movement. But with the quieter drones we have been able to get different angle shots of every animal with 3D sensors and put together a good start on an extremely accurate database."

Otto smiled and continued, "I mean, it is just mathematics, really. If you create the correct algorithm it gives you what you need. Pick the landmarks then the ratios start creating information."

"As you can see," Steve said, "Otto is modest. He has taken existing facial tech platforms and expanded and enhanced them to an unheard-of level."

"I'm picking up on that," Charles agreed. Then he turned to Otto and asked, "Does light affect your ability to use your technology?"

Otto shook his head and replied, "No, in addition to a combination of geometric and photometric algorithms, the 3D sensors I mentioned provides usable information that is not affected by lighting."

"You don't have to tell them to not smile also," Lauren said. When no one said anything she continued, "You know, like passport photos?" When no one said anything she added, "Okay, so what else do the cameras do?"

"Not only does it track skin patterns but also skin texture. Different dinosaurs have different skin textures and feather placement. Oh, and heat radiation. We can differentiate dinosaurs by what areas give off the most heat. Is it a *Tyrannosaurus,* an *Albertosaurus*…you get the picture. The more factors we can associate with a certain animal the higher percentage of an identity."

"It's all amazing," Lauren agreed. "What do you call your invention? *Rex*ignition?"

Otto smiled as he answered, "No, I call it Woody."

"Woody? Too many beach films when you were younger?"

"No, Woody Bledsoe was one of the first to use a computer for facial recognition. It just seemed like a good way to honor him."

"Got it," Lauren said.

"Wait, that's not the best part," Charles told her. "Otto, please explain your fascinating X-ray component. Well, not X-ray exactly, we call it DTP."

Otto smiled again and said, "You are being too kind, sir."

"I'm Charles and this is Lauren and I'm not being too kind. This is technology that is way ahead of everyone else's. Light years."

"Well, again, thank you…Charles," Otto said as he dropped his head slightly. "I am quite flattered you find it so interesting." He reached into some holocontrols and the *Stegosaurus* was turned into a skeleton. "Lauren, this is what Charles was talking about. I created a dynamic Deep Tissue Program that allows continuous extrapolation of measurements from the dinosaur."

"Deep Tissue Program, DTP. Got it. How does it help?"

"Well, many dinosaurs have been visualized and created from a single bone. A toe bone can tell a learned scientist like yourself if it came from a *tyrannosaur* or a *Hadrosaurus*. But many bones can only provide generalities. If an animal was a theropod or a sauropod for instance. The size of the bone gives you other dimensions based on previous skeletons that have been found. Of course, it doesn't give you exact features, but enough to speculate. I didn't want to speculate anymore. I wanted to be able to see a skeleton; the bones, their size and shape, how they connected, and where they were located with precision measurements.

"Now you can go into any museum that has a box of unknown dinosaur fossils and if it is in our database know exactly what type of dinosaur it came from. No more sudden realizations by frustrated paleontologists that they have the same bone fragment in their box as they do in another country. No more generalities, now there will be precision."

Lauren watched the skeleton slowly walk across the screen and nodded her head, "I have to admit this is unbelievable. A step I never even considered. Congratulations, Otto."

"Again, thank you. I always hope my little experiments and inventions are worthwhile."

Steve turned and said, "Otto, I've never met anyone quite like you. Everything you have done for EXECON has been more than worthwhile. You are worth your weight in gold." As Otto smiled, Steve continued, "Okay, we're here. Solar panels, windmills are functioning. Let's deploy air and ground and get the satellite up. Ben, I want image for 200 yards in all directions to begin with and then bump it out 100 yards at a time until we find something interesting."

"Already on it," Ben replied. "Also, I'm going to check the lagoon this time, let's see if the big boy is around. Maybe we can get it out of the water for Ron."

Ron walked into the control room at that moment and asked, "Did I hear someone say my name?"

"Yes, you did," Lauren said as she sat down. Then she turned to Charles and asked, "Now how do I work these controls?"

Steve smiled at Ben and as Lisa joined Ron they watched as Steve moved some holocontrols. They could hear things locking into place outside of the unit and suddenly there was a loud whooshing sound and Ron asked, "What was that?"

"A small satellite," Ben answered. "Gives us a forty-mile radius of observation for anything that looks interesting. Say there is a herd moving, we may want to stay here for a couple of days and see if it gets close enough for an out and back.

"Air and ground drones are out to see what is really close. We want to see if Ron's animal is a regular here and what about those juvenile *Rexes*, are they still close by?"

"So, we returned to where your men were killed? How many days later?" Ron asked.

"Three days," Ben said. "Seemed like a good number."

"Why?" Lauren asked.

Ben grimaced and replied, "Well, not to be too graphic about it, we hope the animals are still in the area…but the bodies are not."

Lauren just nodded. She didn't want to see any bodies or body parts or anything else. Then she took a deep breath and asked, "What's first?"

"An actual first," Steve said. "The Unit is going to take a Walk."

"What?" Ron asked. "I thought Ben said we were going to lure the animal out of the lagoon first."

Ben spoke up, "No, I said we were going to look for the sea monster. We're going into the lagoon and maybe even further out into this ocean. It's the Inland Sea, right?"

"Western Inland Sea, right," Ron said. "But, this thing can go into the water?"

"Sure can," Ben replied.

"But you said this was going to be a first," Lauren said.

"Yes," Steve agreed. "The first real time we've gone into water. But we've run hundreds of simulations and there has never been a problem. Right, Otto?"

"Yes, sir."

"Simulations?" Lauren and Ron said at the same time.

Steve and Ben laughed, and Ben told them, "Don't worry, we'll be just fine. It has withstood hurricane force winds and once a *Triceratops* even ran into it by accident. It will hold up."

Lauren looked at Charles with a what-have-we-gotten-ourselves-into expression, but he just smiled back. "Science will prevail," he told her.

"That's what they said about the Titanic," she whispered.

As the Unit suddenly started forward Lauren asked, "Who's driving, and will we come back to the same spot?"

"Otto's computer is driving," Ben told her, "and it will guide us back to the exact coordinates we just left. Lauren, I know you weren't expecting this, and it sounds dangerous, but there will be no problems. Well, no problems we can't solve."

As the Unit got closer to the lagoon, Ron walked up behind Ben and put his hands on his chair. Lauren saw that he was shaking with excitement. As the water slowly rose higher Lauren kept expecting to at least hear water running into the Unit or at least past it. But there was no sound. Just an eerie silence as the Unit was slowly covered by water.

"What readings do we have?" Steve asked. "And can we get some lights?"

As the lights turned the dark water in front of them into a brown and yellow watercolor, Ben said, "Temperature is 73, S is just 11 at the moment. Everything else coming in as expected."

Lauren watched as holographic numbers appeared under an ever-changing list of names. She saw temperature, salinity, halite, bromide, pH, and a long list of numbers under headings of anions and cations. Then it was all a blur as readings were coming in so fast that only the computer could handle the calculations. "You're investigating the make-up of Inland Sea too? I thought we were just looking at the animals," Lauren said.

"Oh no," Ben replied as he turned to face her. "Flora, fauna, chemical balances, temperatures, stratification, the list goes on."

"Fascinating," Ron exclaimed. "Like Lauren I didn't realize this would be such a comprehensive study. I'm sure it will be beneficial, answer many questions."

"Look at this," Lisa said excitedly, and everyone looked at the monitor.

The dirty, swirling lagoon water was disappearing and suddenly an amazing undersea panorama lay before them. "Stop here," Steve said, and the Unit halted at the top of a long shallow slope that disappeared into a dark blue background that seemed a mile away. Between the surface and the floor of the sea there was a constantly changing kaleidoscope of blues and golds as the sun shimmered off of the waves and currents. Shafts of light highlighted and threw into shadow in the blink of an eye a multitude of creatures that moved before them.

"I didn't know there were so many shades of blue," Lisa whispered. "It's like being inside a dream. And look at all of the fish." Then she turned to Ron and asked, "What will we see here?"

"I can guess at a few things," Ron replied, "but I specialize in land animals. Lauren?"

Before she could start, Danny spoke up, "Let me see if I can recall a few things. Let's see, there are a few animals that are still around in our time though they might not look exactly the same, like, bony fish, cartilaginous fish, squid, lobsters, clams, sea snails, turtles – though they're much bigger here. Uh, starfish, nautilus, crabs, coral and...oh, yeah, sponge. Got to have sponge.

"And crocodiles, sharks, jellyfish, shrimp and some sea birds including one that can't fly. I can't remember if it looks like a penguin though. Sorry. But there are some early birds that had teeth. I think they were sea birds."

As Danny stopped, Charles asked, "Why do we have to have sponge?"

"Because it is our most distant cousin," Danny answered quickly and then continued, "Now you're also going to see things no human has ever seen. Like *Mosasaurs*, and those long-necked things, I can't remember if they were *Plesiosaurs, Pliosaurus* or *Elasmosaurus*. It depends on what time period we are in. There will be *Squalicorax*, no wait, that's just a type of shark. Lots of fish that are extinct and…more sharks I guess. I'm stuck on sharks. Sorry, I'm no Verne hero."

"Who?" Charles asked.

"You know, Jules Verne? In all of his stories there is always someone who knows every fact about every country, plant and animal. I started sounding like him, I think."

"Well, I think you did great," Lisa said. "But how do you know all of that?"

"The ending of my book. We don't know how Taggit died for sure, he could have just drowned. But that wasn't very exciting, so I had him torn to bits by a lot of sharks. I had to look up a lot of information. Some I remembered, some I've forgotten."

"I would have had a *Mosasaur* get him," Lauren said quietly. "And he would have died screaming."

As the room got quiet Lisa looked at Steve and Ben and asked, "Is Danny right?"

"He is," Ben replied. "Look at the screen now." He had activated the DTP and now animals were tagged either to their species or as unknown. Some of the unknown animals had bones highlighted that tied them to a specific taxon but provided no other information.

"Look at all the 'unknowns'", Lisa said.

"Not surprising," Ron told her. "At best, we have found 50 percent of all the dinosaurs that lived. But I seriously doubt we have uncovered that many. An animal, or even a plant, has to die in the right place, at the right time and under the right conditions. Then the fossil has to withstand normal Earth movements and forces along with man's interference through construction and carelessness. I would think aquatic creatures would be even harder to find. What those 'unknowns' out there represent are gaps in our knowledge about extinct species."

"And this knowledge will soon be yours," Steve said. "All of you."

Lauren started to say something to Charles, but he was using his work station to follow around a large blue fish with pale yellow stripes running horizontally along its sides. He glanced up and asked, "What is this? Some kind of oversized piranha?"

"There's only a few sea animals I know," Lauren said. "But you did find one. That is *Xiphatinus*. It's not a piranha but as you can see by the teeth it is a hunter."

"That is one ugly fish," Ben remarked.

"Something big coming in," Ben said suddenly. The room grew quiet again as a dark shadow appeared on the right side of the screen and slowly started getting bigger as it approached the Unit. "It's the big boy from the other day. It's coming back to the beach."

"We're in its way," Lauren said. "Are we camouflaged?"

"No," Ben shook his head. "We look like a big dark rock. We don't want it running into us by accident." Then he touched a hologram in front of him and asked, "Is the bubble ready?"

"It is," Major Donald answered.

"Who won?"

"Lost is the lucky one."

Another screen appeared in the upper left corner of the larger view screen showing a large plastic-looking bubble. The blurry form of a person could be seen moving around inside it and as Ben asked, "Can you show me phase 3?" the outside of the bubble seemed to disappear and Lost could be seen sitting inside.

"Great. Phase 1?" And the bubble completely disappeared. "Good, now back to 3 and how are you feeling?"

"Ready for a bite, Paycheck."

Lauren jumped up from her chair and shouted, "What? You're going to have this animal attack her? Didn't you just lose a person doing that?"

"And that's why we won't lose her," Steve said. "This new sphere can take the bite of two of these things at the same time. There will be no problems."

"I just can't believe it. Why does a person have to be inside it?"

"Remember, we have to be able to show our military contacts that a person can actually live in this. It can't be theoretical. They want proof."

"Don't worry," Lost called out. "I've been looking forward to this all day."

In a flurry of bubbles, Lost moved away from the Unit and out over the coral reef in front of them. Fish scattered in all directions in a frenzy of color and even the dark shadow, which was beginning to take the shape of an extremely large crocodile, turned slowly away from them. "Try the lights," Ben said. As Lost activated a series of flashing lights on the sphere the giant animal turned around and in just a few seconds bumped the sphere.

As she was bumped, Lost said, "Well hello to you too, big boy. Come back and let's get acquainted." As if on cue the animal turned suddenly and snapped at the sphere. But its jaws didn't close around it. It shook from side to side and clamped down again, but the sphere held its shape.

"We're good," Steve said. "Go ahead and juice it."

Immediately the animal let go of the sphere and recoiled backwards. It shook its massive head and then turned and swam back toward the deep-water shadows. As Ben and Steve shook hands and patted Otto on the back, the sound of the Team cheering could be heard.

The sphere returned quickly and after it docked Ben said, "Let's go see Lost."

Steve and Otto stayed in their chairs and as everyone else left the control room Ron stepped forward and asked, "Can you show me a video of that animal using the Deep Tissue Scan analysis?"

"Ron, it would be my pleasure," Steve replied and as the display came back in the lower right corner of the screen he continued, "Sorry, doesn't look like there's much there."

"But there is, there is," Ron told him. "The animal itself is not identified but some of its bones are linked to other animals. I was right in my guess that it might have something to do with *Sarcosuchus*, but not much. No bulla tells me that. But see how there is a vertebra associated with *Sarcosuchus* and an ankle bone and cranial bones associated with *Deinosuchus*? What can't nature and evolution do?"

"So, what will you name it?" Steve asked.

Ron shook his head and replied, "No, I won't name it. But hopefully someday in Texas, Oklahoma, maybe even Kansas, they'll dig this up."

"Anything else you want to see?"

"No, but I do have a question. Just a few days ago you told me you didn't have anything that could withstand the bite of this animal. But today you do. What happened?"

"Otto," Steve said emphatically. "Anything else?"

"No. I'm just going to look for a while."

As Lost walked into the locker room the Team crowded around her. As they slapped her on the back and hugged her she couldn't stop smiling. "You did it," Ricardo told her. "Good job."

Lost just kept nodding her head and just laughed when Lauren asked her, "Why? Are you crazy?"

"A little bit," Lost replied. "But it's like landing on the moon. No one else has ever done it. Even though others will, I'm the first and that can't be taken away. Also, it's science. All of it. And if you believe in science then you know everything is going to work like it should. And now we have you guys."

"Us?"

"Yeah. As you put the science into the animals we'll have a better understanding of what to expect. That means fewer surprises and that means fewer problems. Science."

Before Lauren could reply, Steve was on the speaker saying, "We're getting ready to move back on shore. Better have a seat."

Ben, Lisa, Lauren and Charles returned to the control room and watched the view screen as the coral reef disappeared and the water turned brown and black again. The dark water ran down the Unit as it moved slowly up onto the beach and back toward its starting point. There were some clicks as the Unit settled into place and Ben turned to Lauren and said, "Like I said, no problems."

Lauren nodded her head and replied, "I have to admit it, the whole thing went off without a hitch."

"Can I take that as a compliment?" Ben asked.

Lauren laughed and said, "Yes, that was a compliment."

"But, you are still worried about things, right?" Steve asked.

"Yes. I guess deep down inside there is still the doubt. Sorry."

"Don't be sorry. I asked that you be completely truthful with me and I meant it." Steve paused for a moment then asked, "What if we do another short Walk right here? There are possibly three *T-rex* juveniles in the area and also a *T-rex* adult. We can do a quick information gathering and you will have seen us in action twice."

"Doesn't everyone want to go home?"

"Well, if you are asking," Ron jumped in, "no, I don't want to. This is fascinating."

When she looked at Charles he just shrugged and said, "I'm in no hurry."

"I could go or stay," Lisa added.

Ben asked the Team, "Anyone want to go home?" After a few shouts of "No" came over his speaker he looked at Lauren and shrugged his shoulders.

Danny walked into the control room with a smile on his face and said, "You know, I don't feel so bad now. That was quite a show. Is it okay if I join the Team?"

"Me too," Ron said quickly.

"Is everyone losing their minds?" Lauren asked.

"Well, if Ron is going I want to go with him," Lisa said.

Lauren turned to Charles who said, "If Danny is going I think I should too. He isn't feeling well, he just thinks he is."

Lauren let out a sigh and told everyone, "Okay, you can all go but I am staying here." She asked Ben, "I can watch them, right? And, see what else is going on around them?"

"Yes, you can. In fact, if you are staying here you could help direct the Team. Let them know what you want them to do and why."

"Your expertise would be invaluable," Steve added.

Lauren sighed again and said, "All right, but I want everyone geared up just like the Team."

"They will be," Ben assured her. "But first I want to take about an hour to let the Team eat something and to check the entire area. You can stay and watch if you want to."

"What are you going to do?"

There were several metallic noises for a couple of seconds and Ben said, "Drones and bots are now out, and you heard earlier one of the satellites is already up. I'm going to start tracking all animals out as far as I can see their heat signatures."

"You can see all of that?"

"Most of it." Ben held up a hand as Lauren started to say something and smiled as he continued, "But the computer sees better than me. We get something fast or large moving anywhere close by and it alerts us. We have an animal approaching the Team, we get alerted. We don't trust me only, I have to have a backup."

"What backs up the computers?"

"Two more computers," Otto told her.

Lauren didn't know what to say after that, so she told Ben, "I think I'll go sit down for a while with Charles and make sure his insurance is up to date and that I am the sole beneficiary." She looked at Lisa and added, "And to make sure everyone is dressed right."

"Yes Mom," Lisa laughed and then she suddenly stopped. She was reminded vividly of holding Marilyn during the third jump. She turned and took Ron's arm and they walked out of the control room.

Danny told everyone he was going to lay down for a few minutes and as Lauren and Charles walked out with him, Ben turned to Steve and asked, "What do you think so far?"

"Well, that was a perfect start. The underwater test went exactly the way we knew it would. Still, Lauren and Charles are not quite on board yet. There is still a little hesitancy and even suspicion."

Ben nodded and replied, "But you were right on target asking everyone if they wanted to go out. Everyone is caught up in the excitement. I think Ron would have just run out the door immediately. Everyone is going except Lauren and I think she really wants to. I was surprised Charles wanted to and even more surprised when Lisa said she would go."

"I was too," Steve said. "I thought Charles would stay inside and watch what I was doing. And you know, I can't quite figure Lisa out. I know she's afraid but there is a strength there that is hard to read." The room was silent for a moment then Steve continued, "But let's get to work."

As Danny gave them a wave and headed to the bunk room, Lauren and Charles went into the viewing room and sat down. After a few seconds Charles said, "Look, I know I promised I wasn't going to go out with these people, but Danny is –"

"I understand," Lauren cut in. "I don't mind. He does seem to be sick so it's nice you're going to watch him. You know, this does seem to be a safe operation. But still, it can't be 100 percent safe all of the time. The odds are against it, something has to happen."

"I guess that's why you will be in the control room."

"You guess right. I can't let anything happen to you before we go on vacation."

Charles leaned back and smiled as he said, "You know, I thought this would be our vacation. It's tropical, we get a tan, it's got a built-in zoo. What more do we need?"

"No worries," Lauren told him as she took his arm. "When we are in Hawaii I don't want to worry about anything and I don't care if we see any animals or not. Now let's go and see about getting all of you geared up."

They walked into the locker room and found Danny, Ron and Lisa already there. "Tried to lay down but I'm too pumped," Danny told them as Lost was fastening a DOPE on him. "This is going to be exciting." He turned around and as she cinched his belt he asked, "So what do I have?"

"First you have your DOPE. If you throw yourself down on the ground it automatically activates. Make sure you're on ground though, not rock. It digs in and you can't be moved or be chewed on."

"That's useful."

"Most definitely. If you are inside you'll see controls for ventilation, air flow, some food and water and most importantly, shock. You got something you don't want around you, just zap it and send it a message."

"Like you did earlier."

"You got it. The earpiece has your mic and audio and the helmet with the visor protects your head and eyes. Also, a view screen can be activated on the visor by leaning your head forward and to the right. Paycheck can give us a real-time view of what he's looking at. Comes in handy sometimes."

"So, it's not on all the time?"

"No. Might draw your attention away from something more important, like something wanting to eat you."

"Got it."

"Last, your utility belt. You're right handed so that's where your sidearm is. You've seen them already. Just one mag but it holds fifty rounds of our special ammo. However, you do have a magazine of ten of the exploding rounds attached to the outside of the holster. For those special guests that have overstayed their welcome."

"That would be my neighbor, Stanley."

"Feel free to take a couple with you when we get back. Next to your holster in the red canisters are three grenades. Next to them in the two green canisters is some smoke. That gets us to the left side where you have three extra magazines for your rifle. They each have fifty rounds in them. Add the one that is in your rifle and you have two hundred rifle rounds, fifty handgun rounds and ten explosive rounds. That's 260 rounds multiplied by a whole lot of us when we Walk."

"That is a lot of firepower," Danny agreed.

"Just under your left arm is your knife." As Danny pulled it from its sheath Lost continued, "That's an 8-inch blade that has a little extra punch. After you stab it into Mr. Teeth you can slam your hand down on the back of the hilt and the blade will explode forward another 6 or so inches."

"That would do the trick. What's in the long horizontal pack on the back of the belt?"

As Lost adjusted Danny's belt, she paused and then told him, "Stuff we hope we never need. All our medical gear. Patches, 4x4s, gauze, tactical tourniquets, morphine, and even some sponge filled syringes to stop bleeding in really bad wounds."

"Thanks, Lost." Then after a pause he asked, "Why Lost?"

"Because she doesn't know east from west or up from down," Blonk answered.

"Or what time it is, ever," Whitey added.

"She's always just lost," Maybe said. "But that doesn't mean she didn't do a great job today taking the bite."

As everyone agreed, Lauren asked, "What about everyone else? What about your nickname, Maybe?"

"I never answer yes or no right away. I have to think on things first so it's always a 'maybe' to begin with."

"Okay, Whitey?"

He rolled up a sleeve to show his pale arm and said, "This is the tannest I've ever been."

"Before I forget, what about Stork?"

"You did see that tall, gangly guy didn't you?" Blonk asked.

Lauren nodded and asked, "Blonk? Short for Blonken-something?"

"Easier than that," he answered. "I have blond hair and as you can see I am pretty big. My dad always said I was strong as a horse, so he called me Blonk which he said meant white horse. There you go."

"Interesting," Lauren replied. "Ricardo?"

"Don't get him started," Cat advised. "He thinks he is a Latin-lover. His real name is –"

"Never mind," Ricardo cut in. "I am Latin, and I'll leave the rest to everyone's imagination." As the Team groaned he continued, "At least I am not a cat because I sneak around."

"Hey, what's wrong with being able to sneak around?" Cat asked. "I'm just quiet and stealthy –"

"And because you're a Peeping Tom," Junk said. "We all know why you're sneaking around."

Cat put his hands up and said, "Always accused, never convicted."

"Okay, maybe I should stop," Lauren said.

"No, we're good," Junk answered. "I'm Junk because I collect a lot of things I think will be valuable one day. Figurines, art, magazines, antiques. Stuff."

"Stuff that some of us call junk. I'm Ammo because I know the specs on all types of ammunition: handgun, rifle, shotgun, machineguns, cannons, rocket launchers. I like to shoot and blow things up."

"He does. Sometimes he does it just to scare us." Rover slapped Ammo on the arm and continued, "Or at least me. I'm called Rover because I like to keep moving. When we're Walking I like to go out with Cat to scout."

"That's not all I hear you like to do with Cat," Ammo added, and Rover slapped him again. Then he said, "Stoney, why don't you take your shirt off?"

"You know I'm not shy," she said as she took off her shirt and flexed.

"Now take off the sports bra," Ammo shouted.

"You wish. I'm not as big as Blonk and Chesky but you won't find a lot of fat anywhere on me. The guys think I'm like a stone, so I'm Stoney."

"Chesky?" Lauren asked.

He hung his head for a moment then replied, "My father played Polka music. There is a famous Polka band leader named Chesky and he would call me his little Chesky."

As the Team went "awwww" Lauren asked, "Do you play Polka?"

Chesky hung his head again; as everyone went silent he answered, "Yeah, I have an accordion."

As everyone started making jokes Lauren said, "Well, I guess that's everyone."

"What about me?" Sinewave asked.

"Second smartest person in the room? Why would we care?"

Sinewave couldn't help laughing with everyone else and then he said, "I see the way it is. But anyway, smartest kid in my high school. I actually knew what a sine wave was but that's not what got me the nickname. I loved the old monster movies where dead people were brought back to life. There was always an oscilloscope with sine waves moving across it. I talked about it so much that I became Sinewave. And you know that's interesting because you can also call them –"

"Stop him," Blonk said. "I asked what time it was once, and he told me how Big Ben was built."

"Yeah, let's get Charles, Ron and Lisa suited up too," Lost said.

When everyone was ready Lauren said, "Charles, be careful." Then she added, "And the rest of you too."

"Yes, Mom," the Team replied.

Lauren shook her head and asked, "Why do I always get that?"

Before anyone could answer Ben came over the speaker, "If you cowboys and cowgirls are ready, it's time to take a Walk."

CHAPTER NINE
THE WALK

Major Donald immediately entered the locker room and advised Ben, "We're ready to Walk. Going out will be the Team, Sgt. Jameston, Ron, Lisa and Charles."

"Stand by for just a moment," Ben said.

Steve came over the speaker and said, "We've been watching something for a few minutes and they have suddenly turned in our direction. They're not going to be close enough to worry about we think, but they are interesting. We thought Ron, and everyone else, might want to step outside for a look."

Ben added, "The lagoon is empty right now and I'll keep a watch on it. Major, you have a green light to step outside but for right now stay within the curtain. We still aren't a hundred percent sure which way they will go."

"Roger that, Paycheck," Major Donald replied.

"What do you think it is?" Lost asked Danny.

"Well it can't be my neighbor, Stanley, or they wouldn't have let us go out."

Lauren watched on the view screen as the Team moved out of the Unit. Ben immediately said, "Seventeen out, starting the timer."

"Dad's going to like this," Lauren said. "But are you sure they shouldn't come back in?"

"They're fine," Ben told her. "They're still inside the curtain. Just because you can see through it doesn't mean it isn't there. If something decides to come closer we'll just make the curtain look solid and the animal will go around us."

"Won't they just run right through it?"

"No. I mean, what animal just runs into a wall or the side of a mountain? I know in the movies dinosaurs just run through things but they're not that stupid. They don't just run into things to see if they can. They don't want to injure themselves."

"I had never thought of that," Lauren said. "Too many movies I guess."

Steve suddenly said, "Look," and pointed at the screen. Outside, the Team saw it at the same time; the head of an animal seemingly floating above the treetops. Where the trees were shorter they could see the long green and grey neck. Behind the lead animal were two others, not as tall, but following closely.

"What are they?" Ammo asked.

"My guess is *Alamosaurus*," Ron replied. "Maybe a male and female pair with an offspring."

"They're huge," Cat said. "How big do they get?"

"80 to 90 feet long and close to 50 feet tall. They were a Titanosaur."

"Like the one they found in Argentina?" Ricardo asked.

"Exactly, exactly," Ron exclaimed. "Look at their necks. The two larger ones have frills that run about two meters down their necks. The smaller one doesn't."

Lauren came over their headsets, "Adult and juvenile difference?"

"Maybe, maybe. Could be." Ron paced for a second then said, "I wish I could see the sides of them."

"Why is that?" Ben asked.

"Their spikes," Ron answered.

"Spikes?" Steve repeated. "Let me put something up on the curtain for you." A view screen appeared, and they could see a shaky image as a drone was slowly dropping in beside the huge animals. "I'm going slow," Steve told everyone. "I don't want to spook them, and I have to dodge some brush. Hang on for a moment."

Then the picture steadied and as the animals walked by Ron shouted, "Yes. Do you see them? Just above the back hip on each of them? Do you see the spikes?" Everyone excitedly said they did and watched intently until finally the animals' whipping tails slowly moved across the screen and then out of view.

Steve reported, "Ron, you were exactly right. The DTS confirmed that was an *Alamosaurus*. Great job."

Ben came back on and said, "Okay, that was fun. Are we ready to head out now?"

There were shouts of "Let's go" from everyone and an opening appeared in the screen. The Team quickly stepped through it and as Danny followed he immediately said, "Man, I forgot how hot and humid it was. Lauren, how hot is it?"

Lauren asked, "Danny, do you really want to know?"

"So, it's that hot," Danny said. "Never mind."

"I'll stay close to you," Charles told him.

Then Steve came in with "Major Donald."

"Yes?"

"Head northeast. Follow the lead drones and bots and stay alert. We're not seeing the *Rexes* or really anything yet, but those last three *Alamo* guys moved in pretty quick."

Ben turned to Lauren and said, "Let me explain what we have here. On the main screen right now is the satellite view of the area. We'll switch to drones and bots shortly and probably go back and forth between them. You saw Steve do that for the horns. On the screens on each side of the main view are the helmet cam videos of the Team with each of their names at the bottom so we know what the Team member is looking at."

"Do you have heat sensing optics?" Lauren asked.

"Yes," Ben told her. "The drones, bots, satellite and even the Team helmets."

"So, there is nothing showing up right now?"

"Lots of small stuff, we're talking less than a foot long." Ben held up his hand as Lauren started to say something and continued, "And I know some of those could be dangerous but probably not to a group of seventeen. Still, that's why Steve told them to stay alert."

Lauren watched as the Team disappeared into some high vegetation and the satellite view disappeared from the main screen and was replaced by a much closer overhead view. "How do you control all of the drones and bots?" Lisa asked.

"It's not as hard as you think," Ben told her. "They all are linked together for a team concept approach. On the ground, the four bots form the corners of an ever-changing rectangle around the Team. We really only have to move one and the others follow."

Ben waved a hand in front of him and a holographic view appeared. He looked at Lauren and said, "Just move your hand a couple of inches away from your workstation screen." She did so, and the Team holograph appeared before her. Then Ben continued, "Okay, you can see the Team silhouettes outlined in red. In the corners, the green square outlines are the bots and the blue outlined circles are the drones. The bots are numbered one through four and there are five numbered drones.

"Say I want just one bot or drone to move. I just put my finger on it then drag it to the new position." Ben touched bot 1 and moved it to the left of the Team. "Now obviously the bots cannot move as fast as your fingers. You have to allow for terrain contours and obstacles you can't see, so it might be several minutes before the bot is in position.

"You see each of the bots has sensors that keeps them from running into things and gives them the ability to find clear paths. Obviously, all of the bots will encounter terrain difficulties during the Walks, maybe even at the same time. But because they communicate with each other they are constantly attempting to maintain their positions. If one lags behind because of an obstacle or rough terrain their planned shape can change but when the delayed bot catches up they move back into their original formation."

Lauren watched as bot 1 slowly changed position on the view screen. It followed a winding course and Lauren could see from its view there were fallen tree branches and some heavy vegetation it had to go around. It took over a minute to get to the new location.

"Okay," Ben said, "let me show you something else with this one. I'm looking at a pretty uninteresting tree stump at the moment, ah, there we go. See that disgusting looking insect crawling around? The shiny brown one with a million legs and very long antennae?" Ben touched the bot's video screen and a green dot appeared on the insect. From that moment, the bot's camera followed only the insect. Ben held his finger on the green dot and the bot's camera zoomed in until he moved his finger away. "What do you think?" he asked Lauren.

"I like it," she told him. "But why did bot 2 move?"

"Because when I moved bot 1 from the upper left corner it left a hole in the Team security. Since bot 2 is the other lead bot, it moved to the center of the Team and began using its front and both side cameras."

"Got it," Lauren replied. "Team safety is first."

"Most definitely. Now, when I'm finished with bot 1, I just tap it twice and it will automatically start moving to resume its assigned spot on the Team perimeter. Again, it may take a few minutes since the Team may not have stopped while we used the bot. When it gets back, bot 2 will return to the upper right corner of the rectangle and you're back to normal."

"How do they know how fast to go in the first place? Do you set a speed?"

"No, they constantly monitor the Team, also the Team's speed determines their speed. The bots are there to provide vital information, so they can't outrun the Team or go too slow. Though each bot has a camera on all four sides, only the front and outside cameras are activated on the leading bots and the outside and rear cameras on the trailing bots."

"Unless one is doing double duty," Lauren said.

"That's right," Ben agreed.

Lauren nodded and asked, "My guess is that the drones are set up similarly?"

"You got it," Ben agreed. "They form a wider perimeter than the bots but are set up the same. They usually have fewer moving problems because they can adjust their height and distance from the group more easily. They move quicker to a new location since they don't have rocks and ditches to worry about. But they still have to watch out for branches and leaves. So, they may go up and over or out and around things."

Ben pointed at the main view screen and continued, "The view from drone 1, which is above and slightly behind the Team, is on the main screen right now. Remember, the drones are the blue circles and like the bots, each view is numbered to make it easy to know which drone you want to control.

"Now here is an interesting thing you can do with the drones. When I pinch the holographic drone and pull toward me, it raises up. Pinch and push toward the screen and it will lower. And, if you tap it twice it will auto return to its assigned position."

"Okay, so we can control the bots and drones from in here. What about the Team?"

"Good question. If the Team changes direction or its speed, the bots and drones adjust. If a Team member needs a bot or drone for some specific reason they have to let us know. Too many people controlling them could cause confusion. After all, whatever the Team sees is already shown and recorded through their helmet cams. If multiple views are necessary then we coordinate that from in here."

"What if a bot or drone is destroyed?"

"The same as if we move one of them. The other drones have a preset system of replacement which will keep one drone in front and two drones roving behind the Team. If two drones are destroyed the two remaining ones begin to rove, one in front and one behind. Also, if the Team is close enough, we send out replacements. The new drones or bots begin communication with the others when they arrive and then we're back to full protection mode."

"Seems simple," Lauren said. "I can just push and pull or tap."

"Or hold," Ben added. "If you want a bot to stop or a drone to hover just grab it and hold it in place for a second. When you want it to move again just tap it twice like before and it returns to its spot."

"Wow."

Ben smiled and told her, "Just say, 'thanks Otto'."

"Thanks Otto."

"Oh, uh, I just did some research and I, uh –"

Ben cut in with, "Otto, just say 'you're welcome'."

Otto laughed quietly said, "You're welcome."

Major Donald called in, "Steve, we've paused about three hundred yards away from the Unit. Nothing in this area except a kind of trail surrounded by thick brush. Now there are dino tracks leading into the heavy stuff that Ron is interested in. We're still good to go?"

"Yes, still good to go. Nothing around you at all."

"Dad is looking at the tracks," Lauren pointed out.

"Why don't you talk to him about them?" Steve asked.

"Uh, okay. How?"

"Look at his screen and tap the microphone under his video."

Lauren quickly did and asked, "Dad?"

"Lauren? Can you see these?"

"Yes. Those look like *Rex* tracks. What are you thinking?"

"Yes, they are *Rex* tracks. Like we were told, I can see one set of large tracks and they are covered by the tracks of the juveniles. I think we're going to follow them."

"I don't think you want to run into four *Rexes*, Dad."

"That's right but my feeling is at most there will be three. The adult will not be socializing with the juveniles. And I know the juveniles were together on the beach, but I can't see them staying together for long. Just a hunch, but that's why we're here. I think we'll see the tracks go in separate directions."

Lauren looked up and told Steve, "I actually have to agree with him. But just in case can you keep a close eye on that satellite image and have those drones and bots on alert."

"Those drones and bots are always on alert, but we will keep a close eye on everything," Steve told her. "Major Donald, right now there are no *Rexes* in the area and we'd like you to go with Ron's suggestion and follow the tracks."

"We were hoping you would," she replied.

As the Team started forward, Lauren said, "Let's keep those drones and bots close by. In fact, can the drones go up higher? I want to see as much as I can."

"No problem," Ben replied. "I'll increase their area too." All five drones rose up and spread out around the Team. Ben activated the heat sensor readings and suddenly Lauren saw red spots of animals moving all around the Team. But they were all small and none appeared to be moving toward the Team.

As the Team picked up its pace Lauren could hear someone breathing hard and Ben asked, "How are you doing, Danny?"

"It's getting hotter," he replied. "I'm sweating like a –"

"How do I stop all of them? The drones and bots?" Lauren suddenly asked. "All of them."

As Ben immediately said, "Team, stop and take a knee," he also placed his hands on a green square that had a blue circle in it that was not part of Lauren's workstation. The bots and drones stopped, and Ben added, "No talking, stand by." He turned to Lauren and asked, "What do you have? I don't show anything."

"I don't either," Steve added.

"Okay," Lauren answered. "You have to trust me for a second on this one. Can you show me the satellite view and mark where the lead drones are?"

"Sure," Ben told her as the view came up with two points marked drone 2 and drone 3.

"Okay, great. Now then, when I move drone 2 can I see it move on the satellite view?"

"Yes. I'm going to move bot 2 with you."

Lauren took drone 2 and watching the satellite view closely, moved it on a 45-degree angle to the northeast of the Team. When she let go the drone 2 camera was looking down through some thick vegetation. Lauren slowly moved the drone lower until it moved slowly around some branches and through some leaves.

Below the drone was the forest floor and Lauren said, "There it is."

Ben shook his head and said, "I don't see it."

Lauren pressed on her screen and as the drone 2 camera zoomed in Ben suddenly shouted, "Those are teeth."

Lauren replied, "They certainly are. Now keep watching." She pulled the drone up slowly and as she did the outline of the *Rex* suddenly became apparent.

"I see it," Ben exclaimed. "How did you pick that out?"

"It wasn't much different than spotting a bone in the rocks."

"I still don't see it," Steve said.

Ben used both hands to form a square around the *Rex* and then made the area much lighter in color. "And there it is," Steve said. "Ben let's take a closer look."

As bot 1 closed in Lauren said, "Well, I can see from the drone feed that there are scavengers on this *Rex*. It's obviously dead and no danger to the Team. Since there was no heat signature from it I was pretty sure, but, well…"

"You don't have to apologize, Lauren," Steve told her. "I can only imagine your feelings at seeing a *Rex* again, live or dead, and knowing your friends are walking toward it."

Ben turned all the bots and drones toward the dead animal and told Major Donald, "I don't know which way all of the tracks lead but follow the bots and tell Ron some of the tracks are coming to an end. Dead *Rex* ahead."

"We're sure there's nothing else around?" Lauren asked.

"No," Ben told her. "Nothing big at all for at least a mile."

"Major Donald, you're about a hundred feet away."

"We're clear."

"Okay, I'm putting on the enhanced satellite view for you. Got it?"

"Yes."

"Great. Let's see what we have and what we want to bring back."

"Yes, sir," Major Donald replied and then the Team started moving forward. As several of the cameras swept across Ron, Lauren could see he had a big smile on his face.

"Well, somebody's happy," Lauren noted.

"You're sure it's dead?" Lisa asked.

"Yes," Ben assured her. "It's dead." Then he said, "Major, watch for the scavengers. There's maybe ten or so, small but they might be persistent."

"No problem, Paycheck. Hopefully they won't stick around."

"Ron, what are those?" Steve asked.

"What does the DTS indicate?"

"It doesn't. It's a mystery animal."

"I'm glad you said that," Ron replied. "I was trying to figure out what they were from where we are. I can mentally compare them to the fossils we already have on record and to dinosaur artwork. But that can only indicate detail or suggest possibilities. Just guesswork."

"What were you going to guess?" Steve asked.

"*Saurornitholestes*," Ron replied.

"I can see that," Lauren said. "But it's not, and we have the video and data to prove it. Well, I mean, if we were going to do that."

Steve laughed and said, "It will just be our secret." Then he asked her, "What do we need to do here?"

"Let me think for a minute," Lauren said. "Okay. Let's keep the drones on guard duty and away from the *T-rex* body. When the Team arrives, I'll concentrate on what each person is doing, and I'll see what they see on their helmet cams. Dad will have a lot of input also." She paused, then asked, "What's taking them so long to get there?"

"Thick vegetation and uh, your dad is stopping to look at everything," Ben said. "Which is okay," he quickly added.

"Dad, let's get to the *T-Rex* before the scavengers eat all of it," Lauren said.

"What? Oh, sorry everyone."

"Don't worry," Major Donald told him. "We're almost there."

Lauren looked at Ben and asked, "There's nothing close by? Right? Moving I mean. It doesn't have to be big. Is there anything that can attack them?"

Ben moved the drones in different directions and to different heights for a full minute. He rechecked the heat images then smiled and said, "No, there are a few other small animals in the surrounding area, maybe a foot tall, but that's it. Of all the scavengers present only a couple are close to two feet tall. It looks safe, but of course we will continue to monitor. Do you want the Team to go in now?"

Lauren paused again then said, "Okay, yes, send them in." She paused then added, "But tell them watch out again, please."

"I will," Ben told her.

The Team forced their way through the last of some thick roots and were beside the *Rex*. The scavengers either ran away or flew off, though a couple were reluctant and left only when charged by Stoney and Chesky.

As the Team video of the dead Tyrannosaurus came in, Ben told Lauren, "Take over the drones and bots if you need to."

"Actually, there is plenty of video coming in from the Team. So much that it's hard to keep up with. It will take weeks to go over."

"Well, if you decide to join us you'll have something to do," Ben pointed out.

Lauren smiled and asked, "Do you think it is one of the animals from your first visit? It is a juvenile *T-Rex.*"

Ben activated the DTS and several points began blinking then the entire animal blinked once and in the lower corner of her view screen she read '100% Probable'. Ben told Lauren, "Well, now we know it is one of them. What do you think happened?"

"Your answer is right there in the large wound on the back of its neck," Lauren said. "Can you ask someone to pull the tooth out of it?"

"On it," Whitey said. His screen then showed his hand reaching down toward a white object and then holding up an 8-inch-long tooth with well-defined serrated edges.

As the tooth was moved around slowly so it could be seen, Ron said, "It's a *Rex* tooth. No doubt about it. Ben, you said there were three of them, but one was larger than the other two?"

"Yes."

Ron paused for a moment then continued, "Well, it's only a guess, but I think that though there is some theoretical evidence that *Rexes* may have stayed together when they were young, and of course the three you saw were, the older one decided it was time to break away. Maybe one or both of the other ones didn't take the hint and learned the hard way."

"DTS confirms it is a tooth from the larger juvenile," Ben said.

Steve turned to Lauren and asked, "What do you think?"

"Big cats are part of a group to begin with but go their own way after they get mature enough. Could be what happened here, but we really don't know for sure."

"We could step back and find out?" Steve told her.

"Step back?"

"Sorry, go back in small increments of time until we see the incident actually occur. Could give us the information you need."

Lauren shook her head and replied, "No, as interesting as that sounds, I have to say no. We might stop the fight by accident before it began and, somehow, someone might get hurt and I would not want that."

Steve just nodded as he turned back to his station, but Ben said, "We can do whatever is needed, Lauren. There is an inherent risk in everything we do. If it wasn't safe, we wouldn't do it. Think on it then let me know if you change your mind and we'll see if it can be safely done."

Lauren didn't reply as she turned back toward her station and then wished she hadn't. Various body parts, teeth, claws, feathers and skin were being removed from the dead *Rex*. She started to turn away when she saw on Junk's screen a hand come down and lightly touch the Rex just above its eye and then slowly pull away. It was like Junk had caressed a pet, and Lauren wished she had been part of the Team, so it could have been her. Then she got mad at herself for thinking it though she made a mental note to talk to Junk.

"How's everyone doing?" Ben asked the Team.

"We're doing great," Major Donald reported.

"Hey, Paycheck," Cat called in, "why did it have such tiny arms?"

"You have Ron right there. Ask him."

"Hey, Ron."

"I heard your question," Ron answered. "There is a lot of speculation about those arms. Some think they were used only during mating and others think that they were used to grab prey but were short because longer arms would be more susceptible to breaking. Maybe the most logical reason though is that it takes a lot of neck muscle to hold that giant head up and that didn't leave room for a lot of arm control muscles."

"Okay, Ron, answer this," Ammo called out. "Look at these legs, they are huge. How fast could this puppy run?"

"Again, there are several theories. Some say slow, others say up to 25 miles per hour. I think it was more like ten miles an hour, maybe a little faster. If it means anything, we had to run to get away from the ones that chased us, and we did it."

There was silence and then Whitey said, "That's right, you've already done this. Man, you lived it."

"That's right," Ron said. He turned to look for Lisa as he spoke and noticed that she was standing away from the group. She had her hands clasped in front of her and she was just staring straight ahead.

"Lisa, are you okay?" he asked.

"Yes, I'm doing okay. Just processing everything."

"Why don't you come over and stand by me?"

"I'm okay here, really."

Ron paused for a second and then told her, "But you have company."

She quickly looked around and then down. A couple feet away from her were two small dinosaurs. They looked like the ones that Ron could not identify. Lisa quickly moved over to Ron and asked nervously, "They weren't getting ready to, I mean –"

"No," Ron assured her. "They're just waiting for us to leave."

As she watched the screens, Lauren sighed and said, "There is one thing I really don't like about this."

"And that is?" Steve asked.

"Too ghoulish. All the samples and dissecting makes it seem like some kind of horror movie. Sorry. I know it's not and also necessary but still, just something I could do without."

Before Steve could reply, Ben cut in with, "We have a large animal and two smaller ones entering the perimeter from the south. They are moving slow and should not pose any danger to you. Thought you might want to take a look at them. I'm moving drone 1 and bot 3 toward them for a visual check and also activating DTS."

A moment later Lauren smiled and told everyone, "It's a large *Ankylosaurus* and two smaller ones." Then the smile left as she remembered Mitch calling them *Ankle-saurs*.

"What are the little ones called?" Sinewave asked. "Cubs?"

"How about 'clubs'," Lisa suggested.

There was a moment of silence then everyone laughed as Ben said, "Clubs it is. Funny."

Drone 1 stopped above the animals and Lauren said, "Just as I remember. Look at the size of it and –"

"And those clubs are so cute," Lisa interrupted. "Look at them trying to jump around."

Bot 3 had stopped thirty feet from the animals and its movement caught the attention of one of the 'clubs' and soon its face was stuck into the camera lens. After a few seconds though it grew interested in something else and continued walking with the others. The Team stayed hidden for a few minutes as the animals passed through the forest about a hundred feet from them.

A few seconds after they disappeared, Major Donald asked, "Paycheck, are we good to go?"

"You are," Ben answered. "The mom and clubs are continuing to move away from you so head back and get the samples stowed away."

"Roger that," the Major replied and the Team started back.

"Danny, are you feeling okay?" Charles asked.

"Well, I'm sort of doing okay. The excitement of being next to the *Rex* got me going again but now that we're headed back I'm starting to drag a little. I'm good enough to get back though."

Ron came up behind them and asked, "Should we have them send out something to carry you back? Maybe they have a golf cart or something for injuries."

"No, no, no," Danny replied. "First, it couldn't get to us through all the stuff we went through. Next, please keep your voice down. No one else needs to know I'm not feeling well, okay?"

"Okay," Charles told him. "Your secret is safe with us. But when we get back to our time, let's get you to a doctor."

Danny started to say something then he paused before continuing with, "Of course. Probably just a bug of some type."

In the Unit, Ben suddenly leaned forward as he stared at his screen then turned to Lauren and said, "Tell me what *that* is, and should I tell everyone to hide again?" As Lauren looked down at her screen Ben calmly told the Team, "Another large animal is approaching. This one is from the north and it is not mama and her clubs coming back. It's big, moving quickly and I think it is another –"

"*T-Rex,*" Lauren cut in. She was talking fast as she continued to everyone, "This is a large *Rex*. Very large. It seems to be moving with a purpose. I can't tell if it's coming in to scavenge the juvenile or following another scent. But it's moving quick."

Ben jumped in with, "Team, we have a couple of minutes before it will be able to see you. Start southwest right now and keep moving until I tell you to stop. I'm moving drone 1 and bots 3 and 5 to intercept and track. Get moving."

As the Team started, Ben called again, "Ammo, I need your quarterback arm."

"Okay."

"Throw a killdeer as far as you can back toward the juvenile Rex. Do it right now then catch up with everyone and keep moving. Have your finger on the button."

Lauren started to ask what a killdeer was when drone 1 arrived over the *Rex*. "I hate it when I'm right," Lauren said. "This one looks mad."

"Doesn't that face always look mad?" Steve asked.

"I'm not looking at its head," Lauren replied. "See how it is bent forward? When it's just out for a stroll it has a different posture. This one is ready for battle."

Ben stared at Lauren for a second then he was talking to the Team, "Get moving, people. Faster. I'm going to be giving you a countdown so be ready to stop and drop when I say so. We're not covering up yet, just take a knee. You got fifteen seconds. Go, go, go. Ten seconds. Stand by…stand by…down, down, down."

As the Team came to a complete stop the *Rex* paused about a hundred yards away. They could just barely see through the tress that it was lifting its head, sniffing and looking in the direction of the Team and also toward the dead *Rex*. As bot 3 ran past the toes of the *Rex* it stepped quickly backwards and accidentally crushed bot 5. Bot 3 raced in front of the *Rex* and after dodging back and forth a couple of times it sped away toward the juvenile *Rex*. The larger animal took a couple of steps after it then paused and looked back in the direction of the Team.

As it took a slow step toward the Team, Ben told Ammo, "Activate your killdeer. Everyone else, don't move."

Suddenly the cries of a wounded animal sounded behind the *Rex* and it spun around and ran toward them. Then Ben was in their ears again saying, "Give it a few more seconds and it will be at the dead *Rex* and we shouldn't have any more problems. Wait a second." After a short pause he continued, "Ladies and gentlemen, the Rex is now enjoying dinner. I would suggest you resume your return trip and try your best not to attract any more company."

"Amen to that," Rover called out and everyone jumped up and moved quickly back toward the Unit.

Ben called out again, "If you hear any noises, you are just scaring some animals and they are all moving away from you. When you arrive on the beach you'll find some smaller animals wading and getting a suntan. Additionally, just coming into view at the far end of the beach are some duck-bills. They aren't too big and if I remember correctly, they are vegetarians. Right, Ron?"

"They are," he agreed. "I don't think we'll spook them into a charge or anything."

"Major Donald, Danny has fallen behind," Blonk called out.

The Team immediately stopped and Blonk and Chesky ran back to where Danny was bent over, hands on his knees. "I'm okay," he told them. "Just getting winded." He took a deep breath and continued, "I heard Ben say there wasn't anything out here to get me so don't concern yourselves, I'll be there in another minute."

"Begging your pardon, Sir," Blonk said, "but we don't leave anyone behind." Blonk got behind Danny and slipped his arms around him and Chesky picked Danny up under his knees. They fell back in line with the rest of the Team and soon were breaking from the forest on to the beach and then the curtain around the Unit opened up.

CHAPTER TEN
PLANS

As they filed in, hot and sweaty, but laughing and talking, Ben told them, "Samples in the lockers, please." Ben stated, "Seventeen in," then he turned to Lauren and added, "Just like always."

Lauren said, "You did make it look easy." Then she asked, "What's a killdeer?"

"What's a killdeer known for?" he answered.

"Well, it has a distinctive call," Charles said as he entered the control room.

"That's right," Ben agreed. "But what else?"

"The broken wing fake-out," Lauren said. "So, Ammo throws the killdeer to draw away the *Rex*, why wait to activate it? Why doesn't it just go off?"

"Because it will immediately draw animals to where you still *are*. We want them going to where you *were*."

"Okay, I got that."

"But, I have a suggestion," Charles said.

Steve and Otto turned toward him as Steve asked, "What is it, Charles?"

"Use the drones or bots to deliver the sound. They can move around quicker and go straight to wherever you want an animal to go without any danger to a human. The killdeers the Team carry should be backups."

Steve looked at Otto and said, "I guess we're not quite as smart as we thought we were."

Otto nodded and told Charles, "That was an excellent suggestion." Then Otto nodded to Steve and said, "And you are that smart. After all, you made him part of the Team."

"Thanks, Otto," Steve smiled. "But I'm giving that point to Charles. Anything else you would like to suggest?" Steve asked.

"I understand that is the reason you want us here but I, well Lauren and I, we're just checking things out."

"And, so far?"

"Well, today I have been impressed. Underwater, a bite with no harm, the juvenile *Rex* and then easily escaping the big *Rex*. It's been a good day."

"Lauren?"

"I agree with Charles and I have to add that Ben, you were really calm when the big *Rex* showed up. And so was the rest of the Team. I know I wasn't."

Ben shook his head and advised, "No, I wasn't calm or even close to it. But we've trained these situations and you react as you train under stress. The training just took over."

"You're being modest," Charles told him, "but I understand." Then he turned to Lauren and said, "Let's go see how Danny is."

Down in the locker room, Maybe was asking Ron, "How long have you been studying these 'saurs? You seem to know everything about them."

"Since I was a kid I guess. I've always loved dinosaurs and digging them up has been the best job I ever could have had. But now, now –"

"Now you get to see the real thing," Cat finished for him. "No more dusty, old bones. You get to see the 'saurs moving around. Breathe the same air they are. Man, that's got to be exciting for you."

"It is," Ron agreed. "But I have to be careful and not get carried away. I almost did that on my first Walk and today I was paying more attention to everything except what we were supposed to do. I have to keep myself in check."

"We'll go out with you anytime, sir," Blonk told him.

"Lisa, what about you?" Lost asked. "Do you want to Walk with us again?"

"Well, I do, and I don't. I could tell Ron was having a good time and it made me want to be there. But...our jumps, our jumps ended with death. That's still in my mind and I keep thinking it's what will happen to some of you. I know you're good, but life has a way of surprising you." She went quiet for a moment then said, "Sorry to be a downer. Maybe I'll be more involved next time."

Lost gave her a hug and said, "Come out anytime you want to. Remember, you are part of the Team."

"What about you, Danny?" Lisa asked. "Going out again?"

"Probably," Danny replied. "Sorry I'm feeling bad. I thought it was the flu, now I think it might be an allergy and being out in the jungle wasn't helping me any."

"What are you allergic to?" Sinewave asked.

"Getting bit by a *Rex*," Danny replied. "But seriously, it felt just like it did the first time. I was scared too, the whole time, and excited too. It's hard to describe. I did what I had to do but I wouldn't want to do it again." Then he looked at Ron, Lisa, Charles and Lauren and said, "But look who I'm talking to. We all know what it was like." He looked around the room and continued, "But today was different. I felt scared some of the time, but I really felt like all of you would take care of us. So yeah. I'll go out again."

There was a cheer and Rover asked, "Charles?"

"I will go out again. But next time I want to sit with Ben, I mean Paycheck, and Steve. I want to see how things are run. What was it like inside, Lauren?"

"Well, there were no teeth, no heat, no humidity, no sweating and no hacking up dead dinosaurs."

"What was there then?" Charles asked.

"Cabana boy, foot massages and endless piña coladas. I barely made it."

"I knew it," Stoney shouted as everyone laughed. "Paycheck has been holding out on us."

"What have I been holding out?" Ben asked over the intercom.

"Lauren told us about the piña coladas."

"Hey, it was only one pitcher…each," Ben replied. As everyone shouted, Ben continued, "But you can get your own piña coladas when we get back. Right now, hydrate, eat something – we have chicken today, then we'll take all the used gear outside and leave it like usual. Also, we'll do the Walk debrief tomorrow instead of tonight since your New Year's Eve got replaced with training. Boss Man Steve says it was a great day. A bonus day."

"All right," Blonk shouted. "Stork is going to die when he hears this."

"We'll call him when we get back," Rover added.

As everyone started talking, Charles walked over to Lauren and said, "But you didn't answer the question. Would you go out?"

"I may not be as opposed to it as I once was, but right now still a no. But, maybe in the future. What about you? Aren't you still concerned about the theft of your work?"

"Yes, I am. That's why I want inside next time. I know what he took, I want to see what he did with it. Maybe I'll tell him I know what he did and see how he responds. He doesn't seem to be a monster. At least not yet."

Danny walked over with Ron and Lisa following. Charles winced and said, "Danny, you need to go lay down. You look terrible."

"I feel terrible. Like I can't breathe. I might step outside for a moment. Stay inside the curtain where the air is cool."

Ron said, "We'll come with you."

Danny shook his head and said, "No, I'm just going to stretch my legs."

"Okay," Ron said. "But come back in and lay down in a few minutes. Charles is right, you are looking bad."

"I'm just tired from all the walking we did in this heat. But I'll come back in, just save me some chicken."

Danny stuck his head into the control room and asked, "Can you let me out? I'll stay inside the curtain, but I need to stretch my legs. I still don't feel a hundred percent."

"Sure," Ben told him. "If you need anything just ask, I'll be able to hear you."

"Thanks." As Danny stepped outside, the cool air in a more open space felt good for a few minutes. But he couldn't settle down. He took some deep breaths, but he felt like his nerves were working overtime. He paced back and forth for a few minutes then turned toward the Unit and asked, "Ben, is there anything close by that will eat me? If not I'd like to take a walk."

"A walk?"

"I need to settle down. A couple of laps around the Unit."

"Hang on a second and we'll send someone with you."

"No, I just want to –"

"We'll be outside too," Danny heard Lisa say. "Ron and I. We want to walk outside for a couple of minutes."

"I might step out for a second too," Charles said.

"I'm going out too," Lauren found herself saying. "I'm not sure why." She looked at Charles and added, "Right next to the Unit, no further."

"How are all of you able to hear me?" Danny asked.

"We went into the control room to talk to Steve and heard you," Lisa told him.

There was a pause and then Ben said, "Well, I can't really say no to all of you. But, the satellite is powered down and all the bots and drones from earlier have been shut down."

"I thought you could see out to 200 yards just with the equipment on top of the Unit?" Lauren said.

"That's true but you know how quick some of these things are."

"All we want you to say," Lauren told him, "is there isn't anything close by that will eat us and you'll let us know if something wanders our way."

"I can do that," Ben agreed.

"I have an idea," Otto said. "One, if you stay fairly close to the curtain I can expand it out around you in about one second. Once you are inside nothing can get through the curtain. And two, I can send up a drone to scout around us for some aerial support."

"Yes, to the curtain, no to the drone," Lauren said. "I don't know about anyone else, but I plan on being outside for just a few minutes. I'm using it as a baby step for later."

"Okay," Ben said. As the group headed toward the curtain, Ben told Otto, "Be sure to keep an eye on them. I'm going to the locker room to see how everyone is doing."

"I will," Otto replied. Then he told the group, "It is still clear out to 200 yards. I'm opening the curtain and I'll keep a close eye on things." As Lauren shouted, "thanks, Otto", he closed the curtain and then thought it would be better to be safe and opened up the drone program.

They all paused as the curtain closed behind them and Lauren told Danny, "It is hot out here. It almost feels like it is taking my breath away. The jungle, the noise, it's a lot. Do you need to go back in?"

"No," Danny told her. "For some reason, the heat now feels good and I'm breathing better now. But I still feel jittery, like I got to keep walking. You know, standing right next to the *Rex* seemed to help my nerves, but now I'm not sure. I'll stay close by, but I have to walk. Don't worry, I'll be back in a minute."

"Should we go with him?" Lauren asked.

"No," Charles told her. "I've gotten to know Danny over the last few months and he really is a quiet person. He speaks when he wants to, but he likes to listen. Sometimes he seems preoccupied, but he is thinking about retirement and we've seen his father a few times on our jumps. Just think about what we are doing right now. You and Ron are in your element, Danny isn't."

Ron nodded his head and said, "You know, I'm starting to think there is more going on with Danny than he is letting us know. Let's keep an eye on him and get him to a doctor when we get back."

Lisa changed the subject by asking Ron, "How did you really feel about today?"

"It gets in your blood," Ron said. "I've had some bad dreams about the jumps, but deep down I've wanted to go back out because it's the most alive I've ever felt. I know all of you hated it, but I think you liked at least some part of our jumps and what we did today. I'm ready to do it again." Ron paused and asked Lisa, "What about you?"

"I hated every moment of it. Ben and Steve can see for miles, but I just knew any second something was going to attack us. When we had to drop down I knew I wasn't going to get back up. That this was it, one time too many. I'm still shaking."

Ron took her hands and asked, "Why did you do it then?"

Lisa smiled and said, "For you. I wanted to be with you, do things you like to do. To support you. And if something went wrong I wanted to be right beside you, sharing the danger."

Ron shook his head and told her, "No, you shouldn't do that. You have to take care of you first. Next time we'll both sit out and make fun of Charles."

"You couldn't do that, Dad," Lauren told him. "I think you are an adrenaline junkie."

"I do like this," he admitted. "But I don't base jump or run with the bulls. This is exciting because I'm learning answers, real answers, not theory. And I believe in Steve and Ben.

"The last time, we were always faced with uncertainty. We didn't know what was waiting for us much less where it was. Right now, we could walk over to that lagoon and take any water or plant samples we wanted to. We could walk through this jungle and anything we scared up would run away from us. We don't have to climb a tree or hide in an *Ankylosaurus* body. It's safe. We can walk around like we are in our own home."

Ron paused and asked Lauren, "Knowing what we know now, doesn't some of this interest you?"

"Some."

"But you need your answers first."

Lauren nodded her head and agreed, "Yes, I am a little embarrassed that this actually seems interesting to me. And I do want to poke around and find real answers, maybe see something exciting. But I'm still afraid."

"Me too," Lisa said. Then she took Ron's hand and said, "Let's walk past the lagoon and over to the real beach. Where the ocean actually is."

"Are you sure?" Danny asked.

"Ben hasn't called us back in. Until he does I know we're safe. I'm feeling better now."

As they walked off, Lauren asked Charles, "What about your adrenaline? Did that *Rex* get you going?"

Charles shook his head and replied, "I'm not you. I'm just interested in how we got here. That's exciting to me. Danny, well maybe he's just facing a midlife crisis. Lisa is just in love with your dad. It's you and Ron who are interested in the animals."

Lauren took Charles' arm and as they started to follow Ron and Lisa she leaned in close and said, "True, but now that the walks are finished what I'm really interested in is what are Steve and Ben actually up to?"

In the Control Room Otto leaned forward but Lauren had turned away and he couldn't quite hear what she had said. What was she really interested in? He knew he should have sent up more drones and now it was too late. He glanced at the time, he'd give them all a few more minutes. Maybe he would be able to hear more of their conversation.

Ben stuck his head into the control room and asked, "How are they?"

Otto glanced down then advised, "A few *Pterodactyls* at about 200 feet...the usual small animals running around the jungle. That's about it."

"Okay, give them a few more minutes. They got interested today so let them spend some more time outside. I'll be back in a few minutes."

"Sounds good," Otto replied then he quickly checked on Danny. He had almost forgotten about him. He quickly confirmed there was nothing around Danny and went back to quietly keeping the drone out of sight above Lauren and Charles.

Danny walked until he started feeling tired then he rested against a tree. He was still feeling overwhelmed. Even now, the small animals and insects darting around the trees and ferns, the sounds and smells brought back too much, more than he thought they would. He took a breath and was glad to see he was calming down. He didn't have to go out again, he had proven to himself he could. Now he would go out only if he wanted to.

As he started to turn toward the Unit he thought he saw a shadow in the trees to his left. Panic rose in his throat until it almost choked him. He didn't have anything with him. Why hadn't he brought a rifle at least and put on a helmet so he could talk to someone? As he stared at the shadow he could see it walked on two legs. That was bad, probably a carnivore. He knelt down beside the tree, maybe it wouldn't see him. Then he realized it would probably smell his fear.

As he watched, the shadow seemed to stumble and then fall to the ground. He suddenly found himself drawn toward it and the closer he got the more he couldn't believe what he was seeing.

He ran forward and knelt down beside the young man and took in a deep breath. The wounds were extensive, bone was showing in some places and blood was running out of too many rips and tears to count. Danny touched the man's shoulder and said, "I'm going to get you some help."

The man's eyes widened, and he whispered, "You came back for me, you came back." Then as he focused on Danny he continued, "No, you're not Paycheck. Did they leave you behind too?"

"I'm with Paycheck," Danny told him. "I'm with everyone. We can help you."

As Danny started to stand up he was surprised at the strength the man seemed to still have as he grabbed his wrist, pulled him down, and said, "No, they won't help. They left me. They will leave you too. Leave you to die. Leave you to…"

"Who are you?" Danny asked.

As the man closed his eyes and his head dropped to the side Danny started to ask again, but then he realized there wouldn't be an answer. Danny stood and stared back in the direction of the Unit. He had to find Charles and Lauren.

Steve liked his office in the Unit. True, it was small, but it got him away from everyone, especially Ben. He didn't know why but Ben was really starting to bother him. Then he leaned back in his chair and smiled. Sure, they would still have some suspicions, but today had gone a long way in converting Charles, Lauren and Danny.

The satellite they had launched when they were here three days ago was still in place and had fed him some unbelievable information. He looked at the numbers, made the calculations and imagined the profit. There was a knock on his door and he quickly said, "Yes, what is it?"

Dr. Otto entered and immediately told him, "I have something you need to look at. I just recorded it and it's ready for you to watch on your screen."

Steve brought up the control room view on his computer and saw Charles and Lauren as Danny came up to them. He was out of breath as if he had been running and it took him a few seconds before he could say, "I just saw a man in the forest."

"A man?" Lauren asked. "What man? Someone from the Team?"

"No, a man I'd never seen before," Danny gasped. "No one from our group. He was from a different group brought here by Ben and Steve. He was dying from some type of animal attack, but he lived long enough to tell me that he was left behind by Paycheck. Left behind by Ben."

"Wait a minute," Lauren exclaimed. "Why didn't I think of this before?"

"What?" Charles asked.

"There were four people who went on the Walk they did right here. First, Ben told Lisa and Dad that one of them made it back but now I remember that he told all of us that four of them didn't make it back. When he was talking with Dad it was three because one did make it back, but they left him behind so now it's four. He couldn't keep his story straight."

"Not a bad assumption," Charles replied.

"Just like you thought, Charles, they aren't okay," Danny said. "They kill the people who work for them. People like us."

"And Dad and Lisa," Lauren said.

"Yes," Danny agreed. "All of us."

They both looked at Charles who nodded and told them, "Okay. So now we know what's going on. We're getting ready to go home so we don't raise any suspicion. It's been safe, and they are still talking about how they need us. When we get back home we'll let Ron and Lisa know what's going on then try and figure out what we can do. Okay?"

"I don't know if I can control myself," Lauren said. "They're no better than Taggit. I want to go in there and toss them out and leave them behind. Can we take over the Unit?"

"They have the Team," Danny said. "Even if they don't know about everything, why would they believe us instead of Ben and Steve?"

Charles added, "I can tell you how most of this works but I'm not sure about all of the controls or how to get past any security controls. I can't operate this Unit. We just have to be friendly, smile a lot, and get home."

"You make it sound easy," Lauren told him.

"Well, we can hang with the Team. We have questions, right? Ron and Lisa will still be their normal friendly selves, and no one will be the wiser. It's just a few more hours at the most."

As the video stopped, Otto told Steve, "I thought you would want to know."

Steve nodded and then called to Ben on the intercom, "Can you meet me in my office for a moment?" As Ben walked in Steve told him, "We're going to get everyone back in and be ready to go in five. Sound good?"

"Sounds good."

"Oh, wait," Steve said. "We haven't dumped our equipment yet. Everyone needs to help so we can get this done quickly." He smiled as he added, "I know the Team is anxious to get home to get their bonus and visit Stork."

"This will be quick," Ben said and headed for the locker room.

Steve looked at Otto and slowly started, "Okay, this is the day I have talked with you about a few times."

"Cleaning day," Otto replied.

"Yes, cleaning day. You have told me you understood and that you would be able to do everything I ask. Are you still sure?"

"I am, sir. You are the smartest person I've ever known. You understand there are hard decisions and you have made them every time. I'm with you."

"Okay. I'll start things, stand by to finish them."

As Otto stepped back into the control room, Steve spoke into his desk microphone, "Ron, Lisa, Charles, Lauren, Danny, the area is still clear. If you still want to see something interesting continue walking down the beach about 100 feet and then walk up to the edge of the trees."

"What is it?" Lauren asked.

"Something you won't forget," he told her. Then Steve sat back in his chair, took a deep breath and closed his eyes.

"Okay Team," Ben shouted as he entered the locker room. "Let's get the gear outside. The sooner it's done the sooner the fun."

"You know what to do," Major Donald shouted. "Let's go."

As the Team collected their gear Danny walked inside and said, "Guys, I'm going to lay down. Not feeling good at all."

"Is your stuff in the bunk room?"

"Yeah, it is. I'll get it then lay down on the way back."

"I can get it now," Lost said.

"No, that's okay. I'll have it out in a minute."

The Team and Ben quickly gathered their gear and were about to start out when Steve came over the intercom shouting frantically, "Team, Ron and everyone are trapped at the end of the beach. Can we rescue them?"

"Quick gear," Major Donald shouted, and everyone put their helmets and DOPEs back on and ran outside.

As they passed the curtain Ben pointed and said, "There they are."

Major Donald was in the middle of the group and as she glanced around she said, "Junk and Sinewave watch the ocean, Blonk and Rover you have the forest side and Cat you have rearguard. Everyone else be ready to go hot and don't hit any of the friendlies."

"What are they doing?" Lauren asked as she looked back at the Unit.

"Something's wrong," Charles replied as everyone turned and saw the Team running toward them.

"Take a knee," Lisa told everyone. "When they get here they'll get us back."

"If they're quick enough," Lauren said as she eyed the tree line nervously.

A few seconds later the Team was around them and Major Donald told them, "Move inside our circle and let's start moving back to the Unit. Take it slow everyone and keep your weapons at the ready." As they started moving she asked, "Steve, what is it and where is it?"

"I can't tell for sure what it is," he told them. "But it's big and it's moving parallel to you. It must be just out of your sight."

"You heard him, focus on the tree line. Anything that comes through it doesn't get to us," Major Donald instructed. "What did you guys see?" she asked Ron.

"Nothing, we didn't see anything. Steve must have seen it on his computer."

It took several minutes to return to the Unit and as they got closer the Team was surprised to see Chesky, Ammo, Whitey, Maybe and Ricardo were still inside of the curtain. "What happened?" Blonk asked. "How did you get locked inside?"

"I can answer that," Steve told him as he walked outside the Unit and up to the curtain just opposite of Major Donald. "I asked them to. You see this was a great day. We accomplished a lot and like always we did it safely and without any major problems. But we did run into one problem."

"Well, let us in so we can get away from it," Blonk said. "Then it won't be a problem."

Steve threw his head back and laughed. Something about his laugh caused Lauren to snap her head up and as Lisa buried her face in her hands, Steve continued, "You're thinking about the wrong problem. It's you, all of you, who are the problem."

Major Donald quickly asked, "What do you mean?"

Then the inside group began laughing and Lauren groaned, "Oh no."

Steve nodded and said, "Yes, Lauren, 'oh no'. Sorry, but you're going to be left behind again but unlike last time you won't have a rescue plan to save you." He looked at Charles and told him, "First I destroyed your main time unit, the one out back of your house. It's not coming after you. And the little one you had hidden in your elevator shaft isn't working either. Sorry. All of you will be staying behind."

"What are you talking about?" Ben asked hotly. "Let us in, right now."

"No," Steve replied. "You have become weak, a liability. I've seen it several times recently and I can tell it's only a matter of time until you do something stupid and ruin everything. Sorry brother, it's just business."

Ben walked up to the curtain and pleaded, "Steve, let me in. There's no reason to do this. Come on, let us all in."

Steve stepped up until he was just a few inches across from his brother and slowly shook his head as he said, "Sorry, I can't do it. You've been a great asset, but now, well, not so much. And Charles and Lauren know too much now, they know about Skate. His body is just a few hundred feet south of the Unit. He actually spoke with Danny. I guess he lived for a couple of days anyway."

"Steve, let us in. We're not the same, you're not the same. We're legitimate now, remember? It's what you want to do."

"There's a lot of things I want to do, Ben, but worrying about Charles and Lauren is not one of them."

Ron stepped up beside Ben and said, "Steve, Lisa and I don't have any idea what is going on here. Let us all back in and we'll discuss this, reasonably, calmly. Charles and Lauren will never say anything about whatever is going on."

Steve sneered and replied, "You don't really know your own daughter, do you? She's already writing her speech. No, Ron. Can't do it."

"Please, Steve. Let us in. None of us can talk about anything. Who would believe us?"

For a brief moment, Steve looked down but then he shook his head as he said, "Sorry, I can't do that. It would be hard enough between us but look at the Team, sides have been chosen and there is a new leader – "

"That's right," Chesky interrupted. "A new leader. We won't be doing anyone's dirty work anymore, things will be different. No one outside comes back."

"Is that what you want?" Major Donald asked Chesky. "Everything can be worked out. All of you, this can be worked out. I don't care who the leader is, you can be Team leader. Think of all we've done. Our friendship. For God's sake, let us in, don't leave us behind. You'll be killing all of us."

"Yes," Ricardo agreed. "But we'll also be getting all of your money."

As the inside group began laughing the rest of the Team started shouting at them. Blonk and Stoney picked up some weapons and fired them at Steve, but the bullets were simply absorbed by the barrier then dropped harmlessly to the ground.

Major Donald shouted, "Stop. Everyone stop. Now." Both groups got quiet as she looked at Steve and asked, "Is this really the way it has to be? When we get back we'll all go our own ways, no one has to know. No one has to die in this place."

Steve stepped up even closer to the curtain as he replied, "I'm afraid it is, Major. If you're not part of the Team, you get left behind." Then there was a low swishing noise in his ears and it took Steve a second to realize he was now outside the curtain too. He turned quickly and shouted, "Otto, move the –"

But he was cut off by a loud laugh as Otto followed with, "No, Steve. You're not part of the Team anymore either."

CHAPTER ELEVEN
DAY ONE

"So that means you get left behind too," Otto said.

Now Steve got mad as he shouted, "What do you mean? Let me in right now, Otto. Right now. You can't –"

"Oh, but I can. I can do anything you could and more." There was another laugh and Otto continued, "I know to you I was just the fawning Otto. Following directions with a nod of the head and a smile on my face. Always willing to please the great Steve Weston. The genius. Our leader. The fool.

"And I mean really, a fool. Did you think all the time I was with you I couldn't figure out how to run the Unit? You just didn't realize that I'm actually smarter than you are. I invented almost everything in the Unit and Charles invented the rest. I had to recheck every change you made to be sure your calculations were right. I never told you that some of them were wrong and that I corrected them. After that, all I had to do was act the part you needed from me and let you keep doing all of the work."

"You did not -" Steve started.

"Yes, I did," Otto said. "Look at the Team that is still inside the curtain. Do you think you chose them? I did. I made the Team I wanted, to replace the one you had already started."

"Why?" Major Donald asked. "We are…were, a great Team."

"Because you wouldn't have done what my Team has done."

"And what is that?"

"Leave the weak behind."

"So, you can do what?" Ben asked.

"The same thing your loving brother was going to do, get rich."

"We were all going to get rich," Ben said.

Otto sighed and said, "Well, Steve was, I'm afraid you weren't. Ben, do you know why a satellite was sent up before almost every Walk, and why it was made to last longer than your other equipment?"

"Well, it was made of stronger material because of the effects of a higher altitude and we needed a big picture to protect the Team."

"That's what I mean. You really didn't know anything about what was actually going on. Why don't you tell him now, Steve?" When Steve didn't answer Otto continued, "Oil, Steve, oil. He was charting likely oil deposit areas by creating a gravitational map which would take a lot of guesswork out of where to start looking. In our time he's already purchased land in several states and other countries so that work crews would be able to go back in time in those areas and tap into these oil deposits. Think of it, creating fake drill sites in our time but actually getting the oil from hundreds of millions of years ago. I have to admit that was smart.

"So, you see Ben, all of the equipment you have been testing has really been to see if it will hold up against dinosaur attacks on workers. The curtain you are now on the wrong side of will stop any dinosaur. Any of them. The DOPES will stop claws and teeth from multiple attackers. There were never any military contracts. Who in the military would have been able to keep this a secret? Time travel? Come on.

"No, Ben. It was simply Steve wanting to provide oil and take away the Middle East control. He could sell it cheaper and then where would everyone want to buy? EXENCO.

"Oh, maybe he was still going to help out the military and law enforcement later, but I would bet he wasn't. After all, Steve had already decided you were going to be left behind at some point. Just like the two of you had left all those others behind. More money for Steve then."

"Money," Lauren hissed.

"Yes, money. Just like with Taggit. You know, I was surprised at how easily Steve conned all of you. But, I guess since Ben didn't actually know everything that was going on he always sounded truthful to you. Charles, I do have to say I am very disappointed in you."

"I have to admit I am too," Charles replied. "I knew he was up to something, but I thought he was a better person than Taggit."

Otto asked sarcastically, "A better person?" He paused and asked, "Ben, do you know what happened to Stork?"

"Sure, he broke his ankle yesterday. He was taken to the hospital and then – "

"No, he wasn't. Ask Steve what happened."

Ben turned toward his brother and Steve backed away saying, "I don't know what he's talking about I – " A holograph image of Stork being chased and killed by Tiny suddenly appeared on the curtain. Everyone gasped and then as the image panned up they could see Steve looking down at the scene. He was smiling.

As the video disappeared Otto said, "Ben, your brother is not a nice man, as you already know since you are not a nice man either. I assure you, to Steve you had been useful before, but now that he was close to his real purpose he didn't think he needed you anymore. And he was right."

Ben turned away from Steve as he asked, "And his real purpose was oil? Not to help anyone else?"

"No, that is thinking small. You know, I can see why Steve was going to part ways with you. Like I said, Steve has been mapping out prehistoric oil fields where the oil is only protected by time and animals and conditions that, thanks to me, are now controllable. We can keep workers and equipment safe behind our field proven technology. One site will – "

"But won't that use up the oil that would have been discovered in the future?" Lauren interrupted. "Or, are *you* going to discover oil and – "

"Right on time," Otto said. "That is exactly what I thought you would ask. Always the time line worrier. No, there are millions of gallons of oil here that will not be available in the future. We'll start a company through EXENCO and start providing oil in such a way that – "

There was a loud noise and Otto asked, "What are you doing in here? Leave me alone." Then he shouted, "Chesky in here, quick."

Chesky, followed by the others, ran into the Unit and loud shouting was heard over Otto's microphone. They could hear movement all over the Unit and then suddenly Danny was being carried outside and thrown onto the ground. As he rolled then tried to stand up the curtain dropped back past him, and Lauren ran to Danny and helped him up. "I'm okay," Danny said.

"Of course, he's okay," Otto said. "Steve taught me to let the animals do it. But, I'm not without compassion. I'm leaving food, water and some equipment for all of you. Who knows, maybe you'll start your own city right here and live happily ever after. However long that might be. So now - "

"Can you wait a moment?" Danny asked.

"No."

"Please. I need my medicine. It's on a table next to the cot I was napping on. It won't take you a minute. You've got the time."

There was silence for about thirty seconds then Ammo stepped out of the door and as a small opening appeared in the curtain he threw Danny's medicine to him. Danny couldn't get his hands up quick enough and the container hit the ground. "That's for you, Sarge. I'm sorry it had to end this way." Then before Danny could say anything, Ammo stepped back inside the Unit and the door closed.

"They're leaving," Lauren said out loud and as everyone watched, the Unit began shimmering and an instant later it was gone. Everyone stood completely still for about 10 seconds as they hoped by some miracle it would return for them.

When it didn't, Steve said, "Ben, I need to – " He didn't finish though as Ben hit him in the side of the head with a right hook. Steve dropped straight down, and Cat walked over to him, pulled out his pistol and pointed it at his head. Charles quickly said, "Wait, don't shoot him. We may need him. We need to know what he knows and if he has any ideas."

"What do you mean?" Major Donald asked.

"Maybe he worried about something this like happening. Our last jump with Taggit went wrong so maybe he has a plan."

Cat poured some water on Steve's head instead of shooting him and Steve spluttered back to consciousness. He glared at Ben but didn't say anything. "Do you have a backup plan for this?" Charles asked.

"How was I supposed to know something like this would happen?" Steve whined as he rubbed his head.

"You read Danny's book. You had to know something like this might happen. You had to have planned for something. Are you saying you just trusted everyone?"

Steve sighed and said, "I guess I did."

"No, you didn't," Ben said sharply. "You just thought you were smarter than everyone else. How could anyone do to the great Steve Weston what Taggit did to Charles and his group? Why have people around you that you can trust and share your thoughts with? Just keep everyone at arm's length and not believe for an instant you could be fooled. Why not just get rid of everyone not as smart as you? That would be everyone, even your brother. Right?"

"No, Ben, I was going to come back - "

"No, you weren't," Ben replied. "Whatever lie you were going to say, you weren't going to come back."

Major Donald shouted at them, "Quit arguing and let's see what was left behind."

As everyone started toward the cases, Charles looked at Danny who was checking his watch. "You can look at the time all you want, Danny. They're not coming back."

"I already know that," Danny replied.

There was an edge to his voice that caused Lauren to ask, "Why are you so sure?"

"Because it has been way over a minute since they left. That's all I was checking."

"Why is that important?" Charles asked.

Danny didn't answer. Instead he turned to Ben and asked, "I wasn't sure, could you activate a killdeer through the closed curtain?"

"No, there had to be an opening..." Ben started to answer and then he paused and continued slowly, "...say an opening just big enough to throw a medicine bottle through. How did you know they would do it?"

"I didn't," Danny replied. "But I had to take the chance. I mean, I was pressing the button either way, but I was afraid the signal wasn't getting through."

"I'm not following," Blonk said. "What did you do?"

"I heard what Otto was saying so I knew he wasn't aware I was still inside. I grabbed him but, sorry, I'm just too weak right now. I just couldn't get past him to the controls, so I turned and ran from one end of the Unit to the other. I set two grenades for two minutes and threw them into the room where I had been sleeping. I threw the killdeers in the break room and hoped I would either have a chance to deactivate them or activate the killdeers, so no one would accidentally find the grenades and shut them down. Then they grabbed me -"

"And threw you out the door and you tricked them into letting you activate the killdeers."

Danny nodded and looked at Charles and asked, "What would be the effect on space, time, whatever, if a grenade was to go off while the Unit was time traveling?"

"As soon as the explosion started, within the first few milliseconds, the Unit and everything in it would have been reduced to small particles no longer capable of traveling through time. So, there would have been a sudden micro-dust storm that lasted a day or so as they entered real time and then everything would have gone back to normal. All of it would have probably still been during the Cretaceous Period so who would know?"

Otto laughed out loud and asked, "Chesky, did you see the look on their faces?" He paused then added, "I mean Major Chesky."

"I did," Chesky replied. "Too bad."

"Yes, too bad," Otto agreed. "But necessary. I never could understand why Steve had such weak people on his Team. And then to add even more with Lauren and all of them. I wonder how long they argued about eating or not eating something because it might change the time line."

"You almost brought a tear to my eye when you threw Danny his medicine," Maybe told Chesky. Then she asked, "Do you think his prescription has run out yet?"

"About a million years ago," Whitey said.

"More like - " Otto started when he stopped and asked, "What's that noise?"

"A killdeer," Ammo told him. "One is accidentally going off."

"They can't accidentally go off," Otto told him. "Where is it? Someone could still be on the Unit."

"This way," Ammo said and led them into the locker room. The killdeer was laying on the floor and when Ammo turned it off they could hear another one. "That one is over there in the corner."

"Who did this?" Ricardo asked as he turned it off.

"Danny," Chesky said quietly.

"Why? What good did it do?" Otto asked.

Chesky sat down and smiled as he said, "Actually, it did a lot of good."

"What do you mean?" Otto asked.

"I mean you're not that smart either. Danny won."

"How did he win?" Otto asked.

Chesky looked up at everyone and simply said, "Boom."

"Then no one can come back for us now," Steve shouted. "Why did you do that?"

As Ben spun toward Steve he stepped back but it wasn't Ben that got to him first. Lauren swept his left leg and as he fell backwards she slapped him as hard as she could on the bridge of the nose. Steve landed flat on his back and didn't move.

Ron looked down at Steve then up at Lauren and asked, "You, you didn't kill him with your Small Circle Jujitsu, did you?"

"No. Well, probably no. Just didn't want him making a lot of noise."

As Major Donald walked past Lauren, she said, "You heard her. Keep the noise to a minimum. We don't need any unwanted guests. Right now, I suggest we take stock of what was left behind and start thinking about tonight." She turned to Lauren and asked, "Because they hunt at night, right? We're going to need some kind of shelter?"

"Yes," Lauren agreed. "Some of them are nocturnal." She looked around briefly and continued, "We can't build anything, and it would take a while to find a cave."

"We don't need to," Sinewave called out. "I found a camp DOPE, actually two of them."

"Well, that's something," Major Donald told him. "Keep looking and let's divide what we have into areas of shelter, food, water, weapons and miscellaneous. After that we'll have a better idea of what we need to start looking for to - " She stopped and took a deep breath and continued, "To survive as long as we can."

"Major, I have a suggestion," Junk said. "The bots and drones we just used are here along with some handheld controls. Let's set up a perimeter with them and let Sinewave monitor them with his helmet."

Major Donald nodded and replied, "That sounds good, but I don't want one person looking at eight screens. Or even three. Sinewave get two of the drones up and keep them moving. Junk send out two bots. One south and one along the same trail we followed earlier. Blonk, you watch this beach and let us know if something walks out of the jungle north of us. The rest of us, let's get busy with our sorting."

The rest of the Team along with Ron, Lisa, Lauren, Charles and Danny started quickly moving items into different piles when suddenly Lisa moved a box then stepped back and started to scream. Instead, she put her hands to her mouth and looked at Ron. "What is it?" he asked.

"People," she whispered. "People."

Everyone ran over to where she was, and Lauren said, "Oh, my God. It's Aria and Tony. What are they doing here?"

"Well, I believe Tony was working for Steve and Ben," Charles said. "I'd ask Steve but he's still out. What about it, Ben?"

"I've never seen the woman before. Tony worked for Steve, not me. I told Steve I didn't trust him."

"But you didn't try and stop him, did you?"

Ben lowered his head and said, "No, I didn't. I knew what was going on, but I never thought it would lead to this. Never."

"But it always does," Lauren said. "Are they still alive?"

"Yes," Ron told her. Then he looked at Steve and said, "Just two more people you were leaving behind." Then he looked at Ben.

Ben shook his head and replied, "No, I swear, no. I have no idea how they even got in the Unit. He must have been working with Otto on all of this."

At that moment Aria sat up and slowly shook her head. She looked around and as a look of panic crossed her face she asked Lauren, "What is all of this?"

"Okay, everyone," Major Donald cut in. "Get things sorted while Lauren answers the question. Someone might want to wake the Tony guy. That way you don't have to explain things twice."

As Ron found some water to pour on Tony and Lauren comforted Aria, everyone else continued dividing everything into small piles. After a few minutes Sinewave said, "This is it. All of it."

"Tell me the good news," Major Donald said.

"Well, some of it is good news," Sinewave replied. "First, we all just ate so we're good for a while. We have enough bars to last everyone a good two weeks. If we ration them or supplement them with hunting, then more. The water we have is just going to last a few days but there are several water purification kits and straws and a couple of water storage containers. So as long as there are rivers or ponds and even rain, we're okay there. Well, for a while. Also, I was surprised that there are also some real plastic bottles of water. A whole case."

"Why were you surprised?" Lauren asked.

"You know, the whole 'a water bottle takes a million years to decompose' thing."

"Well, what's a million years when we're stuck 70 million years in the past?" Junk asked.

Sinewave nodded and said, "Yeah, I guess you're right."

"Let's get back to the inventory," Major Donald commended.

"Yeah, okay, the drones and bots we were using are about eight hours into their countdown. So, we have another forty or so before they start breaking down. There are one more of each so that gives us another couple of days of knowing what is going on around us. The drone is light, but the bot weighs at least fifty pounds. That will be a lot to carry in this heat.

"There is some good news about the satellite. Its view popped up on my portable screen too. I thought you could only see the satellite view from inside the Unit. So, we got an extra perimeter of viewing. The bad news is I can't lower it any so, even though it can show infrared images at its altitude, I won't be able to identify any animals. They will just be red blobs. And it could fail at any time. I don't know what its life is. Paycheck?"

"Six, sometimes seven days. We sent it up three days ago, so it may help for a while."

Major Donald nodded and said, "Okay Sinewave, keep going."

"For weapons, we have the guns we have right now, and I'm including the ones Ron, Lisa, Charles and Sarge had. They were part of the pile of stuff we had already brought outside. That's a dozen rifles and handguns but they are in the same time countdown as the drones and bots. There are another fifteen rifles and handguns which will give us an extra forty-eight hours of protection when we open them up. Obviously we won't do that until we need to."

"Why so many?" Major Donald asked Ben.

"In case the Team had to stay longer than expected and maybe one for me and Steve if we had to have one," Ben answered. "I tried to plan for a few contingencies, but I was always told we didn't need to plan for anything happening. Steve thought we would never need them."

"Well I'm glad you did," Sinewave said. "If we give Lauren, Ben and Steve guns right now that takes us down to twelve extra. If you include the mom and son we'll have ten left. Depending on where we are, in a cave or something, we may not have to get them all out at the same time. Maybe a couple of guns that will be used for hunting and then guarding. I don't know, just thinking out loud.

"Moving on," Sinewave continued, "there are the helmets and equipment belts that includes grenades and knives, that we are wearing now and the same number of replacements. Of course, they're in the same count down as the rifles. Oh, and ammunition, there is a lot of ammunition that should last as long as the guns."

"Unless we run into something," Lost pointed out.

"True," Sinewave agreed. "For shelter we have our current DOPEs, fifteen replacements but we should definitely give one to Ben, Lauren, mom and son and Steve too. Again, that takes us down to ten DOPEs. But, we have the two Camp DOPEs. And under miscellaneous I have rope, webbing, netting, lights, some tools like saws and pry bars, some handheld radios, night vision goggles and some raingear, though not enough for everyone. I'd like to say there is more, like the pieces to put together another Unit, but there isn't."

"Anything else?" Major Donald asked.

Sinewave was silent for a moment then replied, "In a few days we'll have to start living off of the land. Hunting without knowing what's hiding behind the next bush that might be hunting us. In time we're going to have to defend ourselves with spears or maybe bows and arrows that will probably bounce off these animals. We'll have to make sure we always have a fire burning and we'll have to find a cave to live in because there is no safety on the ground. And quite frankly, even in a cave, we probably won't be able to defend ourselves against determined attackers for very long."

At that moment Aria began sobbing and saying, "I can't believe this. I just can't. This is a nightmare."

"It is a nightmare," Lauren agreed. "We're stranded seventy million years in the past and we're never going to - "

"You son of a bitch," Tony shouted and started running toward Steve who had just sat up.

He was intercepted by Stoney who grabbed him by the front of his shirt and as she curled her arm she lifted him up onto his toes. "You're not doing anything," she told him.

"Why not?"

As she threw him to the ground she said, "It's not your turn."

It was quiet for a moment then Major Donald said, "Okay, the equipment we have is better than nothing. We can -"

"Something coming from the south," Sinewave said.

Danny looked up and wondered for a moment if it would be the young man he saw. But he knew it couldn't be and as the Team got their rifles ready something could be heard walking loudly through the trees toward them. Suddenly a pair of duckbills emerged, possibly the ones they saw earlier on the beach, and Ron said in a low voice, "Remember, if we don't scare them we should be okay."

Aria stopped crying and no one moved. The animals paused and dropped down to all fours as they eyed the group of people for a few seconds. Then they continued walking slowly past them and turned onto the trail that went past the dead *T-rex*. As they moved, their green and yellow mottled skin began blending into the jungle and they seemed to just disappear. As they moved out of sight, Blonk asked, "Ron, what if they scare us?"

Aria started crying again as she said, "This is terrible. We are going to die here."

"Not without a lot of kicking and screaming," Major Donald said. Then she continued, "Like Sinewave said, most of us already have weapons. Now we need to get Lauren, Ben, these two and Steve geared up."

"You have got to be kidding," Cat said. "Gear up Steve? And what about Paycheck and this kid? They weren't exactly saints during all of this."

"I understand," Major Donald replied. "But everyone should be able to defend themselves and each other. The more firepower we have the better. We aren't going anywhere. We are stuck here for the rest of our short lives." Then she looked at Ron and said, "You are the expert. What do you think? What are our chances?"

Ron started slowly, "For a few days we can defend ourselves to some degree. I hate to hand out so many weapons at the same time, but we do have to watch out for each other. We have to have weapons as long as we can. I've heard that rifles offer better accuracy so give those to the ones who really know how to use them. We have to depend on those who can shoot the best to protect us. Work in groups."

"That's going to be hard to do," Steve pointed out. "Why would I trust one of you to shoot something trying to get me when you might be busy protecting yourself? We'll all want guns all of the time."

"Well, you won't get them," Major Donald told him.

Ron went on, "If we can find a cave we might be able to survive for a while without too many problems. But like Sinewave said, at some point, no matter how we try to keep from using the weapons, they will be gone. The food and water we carry will be gone. Then we'll have to leave safety behind and walk into the forest with only wooden spears or big rocks.

"But we don't belong here. Even though there isn't something waiting to eat us every ten feet, we can't compete safely for food supplies. Even the herbivores in this time are huge and will be tough to kill. We can't fight them, they have evolved to survive in this time against all the predators that we already know we can't defeat."

"So, there's no hope?" Junk asked.

Ron smiled and said, "If we can get some place safe, that we can defend then maybe weeks, months, who knows? Maybe something will happen."

"What will happen?" Steve asked. "Nothing. Our only chance was Otto deciding to continue what I started. Sending back workers to start drilling for oil. Maybe someone would talk and then suddenly there would be more time travelers and even now there would be a chance someone would be coming to rescue us." He turned to Danny and said, "But you ruined all that with your shoot first and ask questions later mentality. You've doomed us."

Danny looked at Blonk and said, "Go ahead. I'm too tired."

Blonk knocked Steve down again and Steve shouted, "Will you people stop hitting me? I can't help it if we are going to die."

"But you could have. You didn't have to do all of this," Charles told him. "We didn't have to be stranded here, living a death sentence. You did this." He paused then continued, "But there might be a way out."

Lauren turned her head quickly toward him and asked, "Just like last time?"

"Yes, and no," he replied.

Ron moved in beside him and took his arm, "But Steve said all of your other time machines were destroyed."

"I'm sure they were," Steve said.

Charles stepped toward Steve who backed away and put his hands up. "I'm not going to hit you," Charles told him. "But you aren't quite as smart as you like to think." He paused and asked, "You only destroyed the time machines in the shed and the house, right?"

"Yes, all of your time machines."

Charles smiled and turned to everyone else and said, "Look, I made a mistake and the fact that Lauren, Ron, Lisa, Danny and myself are here is my fault. I thought we had a handle on things. But I always expect the worst. I always have to have a backup plan or two."

"There is another time machine?" Major Donald asked.

"There is," Lauren answered. "But it's not at the house, is it?"

"No, it's about five miles northeast of here in a group of condos I bought." He turned to Steve and continued, "You see, I realized there were limitations to both of my older machines. Too stationary. I gutted the condos and put another time machine in a much wider and taller area to maneuver in. Not as large as your warehouse, but big enough."

"Just five miles?" Cat said. "We can be there in two or three hours."

"No, we can't," Ben said.

"I agree," Lauren added. "This jungle is too dense."

"We have the trail," Rover told her.

"We do," Lauren agreed. "And we can use it to start east for as long as we can. But walking on a trail would be inviting trouble."

"Lauren is right," Ron told everyone. "We ran into a lot of carnivores on our jumps. I couldn't figure out why until I realized later we were always near water or a trail that was being watched by predators. We don't want to fight our way to the time machine. Some of us would not make it. Probably none of us. We all need to make it back."

"All of us?" Steve asked.

"All of us," Ron said turning toward him. "Though I don't know what will happen when we return." Steve started to say something then he just folded his arms across his chest. Ron turned away from Steve and continued, "But if I understand right, we have at least three more days of protection total with our guns and the bots and drones. That should be enough time to make it."

"Should be," Lauren agreed. "But there is a lot of unknown in the way."

"So, what direction do we go?" Major Donald asked Charles.

"Northeast."

"How do you know?"

Charles held up his watch and said, "This computer has the coordinates of the time machine embedded in it down to a yard. When I activate a special program the time machine will travel back to where I'm at. The easiest way to start would be the way the duckbills went but I guess it isn't the safest."

"It might be right now," Ron said. "I think if there are any predators watching the trail they are following the *Kritosaurus*, those duckbills to gage their weaknesses. At least until they decide either to attack or not. We probably have some time to move along the trail. We should get started and try to move as fast as we can for as long as we can. We need to cut into the five miles today."

"Dad's right," Lauren agreed.

"Okay," Major Donald said, "Let's grab the gear and let's go. All of us. There's seventeen of us and I want all of us to make it back. So, don't leave anything behind because we might need it. Sinewave and Junk keep the drones and bots moving, especially the drones. If the bots fall behind they'll have to catch up. Let's go."

Blonk bent down and picked up the extra bot as everyone started picking up items and slinging them over their backs. Even Aria, who seemed completely lost but understood she had to help, picked up some line and netting and tried to fit it around the DOPE she was now wearing. Lauren tried to explain the guns and the DOPE to her, but it was a hurried explanation.

Steve had quickly grabbed the DOPE he was going to wear and had three more when Stoney tore two of them out of his hands. "You get one extra," she told him. He glared at her but didn't say anything.

Major Donald put Cat and Blonk on point and the rest of the Team fanned out and covered their areas on the flanks and rear. Then they moved out.

As they drew near the dead *T-rex* site, Major Donald asked, "Do we stay on the trail?"

"Anything?" Ron asked Sinewave and Junk.

"Nothing," they both told him.

"Then yes, let's keep pushing it. We can rest later. But Sinewave - "

"Believe me, you'll know if something starts our way," Sinewave cut in.

No one talked as they continued rapidly along the trail for another fifteen minutes when Sinewave said, "Nothing's coming toward us but we're catching up to a group of animals. Small ones, but definitely staying together."

"Let me look," Lauren said. After a few seconds she said, "Okay, they look like scavengers or possible predators. They are all gathered around something and I don't want to find out what. I think we should start northeast now."

Major Donald didn't say a word, she just turned and guided the group into the jungle. It wasn't too dense to begin with, but they could see dark thickets of vegetation ahead of them. Blonk suddenly paused and held up his fist and everyone stopped. Sinewave stared at his screen then shrugged his shoulders and looked confused, but no one moved. After a minute, Blonk waved his hand and they started forward again.

Twenty minutes later they stopped in front of a wall of interwoven plants and Major Donald said, "Sinewave, take one of the drones up and see if there is a place where it is thinner."

"We have the machetes," Steve said.

"I know, but swinging machetes make more noise than all of these insects around us and even trying to be as quiet as we can the seventeen of us are going to make a lot of noise." Major Donald turned to Blonk and asked, "Why did you stop us?"

"I thought I'd let the biggest snake I've ever seen get out of our way first."

"It didn't have a red head, did it?" Ron asked anxiously.

"No, it was brown like the rest of it, but the head was bigger than a football."

"Major," Sinewave said, "if we cut to the right it looks like this thins out."

"Junk, take the bots that way and we'll follow. Sinewave, take the bot up in front of us and see if you can guide us through."

"Will do, wait…no I won't."

"What? Why not."

Sinewave didn't have to answer as suddenly a shadow passed over them and a large winged creature came into view. Its body was light gray on the bottom and they could see it was greenish-brown on the top of its wings as they flapped. They could also see it had the drone in its beak until it snapped in half and the animal let it drop to the ground.

Major Donald looked at Ron who said, "It was a *Pterosaur*, probably *Navajodactylus*. They are going to be territorial, so you'll have to keep the drones low, but that might not be enough to keep them from being attacked."

"Understood," Major Donald replied. "Okay, let's see if we can find a less dense area and keep moving. Remember, be as quiet as you can."

They kept moving with only short breaks for another two hours, but they still had a hard time getting through the thick jungle. Finally, Lauren said, "This is actually a good place to stop for the night."

CHAPTER TWELVE
DAY TWO

"Why is that?" Ben asked.

"First, we have a small, fairly level clearing here that we can all fit into. Next, we have thick brush all around us and the tree trunks don't have a lot of space between them. This isn't a place something big would have an easy time getting into."

"Just set up a Camp DOPE," Steve commanded.

"No," Major Donald told him. Then she continued, "As a matter of fact, I might not sleep under my DOPE either. I want to save it for a true emergency. Also, Sinewave, can we set up the bots, so they maintain a perimeter for us?"

"Maybe one at a time to last the night but their batteries are getting low. We need the sun for their solar panels but in here it's too shadowy."

"Okay, that means we post a lookout in each corner of this clearing. We'll use the night vision. There are eight of the Team left so we'll do two hours on and off until daylight."

"No," Danny said. "All of us are tired. Let me get some sleep and move me into the rotation."

"Me too," Charles said, followed by Lauren, Ron and Lisa.

"But you can put me in sooner," Lauren said. Again, Charles, Ron and Lisa agreed.

Danny nodded, "Better to have everyone get at least six hours of sleep."

"Count me in too," Ben said.

"Me too," Tony said quietly.

"Okay," Major Donald said. "Cat, Blonk, Rover and I will take the first watch. Stoney, Lost Ben and Tony will take the second. Charles, Lauren, Ron and Lisa will follow them and since Sinewave and Junk have been staring at their monitors all day they can finish up with Danny and..." she paused for a moment and looked at Steve who just turned away.

"I will do it," Aria spoke up. "I don't know exactly what to do though."

"I'll watch with you," Major Donald said. Then she ordered Sinewave to shut down the bots and drone, then she paused and told everyone, "Look, we made it through the first day. We have the equipment and expertise and now because of Charles a plan that will get us out of here. We stay close, work together and watch out for each other and we'll all get through this. It won't be easy, but I think we can do it. Teamwork."

"Teamwork," everyone replied.

"Okay. So, let's eat something then decide how you are going to sleep. If you want to use your DOPE go ahead, it's okay."

"By the way," Charles said, "we covered a mile and a half today."

As everyone smiled and opened their ration packs, Lauren walked over to Danny and asked, "How are you holding up?"

"There were times I did not think I would make it," Danny admitted. "But the thought that each step was bringing us closer to getting home kept me going. Still, I'm glad we finally stopped."

"I am too," Ron said as he joined them. "I hope this food gets me going again."

Ben was sitting a few feet away and told him, "It will. There's about 2,500 calories in your meal and the water has extra vitamins, minerals, well...everything. You'll feel like a new man tomorrow. Both of you."

Danny smiled and said, "That will be different."

"Danny, why don't you take that long sleeve shirt off? It has to be cooking you," Charles said.

"Can't. The medicine I'm taking to get rid of this cold or flu or whatever makes me susceptible to sunburn. Besides, the sleeves get soaked with sweat that helps keep me cool when a breeze kicks up."

"When we get back we're taking you to a different doctor," Lauren told him.

"Let's do that," Danny agreed.

"Doing okay?" Charles asked Lauren.

"Yeah, hanging in there. Especially since you and your suspicious streak came through again."

"Amen to that," Danny said. "What will we do if your machine isn't there for us? Are we going to have to know when to show up like last time?"

"No, it will take just a few minutes to get to us," Charles said.

"Ron, I want you to take it easy tomorrow," Lisa said. "I know you're in the field a lot but still, it has to have been a while since you've walked like we did today."

"It's true," Ron told her. "But like Danny, knowing a way home waits for us is keeping me going." He hugged Lisa and said, "We'll be okay. We'll make it. Just like last time."

Tony leaned over to Aria and said, "Mom, you need to eat, or at least drink something."

"I can't," she said. "I still don't understand why we're here and I know I'm going to die. I can feel it."

"No, you don't," Tony insisted. "You're just scared. We all are. But remember how much you look up to Lauren? She's here and she's helping to lead us. All of them are smart and know what they're doing. Even the soldiers. They've done this before. It's going to be okay. You should sleep in a DOPE and you're not going to die, Mom. I won't let you. I can't. I'm the reason you're here so I can't let anything happen to you."

Aria looked at him as she started picking at her food and said, "Tony, you are not the reason I'm here." She nodded her head toward Steve and continued, "He is. And Tony, when death comes, you won't be able to stop it."

The Team ate without speaking until Stoney said, "Major, you're doing great. I know you're going to get us through this."

"We believe in you," Rover added as everyone else agreed.

"I...thanks, everyone," Major Donald replied. "I'll keep doing the best I can, but I meant what I said earlier. It's going to take all of us. We all have a part, especially Ron and his group."

Stoney looked at Steve and said, "Not everyone."

Steve ate quickly as he tried to think of how he was going to straighten things out. He had decided it was actually a good thing that Otto wasn't going to be coming back. One less obstacle. First, he would have to lure Ben back. It would be hard but not impossible. It would probably just take a lot of money. The same with the Team. That's all they were interested in anyway. Now Ron and everyone of that group was a different story. They could only be quieted by action. And lies. He would do everything he had said he was going to do. Let them see it and let them think he was beaten.

What could they do then? Tell the authorities he had let one of his workers be eaten by a dinosaur? That they had traveled in time? The very things they did not want to do. No. They could hate him all they wanted to as long as they left him alone, so he could finish what he had started. Now it might be a few years down the road, but that didn't matter. Time was on his side.

Ben watched his brother from across the clearing and thought, "You're not going to get away with anything when we get back."

The group quieted down as everyone started eating and as they finished, Lauren told everyone, "Let's keep the talk to a minimum now and if you have to talk, only whisper. Try not to move around too much.

I can guarantee that something is looking at us right now. It's probably small though and even if it is a carnivore there are too many of us for it to be interested in. But, we don't want to attract a pack of animals or anything large."

"Thanks for the bedtime story," Blonk said and then it got quiet except for the sounds of everyone trying to make a bed by spreading out their DOPE to sleep on.

"I'm just going to say this one last time," Steve said. "All of us should sleep in a DOPE." When no one responded he told them, "I have the DOPE you gave me and one of the extra ones so I'm sleeping in one." He looked about defiantly then dropped down under his DOPE.

Despite their fears, everyone was so tired that they fell asleep quickly. It was a fitful sleep though and everyone woke up at some point not knowing where they were. But in the faint moonlight that streamed down through the overhead canopy of leaves they could make out the silhouette of figures wearing night vision goggles standing still and watching. Then they would drift back to sleep until it was their turn to watch. Though the night passed slowly, it passed without incident.

As the sun began to slip through the leaves everyone began moving around. Sinewave pushed the bots to a well-lit area to charge their solar cells and everyone gathered in the center of the clearing and began eating. After a few minutes, Lost said, "Blonk is still sleeping. Should we wake him?"

"No, let him sleep for a little while longer," Major Donald said. "He must need it."

"Did anyone see anything last night?" Ben asked. "I saw several small animals, but nothing came close."

"I saw all the stars too," Lisa said. "I forgot how many there are, how we could see them the last time we were jumping. No light to mask them, billions of stars."

"You're right," Ron agreed. "They were beautiful."

Then Steve cut in with, "What's the plan for today?"

"I'm keeping Sinewave and Junk on surveillance," Major Donald replied. "The rest is just like yesterday, keep moving the way Charles points us. It will be slow going because the stuff we are in is thick. It's good and bad, keeps us from being attacked but slows us way down. I'm hoping for another mile and a half by tonight."

"You really think we'll have to spend another night in this place?" Aria asked.

"I'm afraid so," Lauren told her. "We'll move as fast as we can, but it will be slow going."

"We'll all sleep better tonight," Major Donald said. "We can deploy the Camp DOPE then no one has to stand guard. The next night too and hopefully we'll be there the day after tomorrow. Maybe sooner," she added as she saw Aria drop her head.

"Time's wasting," Lost said. "Let's get this show on the road."

"Yes, wake up Blonk and let's get going," Cat told her. "Maybe we won't have to be here another night."

Lost walked over to Blonk and started, "Okay, lazy bones, let's…" then she trailed off. Blonk's head was rolled forward and his tongue was hanging out. But his tongue was moving. "No time for games big boy –" she started again when she suddenly jumped backwards and shouted, "No, no."

Everyone rushed over, and Major Donald asked, "Lost, what's wrong?" Lost just pointed at Blonk and turned away. Everyone could see something moving in Blonk's mouth and suddenly a centipede crawled out. It had a bright red head with antennae that were four inches long. Its black and purple segmented body was at least two inches in diameter and as it slowly moved down Blonk's body it took several seconds for its almost two-foot length to drop completely onto his chest. On its last segment, there was an inch-long stinger. As it crawled off of Blonk and toward the brush, Rover drew her knife and as she stepped forward it reared up on the last third of its body and hissed at her. She cut it in half with a quick slash and then stomped on it several times until it stopped moving.

Major Donald touched Blonk's shoulder and he slid off to the side and fell face forward onto the ground. In the small of his back, just below his ballistic vest a gaping hole had been chewed through his uniform and into his body. There were several smaller insects in the wound and it appeared they were feeding. Rover quickly cut them out with her knife and killed them.

There was silence and then Major Donald asked Ron, "How did this happen?"

Ron looked pale as he answered, "Even today, some centipedes are poisonous. In South America, the Amazonian Giant Centipede has been known to kill small children. I can only guess, but Blonk was probably stung and possibly paralyzed by that larger centipede. Once they started feeding they probably severed his spinal nerves and ate their way into several major organs."

"What a terrible way to die," Lisa said.

"There's no good way to die here," Lauren replied.

Major Donald turned to Steve and asked, "How did they get through his DOPE? It's supposed to stop a dinosaur."

Steve took offense and answered, "Don't question my inventions. When the DOPE activates, sensors send a low current electrical charge through the material that changes its molecular structure, so it can't be damaged." He turned to the group and continued, "I told you everyone needed to sleep under their DOPE, but no one listened. This is not my fault."

No one felt like reminding Steve that it *was* his fault and it was quiet until Sinewave said, "We need to bury him."

Major Donald shook her head and told everyone, "No. If Blonk is going to be the only one of us that dies then we have to go now. We have to go fast and stick to the plan of making another mile and a half today."

"But - "

"What are we going to bury him with and how will we bury him deep enough that something isn't going to dig him up anyway? He'd understand," Major Donald said. "Stoney get his gear and everyone else grab yours. Take a moment to say goodbye to Blonk and then let's go."

Stoney and Cat slid a broken branch through the handles of the bot and started carrying it between them. There were some tears, and a few looks back as they moved out. Then all they could think about was getting through the thick brush. They found making any progress was extremely difficult and they had gone only about 100 yards after an hour. After a quick break they started in again and suddenly found themselves in an open area. The bots were now able to keep up with them and the drone was able to move through the trees and see what was ahead.

They stopped after about fifteen minutes when they came to a twelve-foot-wide and forty to fifty feet deep ravine that ran out of sight in both directions. "Okay, let's take a break here," Major Donald commanded. "Sinewave see if there is a way around this on one end or the other."

As the drone sped off Danny sat down, and Aria came up to him and said, "Thanks for walking with me at the back. You don't have to though."

Danny smiled and told her, "Actually, I do. I can feel myself getting slower and that's where I keep ending up. I hope you don't mind walking with me."

She shook her head and told him, "No, I don't mind. Maybe we help each other."

Danny smiled and said, "Yeah, maybe we do."

As the drone floated back down, Sinewave shook his head and said, "Sorry, Major, it goes for a long way in each direction."

As Major Donald stood up, Stoney said, "I think I can get us over it right here."

"How?" Major Donald asked.

Stoney walked along the edge of the ravine to a tree that was about twenty feet tall with a four or five-inch diameter trunk. She pushed on it in different directions for a few seconds then asked, "Can someone cover the other side for me?"

Immediately, Rover, Lost and Major Donald brought their rifles up and pointed them toward the other side of the ravine. Danny and Sinewave kept their rifles pointed in the direction they had come from.

Stoney quickly climbed as high as she could in the tree, up to where it didn't seem like the branches could hold her. Then she leaned forward, and the top of the tree carried out over the ravine. Then she leaned back and as the tree went backward as far as it could she leaned forward again. As she kept moving the tree began swaying back and forth and each time it went further out over the ravine. Just as the tree passed the center of the ravine she climbed further out toward the end of it and the tree kept moving forward. But instead of crashing down onto the farther edge it just settled down as the tree slowly pulled loose from the ground. She brought her rifle up and asked, "Sinewave?"

"Nothing," he told her. "I don't see anything but you over there."

"Okay, I'm coming back." She moved over to a similar tree that was near the far edge and in a few minutes, it dropped her down beside everyone. She stepped away from the tree and said, "Let's move this over so it's next to the first one."

No one moved for a second until Ron said, "That was the most amazing thing I have ever seen." Then everyone started talking and the two trees were quickly rolled until they were side by side. "What now?" Ron asked.

"Watch," Stoney told him as she straddled the trees and scooted forward about two feet. "Lost, toss me some line." Stoney caught the line and wrapped the two trees together. She moved halfway across the ravine and repeated the wrapping and then did it one more time near the end of the trees. As she stood up on the other side she said, "That's the best it's going to get. Lean forward as you scoot, don't lean back and lose your balance. Don't look down and it will only be a few seconds and you'll be across. Who's first?"

Major Donald stepped forward and crossed over quickly. No one hesitated as they stepped up for their turn. Danny helped talk Aria across and Steve was the last to go. He was also the heaviest and he and everyone else thought the trees would break at any moment. But they didn't and when he was across Stoney said loudly, "Cat, it looks like I owe you five dollars."

Then Cat asked, "What about the bots?"

"They can't cross on their own and they weigh too much to balance them," Major Donald said. "We'll have to make do with the drone only."

"That's not good," Steve said. "This Walk was going to be safe because we had the drones and the bots."

"Why don't you go get them then?" Major Donald asked him.

"We weren't going to have them much longer anyway," Sinewave said. "I took their batteries for the drone. We'll be able to use it longer that way."

Steve shook his head and said, "We better keep a good lookout then."

"That's right," Major Donald agreed. "Remember Team, drink as you need to and watch those flanks."

They moved forward quickly for another ten minutes and then the bush grew thicker and they slowed down. They fought their way through it for forty-five minutes then they came to a small open space and Major Donald said, "Time for another break. We've been going all morning. How are we doing, Sinewave?"

"Almost a mile," he said excitedly. "And I'm seeing another trail in front of us. I'm bringing the drone back in to change its battery, but I can scout it out and see if we might want to take another chance. What do you think, Ron?"

Ron was sitting against a tree with his eyes closed but he answered, "I still can't say for sure," Ron replied. After a pause he continued, "But staying in this thick stuff is getting to me and I'm sure a few others. Maybe all of us. It would be great if we could get some distance on the trail, but I'm still concerned about what might see us." He opened his eyes and leaned forward and continued, "But, this shouldn't be up to me only. We must take everyone's opinion into consideration."

"Can we be attacked in this dense stuff?" Major Donald asked.

"Yes," Lauren answered. "Predators in our time use the jungle or tall grass for stalking and their attacks. We could be attacked in here from close quarters with little time to react. It's just less likely. The trail will allow a lot of things to see us even from far away."

"But the drone will help us spot things," Lost said. "Give us more of a chance to defend ourselves?"

"It would help," Lauren agreed. "But if a pack comes after us, well, this isn't the same team as before, is it?"

"I know you don't really want anything from me," Steve started, "but I'm going to say something anyway. We are all tired. But, if we can get on the trail and make some distance like we did yesterday it will boost morale and help us all keep going. We can have our rifles ready and Sinewave can watch the drone screen. Tonight, if we've gone two miles or more we'll all feel better about tomorrow. I know I would."

"Major Donald, what do you think?" Danny asked.

"Show me the trail," she told Sinewave and he opened it up on her helmet screen. After a minute she said, "The trail is about a hundred yards in front of us. But it's not like a path through a field. It's at least one hundred feet wide, maybe wider in some spots. It's well used. As soon as we step onto it we'll be seen and if we cross over to the other side something could ambush us in there." She paused as she thought for a moment then said, "But I also think we should take the trail. It runs in the general direction we need to go. We should move as fast as we can as a group and everyone should be on their guard. After all, it's not if we might be seen, everything will see us. We go as long and as far as we can and then cut back into the jungle."

"Something might be waiting for us," Lisa said.

"There's always that chance," Major Donald replied. "But everything we do runs the chance of something bad happening."

"Everything," Stoney agreed as she stared at Steve.

"Then let's go," Sinewave said. "Right now, the trail is clear."

Everyone stood up, took a quick drink of water, and Major Donald stepped out in the lead as they chopped their way to the trail. It was almost an hour before the trees started thinning and she paused for a second to put away her machete and bring up her rifle. Slowly she walked out onto the dirt trail and everyone followed.

Immediately they felt like they were being watched. Major Donald said, "The trail is not flat, it's rutted up. Watch out for uneven spots and take care of each other. Let's go." Then she started off at a slow trot and the group fell in behind her.

For twenty minutes, no one said a word and most of the group stayed tightly packed together. Aria and Danny were last and then Ron and Lisa who had dropped back to stay close to Ron. Sinewave shouted, "Major," just as everyone heard the rumble and stopped on their own. They were unsure which way to run when one hundred feet in front of them a *Triceratops* burst from the jungle on the right side of the trail.

It was huge, twenty feet long and almost nine feet tall at the hips. It whirled around as two smaller *Triceratops* followed it and then four much smaller ones. As this new group passed it, the larger animal charged back toward the side of the trail using its 3-foot long horns against six animals that were chasing them.

They stood on their hind legs and as they reared up to attack, the largest predators were eight feet tall and almost twenty feet long. The smaller ones in the group were covered in short feathers but the larger ones only had feathers on their forearms. Five of them dodged out of the way of the *Triceratops* but one was gored and thrown backwards out of sight.

Suddenly from the left of the *Triceratops* five more of the feathered animals ran into the trail and stopped. This caused all of the *Triceratops* to wheel and run straight toward Major Donald. She turned to her right and shouted, "Run", and everyone did. They turned to the right, burst into the thick brush, and fought their way through it as fast as possible. As the *Triceratops* continued down the trail some of the predators turned their attention toward this new prey and ran into the jungle after them.

Sinewave shouted, "Turn and fire. Fire." The ones that heard him turned and immediately their bullets were cutting through leaves, vines, trees and animals. In just a few seconds every animal that was in front of them was dead. Those that didn't hear Sinewave; Lauren, Charles and Tony, kept fighting though the brush. Through the intertwined vines and creepers, they could see a clearing.

Danny, Aria, Ron and Lisa had been closer to the right side of the trail and were the first to go in and after just a few feet they suddenly found themselves stumbling into a dusty, fern filled, clearing. As a shadow passed Aria she saw Ron flying forward and as he landed face down on the ground his DOPE activated. At the same time, she heard Lisa shout "Ron", and Danny shout "Aria". Then a large shadow passed over her and she stopped. She couldn't remember what they had told her about the pack on her back. And she didn't think about her guns. All she could think about was Tony. Then two feathery arms grabbed tightly around her and long, curved claws dug into her stomach. She tried to scream but she was being held so tight she couldn't even breathe.

As Lauren, Charles and Tony ran into the clearing, Tony looked over just in time to see Aria pulled into the monster's feathered arms. Her feet were kicking wildly. Its head darted quickly down and as it stood back up Aria's limp body hung from its mouth. Then it turned and disappeared back into the jungle with three others chasing after it.

Tony screamed, "Mom" and started to run after her. Charles grabbed him and as he was about to break free, Ben grabbed him too. "No, no, no," was all Tony could shout over and over again until he collapsed on the ground. "She was right, she was right. I couldn't do a thing," he sobbed.

As Danny stopped and put his arm on Tony's shoulder, Lisa looked wildly around and called out, "Ron, Ron."

Lauren touched Charles on the arm and when he nodded that he was okay she shouted, "Dad."

"Over here," Ben told them. "He's in this DOPE." He quickly deflated the DOPE and said, "He's still breathing, but he is unconscious."

At that moment Ron gasped and said, "I was unconscious but now I'm not. Though now that I'm not unconscious I wish I was."

Lisa knelt down beside him and asked, "Tell us what hurts."

"Everything."

Lauren and Danny knelt down beside him and Danny reached behind him into his med pouches and said, "Ron, I'm going to do a quick assessment of you, so we can tell what kind of injuries you have. First, I don't see any blood so that's a good start. Now then, as I go through this let me know what hurts when I touch it."

As Danny finished, Ron asked, "What do you think?"

"For sure a broken left forearm, probably both ulna and radius, left side broken ribs, and your left shoulder is probably dislocated. I'm pretty sure you don't have a concussion but I'm not a doctor. I don't know if it was the helmet or your hard head that saved you. You have a few scrapes here and there all over and you are going to be sore tomorrow. Oh, and the left side of your body is not going to work right for a while."

"What about you, Lisa and Aria?" Ron asked.

"Apparently, they only wanted you and Aria," Danny told him. He paused and then said softly, "And Aria didn't make it."

"I should have been with you," Lisa said. "And why didn't we just turn around and shoot them?"

"You're not trained to turn and shoot, so you didn't even think about it," Danny told her. "And we really didn't know they were behind us until they were on us. It's just the way it happens sometimes."

"He's right," Ron told her. "Don't worry about me. The worst is done, and we're still headed for the new time machine." He looked at Lauren and said, "I'll be okay, really."

Lauren was so glad he was still alive she just stood up and took a deep breath. She could argue with him later. She glanced around and saw Steve was laying down on the ground a few feet from them catching his breath. Then she saw that Cat, Stoney, Junk, Rover, Lost and Ben had formed a ring around them and had their rifles up facing the jungle. She brought her rifle up quickly and asked, "Are they coming back?"

"No, just wanted to set up in case they did," Lost answered.

"Got it," Lauren answered. Then she asked, "Major Donald, what should we do now?"

"Major Donald is dead, Lauren," Junk said.

"What?"

"Sinewave too."

"How?" Lauren asked.

"It looks like Major Donald got caught up in the *Triceratops* stampede. There's not much left of her. Sinewave took out two or three of those…what were they?"

"*Dakotaraptors,*" Ron and Lauren said in unison.

"Yeah, he got taken out by one of those," Junk told them. "Just unzipped him right down the middle. His equipment was destroyed and so was the drone control. We're blind now."

"How's everyone else?" Ben asked.

"Bumps, bruises and a few lacerations," Junk replied. "We'll live."

He looked at Lauren who said, "Same here."

"Steve? Tony? What about you?" Ben asked.

"I'm okay," Steve said.

Tony was unable to say anything, so he just nodded then turned away from everyone.

"I'm not taking over," Ben started, "but I do want to point out a few things." As everyone looked at him he continued, "We've covered a good distance today and we could stop now. But we're close to this trail and I don't like the fact that those *Dakotaraptors* were in this area. Maybe it's their territory. Ron, I know you're hurting but I think we should keep going. Get off the trail and away from here, maybe another half mile if we can."

"Ron, what do you think?" Lost asked.

As Charles and Lauren helped him to his feet, Ron said, "I agree completely. Splint my arm and wrap my shoulder then give me some medicine for my pain and let's get going. Lauren, do you agree?"

"Yes, and keep a watch out for those *raptors*. We've been hunted before."

"Then…then Mom is just gone?" Tony asked.

As Danny worked on Ron, Lost put a hand on Tony's shoulder and said, "Yes, she's gone. And if we don't want to be left behind too we need to get moving. We can all grieve later but right now we have to go."

"Still going northeast, Charles?" Stoney asked.

"Yes."

"Make sure you're loaded," Stoney said then she turned away and cut back through the brush and out onto the trail. As everyone else followed they saw eight *Dakotaraptors* and two *Triceratops* lying dead to their left. They were already covered by a thick cloud of flying insects and one of the *Triceratops* had several small blue and yellow dinosaurs eating it.

They paused for just a moment as they thought about Sinewave and Major Donald then they quickly crossed the trail. Again, they found the brush thick and hard to get through, but it took their minds off what had just happened. They didn't slow down and after a while the going became easier as the trees and ferns were more spaced out. Lauren stayed with Ron, but he and Danny were able to keep up. Stoney paused for a second then turned to her right and led them into a small space that was surrounded by a low hedge of thicker ferns. As she dropped to a knee she told everyone, "This isn't as good a spot as last night, but it's hidden a little."

"It's great," Ron told her as he sat down on the ground. Everyone else dropped down too and told her it was a good spot.

"Time for the Camp DOPE," Steve said. When no one moved he repeated, "The Camp DOPE, let's get it set up."

"We can't," Cat told him. "Sinewave was carrying them, and they were torn up."

"That's just great," Steve said angrily. "What are we supposed to do now?"

"We have our DOPEs," Cat told him. "We'll use those tonight. Be sure to lay down your pad once you're inside, it will keep the bugs away from you."

"Let's eat and make sure you drink, a lot," Ben added. "And I think we should all check ourselves. Our adrenaline has to be going so we may not know where some of our scratches and bruises are. Let's get everyone treated before turning in."

Everyone began eating and then checking their water. They drank some but saved most of it to drink through the night and for the next day. They helped each other put medication on their injuries and Stoney found she had a two-inch thorn stuck in her arm she didn't even know about.

As Lauren checked Ron, he said, "I'm okay," and she shook her head.

"You may be now but wait until the morning. You are going to be in a lot of pain."

He nodded and told her, "I know, I know. But I've been hurt before. I'll be okay. We're closer, a lot closer to the machine. We'll be there tomorrow."

Lisa held his hand and said, "I hope so. We all need to go to the doctor now."

"Especially you," Lauren told Danny as she moved over to him. "Let's see how you're doing."

"No, I'm okay too," he said as he drew his arms in. As he did, a tear in his shirt spread open and Lauren gasped. He looked down, closed the torn cloth and said, "Now that's our secret, okay?"

"But, it looks like - "

"It looks like what Jimmy had. I know. Like I said, let's talk about this later. Okay?"

Lauren nodded and looked at Danny for a few seconds then walked over to Charles and asked, "How are you doing?"

"I'm hot, tired, hungry, thirsty and hurting in places I didn't know could hurt. But that means I'm still alive. What about you?"

"Same thing."

Ben stood up and when he saw Lauren he asked, "Do you think those *raptors* will follow us? You said it had happened before."

Lauren shook her head and told everyone, "I thought they might before I saw all the dead ones on the trail, but not anymore. You destroyed their pack. There were half a dozen dead on the trail and I wonder how many wounded ones ran off. I don't think they are a concern now."

"That's good to know," Ben said. "Now, I think I'm going to sleep. We lost four people today. I don't know about the rest of you, but I've had enough of this day."

As everyone agreed with him, Cat said, "Remember, spread out your pad to sleep on inside your DOPE."

Then Charles told them, "We covered a little over two miles today. We're just a little over a mile and a half away."

As everyone activated their DOPE they all went to sleep telling themselves, "We're almost there."

CHAPTER THIRTEEN
DAY THREE

When day broke they couldn't really tell except the jungle got noisier. The sky was dark, and it was raining heavily with a strong wind whipping it sideways at times. Rover came over the speakers with, "It's dry where I'm at right now."

"It is," Ben agreed and asked, "Does anyone want to stay indoors for a few more minutes?" Everyone agreed, and it was forty minutes before the rain let up enough that some of them came out of the DOPEs.

"We should collect some water," Ben suggested.

After filling their water bottles with rain water, Lauren and Lisa went to Ron who was sitting up and adjusting his sling. He looked up at them and admitted, "It does hurt a lot. But if we have some more of whatever it was I took yesterday, I'll make it. We can all do another mile plus."

Lost was bouncing up and down as she said, "A mile and a half. That's all. That's all." Then she jumped out of the way of a couple of small animals that ran through the camp and added, "Get me out of here."

"Just a few minutes," Ben said. "Let's take stock of what we have left. Does everyone have one more DOPE or are we short?"

"Not quite," Danny said. "I still have two, my extra one and one that I was carrying for Aria along with some of her water and bars too." Tony looked at Danny and nodded his head but didn't say anything. Danny continued, "That means Steve, you, Lauren, Charles and Ron don't have DOPEs."

"Okay, let's hope we don't need them. But I want us to be extra careful today," Ben said. "Okay, now we need to - "

"Let's go," Steve interrupted. "We're wasting time."

"We may be," Ben replied. "But there is one thing we have to do."

"What's that?"

"We need to drop our rifles, pistols and all ammo on the ground then open up new gear. We do not want to run into anything today with weapons that will not work. I know we don't have enough for everyone to get a pistol and a rifle, so make it work."

"My rifle is already turning," Cat said.

Lauren walked over to look at it and was surprised to see that it looked like sand was slowly falling away from it. "Just like I said," Ben told her. "Now, leave the old DOPEs and put on new ones. New helmets too. Help each other and make sure they are on tight. No mistakes."

When Ben noticed no one was helping Steve he went over to him and as he adjusted a strap Steve told him, "Ben, you're slowly taking charge here. You're doing great. Get them on our side again before we get back."

Ben leaned in close to Steve and said, "You really are stupid. I'm not doing this for us, I'm doing it for them. When we get back I'm making sure you can never do anything with time travel again and then I'm leaving EXENCO. Do you understand?" Then he turned and walked away. Steve stared after him until he noticed Stoney was watching him, then he started checking his helmet.

Ben didn't say anything else and the group was quiet until Stoney asked, "Charles, which way?"

He checked his watch then showed it to her and pointed with his hand as he said, "Still basically northeast, but a little more east this time."

She lined her compass up and asked, "Are we ready?" Without waiting for an answer, she led them out of the little clearing.

They had little trouble as the vegetation was not as tightly packed as before. Then after three hundred yards a wall of tight leaves and branches appeared before them running in each direction as far as they could see. Stoney didn't pause, she just started hacking her way through it. They fought their way through for two hours when Stoney stopped and turned to Ben who was right behind her and asked, "Do you hear that?"

Everyone gripped their rifles tighter until Ben said, "Yes, I do. It sounds like running water."

They pushed on until Stoney stopped again and groaned, "No,". They were standing on a high embankment and in front of them was a fast running stream about thirty feet wide.

"We can get across this," Steve said.

"I don't think so," Stoney said as she pointed to the far bank of the river. "Those aren't logs." And even as she said that, three huge crocodiles slid into the water. Lying on the bank were another dozen with their mouths open, just waiting.

As everyone moved back into the jungle Ron, Lisa and Danny caught up with them. Ron and Danny sank to the ground and Lisa said, "Thanks for stopping."

"I'm sorry," Stoney said. "I actually didn't know you were that far back. We'll rest here for a while."

As Lauren walked over to Ron, Charles said, "When we've all rested I've got something to tell everyone."

She paused and then said, "That's right. You said you always have a backup plan...*or two*. What is it?"

"Let's rest and I'll let everyone know together. I'm not done being smart yet."

"I can hardly wait."

While everyone got something to eat and drink, Cat motioned for Rover to join him and said, "Let's check upstream. Maybe the water is not as wide there."

"Do you think we should? Leave the group I mean?"

"No one is in charge now, so we need to improvise. I'm not going to waste time when we are this close. Let's think about what Ron has been saying. The *'saurs* go to the water, but they can't drink here, the bank is too high. We'll be safe as long as we're up here and the crocs are down there. We'll still watch out, but I tell you, I can't just sit here and make plans. I've got to move."

"I do too," Rover admitted.

"What's going on?" Junk asked as she walked up to them.

"Come on," Cat said. "We're taking a short walk along the bank to see what we can find."

"Hey, if this about some kinky sex thing...well, okay." Rover giggled and slapped her arm and they began walking along the rim of the bank.

Within a few minutes Cat said, "See? See? What did I tell you?"

"What?" Junk asked.

"Look at the island in the middle of the river."

"You mean the big rock?"

"Yeah, the big rock. If we can get to that it looks like a jump of maybe four feet to the other bank."

"But how do we get to that rock?" Rover asked. "It's still ten or twelve feet away and there are those crocs down below."

"Look at the tree from this bank leaning toward the tree that's growing out of the base of the rock. What if we made a bridge like Stoney did? The tree on this side doesn't look that hard to climb and I'll bet we can tip it into the branches of that leaning tree. Or, we can find some other long branches or tree trunks that will reach that other tree and we just build a bridge. Come on, let's see if we can do this."

Before Rover or Junk could say anything, Cat moved ahead and immediately said, "See? Like this one right here. Give me a hand." They helped Cat pick up a small tree that had fallen over and was about twenty feet long and still looked strong. They hacked some smaller limbs off of it then threaded it over a large branch of the tree on their side of the stream. As they kept pushing, it took all three of them to hold down the base of the tree to keep from just falling into the water, but they kept inching it forward. When they were no longer able to keep it from dropping, they let their end up as slowly as they could, and it settled onto a branch of the farthest tree.

"That's a good three feet past that other branch. It's going to be stable," Cat told them. Then he added, "We need another couple of trees, or maybe three."

"We could just barely control that one," Rover pointed out. "Let's go get the others."

"No, we can do this," Cat said. "Let's find another tree and after we get it started I'll go sit on the tree that's already in place. I can hold the tree up from out there which will make it easier for you guys to push it toward me. I'll just keep feeding it over toward the other tree. Understand?"

Junk said, "Well, that sounds like it will work. Are you sure this tree will hold you?"

"It was not rotten at all. If it was going to break it would have broken when the end of it was just floating in space out there. Let's at least give it a try."

They quickly found two more trees that would work, and they pushed one about halfway onto the first tree. Cat eased his way out over the water then used some webbing to tie himself in place. Then he lifted up the tip of the second tree and it only took about a minute to settle it in place next to the other one.

"Yes," Cat said as he dropped back down beside Rover and Junk. "This is great. We get this other tree out there and we have our bridge."

"Then we only have to worry about what's on the other side," Junk said.

"We'll worry about that when we're over there," Cat said. "But at least we'll be over there instead of still stuck over here. Junk help us get this one started then go get everyone else. They're going to be amazed."

"Okay," Junk replied enthusiastically and they all got the third tree started and Junk started back to get the others.

As the new tree became wedged between the other two, Cat shouted, "Rover, come up here and help me get the tree started again.

Then I think it will be easier if you just stay on that end of the bridge and just lift and push."

"Will do," Rover said as she climbed up and helped pull the tree away from a small branch it had gotten stuck on. She smiled and said, "Piece of cake."

After about twenty minutes, Charles stood up and said, "I have something important to tell everyone. We don't have to worry about the stream."

"Are you going to fly us all over it?" Steve asked sarcastically.

"No. I'm going to make it disappear," Charles replied.

Steve sat up and stared at Charles who said, "I'm glad I have your attention. Now the - "

"Wait," Ben said. "We're missing someone." He paused then asked, "Where's Junk, Cat and Rover?"

When no one said anything, Ben picked up his rifle and started, "Okay, we need to - "

"There's something coming at us through the trees," Stoney told them. "Maybe it's them."

As Junk stepped out of the trees she saw everyone had their rifles pointed at her. She stopped and said, "Guys, it's me, that's all."

"Where are Cat and Rover?" Stoney asked.

"That's the good news," Junk smiled. "We've built a bridge over the water. We can cross over and get to the other side and keep going."

"What?" Ben asked. "Where?"

"About 200 yards from here. It looks like the one Stoney made. We can stop sitting around and zip right over."

"Looks like you'll have to make your big announcement later," Lauren told Charles.

"That works for me," he replied. "Anything that gets us on the other side of this water."

"And the crocodiles," Junk said.

Ron was being helped up by Lisa but when he heard Junk he jumped up on his own. "Did you say crocodiles?" he asked.

"They're all along the far bank," Ben said. "Big ones, maybe thirty feet long. I wouldn't want to get in the water with any - "

Ron pushed past him and as he did he shouted, "How high is the bridge you made? How high above the water?"

"About ten or twelve feet," Junk told him.

"No, no, no," Ron shouted louder. "Show me," he told Junk, but he didn't slow down. She had to sprint to get in front of him to lead the way. Everyone ran after them as fast as they could asking "what's wrong?" but Ron kept going. As the bridge came into view they saw Cat and Rover sitting in the middle of the bridge, they were both facing toward the island rock. Ron stopped and put his hands on his knees and said, "Tell them to get off the bridge." Then he shouted again, "Tell them."

Cat and Rover turned their heads toward the group and started waving. When they heard the shouts of "Get off the bridge," they looked at each other and shouted back, "Why?"

Suddenly a crocodile launched itself out of the water like a rocket with streaming cascades of water falling from its sides. But its jump wasn't quite far enough, and it just barely nosed the bottom of the tree bridge then fell back with a large splash.

Cat reached down to untie himself but started fumbling with the webbing as the second crocodile launched itself. It crashed into the bridge and Rover, who had not thought to tie herself onto the trees was thrown into the air but caught the bridge as she fell. She dangled from the side of it kicking her feet as she tried to get back on the bridge.

Just as Cat twisted around to try and help Rover, another crocodile jumped and caught both his leg and the bridge in its powerful jaws. It hung there for a few seconds like a macabre statue. Cat screamed in pain then the bridge snapped, and the crocodile, with Cat still in its huge jaws, disappeared in a splash back into the water. At the same moment, Rover was flipped backward off of the bridge and the instant she hit the water she was dragged under by a huge crocodile that immediately started rolling in the water. Then the river grew quiet again.

Ron dropped to his hands and knees and said, "Too late. I was too late."

"What just happened?" Junk screamed. "How did that happen?"

In between gasps Ron said, "Modern day crocodiles can jump out of the water almost the length of their body. I feared these crocs could do the same thing. You didn't know, and I didn't hear anything about crocodiles. If I had only known sooner."

"We know now," Stoney said. Then she looked at Charles and asked, "What were you going to talk to us about?"

"Jumping out of here."

"Jumping?"

"Yes, jumping, time travel, walking, whatever you want to call it. I can - "

"Wait," Ben said. "We're acting like we're on a camp out. We have been since we got up this morning. Stoney, I want you to take charge. Let's get back to our gear, set up a perimeter and listen to Charles."

Stoney didn't say anything for a moment then Lost nodded at her and she started, "Okay. Like the man said, let's get back to camp. Lost, you're on point and Junk, you have rearguard. Everyone else get your rifles up and be ready. Let's go."

It only took a few minutes to get back to the camp. Lost, Stoney, Junk and Ben set up to watch the jungle but were close enough that they could hear what Charles had to say. He stood up as everyone else sat and started, "I always have a backup plan. Especially when I suspect something is going on. I had one for Taggit, and now for Steve. But I didn't think one was enough this time. I thought Steve might have known about my condos and done something to them. So, Steve, did you?"

"No. I knew about them, but I thought it was an investment property. I didn't receive any information concerning them." As he finished talking, he glanced at Tony.

"That's because I already had my suspicions about Tony and his mother."

"My mother didn't - "

"I know she didn't," Charles cut him off. "But I didn't at first. So, I just decided to be suspicious of both of you. It was easy enough to set a trap and find out that you were working for someone else. I started doing simple experiments in the house and advanced ones at the condos where I had a security system that I built myself. But still - "

"But still, you were nervous," Lauren finished for him. "Was the next person we met going to be another time traveler, like Taggit?"

"Exactly. And that person might know all my secrets, the main machine, the little one in the elevator shaft and the new condo complex." Charles pointed at his boots and said, "So I built these."

As everyone looked confused, Lauren stepped toward him with a smile on her face and asked, "What do these do?"

"They'll jump us a million years."

"That's seventy jumps," Steve said dismissively.

Charles shook his head and replied, "You're missing the point. In a million years the landscape might be so different that we can continue walking to my other time machine."

"Sure, the five of you," Steve shouted. "Are you leaving the rest of us behind or are you going to promise to come back and get us...if we're still alive?"

Lauren turned to Steve and said, "Will you shut up and let him finish or I'll make sure you do get left behind." Steve turned red, but he didn't say anything else.

"Back to the point," Charles said. "*All of us*, will make the jump. I'll explain more in a second, but I do want to stress that. We'll all go. Hopefully the landscape will have changed, and we can get to the time machine without as many problems."

"What if it hasn't?" Lisa sked.

"Then we have two more jumps left. I know it doesn't sound like much, but three million years can change the landscape dramatically. Hopefully for the better for us."

"That's right," Ron said. "The Rocky Mountains that we know in our time are still rising as part of their last phase, the Laramide orogeny. And the Western Interior Seaway is receding right now."

"That's why I'm hoping this river is gone and at least some of the thick vegetation," Charles said. "But we don't know. The river could be wider, and the jungle could be worse."

"I don't see how it could be any worse than it is right now," Danny said.

"There is one last thing," Charles said. "These boot units are charged by small solar panels that are on the inside of the boot right now in a protective pocket. After our jump, we'll need to take the panel out and expose it to the sun. I usually just clip mine on my shirt or a pants pocket."

"How long does that take?" Lauren asked.

"About twelve hours, and I'd like to have them all charged to the maximum. They have an indicator, so we'll know."

"What if they aren't?" Lauren asked.

"Then we'll still jump, but it won't be for anything close to a million years."

"What if it's cloudy or raining?" Danny asked.

"Solar panels will still work whether the light is direct or indirect. Obviously, it will be better and faster if it is direct, but cloudy or not, the sun will still get the job done."

"When can we go?" Ben asked.

"Right now," Charles said.

"Let's get our gear," Stoney said. "I don't want to spend another second more than I have to in this place."

When everyone had their equipment on them, Charles instructed Lauren, Ron, Danny and Lisa to stand with him in a circle, so they could move their arms out and touch each other's shoulders. "Lisa, you'll have to hook your arm through Ron's injured arm to complete the connection."

"Why?" Ben asked.

"Because if we all tried to jump at the exact same moment in time...well, we can't. Even a microsecond of difference would result in each of our jumps ending at a different point in time. Maybe years or hundreds of years apart. But, when we are linked all I have to do is send one signal and all of us jump and end at the same time."

"You make it sound easy," Laura said.

"It will be," he replied as he smiled at her. Then he continued, "Okay, spread your feet apart and everyone else move to the inside of the circle and step up onto our boots."

"But only five can do that," Steve pointed out. Then he sarcastically continued, "And there are *six* of us."

"We can actually carry *more* than six people," Charles told him. "If you step on the inside half of both of Danny's boots, that leaves room for another person to step on the outside half of one and then to the outside half of the person next to them and so on."

"We could have taken ten people," Lisa said.

"Exactly," Charles agreed. "Now Steve, I do suggest you step on the inside of Danny's boots since he's probably the only person here that wouldn't *accidentally* push you off." Steve muttered something under his breath, but he did stand on Danny's boots.

As Tony walked slowly toward the circle he stopped and dropped to a knee and then put out a hand to help him with his balance. "Tony, are you feeling okay?" Ben asked.

"Yeah, well, no. My legs are like jelly and this pack feels like it weighs a hundred pounds. Sorry, I'll get there."

As he stood up he stumbled, and Lauren said, "Some of us may be having bad reactions to our scrapes and scratches." She glanced at Danny then continued, "We'll take a look at you Tony when we finish the jump."

"Here, give me your gear," Ben told him, "then get on my boots."

"Thanks, Ben. And thank you too, Lauren," Tony said as he handed Ben his gear and got into place.

Charles took his hand from Lauren's shoulder and told everyone, "When I activate the start sequence with my watch we'll have ten seconds before the jump starts. That will give me time to get my hand back in place and for everyone to make sure you are feeling stable. The jump will take at least five minutes so don't tense up. The blood has to flow to your legs and then make it back up to your brain again. We don't want anyone to faint. So, everyone feeling good?" After everyone agreed he touched his watch and placed his hand on Lauren's shoulder.

And immediately Tony stepped away from Ben and into the center of the circle.

"Nobody move," Charles shouted. "Tony, quick, get back on."

"No, I can't," Tony said. "How can I go back after what I did to Mom? I can't. You can. Thank -"

And then the jump started, and he was gone.

Tony stared at where Ben had been for a few seconds, then he turned and started walking back to where his mother had died. He didn't stop to drink any water or rest. He never looked around. And as the day grew hotter he became tired and slower. So, he never noticed the shadows that walked beside him and then quietly closed in.

Around them a gray mist formed and overhead a constantly shifting yellow line appeared. No one said anything though Lauren began sobbing. The five minutes passed quickly and just as suddenly as the jump started, it ended.

Charles turned to Lauren and told her, "I'm sorry, there wasn't anything I could do," and she nodded.

Everyone else quickly looked around and Lisa pointed out, "It has changed."

They were in an open space and though there were still trees and ferns around them they were more spread out. All that was left where the river had been was a slight depression in the ground to indicate what had once been there. It was covered with trees and ferns and on the far bank there was now a forest. The trees were tightly packed together but it still looked easier to walk through than it had a million years ago.

But the sight of small dinosaurs skittering through the ferns and trees quickly reminded them of where they were and the dangers that were still present.

Their weapons came out and Stoney said, "Stay low behind these ferns."

"Also," Charles added as he ducked down, "the sun is in the west, it's late afternoon. Depending on how long the day is we may get a few more hours of daylight in but I don't know how many. We'll have to see, but we'll walk what we can." He then showed Lauren, Lisa, Danny and Ron how to remove the solar pack from their boots and had them clip it to their shirts.

Lost whispered, "In this heat we will need to fill up on water soon. We could use a little river or pond right now."

"We may not need to fill up again," Ben said. "We're close enough to that other machine that I'll keep going no matter how thirsty I am. Should we start?"

Before anyone could answer, a group of five dinosaurs appeared where the far bank had been a million years ago. They were black and gray, about six feet tall, walked on their hind legs, had various short horns on their faces and top of the skulls. Their very short light brown and dark brown feathers on their backs and upper arms allowed them to blend into the forest behind them. As they lifted up their noses and sniffed, Ben asked, "Do they smell us?"

"No, the wind is blowing toward us," Lauren whispered. "But they still might see and hear us."

"Predators?"

"I don't recognize them," Lauren replied softly. "They're theropods so I'm guessing it's a good chance though not a hundred percent.

"Dad?"

"I was hoping we were looking at *Dracorex* or *Stygimoloch* which are a type of *Pachycephalosaur* and herbivores, but I'm not sure either. On the carnivore side, *Carnotaurus* has been extinct by now for a few million years. It had skull horns, though not as many. But are these animals products of some type of evolution along that line or completely different animals? I think we need to stay right here until they move on."

"That was a lot of help," Steve said.

"Why don't you take a little run over there and see if they eat you?" Stoney suggested.

"You'd like that, wouldn't you? All of you," Steve replied.

Stoney put her face right next to his and said, "First, keep your voice down or I'll just throw you out where they can see you. Next, yes, we would. Now shut up and don't move."

For over an hour three of the animals stayed in the area chasing each other, digging at the ground and snapping at animals that were running through the tree limbs. Everyone sunk a little lower behind the ferns that were hiding them as they realized the animals were carnivores.

Suddenly there were cries from the tree tops above the animals and the carnivores quickly ran a few feet into the forest and walked along staring into the leaves above their heads. There were two smaller animals, three feet long with thin bodies, chasing another animal through the branches. It was larger than the other two, almost four feet long, and as they bit at its back legs it slipped from a branch and fell to the ground.

It was on its feet immediately and started to run back to the tree it had fallen from, but it was too late. One of the carnivores grabbed it and then another one. Its cries stopped abruptly, and all the predators snapped savagely at its body and each other. A few seconds later the three animals ran off and the two that had been chasing the larger animal dropped out of the tree and ate what was left. Then they climbed back into the trees and disappeared.

No one moved or said a word for several minutes then Ron whispered, "Those animals appeared to be working together. The ones up above knew they could make that bigger animal fall and that the three on the ground would kill it."

"Then they would get their share after the bigger ones left," Lauren added.

Ron nodded and asked, "Symbiosis, or is it mutualism? Sorry, I can't remember which. I guess it doesn't matter."

"No, it doesn't matter. It just meant that something got killed," Lauren replied.

Ben asked, "Do you think it's safe to start out?"

"Yes," Ron said. "Everything in our immediate vicinity has just eaten."

Stoney stood up and said, "Then let's get out of here." She pointed at the woods across from them and asked, "That way?"

Charles nodded and replied, "Unfortunately."

She led them across as quickly as possible and as they entered the woods they found the trees were quite different than the ones on the other side of where the river had been. They were taller and thicker and because the trees were so close together the limbs of one tree were interlaced with the limbs of the surrounding trees like bridges running from tree to tree.

It was cooler under trees with their thick canopy leaves and they continued on as fast as they could until they came to the edge of a small pond. Some small *Hadrosaurs* looked up at them for a moment then went back to drinking. Ben said slowly, "Though I'm tired I want to keep going. But...I think we should follow their lead. Let's fill everything that can hold water then strain it and purify it. We're getting low and considering the sun is setting I'm not sure we want to keep walking in the dark."

"No, we don't," Ron agreed. "But after we get our water, let's get away from the pond. There will be other things coming to drink after dark."

It only took a few minutes to fill all the water bottles and canteens and drop in the purification tablets. They didn't see any animals around the pond that concerned them, but they felt exposed. Stoney moved them back away from the pond and toward the center of the trees. She found an open space and asked, "Will this do?"

"No," Ron said. "Not without DOPEs for everyone." He looked and continued, "But we've survived in a tree before."

"There are things in *these* trees," Lisa reminded him.

"True, but we are a lot bigger than the animal they chased earlier. And, we have guns."

"Do we have to stop?" Lost asked. "I feel like we're so close."

"We are," Charles agreed. "But it's too risky. Better to spend one more night in a tree."

"I'd like to stay on the ground," Steve said. "I hate heights and I just need a DOPE. I'd rather stay down here."

"That won't bother me any...if anyone will give you one," Stoney said as she grabbed a low hanging branch and quickly climbed into a tree. Danny paused for a moment then threw Steve his extra DOPE. As everyone else started up after Stoney, Steve deployed his DOPE a few yards from the tree.

Everyone climbed as high as they could, and it didn't take long to find areas where branches intertwined that created wide enough spaces for a person to sit or even lay in. Stoney and Ben were the highest, about forty feet from the ground, then Junk and Lost were just a few feet lower. Charles and Lauren were below them and Danny, Ron and Lisa had stopped at about twenty feet and were the lowest. It took a long time for Ron to get in place because of his arm. He didn't complain about the pain though, he just kept apologizing for being so much trouble.

As they ate their food, Stoney asked Charles, "How much further?"

After a check of his watch Charles replied, "A little over half a mile. As soon as it's light we can start. Depending on how bad the terrain is we should be there in no more than an hour. Probably a lot less. That pond bothers me though, I'm afraid we will run into something we don't want to."

"I wish we still had the drones," Lost said. "Then we would know which way to go."

"I wish we still had everyone we're leaving behind on this death march," Stoney told her. "We've lost a lot of good people."

"I couldn't believe it when Tony stepped away," Lisa said.

"I did," Danny replied. "He was responsible for getting his mother killed. He got her mixed up with Steve."

"And Steve's still alive," Stoney said. "That's not fair."

"Life's not fair. Ever. And you can't change that," Lauren said.

"Have your weapons ready," Stoney said.

"Should we post a lookout?" Lost asked.

Stoney thought for a moment then answered, "Yeah, we should. I mean we can't see a thing through all the leaves but if anyone hears something use your night vision. It's not going to last much longer but it's something. Are you good to start, Lost?"

"It's why I asked. I can't sleep."

"Wake me up when you do get sleepy," Stoney told her.

"Will do," Lost replied then she slipped past everyone, so she was the lowest in the tree.

As the group grew quiet, Lauren leaned over to Charles and whispered, "You know, I owe you an apology."

"Why?"

"I knew about the condos, but you never said anything about them. I knew you were spending a lot of time there and I thought maybe you had someone else. I was afraid I was being replaced."

He put his head on hers and said, "Not in a million years or even seventy. You're still all I want."

She hugged his arm and said, "You too."

Suddenly Lisa said, "Do not leave the tree tonight. I'm not asking, I'm begging everyone, don't leave the tree. Marilyn did, and she didn't come back."

No one said anything, but Ron squeezed Lisa's hand. As everyone drifted off to sleep, Ben asked himself how much he was to blame for everything and wondered how he could make things right. There were only ten of them now.

Steve was wondering if he could steal Charles' watch.

CHAPTER FOURTEEN
DAY FOUR

Steve looked at his watch and wondered why he was awake. It was only a little after midnight and it was bad enough sleeping in the DOPE, he didn't need to keep waking up. Then he heard the noises and saw the shadows moving and he knew. One of the animals jumped on his DOPE and then two more. They tore at it for a few seconds then quickly moved on. He keyed his mike and said frantically, "Ben, Ben, they're coming after you. Ben, Ben, do you hear me?" When there was no answer he shouted, "Ron, Lisa, Charles, Lauren, can anyone hear me?" His only answer was more static.

Charles was having an odd dream. His house now had a lake in front of it, a large lake. Ron and Lisa and Danny were with him and Lauren in a small boat gently floating on the waves. But then the boat started to rock. Not bad at first, then from side to side threatening to throw everyone out of the boat. And now he could hear waves pounding. On a pond? It didn't make sense. Then he heard someone in the boat ask, "Is someone saying something?" But no one had opened their mouths. Who was talking? He slowly started to wake up.

Lost started tapping the side of her helmet. What was the static from? She tried to remember something that Major Donald had told them once during training, what was it? Then it came to her, toward the end of the life of their communication units the mike might be the first to go. Something to do with the wiring and the dissolving parts. You might just hear a lot of static. Was someone talking? She keyed her mike and asked, "Is someone saying something?"

Then she heard a noise. It wasn't very loud, and she wasn't sure what it had been. Something scraping against the tree? Hissing? No, it was breathing. She turned on her night vision and in the eerie green glare she saw it not more than a yard away. Its head was long and pointy and there were sharp teeth in its half-opened mouth. Its large, unblinking black eyes were fixed on her. She slowly started leaning back and moving her rifle in front of her. Inch by slow inch the rifle barrel came around until it was pointed straight at the pointy head. Then she pulled the trigger.

The animal made no noise, but its falling body did as it crashed through the leaves and branches and fell to the ground. And then there were two more where the first had been. She shot one of them but the other leaped forward and bit into the arm that was holding the handguard of her rifle. Lost screamed in pain and let go of the rifle as she reached for her pistol. Before she had a chance to draw it the animal wrenched its head backwards and Lost was pulled forward and out of the tree.

The scream woke everyone and as Charles opened his eyes he could see a dark shape standing by his feet. He switched on his night vision and realized the boat rocking in his dream had been caused by an animal walking toward him from another tree on the intertwined branches. He sat up and shouted, "Lauren", as he jerked his rifle up in front of him. The animal sprang forward and fortunately bit down on his rifle instead of him and began twisting its head side to side. Charles was trying to fire his rifle when Lauren shot it dead.

Then it seemed the tree was full of animals. They were about four feet long from head to tail and they were fast. Stoney and Ben were afraid to shoot down at the creatures climbing up at them for fear of hitting the others below them. They had to hit them with their rifles until they were too close and then they started knifing the animals. Each of them was bitten several times but because the limbs were smaller where they were there were fewer of the predators attacking them. Then one sprang up and onto Stoney. Ben was able to shoot it with a side shot and it dropped from the tree.

Junk sat up and her night vision showed the ghostly green images of the fast-moving animals coming toward her. But she knew Charles and Lauren were right below her, so she couldn't just start blasting away. She started to stand up, so she could move further out on a branch, but her foot slipped between the branches she was standing on and became stuck. She was able to strike at the snapping heads with her rifle butt and even shoot a few at an angle that was out and away from the tree, but her stationary foot was an easy target and the animals concentrated their attacks on it. She fought until her arms became heavy and she suddenly wondered why she was laying down. Then she went to sleep.

Charles and Lauren couldn't shoot down either, but a lot of the dinosaurs were crossing over straight at them from the surrounding trees.

They shot many of these attackers, but others kept replacing them. Some animals were leaping up and over them though to get at Ben, Stoney and Junk above them, so they weren't attacked by every animal they saw. But they were also distracted by falling bodies as predators were killed in the branches above them. Finally, they were surrounded so Charles and Lauren had to hit some with their rifles and kick others away. They had not been badly wounded yet, but they were getting clawed and bitten also. Then they heard Lisa screaming.

Danny came out of his sleep with his rifle up and night vision on. It took a second and then they were being attacked from every side. The animals seemed to concentrate on Ron and Danny realized it was because he was injured. Danny was firing as fast as he could, and he was amazed at how Lisa was protecting Ron. She was shooting them with her rifle and hitting and kicking at the same time Ron was shooting them with his pistol. But Ron couldn't swing his arm from side to side very fast and was getting bitten by a lot of the animals. Danny was slowly making his way closer to Lisa to help when a dead dinosaur dropped from above and struck him in the head and right shoulder. He stumbled forward and dropped to both knees as he almost fell from the tree. While still kneeling, he continued to fight off animals. Then he heard Lisa screaming.

Ron awoke instantly but his legs were already being bitten and they were pinned to the branches he had been lying on. He never even thought about using his pistol until Lisa shouted, "shoot them" and then he drew it out. He found he could shoot to his right without any problem, but he couldn't shift so he could aim at the animals on his left. Lisa was helping, she was shooting everything, and he saw her kick at least two of the attackers away from him. But slowly at first, then quicker, he could feel himself being dragged out of the tree. "Lisa," he cried as he twisted toward her and she suddenly realized what was happening. She dropped down beside him and wrapped her arms around his shoulders and began pulling him back.

When she heard Lost scream, Lisa had been confused for a moment. Then it all came back as dark shadows moved all around her. She fumbled with turning on her night vision then recoiled at what she saw. Then she saw Ron was being attacked and she reacted. She had no idea how many she shot but they just wouldn't go away. Ron was doing his best, but they were on top of him and also under him clawing at him from below the branches. She could see the rips in his pants and the blood on his legs. Then Ron turned, and she could see the fear in his eyes as he screamed, "Lisa." He was being dragged away. She moved next to him and held on as tightly as she could, but it wasn't going to be enough. He was slipping through her fingers. She began screaming, "Ron," as she knew she wasn't going to be able to hold him.

Then Lauren was beside her, shooting every animal she could see. But Ron was still being dragged away and had now been turned onto his left side as he tried to hold onto a branch above his head with his right arm. Lauren worked her hand under his left arm and began pulling up hard on him. Ron stopped moving away from them and Lisa thought they were actually pulling him back up when she was attacked from behind and bit on the left side of the face.

As Lisa recoiled, Ron dropped down and he slid toward the edge of the branches. His hand slipped from the branch he was holding but caught another lower one. He looked up at Lauren and shouted, "Let go. You can't hold me."

"No. I can hold you."

Charles dropped down beside Lauren and reached to wrap his arms around her. "I've got you," he shouted.

Then, in the green glow of the night vision goggles, in complete silence, in slow motion it seemed, Ron dropped out of sight and Lauren, who refused to let go, was dragged out of the tree with him. Charles looked down and watched as they hit several branches, spinning them over and over, then they disappeared below the lower leaf covering. All the animals in the trees followed them down.

Charles couldn't move for several seconds and then as he heard the fighting and feeding below, he started down the tree. He had to save them. Then he was grabbed by two powerful arms and pulled up. "Ben," he shouted, "leave me alone."

But when he turned he found it wasn't Ben, it was Lisa and she was crying as she said, "No, you can't go down there. It's too late for them."

He stared at her bloody face and tried to pull away but was surprised at her strength and wondered why she didn't want to go down the tree too. "We have to," he shouted at her. "We have to."

"No, we don't. We can't. At least you can't."

"Why not?"

"Because now you've got to rescue us."

Charles stared at her for a few seconds and then said, "We're heading for the time machine. I am going to rescue us. But Lauren and Ron, maybe I could have - "

She shook him and said, "No, you couldn't have. As soon as they both were pulled from the tree they were gone. Probably before they even hit the ground. But I'm not talking about us. Not whoever is still alive."

"Then what are you talking about?"

Before she could answer, drops of blood began falling on her and she told Charles, "Let's see who needs help and then we'll talk."

Charles called out for Lost but didn't get an answer and couldn't see her below anywhere. "She was probably the first to go," he said to Lisa.

Danny joined them and answered, "Probably."

"I'll check Danny," Charles said. "Lisa see who's hurt above us." He climbed over to Danny and asked, "How bad are you?"

"My hands, arms and legs," Danny replied. "But nothing to the body, at least nothing opened me up there. I thought my shoulder had been dislocated or broken but now I don't think so. I'm still pretty charged up on adrenaline though so can you check?"

Charles pulled up Danny's shirt and said, "You're right, nothing I can see to the body, but your arm and leg wounds are deep and still bleeding. And what are these blisters?"

"Things to talk about, "Danny said. "Well, I guess none of the arteries got hit in my arms or legs so right now I just need stitches. We'll stop the bleeding the best we can then when we get back I'll head to a hospital. I'll be hurting like Ron was, but I'll be okay. Well, for a while longer anyway. What about you?"

Charles paused and then said, "I actually don't know. I'm drawing a blank since…"

As he tailed off, Danny took his arm and said, "I understand, let me take a look." After a quick check Danny continued, "Lucky, like me. Stitches later, hospital when we get back."

Charles just nodded his head and stared down toward the ground. It had grown quiet. "Do you think they will be back?" he asked.

Danny shook his head and said, "No, I think they've left. Let's go up higher and see who else needs help." They climbed up as quickly as they could and found Lisa with Junk. "Is she dead?" Danny asked.

"No, at least not yet. She's still bleeding though."

Ben called out from above them, "Turn off your night vision, I'm going to turn on a flashlight. We need to risk it. I want to know what everyone's injuries are then we need to patch them as best we can."

His light shone on Lost and immediately Danny and Charles could see that Lost's left foot was no longer attached to her leg. It was wedged between some branches. Danny pulled a combat tourniquet out of

Charles' belt and placed it on her leg a few inches above where the top of her boot had been. "What other injuries does she have?" he asked.

"Actually, not much else," Lisa said. "A couple of bites on her arms but they are not bleeding much. They just concentrated on her foot."

"Okay, come on up here," Ben told them. There wasn't much room, so Lisa and Charles climbed up and left Danny with Lost. As they got closer they could see Stoney in the glare of the flashlight that Ben had. Both her legs had numerous lacerations and bite marks and there was one deep cut that still had blood trickling out of it into a large pad that ben had placed on it.

As they watched, Ben pulled the sponge syringe out of his med belt and shoved it deep into the leg wound. Stoney clenched her fists and then arched her back as Ben drove the tiny sponges into the wound. When he pulled the syringe out the bleeding had stopped. He quickly wrapped her lower legs with the gauze from his belt and hers. Then he looked at Charles and Lisa and asked how they were.

"I'm not too bad," Charles answered. Then he realized no one had checked Lisa and he asked her, "I can see the bite on your face and it's bleeding pretty good, but it doesn't look like it got your eye. Anything else?" She just shook her head.

"Where are Ron, Lauren and Lost?" Ben asked.

"They're gone," Charles said quietly. Ben didn't say anything, he just sat back and put his head in his hands. "What about you?" Charles asked. "Are you hurt badly?"

Ben shook his head and replied, "Just my legs. Nothing jumped on me like Stoney. She's got a bad leg wound, but I stopped the bleeding, at least for now."

"What do we do now?" Lisa asked.

"Let me do something with your face wound," Ben said. After he cleaned and wrapped it he said, "Okay, the wound is not too deep, especially below the eye." Then he asked Lisa and Charles, "You've checked everyone else, right?"

"Yes."

"Okay, we need to recheck everyone and bandage up everything that needs it. We need to stop all the bleeding and then figure out how to get everyone to your time machine. We need to go home."

"Hey, do you hear that static on your headsets too?" Danny called up to them.

Ben listened for a moment then said, "Well, it looks like Steve made it through all of this."

"Why didn't he warn us?" Stoney asked.

"He did," Charles told her. "I remember now. I was having a dream and it was Lost's voice who asked if someone was saying something? As low as this static is I guess it didn't wake any of us up, but Lost would have heard it. And her scream did wake me up."

"It woke us all up," Ben said. "And we almost didn't put a lookout down there."

"She thought of it," Danny reminded them. "She volunteered for the first watch."

Ben nodded his head then said, "Let's get moving." After everyone was rechecked and bandaged they began starting down the tree.

Steve looked up again as it started getting lighter. He could see shapes moving high in the tree, but all the blood smeared on the DOPE made it hard to tell exactly what it was that was moving. He shuddered as he recalled all the animals that gathered around him. Some were leaping into the tree while others stayed on the ground and would periodically come over and try to tear apart the DOPE. But it held together even when five of them were clawing at it while others were standing on it.

Then a human body had hit the ground right beside him. He didn't know who it had been but within a few seconds it wasn't there anymore. It was ripped to pieces and he watched in horror as body parts were fought over then carried away. Then dozens more began leaping into the tree. How could anyone survive up there? He could hear the screaming, it sounded far away coming through the DOPE, and all he could hear through his headset was static. The equipment was starting to decay.

He grew frightened that the DOPE would fail, and he would be left in the open but then dinosaur bodies began falling from the tree. Maybe Ben and everyone else were winning, they all had guns. That reminded him he could shock the animals that attacked the DOPE. He had been too afraid to even remember it.

As two more human bodies hit the ground he tried to see who they were but before he could they disappeared too. The predators began fighting and as they rolled over the DOPE they smeared it with blood. Then he shocked them, and they ran off and others began to follow. After that, anytime an animal touched the DOPE he shocked it too. Soon there were fewer of them, maybe he was scaring them away. He paused, or maybe everyone was dead. He strained to see up into the tree, but it was completely dark.

Then a flashlight came on and he knew someone was alive. He started to get out of the DOPE but then he wondered why they were shining a light? Wouldn't that attract more 'saurs? He decided to stay inside the DOPE until he knew for sure what was going on. What had happened? He had tried to warn them.

Then he saw the shadows coming down the tree. They were going slow and as the sun climbed a little higher in the sky he could see they were human. Someone had survived. He started getting out of his DOPE.

Danny climbed slowly down the tree as Ben looped a line under Junk's armpits and then wrapped it several times around a cluster of limbs. Lisa stayed just below Junk and guided her down the tree as Ben and Charles slowly let line slip over the limb and lowered her. It took almost ten minutes to get her to the ground where Danny helped lay her down.

Danny started as he heard a faint hiss behind him but when he whirled around he saw it was only Steve coming out of the DOPE. "You're hurt," Steve said, then looked at Junk lying on the ground and asked, "Is that Lauren? Is she okay?"

Danny shook his head and told him, "No, it's Junk. Lauren and Ron are dead."

Steve paused then said, "I'm sorry." He knew he couldn't say anything else. They were trapped 70 million years in the past because of him, and he had planned to leave them to die anyway. But it made him think, if they could die, so could he. "What can I do to help?" he asked. Time to be helpful he thought, watch for an opening to take advantage of later, but be helpful now. He looked up and saw it was Stoney being lowered down. She never took her eyes off of him.

As Charles slowly climbed out of the tree, he stopped and told Lisa, "I can't go down the rest of the way. I don't want to see them."

Lisa put her face close to his and said, "Charles, they be won't there. There's nothing left of them. They're gone. Just like Marilyn." Then she climbed out of the tree.

Once everyone was on the ground Ben checked them again, stopped any new bleeding then gave them all a shot using a syringe from their med packs with a red P on it. But even though the bleeding was stopped for now, Ben knew everyone would start bleeding again when they started moving toward the time machine. And that would cause a huge problem. Not of someone bleeding to death he hoped, but of animals being drawn to the scent.

Lisa was sitting down at the base of the tree with her head in her hands and Charles sat down next to her. He put his arm around her and she leaned into him. Danny sat down next to Charles and Stoney reached out from where she was lying and placed a hand on Lisa's leg. "We'll be okay," she told Lisa.

"No, we won't," Lisa said with an edge to her voice. "We won't be okay. We won't make it the rest of the way. Look at us. We're all injured, worse than what we think. We need to be in a hospital right now, not in a few hours or maybe even days. As soon as we move we're all going to start bleeding again. Junk will be dead in just a few minutes and Stoney, you'll be dead soon after. Then the rest of us will die later. Ben, what was the injection you gave everyone? What was in the syringe with the P on it?"

"Penicillin," he told her.

"Why?"

"For infection. I mean, everyone is injured."

"But why, specifically?"

"The rotting flesh from previous kills of those animals was probably still on their teeth and claws. Penicillin is a first line defense."

"Shouldn't our wounds have been cleaned thoroughly and shouldn't we be receiving a laundry list of medications to prevent further infection from these types of injuries?"

"Yes," Ben agreed.

"As soon as possible?"

"Yes."

"Even if we make it back somehow do you think Junk and Stoney will be able to fight off any life-threatening infections in their current states?"

"I really think - " Ben started but Lisa cut him off.

"You're wrong. Whatever you were going to say, you're wrong. We need to stop thinking about getting out of here and saving ourselves. We need to think differently. We have to concentrate on getting to the time machine and then get Charles back to our time. He has to get there."

"Why?" Stoney asked.

"Because he has to go back and change all of this. Only he can do it."

"Go back and change what?" Charles asked. "What am I supposed to do?"

"Go back and save everyone. Not just on this jump but earlier too. You have to save Pete, Marilyn and Mitch. Even Jimmy and Taggit. Everyone."

"That's insane," Charles argued. "How can I save all those people and why would I want to save Taggit?"

"Because then you'll save Danny too." She looked at Danny and said, "Tell them. Tell everyone. How much longer do you have to live?"

Danny dropped his head and replied, "I don't know."

"Why are you dying?" Charles asked. "Is it those blisters?" When Danny didn't answer he asked Lisa, "Why is he dying?"

"Show everyone," Lisa told him.

Danny slowly opened up the tears in his shirt. Where Ben had cleaned the wounds, everyone could see the yellow blisters. "Charles and Lauren saw them earlier. It's like Jimmy," he said.

Charles repeated, "Like Jimmy." Then he asked, "Have you been to a doctor?"

"Not at first. I kept hoping it wasn't what I knew it was. But when they started spreading and I started losing energy I knew it was bad. The doctors couldn't understand it. They kept asking where I worked, where had I been and what I had been doing. What was I supposed to say? Playing with dinosaurs?

"As soon as each one said they needed to take a biopsy I just disappeared. Who knows what they would find? Something they couldn't classify? Something so awful that if it got out of these little yellow blisters in our time might cause some type of an epidemic?"

He took a deep breath and continued, "Whatever the blisters are I also have these little dark spots all over my lungs and kidneys. Maybe a few on my brain too. They're still checking on that. But you know, I can tell. I can tell that it's taking my life away from me." He looked at Lisa and continued, "And it won't be long. And like Aria, I see it coming."

"I've got a doctor that won't ask questions," Charles said. "Remember when we got back last time?"

Danny shook his head and told Charles, "Too late. I waited too long. You can only lie to yourself for so long."

No one said anything for a few seconds then Lisa said, "Jimmy got his blisters from that thorn that was stuck in him. Remember? How many times have we been scratched this time moving through the thick jungle. What about when we ran from the *Triceratops*? I think I remember pulling thorns out of me after that, but I was so terrified I can't recall. All of us could already be dead, we just don't know it yet."

"What are you suggesting then?" Steve asked. "What is Charles supposed to do?"

She took Charles' hand and looked him in the eye and told him, "There's only six of us left. You've got to go back and talk to you. The you before you started making jumps. You've got to talk yourself out of helping Taggit, maybe even stop your work on time travel. If you do, then none of this occurs. None of the people who have died millions of years ago will have to."

"No, no, no," Steve shouted. "He can't do that. Everything has already been done. You can't change that. No one can."

"Why not?" Ben asked.

"Think of all the timelines that would be altered. All of the people who have died in this life would suddenly be changing the lives of people that they shouldn't be in contact with. I'll use Lauren's own arguments, over two dozen people would live radically different lives that would produce millions, maybe billions, of different variations. It shouldn't be done. It can't be done."

Stoney struggled to sit up and said, "Let's ask Lauren." When no one replied she continued, "Let's ask Ron or Major Donald. How about Lost or Blonk or even Otto. What do you think they would say? You caught all of us in your spider web of lies and deceit. And murder.

"Let's ask Stork. His only mistake was hurting his ankle. And you killed him for it. And what about everyone that came before us, that we were supposed to be so much better than? Or was it we were so much more stupid than they were? Let's go ask them.

"I don't think any of them would care if you never started thinking about time travel. None of us would care if we ever worked for you, or even met you for that matter." As she slowly lay back down, everyone was quiet.

Then Lisa pointed out, "We barely even talked about the others when they died. It was just accepted that it was part of their dangerous profession. They took the bite. For what? Otto and the others followed your lead Steve and they are all dead. Right now, they're still being blown apart and will be for millions of more years.

"Blonk was killed by insects. Bugs. Is that how he thought he would die? He talked about his dad, he wouldn't have wanted his son to die that way. Major Donald was killed in a stampede and we didn't even pause to at least scrape what was left of her off the trail. We had to go so we left Sinewave behind too. Cat and Rover were trying to help us. Maybe they were in love too. But that was a million years ago and even the crocodiles that ate them have turned to dust.

"Today, the last sound that Lost made, a scream of terror and pain, helped save most of us. But not all of us. My love, Ron, and my friend Lauren, fighting until the end to save her father, were butchered right where we are sitting. And the rest of us, are we already dying from some disease that we should never have been exposed to?

"I guess I'm getting cynical, or hard, or mad, but we shouldn't have been here. No one should ever be here. So, I'm not apologizing, but I am agreeing with Stoney. If we asked everyone who ever died because of Steve I'm sure they would all agree they would rather be alive. And Charles, I love you, but you should never have invented your time machine."

Charles hung his head and replied, "I now think you're right. It has caused nothing but death. Maybe I didn't think about it as much as I should have after the jumps for Taggit. After all, the good guys, us, we made it through. But over the years I've thought about Pete, Marilyn, Mitch, and Jimmy. I've thought about them a lot. Sure, they died because of Taggit, but they died because of me too. And now all of these others. It's overwhelming."

"It's overwhelming because you are over thinking this," Steve said. "People are killed and injured in car crashes every day, but unless there is some type of defect with the car it is a driver, or weather, or some unforeseen circumstance that caused the problem. I admit, whole heartedly, that all of what we are caught up in right now is my fault. All of it. And I will make it up to all of you and to the families of all those who have died. I will take care of - "

"Will you listen to yourself?" Ben stopped him. "Bags of money aren't going to ease the pain of Charles, Lisa and Danny. It's not going to stop the grieving of the parents and friends of all those that are part of the long list of unnecessary dead. I bought into what you were saying once. Who would care? Who would miss any of the Walkers? They were poor displaced people that we were actually doing a favor for. Now we know better. Right beside us are people who shouldn't die and gone are people who should still be alive. If it can be undone, then all of us should help." Steve just shook his head and didn't say anything else.

"How is this going to happen?" Stoney asked.

"We get Charles to his machine," Lisa said. "We get him there no matter what happens to any of us. If he succeeds, then none of this will ever happen." She took a deep breath and continued, "I know it means I'll never meet my Ron or any of the rest of you. I know it will alter things that have happened in the last few years and it will be forever. But I'm willing to do it, all of it, because I'm certain of one other thing."

"What's that?" Charles asked.

"That there will be another Taggit. Another Steve. And another and another if you don't stop things. There will always be someone willing to risk someone else's life by traveling in time. And that someone else will always pay with their life."

"Okay," Ben said. "But we just can't leave Junk here. I...I don't doubt she's going to die. But she's not dead yet. Let's build a sled or something to lay her on and then we'll pull her after us."

"Like a travois," Lisa said.

"There you go," Ben replied. "Exactly. We need to make it quickly."

They found some long branches and tied some shorter ones across them with webbing to create a strong frame and make a place for Junk to lay. Ben placed Steve's used DOPE on the cross pieces and then they gently laid Junk on it. She didn't make a sound and was just barely breathing.

"You should just - " Steve started then he stopped.

"Just what?" Stoney asked.

"She's dead, or near enough," he told everyone. "We should leave her here like a killdeer. Her body would attract predators and keep them away from us."

"I am not even going to dignify that with an answer," Ben said angrily. "She's not dead."

Ben and Lisa grabbed the poles of the sled and began pulling Junk. "This is pretty easy," Lisa said.

"This type of sled, or travois, has been used for centuries by Native Americans," Ben told him. "First by people and dogs and then later by horses. You can actually pull more weight by this method than you can carry on your back."

At that moment there was a loud roar that seemed close, maybe within a hundred yards or less. "What was that?" Stoney asked.

"The day shift," Ben said. "Let's get going."

Steve watched as they pulled Junk away with Charles and Danny walking ahead of them. He wondered whose mind he was going to change first and how he was going to do it. He smiled, there was always Tiny. He bent down to pick up his rifle and when he stood up he was surprised to see Stoney was still there. Might as well start with her he thought. "Stoney, how can I help you?" he asked.

"So, what are you going to do?" Stoney asked him.

"Help you, whatever. I can carry some of your equipment."

"You know what I mean. What are you going to do when we get back?"

"Whatever I'm supposed to," he replied.

"No, you're not," she told him. "You're not going to suddenly become a good guy. You'll play along until you can figure out some way to gain control again. To manipulate everyone and then get back to business as usual."

Steve became angry and said, "I said I would go along with -"

"Why did you have Tiny?" she asked him.

Steve seemed confused by the change of subject but finally answered, "I brought him back just to see how he would interreact with - "

"Interact?" Stoney interrupted. "You had him eat things is my guess, including people. No crime scene left when he was done."

"Now, wait a minute. I -"

"Do you remember Nancy, worked in Payroll?"

Steve went red and spluttered, "I, well I, I'm sure -"

"She wouldn't go out with you if I remember the gossip right. And then one day she just disappeared. Did you feed her to Tiny too?"

"You have no proof of any -"

Stoney cut him off with, "You didn't say I was wrong." Then she shot him in the right leg. He looked down and then back up at her in surprise. "Missed," she complained. Then she shot him in the left leg. The bullet snapped his femur and he fell awkwardly to the ground. "There we go," she said.

"Why?" he screamed as he grabbed both his legs.

"You're kidding," she sneered. "You've killed my friends, tried to kill me, have killed who knows how many times before and you ask why? You should be wondering why I didn't do it sooner." She turned her back and as she started walking away added, "But you said we need a killdeer today. Remember?" Steve kept screaming.

Stoney moved slowly and as she caught up with the sled Ben stopped and looking behind her and asked, "Where's Steve?"

Everyone turned to look as Stoney kept walking past him as she answered, "He didn't make it."

For a moment Ben thought he heard shouting coming from the trees, but then small animals began running from the woods. Not to attack them, just running away from where they had been and continuing past them without even looking at them. He turned to the rest of the group and said, "We better get going. They're running away from something." He nodded at Lisa and they began pulling the sled and again then over at Stoney who just kept walking. He smiled for a second and never looked back.

Steve rolled over on his stomach and reached behind him trying to get to his med pouches. Then suddenly he was being lifted up. He thought for a second that Ben had come back for him but then he realized he was at least ten feet in the air. Then the pain swept over him. He arched his back and turned his head and saw his shadow on the ground. His arms and legs were flailing as he tried to get away from the pain. But he couldn't.

CHAPTER FIFTEEN
WALKS

After an hour of slow walking they began to leave the forest behind them. As the trees began to thin out they were exposed to a cloudless sky and the sun beating directly down on them. "It's hot again," Danny said.

The trees were replaced by wide open spaces of flowering plants and ferns. There were no trails through these areas, so Charles used a long stick to beat the plants in front of them to scare away any animals or snakes. Anytime she heard something moving away from her, she paused.

"This is scary," Lisa said. "I remember the snake from our jumps and then Blonk stopped us because of the one he saw. We can't see anything through all of this."

"You're doing great," Ben told her. "Charles, just keep making noise and everything will stay away from us."

"Or hear me and come to see what's making the noise," he replied.

"I need a rifle," Stoney said.

"I have one more," Ben said as he opened a pack and handed it to her. "I couldn't find any pistols or helmets that weren't damaged. Only one DOPE survived, and it is still wrapped up and we have a lot of ammunition. We have food and still have some water though I hope we get to the time machine before we need to worry about needing more."

"Stoney, how's your leg?" Lisa asked.

"It's still there," she replied and didn't say anything else.

They had slowly been making their way toward a low ridge and now as they climbed to the top Lisa said, "It's beautiful. I wish Ron and Lauren were here."

"I do too," Charles agreed.

Before them lay a valley filled with a sea of green vegetation. There were more flowering plants and short ferns; some about five feet tall and bushy and others shorter and more spread out. There were what they thought were short palm trees and intermixed with them some larger trees that looked similar to the modern oak.

As they started down into the valley Charles stopped and ran his hand along some eight-foot-tall green blades and said, "This looks like grass. But I remember Ron said grass hadn't evolved yet."

"It could be grass, or a grass of some type," Lisa confirmed. "I remember Ron talking about some new discoveries that indicated grass was much older than was thought. He said it was significant because paleontologists would view the diet of the herbivores much differently." She touched the grass too and continued, "He would have loved this. He would have probably laid down in it." She paused for another second then turned abruptly and started moving again.

"We could hear a lot of insects in the jungles we were in," Danny said. "But because this is so wide open we can see them too. Look at all the bees moving around all the different colored flowers. They're huge. This isn't what I thought it would look like. We didn't run into anything like this with Taggit. Look at the bees going from flower to flower like they do in our time. I wonder if they make honey?

"And the butterflies," Danny pointed out. "They're not very pretty, but there they are."

"I thought those were moths," Lisa said.

"Maybe they are," Danny said. " They are smaller so maybe that's what they are. But they do seem to be interested in the flowers and I don't think moths are."

"What did you think all of this would look like?" Ben asked Danny.

"Nothing but jungle. Jungle and animals. Some would just walk by you while some wanted to eat you. But this, if it weren't for the predators, this would be paradise."

Lisa turned around and said, "There's no such thing as paradise." Then she held up her hand and said, "Look how far behind us Stoney is."

Everyone stopped, and Ben went back to where Stoney was. As he hooked her arm over his shoulder he said, "Don't let us get too far ahead. We need to stay together."

"I just started falling back as we were going up the hill," she told him. "And by the way, I think Junk is dead now."

"Why?"

"She's not bleeding anymore."

Ben walked a few more steps then stopped and asked, "Had she been bleeding? I mean, was she leaving a trail?"

Stoney seemed very weak as she replied, "Yeah, I guess she was."

As soon as he got back to Danny and Lisa, Ben checked Junk and shook his head as he said, "You're right, Stoney. Junk is dead." He stood up and asked, "What should we do with her? What do you think, Charles? Charles?"

"What? Oh, sorry. I was thinking about Lauren and all that has happened and what I need to do." He looked around as if he were seeing the valley for the first time and then looked down at Junk. "What did you ask me?"

"What should we do with Junk? She's dead."

They were by another thicket of the tall grass and Charles said, "Let's put her in here. She'll be found sooner or later, but let's try to make it later." Ben picked her up as Lisa slapped at the tall grass to chase out any animals. He stepped a few yards into the thicket and gently laid her down then he stepped back out and started to lead the way.

"Stop," Lisa said. "I don't want to just walk away anymore." She turned toward the grass and said, "Junk was one of the nicest people I've met. She helped us become part of their Team by understanding what we needed to do and helping us do it. She didn't deserve to die now or like she did." She paused and then finished with, "This is for everyone else too. May we all get back the lives we lost."

As they started walking again Danny asked, "Stoney, why don't you lay down on the sled for a while. Save your strength."

"No, I'll keep – "

"I insist," Danny said as he smiled at her. She didn't resist as he led her to the sled where Ben and Charles helped her lay down.

"That was nice, what you said back there," Ben told Lisa. "We should have said something for everyone. But the first death was business as usual and the next death wasn't ever expected. We forgot the value of life, lost it somewhere in time and never got it back."

"We can't do that again," Lisa said. "We have to remember how valuable we all are."

"Charles," Danny started, "if you don't change the timeline, are you afraid that human bones will be found? We've had a lot of people die."

"No, not in the conditions we've been through. Everyone…" he choked for a moment, "…has been eaten quickly. Even Junk will be gone within a few hours. The acidic level of jungle floors will break down any leftover bone long before it could be fossilized. And here, in this place, there are too many animals for any part of Junk to survive. No, I don't think anyone will ever know we were here."

He paused then continued, "But I won't fail. One way or another I will change things."

"Can someone talk to me?" Stoney asked. "My leg is hurting and I feel like I'm slipping away. Talk to me. Keep me in the here and now. Tell me about the ocean we were in."

Danny started, "If Ron or Lauren were here they could tell you more about it than I can. But I can talk about it a little. This whole area that we are walking in, and really have been in since we first arrived, used to be underwater. The Western Interior Seaway stretched basically from the Gulf of Mexico all the way to the Arctic Ocean. That's about 2,000 miles or so. It was about 500 miles wide, or maybe more, and it split the United States and Canada into eastern and western parts. Back then, most of the southern states were at least partially covered by water. There was no Florida I remember, and a lot of Mexico was underwater too.

"That's why you can find fish and shell fossils in states where you wouldn't think they would be. And I mean all kinds of fossils. I went to a few commercial places where you could dig up your own fossils. I have several different types of fish and some shark teeth and in one place I was really lucky and found most of a sea turtle shell. After our last jumps I really got into fossils for quite a while."

"I didn't know that," Charles said. "Why didn't you tell Ron and Lauren? They would have loved taking you out on a dig."

"Hey, this is about me, remember?" Stoney said. Then she continued, "Danny, why didn't you tell us?"

Danny smiled and replied, "I thought about it, but I thought they might think it was funny or something. I don't know. Mostly it was I didn't want to be around any of us for a while. Too many memories."

"Stoney, ask him about the sponge," Charles said.

"You heard the man. What's so important about sponge?"

"Let me see if I can get this right. All animals have a common ancestor and then like a tree, a tree is the usual way to explain it, other animals started branching off of it. The sponge was first, the first branch. So, the sponge is the sister...the sister group, of all other animals. I just thought that was interesting."

"You liked Aria, didn't you?" Stoney asked. Danny didn't answer for a minute and Stoney continued, "I'm sorry. I shouldn't have asked. I just thought I noticed something."

"Yes, I did," Danny answered. "She was understandably overwhelmed by things, didn't understand why all of this had happened to her and Tony. But she was strong, and she did her best, she even took a watch. I didn't get to talk to her much, but yeah, I wish I could have gotten to know her better."

"We need to stop," Ben said. "Stoney is bleeding again and so am I."

As they set Stoney down, Charles pointed out, "You can tell this used to be underwater. Look at the rock formations and how some of them form bridges. You can see where water has slowly cut underneath -"

"Ben, you didn't tell them about Junk's blood trail," Stoney interrupted.

"What?" he asked.

"Remember, I said Junk was bleeding but she had stopped. We have company."

Everyone turned around and then instinctively ducked down. There were five small dinosaurs on top of the ridge, but they were bent down like they were following a trail. They couldn't tell what kind of dinosaur they were but when they got to the tall grass they darted into it.

"We're okay," Danny said. "They didn't look that big. Let's keep going."

"No, we can't," Charles said. "Look."

The others looked back again at the ridge and saw four larger animals following the same trail as the first five. Then they ran into the grass too. Because of the distance it took a couple of seconds for the sounds to get to them. Sounds of fighting.

"Something is not going to eat which means they will still be hungry. We need to hide," Charles said.

"I have a plan," Ben told everyone. "Let's go." Lisa and Charles started dragging Stoney as Danny moved up beside Ben and asked, "What's the plan?"

"Over here. I saw it after we put Junk in the tall grass." He led them to a low rock formation and ducked inside an opening which was about three feet tall and two feet wide. After shining his light inside for several seconds, he said, "Okay, come in and let me explain this to you."

Danny followed then Charles and Lisa pulled the sled through the opening. They were in a small tunnel, about ten feet long, that led completely through the rock they had crawled into. The tunnel started off with a ceiling of about four feet and slowly got smaller until it ended with a small exit, about two feet in diameter.

"Look, we can block the back opening with some of these rocks that are lying around," Ben said. And we can block the entrance we came in with the wood from the sled. We'll be safe for a while."

"That sounds good to me," Danny told everyone.

When everyone else agreed, Ben moved Stoney gently off of the sled and then crawled quietly outside the tunnel entrance and pulled some flowers and ferns across the opening to hide it. "If they can't see it hopefully they won't figure out it's here," he said. Then he untied the sled limbs and used some of the webbing to make a barrier across the entrance. He put some stones around it to hold it in place.

"I agree," Charles said and then he crawled toward the end of the tunnel and blocked it off with several large rocks. "There. It's not completely blocked, air can still move through, but an animal will have to dig their way in. That would give us time to shoot it."

No one spoke for a few minutes and then Danny said, "You know, I actually do feel safe in here. I know we have to go back out in a little while but I'm starting to relax."

"I am too," Lisa admitted.

"I'm cold," Stoney said. Immediately everyone moved closed to her and she told them, "Thanks."

Then Ben said, "You know, we were all sweating in the hot sun and since it's cooler in here we're all going to start feeling colder. There is a breeze coming in from the west, so I could light a small fire to keep us warm and the smoke would keep moving away from us and out the smaller end since it's not completely blocked."

"That sounds great," Lisa said. "But I'm not only getting colder, I'm starting to really hurt. I think the adrenaline is wearing off from the attack."

"I think it is too," Charles agreed. "I know we've only come about a half mile, but I can feel every cut and bruise on my legs."

"We all lost blood too," Ben reminded them. "Not as much as Junk or Stoney but we're all still badly injured. Adrenaline can only take you so far."

"I hate to suggest this," Lisa started, "but should we just stay here tonight? I'm starting to be in a lot of pain right now, as I imagine all of you are too. I know we're close, but we were getting slower out there. I'm afraid if we go back out we literally won't have the ability to walk another half mile. I think we would though if we ate and rested here out of the sun. Let's start first thing in the morning."

Danny immediately spoke up, "I was thinking the same thing. I couldn't make it. I just couldn't. I don't have any energy left at all."

Everyone looked at Charles who said, "I don't know if I could make it either, but I was willing to try. If we stay here we're putting off for another night getting to the time machine. We need to get back to get medical attention and to start making things right. But, I want us all to make it back. So, since I'm not sure I could even get there, let's stay here tonight. But we have to get there tomorrow. We have to."

"We will," Danny said. "But you're not thinking right. Only you have to make it there. If we have to go with you to see you make it then I'll have a half mile in me tomorrow. I think everyone else will too. We have got to get you to your machine."

"I got a half mile," Stoney said.

"Me too," Lisa and Ben added.

Ben treated everyone again and promised, "I'll give everyone the last of the pain medication later, so we can sleep tonight. Until then though you'll have to just bear it. Sorry, it never occurred to us that we would need medication for a lot of people for a long time."

As they started eating, Stoney said, "You know what really bothers me? I liked Otto. I thought he was interesting to be around. He could dumb things down so that we could understand them. He had a personality, unlike Steve. Sorry, Paycheck, but I always found your brother to be cold and distant. There was just something about him. I mean, I can't look back and say I knew this was going to happen, but he was always odd."

"I have to agree with you," Ben said. "But I've known him all my life and he was always strange, but in a strange way I understood. He was smart, a genius, so of course he thought differently than me. He went to college, so I accepted his attitude. To me, he was just my little brother. But now I can look back at certain things that I should have picked up on and not just accepted as Steve being Steve.

"And I liked Otto too. Smart and he could think of things in a way that I found amazing. And like you said, he could explain them, and he actually wanted to explain them to you. I knew he was smarter than Steve but of course I never told Steve. But I can't think of anything that Otto did that set off any alarms then or even now. What happened?"

"Greed. Power," Lisa answered. "If Lauren was here she could tell us. All the things she was worried about, but we were looking in the wrong direction. Well, no we weren't. Steve did try to leave us behind first, but Otto was smarter, or just worse."

"What about everyone that went with him?" Charles asked Stoney. "Did you get along with them?"

"Yes. There were cliques of course, but we all spent some time together at the beach or just watching a game. I thought Maybe was a little arrogant and sometimes her not knowing what to do act got a little old, but there was nothing that led me to believe there were two different teams. I was completely surprised." She paused and looked at Danny and said, "But you got them."

"I hope so," he replied. "Think of the damage they would have done if they had gotten back. Plus, well it was bad enough when I realized what Steve was doing, but then to listen to Otto. I had to do something." He was quiet for a moment then added, "Lauren warned us."

"She did," Charles replied. "But we didn't understand how bad Steve was until you told us about the man you found that said he had been left behind. We thought we were in control, no, I thought we were in control. I knew Steve had stolen my work and Tony was working for him, but I thought we could fly under the radar and surprise him." He looked at Lisa and said, "Sorry we didn't tell you and Ron, but we were afraid you would give things away before we got our answers."

"And you would have been right," Lisa agreed. "I wouldn't have acted the same and Ron wouldn't have known how to act. He just kept being Ron, excited and more excited." She clenched her jaws and said, "I miss my Ron, but I will cry later. For everyone. Right now, I'm concentrating on what needs to be done to make sure this never happens again."

It grew quiet and Ben went around checking bandages again and giving everyone some pain medication. Then he told Charles, "I still have the one DOPE that I stored in my backpack. It was in the top of the tree where no animals got at it. You're going to sleep in it tonight and I'm going to position it tight against that entrance, so nothing can get past it."

"Me?" Charles asked. "No. Let's put Stoney in there or Lisa or Danny. Even you if you want, but not me."

"It has to be you," Stoney said.

"Why?"

"Because you are the most important person in the world right now. Don't you understand that? None of us can do what you can do. Save us. Save us all. If somehow something gets in tonight you have to stay alive. So, it has to be you."

Charles tried to say something but couldn't. "Okay," he finally agreed, "but I'm not going to like it."

"I don't need you to like it," Ben said. "I just need you to still be alive in the morning."

"As you go to sleep we need to think about one last thing," Ben said. "Every second may be the last time we see each other. Either from animals or Charles taking care of the time machine. One way or another, to the rest of the world, we will have never existed."

As they fell asleep each one of them thought about each other and all those that were gone. And Lisa couldn't stop the tears rolling down her cheeks.

Ben woke up first and began quietly moving around. He lit the fire again and thought about what he had said. What should he do? There was only one answer.

As Charles came out of the DOPE he asked Ben, "Is everyone still alive?"

"Yes," he replied as he stirred the burning embers of the fire.

Danny and Stoney were the last to wake up and they looked worse. After a few minutes Danny said, "I can't go any farther. I know last night I thought I could but I can't. I'm played out. I don't have any energy and what's more I'm to the point I don't really want to go on." He held up his hand as Lisa started to say something and continued, "This is where I want to stay. I do want to get out of this place though so that there isn't any chance that I'll be found in the future."

"We can't leave you here by yourself," Lisa said. "We need to - "

"He won't be alone," Stoney cut in. "I've decided to stay too. I thought about what Danny said yesterday and I feel the same. I'm dying. I can feel it. There's too much of me gone and I know that there isn't any reason to go back. I don't want to argue about it, it's what I want to do."

Ben looked up from the fire and said, "Actually, it's what we have to do."

"What do you mean?" Lisa asked.

"The more of us that go back, the more we could accidentally cause problems before the timeline is changed. We need to be left here where we will not change history in any way."

"But Charles will need our help," Lisa pointed out. "At least try to get him to the time machine. If you can't, well then you can't. But please, try."

Danny took a deep breath and said, "I'll try."

Charles put his hand on Danny's shoulder and said, "Thanks."

"I'll try too," Stoney said.

Then Ben jumped in with, "Then let's get this train rolling. We have a half mile to go and we don't know the conditions or the company we'll meet along the way. It's early morning and I doubt if it's going to get any cooler than it is right now." When everyone nodded he quickly checked their bandages then started taking the sled apart and laying the pieces off to the side.

Everyone, including Stoney, crawled slowly toward the entrance and as they left the tunnel they had to blink their eyes several times as they got used to the bright sunlight. It was immediately hot, but Danny said, "Not as hot as yesterday."

They moved south for a few minutes and then Charles told them, "Let's move east." Ahead of them were some low hills and the ground was mostly bare, with only a few trees and tall green brush scattered around. They stayed away from the thicker vegetation and whatever might be hiding in it.

Within 200 yards Stoney said, "I'm bleeding again. I'm not stopping but I will probably start drawing something after us."

Danny turned around and said, "That's good."

"What?" Ben asked. "How can that be good?"

"Let's go up this hill and I'll tell you." When they got to the top Danny panted, "You know I could have walked up this in a minute a year ago. It probably took us ten minutes today." He dropped his hands to his knees for a few seconds as Stoney laid down on the ground. Then Danny slowly pushed himself up and said, "Now we are up here where a lot of things can see us. Any predators will see a couple of wounded animals headed to the southwest." He turned to Charles and continued, "Away from you."

Charles couldn't answer for a minute; as he started to tear up he asked, "Is this it then?"

"It is, my friend. I can't do anything else for you except this." Then he held out his hand and Charles pushed it out of the way as he hugged Danny close to him. "Thank you," Danny whispered, "for letting me see my Dad again."

"I'll miss you," Charles said as he wiped the tears from his face.

Then Danny hugged Lisa and told her, "I'm very glad I got to meet you. I hope you have learned you are stronger than you ever thought you could be."

"But I'm going with you," she told him.

"No," he shook his head. "Not yet. Charles will still need you to get him through. Remember, you're the smart one." Then she hugged him back and started to cry.

Ben helped Stoney up from the ground and as they both shook hands with Charles and Lisa, Ben said, "I'm going with them. See if I can keep them out of trouble."

"Here," Stoney said as she handed Lisa the rifle, "I think you may need this more than us."

"That reminds me," Danny said as he untied his boots and handed them to Charles. "We're the same size, you might need these. Remember, they still have a jump in each one."

Ben picked up a piece of wood from the ground and said, "Didn't someone say that in the end all we would have were sharp sticks?" Then Stoney put an arm around Ben's shoulders and they began limping down the hill.

Before they turned away, Charles called out, "Danny, you ripped your pants again."

Danny smiled as he looked down and replied, "And I said it wasn't going to happen again."

Charles stood there for a moment then Lisa pulled on his arm and said, "Let's go." They went quickly down the hill and began walking quicker as they knew with every step they were getting closer to the time machine. But the terrain continued dropping in front of them and as they entered a forest that was across their path they noticed the ground was becoming marshier and soon they were walking through mud. As they crested a hill, Charles said, "Damn." Below them was a small lake.

"Right in the middle?" Lisa asked.

"Of course," Charles told her. "Stand on my boots."

"What?"

"Stand on my boots, I'm only using them for this jump. That way we still have your boots and Danny's boots to jump with."

Lisa stepped on his boots and as Charles started the jump she asked, "Did the cells get enough charge yesterday?"

"Probably not a full twelve hours but we'll still jump a few hundred thousand years."

"I hate jumping," Lisa confessed. "I always feel like we're in a vacuum or something. I'm afraid we're going to run out of air or the walls will close in on us."

"Why didn't you say something?"

"You know me, I'm not a squeaky wheel. I just go along with whatever."

"Not recently. You seem to have found your voice, you're a little more authoritative and take charge."

"I'm sorry, I - "

"No, that's a good thing. Express yourself. You have good ideas and know how to lead. You just don't do it very often."

She nodded and said, "I will. I was hoping I wasn't coming across as bossy or a know it all."

"That's my job," Charles replied.

Then the jump ended, and they found they were on dry ground covered with sparse vegetation and only a few scattered trees. There were still some low hills around them, but Charles told her, "This looks much better. This way, up over the hill and we'll be there." But Lisa didn't move and when Charles turned around, she was crying. "What's wrong?" he asked.

"They're dead. Danny, Stoney and Ben. They're already dead. Hundreds of thousands of years ago. They're dead and we don't even know how it happened." Then there was a roar and she took a deep breath and continued, "But that doesn't matter now. Let's get to the time machine. How much farther? And where was that roar from?"

"I don't know. Down here, surrounded by these hills, the sound probably echoes around so it could have been from anywhere. But we're within a hundred yards of the machine. Let's get over this hill."

They walked past some trees and a rocky outcropping then started up the hill. As they came to the top, they paused. The terrain was different, the ground was still bare in some spots but much of it was covered with waist high ferns. There were a few scattered trees that slowly turned into a dense forest a hundred feet. "I hope one of those trees isn't - " Charles started and then the time machine appeared in an open spot. It was similar to the elevator shaft machine that had rescued them before, but it had a walled exterior.

"I guess you didn't want anything jumping in with us again," Lisa said as they started down the hill.

"No extra passengers or any of their body parts," Charles agreed. "Remember how we had to dig that boulder and bushes up?"

"Yes, and then they weren't even in the landing spot. We did all that work for nothing."

"Nothing to worry about this time," Charles said. Then the *T-rex* walked out of the trees. It was about fifteen feet tall and looked too much like all of the other *Rexes* they had seen. Nothing but teeth and a bad attitude.

"Are you seeing these guys?" Ben asked.

"Yes. Four or five on each side of us."

"Yeah, and a few more behind us too," Ben said. "They are definitely stalking us but even though we are wounded we are still bigger than they are."

"They're waiting for us to stop or lay down or something," Danny said.

"That won't be much longer," Stoney whispered. "I can't go much farther."

Danny stumbled and as he did a small multi-colored predator, not even two feet tall, rushed in. Ben took a quick step and kicked the animal and it disappeared rolling into some brush. "I'm with Stoney," Danny said. "I can feel my heart beating and, and my chest is hurting. Let's sit down by this rock."

Ben knew they shouldn't but there wasn't anything he could do as Danny sank down and Stoney sat down beside him. Four of the animals immediately jumped up on the rock and he knocked one of them off as the other three jumped out of sight. He could hear them chirping to each other but felt he could handle the group if they started in again. But he had to get Danny and Stoney moving again. Maybe they should work their way back to the tunnel. No, they had to keep leading these things away from Lisa and Charles.

As he walked over to Danny he saw him let go of Stoney's hand. "She's dead," Danny gasped.

Ben took a deep breath and realized that Danny wasn't going to last much longer either. Still, he wasn't going to leave him behind. "Danny," he said softly, "we need to start moving again."

Danny looked up at Ben then up at the sun. Then Danny said, "Dad, throw me the ball, Grandpa's watching." Then he leaned back against the rock and his eyes closed. But he didn't stop smiling.

Ben felt for a pulse and then stood up and decided the *'saurs* would have to earn their meal today. He began running and he could hear them coming after him. Suddenly he stopped and before they could scatter he turned and began beating them with his stick. Though a few got past it for a few bites, more of them were left lying in the dirt or limping away.

Then he heard something moving behind him, something larger. The smaller animals were darting away as he turned around and saw it. Eight feet tall, maybe nine, its red and yellow body was slowly moving side to side as it stared at him. If only he had a rifle with an explosive round. Instead he just had a stick. And it wasn't even sharp.

Ben took a deep breath and then he looked up at the sun. He smiled and said, "I'm sorry, for everything." Then he ran right at it.

CHAPTER SIXTEEN
DINO CITY

"I hate it when I'm wrong," Charles said under his breath. They stood completely still as the *Rex* walked toward the time machine. Then Charles added, "We can't let it get near the machine or it might damage it."

Lisa threw her hands up in the air and started shouting and the *Rex* snapped its head and stopped. Then it launched forward, and Lisa shouted, "This way, come on." She turned and ran back down the hill then cut to her left and into the trees at the bottom. She kept moving and when they got to the rocks she moved in close to the wall as she continued to move sideways. "Stay close to the wall," she told Charles.

They could hear the *Rex* coming down the hill and then it grew quiet and they hoped it had lost them. Lisa put a finger to her lips and then they heard the *Rex* snort and begin moving again. It sounded like it was moving away so Lisa peeked out just enough to confirm it. She motioned for Charles to follow her and they kept moving quietly away from the *Rex*.

Charles whispered, "I was just going to send the time machine away. We could have just snuck back down the hill."

"I didn't think of that."

"That's okay, I didn't think about using the rifle. So, we're even."

"Do you have the explosive rounds in it?"

"No."

"Well you better load them otherwise if you shoot that *Rex* you'll just make it mad."

Charles nodded as he changed rounds and they slowly continued moving. It took them about twenty minutes as they skirted the base of the hill until they were back in position to see the machine. They crouched down and didn't move for several minutes as they watched the area. "What do you think?" Lisa asked.

"I don't know. Why was the *Rex* even here? We weren't on a trail and I haven't seen any water. We can't be that unlucky."

"I would agree with you if I hadn't seen it. In any case though, it went one way and we went the other. I say let's get to the machine."

"My thought too," Charles agreed. "Still, let's stay as low in these ferns as we can until we are right next to the time machine. All we have to do is jump in and hit the big red button."

"That sounds easy."

"After the last time, I made it as easy as I could. Still, we're a couple of hundred yards away."

It took them twenty minutes to creep half way to the machine and they were well hidden in the ferns when they heard rocks being moved behind them. They slowly turned and saw the *Rex* had turned around and followed them. As it lifted up its head and began sniffing the air, Lisa said, "Our blood."

They both looked at the machine and Lisa asked, "We can't make it, can we?"

"No, and it won't have a hard time finding us in this stuff. We need to either run for the trees and hope we can lose it or I'm going to have to shoot it."

"Plan B, stay low and shoot it."

Charles slowly brought the rifle up and put its head right in the middle of the scope. He tried to pull the trigger, but it wouldn't move. "It won't shoot," he said.

"Take off the safety," Lisa told him and reached over and flipped the lever on the side of the gun. The *Rex* saw the movement and turned and lowered its head to charge just as Charles fired. The bullet skipped off the angled skull of the *Rex* and ricocheted off toward the hill where it exploded a second later. The *Rex* glanced at the explosion and then back at where Charles and Lisa were hidden. As it stepped forward they both jumped up and Lisa shouted, "Plan A", as they ran for the tree line the *Rex* had stepped out of to begin with.

The trees were fairly close together and slowed the *Rex* down just enough that they were able to stay ahead of it. Lisa shouted, "Jump", and Charles blindly followed as they cleared a six-foot-wide ravine, but the *Rex* didn't slow down and crossed it easily. "This time let's jump down into it," Lisa shouted.

"How deep is it?" Charles shouted back and then it was too late, he was already plunging down. Fortunately, the ravine was only eight feet deep and even better only four or five feet wide. As Charles followed Lisa, the *Rex* tracked them along the sides of the ravine but couldn't step in after them or get his head close enough to snap at them.

Lisa jumped over a partial skeleton and as she glanced down at the bones she slowed and said, "Something's wrong."

Charles ran into her and started pushing her as he shouted, "Yes, I know, there's a *Rex* after us." She tried to say something else, but a loud roar made her realize the ravine was getting wider and it wasn't as deep. Just ahead, the ravine suddenly split with part of it making a sharp turn to the left. Lisa followed and ducked under a barrier and as Charles followed, he looked up and almost stopped. Then he ducked under the barrier and looked back. Then he did stop.

"Lisa," he shouted, "come back."

"Are you kidding?" she shouted as she looked back at him. Then she followed his gaze to the left and right and stopped too. "It's a...it's a..."

"It's a fence," Charles finished for her. He looked down at his feet and continued, "And we're standing on concrete."

As she walked back to Charles, the *Rex* stopped on the other side of the fence and roared for a few seconds and then it turned away. "I don't understand," Lisa said. "Where did all of this come from?"

"Do you hear that?" Charles asked. "It's a - "

"Chopper," Lisa finished. "It's a helicopter."

It landed about a hundred feet from them and suddenly there were people running at them from all directions. They were all wearing light gray uniforms with RABAR patches on their short sleeve shirts .They were heavily armed and had their rifles aimed at Charles and Lisa. They all stopped together and one of them shouted, "Drop your gun."

"What?" Charles asked. "Who are you? What's going on?"

"I said drop your gun," the man shouted again.

"What?" Charles repeated.

"Wait, wait, wait," Lisa shouted as she stepped forward with her hands up. "We're just confused. I'll get it." She turned around to Charles and said, "Raise your arms up, get your hands over your head."

As he did, Charles stared around at everyone and Lisa lifted the rifle sling up over his head and laid the rifle down on the ground. "Okay," she said. "Now, who are you? Why are you here? And no, there is no one else out here. We're all that's left."

"Where are we?" Charles asked.

As the rifles were lowered, the man who had given the commands stepped forward and said, "Don't play games with us. Why would you be in the *Rex* pen with a rifle if you weren't poachers or Riskers?"

"Riskers?"

"I said don't play games with us. Jenson, cuff them and take them to Compound 3."

As Charles was being handcuffed he said, "Let me change my question; *when* is this? What year is it?"

"What?" the woman asked. "What year do you think it is and who are you?"

"I think it's about 69 million years or so ago from my time, Jenson, and my name is Charles Dawson."

The woman's head snapped up and then she looked at Lisa and asked, "And you?"

"Lisa Wells."

Jenson took a small rectangular object from her pocket and held it in front of their faces and as she turned it toward her she said slowly, "Oh my God. Chief Richards you need to get back here, now!"

"What is it, Jenson?" he asked curtly. "Let's get them out of here."

"Look at my scanner," she told him as she held it up for him.

"Yeah, yeah, Charles Dawson and..." He trailed off, looked at Jenson, and asked, "Is this right? Is there a mistake?"

"No, it's him, I mean them."

"Get the cuffs off of them, now. Now," Richards shouted. "You three, help them to the chopper and tell the pilot to get them to Building One. Go, go, go." As three of the others in gray shirts started to help them walk to the helicopter, the others wondered who they had stopped and started to gather around.

Then Lisa said, "Wait a minute. Can't you see that we're injured? We've been on the other side of that fence for millions of years. We have injuries that need to be treated. We've only had penicillin and not much of that. We're tired, hungry, hurting and I don't know about Charles but I'm mad as hell at the way you are treating us. We need help."

"Yes, ma'am," Richards replied. "I can see that now. I was just caught up in...well, we had no idea who you were or that you were even still alive. The chopper will take you to Medical and I'll have Jenson go with you to get anything you need. Anything. Just ask."

"Thank you," Lisa said.

"Yes, thank you," Charles added. "I do have a question, how do you know about us and how did," he waved his arm around, "all of this happen?"

"I'm not the person to ask about that," Richards said. "I'm sure that after you start feeling better there will be a lot of people in to talk to you. They can tell you all about it."

As Jenson led them to the helicopter, Charles asked, "Can you tell me why there is a hole in the *Rex* pen fence? Can't it get out?"

"Mr. Dawson, it's a water runoff for that ravine that cuts through the *Rex* pen. If we don't keep it wide enough it gets jammed during some of the heavy rains we get, and the fence gets ripped apart."

"But the *Rex* - "

"Is too big to get through," Jenson told him.

In just a few minutes, Charles and Lisa were in the helicopter and as it rose they could see a blacktop road that ran through the jungle. "That would have made things easier," Charles said.

As they glanced back, they saw the *Rex* on the other side of the fence and Lisa leaned against Charles and said, "You made it."

He put his arm around her and smiled as he replied, "Yes, we did." But as he leaned his head back against the seat he told himself that was wrong, they weren't back. They weren't back at all.

Then Lisa said, "Look."

Charles opened his eyes and out the window he saw a lot of buildings and roads running in every direction. There were other open areas and some of them contained other dinosaurs. There were also smaller buildings and a helipad that they were getting ready to land on. "What is this place?" he shouted to the pilot.

The pilot turned and gave him a questioning look then shouted back, "Dino City, of course."

As the helicopter disappeared, Richards reached for his phone and told everyone around him, "No one says anything about this to anyone until you get the okay. Got it?"

As Ray Budgem jumped up from his desk, phone in hand, the other two turned away from the map to stare at him. "What did you say?" Budgem asked. "Tell me again and go a little slower." He just shook his head and sat down as he mumbled, "Okay, got it," and ended the call.

Sheila finally broke the silence by asking, "Ray, what is it?"

When he didn't answer, Almar walked around the desk and said, "Ray? Ray talk to us."

"You're not going to believe this. Just a few minutes ago, two people ran out of the *T-rex* enclosure. They were dirty and covered with all types of wounds."

"Serves the Riskers right," Almar said. "We don't need - "

"No, it wasn't Riskers or poachers or anything like that. It was Charles Dawson. *The* Charles Dawson."

"As in *the* Charles Dawson who invented time travel?" Sheila asked.

"*The* Charles Dawson who invented time travel," Budgem confirmed.

"Who was with him?"

"Lisa Wells, one of the people who disappeared with him."

"Right out of the history books," Almar said. "Wow. Should we get the Media people ready for this? Do we - "

"We do nothing right now," Budgem interrupted. "This will go straight to the top. They will let us know what to do."

"What do we do now?" Sheila asked. "People are going to start learning about this."

"That's true," Budgem said as he nodded his head. "There was a security team that responded to them when they set off an alarm." He thought for a second then turned to Almar and told him, "No one leaves the entire complex. I don't care what site they work at, no one leaves."

"And no one comes in tomorrow?"

"Yes, that's right. No one in or out. Right now, this stays right here." He grabbed his phone again and then said, "And as soon as I'm done here I'll block all communication, phones, radio, and no one travels in or goes out. Family, friends, guests, it doesn't matter. My guess is the big boys will travel in tonight. They get in, no one else does. Got it?"

"Got it, Ray," Almar said. "We're on it." Sheila and Almar quickly left the room as Ray made a phone call.

As Charles was wheeled down the hall, he asked, "Which room is Lisa in?"

"Right next to yours, sir," Jenson answered.

"First, please just call me Charles. Next, will I be going everywhere in this wheelchair and third, can I stop at her room so I can see how she's doing?"

Jenson smiled and said, "Well, you have to call me Sharon then. I'm supposed to take you all the way to your room, but you can jump out right now if you feel up to it. And here is Ms. Wells' room. If she's awake you can talk to her, but she may not be. And you may not be too much longer yourself. Do you need anything else?"

"No, but I bet Ms. Wells tells you to call her Lisa."

"She already did…Charles, I just have a hard time doing that. Here you go."

Charles called, "Thanks," over his shoulder and then went into Lisa's room. She was by herself and her eyes were closed so he started to turn to leave when she said, "No, come on in. I'm still awake, at least for a few more minutes."

"How are you feeling?" Charles asked as he checked her bandages.

"With all the drugs, pretty good. I wish they would have let us eat a little more, I am hungry."

"I am too but I'm sure they'll let us eat when we wake up." He glanced around the room for a moment then asked, "Can you hear me? Are you able to understand everything I say?"

Lisa opened her eyes quickly and said, "Those are strange questions. You have my attention."

He lowered his voice and said, "I don't know why, but I have an odd feeling about all of this. Putting two and two together I can understand that when we didn't return from our time travelling that Steve's business would have been looked into. I'm sure my name would have been in any records they found, and they quickly would have realized what had happened. Now, depending on who took control of those records, many different things could have occurred. So, I need you to do me a huge favor."

"You know I will."

"Lisa, you are the smartest person I know. You're even smarter than you know. But I don't want you to talk very much to anyone for a while. Follow my lead, but don't be surprised if I change things here and there when I'm talking. Answer any questions you are asked honestly but, you may have to lie. Also, I want you to study how people answer me, what they actually say, their body posture, do they have to think before they answer."

"See if they are lying," Lisa said.

"Yes."

"Why? What do you think is wrong?"

"I don't know, but I've got the feeling that I did before Taggit and Steve."

"Why?"

"No one will answer any of my questions. No one. They aren't that hard. When did you start time traveling? Where are we? When are we? Either people give me a non-answer, or they change the subject. One or two who don't know what to say would be okay, but not everyone."

"Sharon seemed okay."

"But Sharon has been with us. I don't think she's received any instructions yet."

"I trust your instincts," Lisa told him as she closed her eyes. "When I wake up, I'll be ready."

Charles smiled and nodded and walked to his room. In the hall, he waved at an orderly who seemed to be watching him. The man smiled and waved back. As he started to fall sleep he hoped he was wrong. But he knew he wasn't.

Ray, Sheila and Almar watched the chopper land and waited for everyone to get out. It was after midnight and they were tired, but they knew how big this was going to be. They were surprised there were only two passengers, Rachel Sims and Jack Barman, the money and the mind.

Though the joke was he spent her money and she didn't mind. They owned and operated RaBar Time and no one stood in their way.

As they walked up, Jack said, "Sorry it's late but all of us have to be on the same page tomorrow. No one has talked with them about anything, right Ray?"

"Yes, sir. I - "

"Let's keep it that way," Jack interrupted. He continued to walk quickly to the small meeting room and they sat down around a small round table. "Okay," Jack started again, "what are the workers saying? What do they know? Has anything got out?"

"Absolutely not," Ray assured him. "The security team that found them were immediately given strict orders not to talk about anything to anyone. In fact, they are being kept apart from everyone else. The moment I finished speaking with you we locked the site down tight. I met with all the workers and explained there was a containment problem and that no one could leave, and the next shift was not coming in. Most of them are just happy they are now being paid for every hour they are here. They understand it's to keep the media away from them since it's always news when something happens here. I also sent out a notice to the families and then all communication was shut down."

"Good, good," Jack replied. "Now, about Charles Dawson, first we need to find out everything that happened to him. If it's boring we can spin it but if it's anything like that book the one guy wrote maybe it may actually be interesting. To begin with we'll control all media appearances and that type of thing."

"RABAR doing the right thing for Charles Dawson who has come back from the dead," Rachel added. "This will be gold. We'll form a partnership with him, he can become the RABAR public spokesman." She paused and looked at Jack, "If he will."

"That is the big 'if'," Jack admitted. "Looking at all the records we took from EXENCO indicates he is not as avid a time traveler as he once was. We'll need to really sell him on what we are doing and why."

"He'll want to know everything we do and about our safety record too," Rachel said. "And especially…what was her name?"

"Well, his wife was Lauren," Jack said. "But the person who survived with him is Lisa and I can't remember how she is part of the disappearance. According to her though they are the only survivors." He looked at Ray, Sheila and Almar and asked, "Who remembers their history? Any details of the disappearance or maybe read the book?"

"Probably all of us remember something," Ray answered. "But it has been a few years anyway."

"Find out who Lisa is tonight and let me know by tomorrow's meeting. We'll make it around noon."

"Sir, if I may ask," Sheila started, "what is your main concern about Charles Dawson?"

"Right now, he doesn't know that he has no home or money anymore. Everything he ever had is gone. But we can fix that easily. In fact, he'll probably be richer now than he ever was or could have been. But what if he wants to fix everything? What if he wants to go back and rescue all those people who died, or even just his wife? Then we'll have a huge problem."

"But no one would want him to do that and, he doesn't have the ability anymore," Almar said.

"There are people who don't want time travel," Rachel pointed out. "So, he would have some supporters, probably more if it was to rescue his wife. But I'm sure we can head that off. The vast majority of people will not want him to destroy time travel though, and I hope that would dissuade him."

"You really think he would want to stop time travel?" Ray asked. "There's always risks traveling but not like the unexpected consequences of stopping it altogether. That would completely change billions of lives."

"I also have to ask how he could accomplish it?" Sheila added.

"He's obviously one of the most brilliant men who ever lived," Jack told them. "He seems very resourceful too. In a few years why couldn't he time travel again?"

"Well, the rules and regulations that - "

"He won't care about that," Rachel said. "Not if he thinks time travel should be destroyed. If he's that smart we would have no idea what he was doing."

Jack leaned forward and said, "Listen to me, carefully. From this second on I want them pampered and their every wish granted. I want them happy. Then have them at the meeting at noon so we can find out if we need to be concerned." He looked around the table and then continued, "As far as I am concerned, until we find out what Charles Dawson thinks, he is the most dangerous man on the planet."

Lisa slowly got out of bed and was surprised that she wasn't in more pain. She made a mental note to tell everyone she didn't want as much medicine, she wanted to know when she was doing something she wasn't supposed to. Pain helped stop you from hurting yourself more. She wandered out into the hall and three smiling orderlies rushed toward her.

"Good morning," they all said. "You should have rung us, and we would have come to you."

"No need for that," she told them. "I need to work the pain out by walking. Is this - "

"Yes, that is where Mr. Dawson is," one of the orderlies answered.

Lisa knocked on the door and Charles said, "Come in."

As she stepped in, he immediately went to her and hugged her. Lisa was surprised and confused until she heard him whisper, "Normal conversation." Then louder he asked, "How are you feeling this morning?"

"Actually, pretty good," she replied. "I'm feeling a little stiff and still sore, but better. What about you?"

"The same. I'm sure when the medicine wears off we'll know it."

"What's going to happen today do you think? I mean, we're a surprise to everyone. Are we just going to go home?"

"I can't remember much from yesterday," Charles told her. "I don't know if we have to stay here a few days because of our injuries or what. I'm sure someone probably told us, and I kind of remember someone saying something about 'a couple of days', but I could have dreamt it too."

Lisa replied, "Well I'm glad I'm not the only one. I can clearly remember running from the *Rex*, and all the people, and the ride in the helicopter. After that I just remember tables and IV's and eating something."

"I'm sure we'll find out soon enough."

"Let's go for a walk," Lisa said. "I'm hungry. I think we can walk in the hall."

As they started for the door, there was a knock and a voice asked, "Can I come in?"

"Yes," Charles answered and an orderly brought in a tray of food. "Right on time," Charles told him as he set the tray on a table. "Do you have something for Lisa too?"

"Yes, I do, would you like it brought in here?" he asked her.

"Please. What do we have?"

"A little of everything," the orderly laughed as he came back in with another tray. "We didn't know for sure what you wanted so there is juice, coffee, fruit, yogurt, pancakes, toast, eggs and some bacon and sausage. Does that work, or would you like something else?"

Lisa and Charles were already eating as Lisa told him, "This will do."

The orderly smiled and said, "If you need anything else either buzz us or walk down the hall to the right. Anything at all, just let us know."

"He was nice," Lisa said.

"Everyone is," Charles agreed.

A few minutes later, Lisa asked again, "Take that walk now?"

"If I can move," Charles replied. "Living on nothing but protein bars can make you appreciate a good breakfast."

As they walked toward the door, there was another knock and then a woman in green scrubs came in. She smiled and said, "Well, you both look better than yesterday. I don't know if you remember but I'm Doctor Blacke. How are both of you feeling?"

"Just fine," Charles answered.

"That's great," Doctor Blacke told him. "Could both of you have a seat? I'm sorry, I just need to poke and prod for a minute and check your dressings." It didn't take very long, and she said, "Everything looks fine, but I am surprised you're up. You've both had a close call. Even though you had some penicillin there was some infection starting. We do want you to walk around but please be careful and watch that you don't tear any stitches. Lisa, you have a slight fever, but I don't think it is anything to worry about. I'm going to prescribe some antibiotics and for the pain - "

"I really don't want any more pain medication," Lisa interrupted.

The doctor made a quick note and continued, "I understand. I usually never complete a prescription of pain meds either. I like to hear what my body has to say." As Lisa nodded, Doctor Blacke continued, "But, you will need the antibiotics...*all of them*. Please follow the directions on the bottles and I'll check on you again tomorrow morning."

"So, we need to stay one more day?" Charles asked.

"Yes, just one more I think. You can take the meds at home and your physician can take out the stitches. It's really fortunate that you had the person in your group that bandaged you and gave you the penicillin. Otherwise, I'm sure you would have had a lot more complications. Now, what else do you need from me?"

"Can we walk outside?" Charles asked.

"Again, I thought with all the walking you've done you would want to rest, but you can check out Dino City if you want. Just pay attention to your bodies and if you think you need to rest, then make sure you do."

"Dino City," Lisa said. "That's right, that's what the pilot called it."

"You got it."

"Well, we'd rather be outside, and I think all the walking we did the past few days actually is now helping us. So, I guess we'll explore Dino City."

"Just take it easy and they do have golf carts if you need one. I bet someone would also love to drive you around. Oh, one last thing. If you are up to it, the RABAR executives would like to meet with you today at noon."

"Okay," Charles replied. "Any idea what it will be about?"

"No, but I'm sure it's to bring you up to speed on things. You've been gone a long time." Before Charles could say anything else, Doctor Blacke opened the door and said, "I will be checking on you again before you leave. Please take care."

"We will," Lisa called out.

"Let's try going outside one more time," Charles said. Then he took Lisa's arm and they walked into the hall, found an exit and went outside. "I forgot how hot it was," he sighed.

They paused for a few seconds to look around. In front of them was a large park-like open space covered with mown grass and dinosaur statues. A sidewalk led from the center of the park to each of the eight buildings that surrounded it. Though each building was slightly different they were all two stories tall and were made with stone and had large glass curtain wall facades. There were a lot of people either walking or driving around and they noticed there were streets and sidewalks between each building that disappeared into the surrounding jungle.

"Interesting place," Lisa said. "And we're finally outside. Why?"

Charles leaned in close and said, "You are smart, as I've said before." They continued walking along a sidewalk leading away from the building and after a minute Charles continued, "My room was entered last night after I went to sleep. Things were moved and then someone tried to put them back where they were. I'm sure we're being watched, and I don't doubt our rooms are bugged, maybe even monitored. That just makes me suspicious - "

"And cautious," Lisa said. Then she yawned and stretched.

"Do we need to go back in?" Charles asked.

"No. Just checking to see if there were any drones above us."

"And?"

"We're good. Now, what do you think they're after?"

"I'm still thinking about that, but that made me think about something else. When we were running from the *Rex*, why did you say something was wrong?"

"Wow, you just didn't answer my question *and* changed the topic all at the same time. I need to keep an eye on you." As Charles smiled she continued, "We ran past part of a *Stegosaurus* skeleton. I picked up enough from Ron to know that the *Stegosaurus* and the *Rex* lived in completely different time periods. Something wasn't right. But now I remember when we were in the copter we saw they keep animal pens like it's a reserve or a zoo or something. Maybe they just mixed the animals together for some reason."

Charles said, "That's interesting," then he was quiet for several minutes.

"Going to let me in on things?" Lisa asked.

Charles took a second to answer then said, "No, not right now. I'm sorry, because this is the second time I've kept you in the dark about something, but I need you to act naturally."

"And just go along with whatever you say and do."

"Exactly."

"And watch everyone."

"Yes."

"What am I watching for again?"

"People lying. Or rather indications they are lying. It's hard to do because it is not an exact science. Things you may have heard before, like a person will not look you in the eyes or they nervously tap their foot, are not always signs they are lying. You have to see if the person always taps their foot or has a hard time looking someone in the eye. That means those are just their normal habits. You have to know what they normally do and then see if they deviate from that."

"Like 'tells' in poker."

Charles smiled and nodded as he said, "Well, yes, that's an example. So, look for those things but also watch body posture, facial expressions, do they get louder or softer, does it take them an extra second to think of something to say, do they omit things or get mixed up. But again, you have to establish a base line, do they already do those things, so they aren't lying, they are just being themselves."

"Okay, watch and learn. Don't go all in the first few hands."

"And one other thing."

"What's that?"

"Remind me not to play poker with you."

"Got it," Lisa said, then she pulled Charles around and started back to the medical building. "I'm hot and I want ice cream and the doctor said we should listen to our bodies." Charles put his arm around her as they walked back, and she just smiled at him and said, "Don't say anything else. There are people watching us so just keep your arm around me, smile, and keep walking." Charles did what Lisa said and they walked back inside.

As Charles and Lisa stood at the head of a long table, they watched everyone file in and stand behind their chairs. They knew Jenson, Richards, and Doctor Blacke but not the other five. At a nod from one of the men, a woman standing next to Charles said, "Mr. Dawson and Ms. Wells, it is a relief to find both of you still alive and an honor to have you here with us. But before we go any further, please, let's all sit down, and I'll introduce everyone."

When everyone was seated she continued, "On your right we wanted some familiar faces. You met Security Chief Richards and Security Officer Jenson yesterday and Doctor Blacke today." They nodded but didn't say anything. "This is Ray Budgem, Site Director, this is Almar Ritt and I'm Sheila Travers, Associate Site Directors, and at the end of the table are Rachel Sims and Jack Barman, the founders and CEO's of RABAR Industries." She turned back to Charles and smiled as she continued, "First, we hope that all your needs have been taken care of?"

Charles smiled back and replied, "Please, all of you, accept our thanks and gratitude for what you have done for us. I'll begin by apologizing first to Chief Richards and Officer Jenson for making their day that much harder yesterday. It was my fault that we didn't immediately follow your instructions and caused some alarm and confusion for you. And Doctor Blacke, neither one of us knows exactly what you did for us but whatever it was, you have worked miracles. Our injuries are healing, and we feel better than should be expected.

"Mr. Budgem, Ms. Travers and Mr. Ritt, your staff have treated us like royalty and after what we went through it is deeply appreciated.

"Ms. Sims and Mr. Barman, we want to commend you on the staff at this facility. We're sure they reflect your concerns and values and you do not know how safe that makes us feel. We are now, and always will be, in your debt. And please, as we speak here, I'm Charles and this is Lisa."

"I am honored you feel that way," Barman said. "Thank you Charles, for your praise. We do take pride in all of our businesses and our workers. They are our family and Rachel and I feel that everyone at this site did an exceptional job yesterday. Now before I say anything else, I know you both have many questions. Please, ask."

"Thank you," Charles said. "First, how long have we been gone?"

Barman spread his hands and said, "In our time frame, about twenty years."

CHAPTER SEVENTEEN
LIES AND TELLS

As Lisa dropped her head, Charles said, "Thank you." He paused and then continued, "Before any other questions, I would like to explain to you why we were gone." It took him over an hour to briefly describe what happened during their first jumps with Taggit and then the last time travel with Steve.

When he finished everyone was quiet then Barman said, "That's unbelievable. A terrible story to be sure but one of great personal perseverance on your parts."

"We were lucky," Charles said. "Lucky in so many ways. But I wanted you to understand that to us we've only been gone about a week this last time. There was no such place as this when we left. What is it?"

Barman nodded and replied, "Much of what I'm going to tell you will be a surprise I'm sure and some of it may not be pleasant news. But you need to know it and what RABAR plans to do about it.

"Rachel and I were limited partners of EXENCO. We knew Steve but not very well, he was distant and not a very social person. When he and his brother Ben disappeared, there was a lot of concern. The police began an investigation at his residence and we assisted by checking the records at EXENCO. At first there was nothing out of the ordinary, and then, well you can imagine what we found.

"Instead of reports and data about new energy sources, there was data on dinosaurs and impact and bite forces and people dying. There were orders for unusual equipment and the formation of a group called Walkers and then later the Team.

"In the warehouses we found items that shouldn't have been there. Guns, like the one you were carrying, bullets and something called a DOPE. There was a huge training area with dinosaur images, even a dinosaur holograph, a *Tyrannosaurus Rex*."

"It scared the hell out of me," Rachel said. "While I was walking through the training area it just appeared and it was so life-like. Then we found the real one, the one I guess that ate the team member. Fortunately, it was dead. It starved to death we think before we started looking into things. As you can guess, after that we had to know what was really going on at EXENCO because it obviously didn't have anything to do with energy."

"So, we bored down through every scrap of information we could find. No report, piece of data or memo was too insignificant. And slowly we got the picture though it took us a while to believe it. Time travel. Invented by you, Charles, and stolen by Steve. But you were gone too and I'm sorry to confirm it, but Steve did have your house and the other time machine destroyed."

"I believed him when he told me," Charles said. "So RABAR replaced EXENCO and took over time travel?"

"Yes. Some of what Steve, or perhaps more to the point, Otto was doing was actually ground breaking. The energy initiatives and safety for military personnel were very interesting and we hoped we could follow up on them, but we haven't been able to yet."

"Too many problems?" Charles asked.

"Way too many. All of the dinosaur protection and guns, bullets, those items, are great. But so far we have not been able to stop them from disintegrating within a few days. So, there is no way to make these items available at a reasonable cost and no one would want to purchase items that quickly turn to dust.

"The cheap energy claim had no merit past drilling for oil in the Cretaceous period. Windmills, ocean currents, river flow, all of it, just speculation and fantasy. All of it was just words to lure investors and unfortunately, it seems, your friends, into becoming part of EXENCO.

"The only real promise was in Otto's work. His updates to your ideas, DOPEs and weapons actually worked as seen with the time travel unit. Several of Otto's future ideas, which I guess now were to be completed after his return from getting rid of all of you, seemed astounding. Unfortunately, Otto didn't want anyone to know his secrets. When we accessed his files, they self-destructed.

"So, we were left with the only real ideas that worked. All your records were in Steve's database Charles. And we successfully used them to create time machines and added a new division to RABAR, one that focused on the benefits that time travel might provide. When we were ready, we went public and of course met with a lot of skepticism and ridicule. That soon changed to complete amazement and a public demand for it.

"The government immediately stepped in with rules and regulations, beneficial rules and regulations I might add. We also had employees that tried to steal the technology, so they could set up their own companies, but we stopped them all.

"To shorten a story that is already too long, the government granted us exclusive rights to time travel, we adhere to their rules and we supply the public with what they want."

"Which is?"

"Basically, time travel to prehistoric times only to obtain animals for zoos and study. Believe me when I say that keeps us busy enough and of course has made us a lot of money. We are a business after all."

"You can't be faulted for that," Charles said. "We knew that EXENCO was going to make money and they were going to pay us to help."

"Thank you for saying that, Charles," Rachel said. "And I think this is where I should let you know what we will be doing for you. Obviously, everything we have accomplished is thanks to you and your research. Unfortunately, all of your assets, home, work and money are gone. Stolen by Steve and then absorbed by us and various other institutions.

"First, we will pay you whatever you think we owe you for our use of your work. I hope you understand we weren't trying to steal it, we felt we had inherited it from EXENCO. We were thinking in the one-billion-dollar range, but you let us know. Next, we would be honored if you would become the spokesman for RABAR. We would include with that position several homes, private jet and a staff equal to your needs. Also, I'm sure the public will want to know your story. We would help you in any way necessary and publish any magazine articles, scientific papers or books that you would author. If any of this is not satisfactory or if I have left something out, please let me know."

Charles nodded and replied, "I am stunned and encouraged by your generous offer. When you confirmed what had happened to everything I ever owned just now I was concerned about my prospects.

"I would like to ask for RABAR to consider one other action. Many people died that didn't need to. Ron and Lauren, the Team members, Aria and Tony and people I never met, the original Walkers. Would it be possible to take some of the money you have offered me and give it to their families? When this news gets out they won't have any chance of litigation to get compensation, Steve is gone, and his company dissolved. Unless, that is, you have already done it."

Barman shook his head slowly for a few seconds, then said, "Charles, I'm ashamed to say we never even thought about it. The first few years we were wrapped up in figuring things out, after that was manufacturing and making things public, and then the business grew astronomically, and we had to meet all the restrictions that were placed on us. And we built Dino City.

"I can only plead we were busy and that's not good enough. Even after we knew who had been involved we have obviously dropped the ball. We will make due compensation to family members as soon as possible out of our pocket, not yours."

"Thank you."

"Charles, I hope you don't mind," Barman said, "if I ask you and Lisa a…well, a personal question."

"Not at all, sir."

"Please, I'm Jack. My question is about your wife, Lauren and Lisa, your husband, Ron. If you could, would you go back and save them if it were possible? Maybe save everyone?"

"I do not want to speak for Lisa," Charles said, "but I will tell you what I think. If you go that route, changing the timeline, you run the risk of changing time in ways that can't be understood. Lauren was vehemently opposed to time travel but I'm not. We argued about it constantly. We had already separated before we became involved with Steve and Lisa was never married to Ron. We were all still friendly, and my house was big enough for all of us, but Lisa and I are actually together now, we have been for some time, and I don't need to save her.

"I would not risk changing the timeline for anyone or anything. I'm sure that was a big discussion with other people when you went public. It can't be done. I never went back to save Pete, Marilyn, Mitch or Jimmy. I won't go back now. Do I want to jump again? Yes, I do, and I will. But not to change the timeline."

Charles turned to Lisa and she started slowly, "I wish I could go back and save Ron. We were still friends, but we had recognized that he was a field person. He always wanted to work, and I was…not a party person, I don't like parties that much, but more of a 'let's go do something fun' person. I wish I could save Lauren and maybe save everyone else too. But I was around Lauren and Ron enough to know not to disturb the timeline. No matter what you do, you affect things. And this was the second time something has happened. Personally, I'm never jumping again."

As Lisa dropped her head and wiped her eyes, Barman said, "I'm sorry. I shouldn't have brought it up now. Perhaps we should meet again in a few days, after you are released by Doctor Blacke and things start to settle down."

"Dr. Blacke has told us we are free to leave tomorrow," Charles told him. "So, we can meet whenever you like. I do have one question for you and then maybe I can address something you said earlier."

"Go on."

"Every time we have gotten involved with someone, two things have caused problems; money and safety. It doesn't appear that money is an issue with you so tell me about your safety record."

"We had our share of accidents when we first started. We learned, and it slowly has gotten better. I can't think of any recent accidents, but I can get you all of the records if that will help."

"What happened with the *Stegosaurus* and the *Rex*? Was that an accident?"

"I'm not sure I know what you're talking about."

"There was a *Stegosaurus* skeleton in the *Rex* area. I wouldn't think you would feed the *Stegosaurus* to the *Rex*, too much of a possibility the *Rex* would get injured, so I just wondered if it accidentally got in there and was killed."

"Oh, I understand," Barman said. "Ray, didn't the *Rex* area used to be a *Stegosaurus* pen?"

"Yes, yes, yes it did," Budgem agreed. "There could be a *Stegosaurus* skeleton still out there. Thanks for letting us know, I'll look into it first thing."

Charles started nodding his head and then said, "Okay, that's all I needed to hear. Mr. Barman, I mean Jack and Rachel, I'm on board. I'm not sure what I can do for you as a spokesman, but I am interested in publishing several scientific articles now that time travel is known."

As Barman stood up, so did everyone else. He quickly walked to Charles and Lisa and shook their hands and said, "This is a great day for RABAR, a monumental day. We'll get all the details ironed out in a few days." He turned to Dr. Blacke and asked, "They will be released tomorrow?"

"They will be."

"Then we'll fly both of you to corporate headquarters tomorrow afternoon for a huge press conference. Will you be up for it?"

"I think so," Charles said. "We are still getting over our injuries though."

"A short press conference then. We'll see you both tomorrow."

As everyone walked from the room, Dr. Blacke called out, "I want to see you both in the Medical Building in a couple of hours, okay? I'm going to try and detail what you can do and how much rest you should get over the next few days. And medicine," she laughed, "lots of medicine."

When they got back to their rooms they found they had been moved. "Sorry for the bother," an orderly said. "If we had known you were a couple we would have put you in the same room when you came in." They took an elevator up to the top floor and it opened into a spacious living room that was filled with flowers. "This is our VIP quarters," he told them. "After I leave, visitors must contact you on the intercom to be let up. Then just press this button. If you don't have any questions I'll let you get acquainted with your new rooms."

"How do we get back up?"

"The elevator will recognize you both."

As soon as he left, Lisa hugged Charles close and whispered, "I need to rest. We'll talk later."

"I'm tired too," Charles said aloud. "Let's find the bed and take a nap."

They quickly found the king-size bed and fell asleep.

"That went well I thought," Barman said.

"It did," Rachel agreed. "And you only touched on the 'O' word."

"If they aren't thinking about it then neither are we," Barman laughed.

"I was surprised we didn't have information that they were a couple."

Barman picked up a report and said, "It says here they've been holding hands and he visited her last night and she went in to see him first thing this morning. I get it. What did you think of them?"

"What I expected. He's the science guy, all business, and she's a bit of fluff. I don't see this romance working out for very long either."

Barman laughed, "You're always so cynical."

Rachel laughed too and replied, "It's why we have so much money. What's next?"

"I'm going to make some calls and get the press conference set up. This will be huge. Oh, and I'm going to make sure Budgem keeps a lid on outside communication a while longer."

"That won't make the workers happy."

"Triple time will."

"You're getting generous in your old age."

"Tomorrow, with all of the publicity, our stock will quadruple."

"That's what I like to hear."

"And I need to think about a new head of Security. Richards almost dropped the ball."

"He came through," Rachel pointed out, "and he does do what you tell him. He keeps us up to date on what really happens around here."

"Maybe, but the cleaning crew could probably do that," Barman snorted. "Anyway, one more night here in the slums and tomorrow morning we'll be making news all over the world."

"We've fooled presidents and generals for years. It will be just one more time," Rachel said confidently.

Chief Richards called Officer Jenson into his office and said, "I know the brass thinks that Dawson is being level with them, but I don't. I didn't buy anything he was saying."

"Why not? I thought he sounded sincere."

"He *sounded* sincere, but he wasn't. Something is wrong with all of this."

"What?"

"I can't put my finger on it yet but for one thing, how did they get into the *Rex* pen without setting off an alarm? They only set off the alarm when they came out of it."

"Some type of dampening device?"

"No, at least not on them when we stopped them. And why were they there? Where were they walking to? Why would they have had a dampening device? I've been asking for cameras all the way around that pen for years, but I've had to put up drones and alarms instead. We don't even know where they got in at. We might have a breach in the fence and not even know it."

"Do you want me to go look?"

"No, and something else. I think you connected with them a little yesterday, maybe enough to just drop by and talk to them. And to fix the bug you put in Dawson's clothes."

"Do we have any bugs that actually work?" she asked. "This is frustrating."

"Listen, if I can pop Dawson trying to go back and save his wife, I'll save RABAR a lot of money. A lot. Mr. *Rex* can eat the mistake if you get what I mean, and I'll get a promotion out of it for sure. And a raise. And more money for the Security Department."

"And a raise for me?"

"I'll need a new Chief won't I?"

Jenson smiled as she said, "I'm on it, Chief."

"Good. I'm putting Security on alert until they are gone. I expect *something* from those two."

"Well, they've been in the *Tyrannosaurus* pen, so something else? Are they going to steal a machine?"

"That's not a bad idea, Jenson, not bad at all. To go back in time and save their group they will need one. I'll triple the guards on the machines."

"I'm off to be engaging," Jenson said as she left.

Lisa woke up and found that Charles was already up. "Did you actually sleep any?" she asked when she found him sitting in the kitchen.

"Yes, a little, but my mind is racing. First all the bad luck of the jumps and then the good luck provided by RABAR. Couldn't sleep after that."

"Sounds like you need to take a walk," Lisa suggested.

"Sounds great," Charles replied. They took the elevator and were quickly outside. As soon as they were far enough away from the building, and Lisa had yawned again, Charles asked, "What did you see?"

"At first there was nothing, and I mean nothing. I thought they were either telling the truth or they were the best liars ever because I couldn't read anything. Then you brought up the *Stegosaurus*. I wondered why you asked me about it, but it really worked. Jack changed completely for a few seconds, could have just been he just didn't really think you would ask a question and he was caught off guard."

"But?" Charles asked.

"But Security Chief Richards just about fell out of his chair when Jack asked him about it. But you know, it could have been he just didn't think he was going to be asked to say anything in such an important meeting."

"But?"

"But Jenson sealed the deal. As soon as you brought it up she took a deep breath in and just stared straight ahead. She didn't blink, she didn't move. Then she slowly sat back in her chair like she was trying to distance herself from everything. She stayed that way for several minutes before she began trying to act normal again."

"What do you think?"

Lisa told him, "I think the *Stegosaurus* got in the pen by accident and that people were probably hurt or killed. So, if they are hiding safety facts I think they are hiding the one thing that barley got a mention."

"The oil."

"They want us to think that part went away but it didn't. They offered you a billion dollars. I just can't imagine they have that kind of money from selling dinosaurs to zoos and running dinosaur camps. They want you to work for them where they can watch you and control you. Although you are just a scientist and you just want to make jumps and write papers."

"Liked that part did you?"

"You sounded the part. I think you sold it," Lisa said.

"Hope I didn't surprise you too much about Lauren and Ron. I guess I made it sound like we didn't care for them that much."

"I had decided you might go that way but still, I couldn't breathe for a few seconds. But then I reminded myself that you're going to make things right. You are going to change things."

"I am," Charles agreed. "I am."

"Because you didn't bring up one thing either," Lisa pointed out.

"You mean my time machine that will be waiting for us in the *Rex* pen?"

"You got it. So, what's next?"

"Well, we can't leave with them tomorrow. Who knows where the time machine would be trying to appear in the twenty years in the future time period?"

"So, it has to be tonight."

"Yes. I'm unsure what to do though. We have to get into the *Rex* pen and then stay alive long enough to get to the time machine."

"No," Lisa said as she shook her head. "You have to stay alive long enough to do all of that. I can be part of whatever diversion we can think of."

"We'll see," Charles replied.

"Let's change the subject, there's Officer Jenson coming our way."

"Officer Jenson, how are you?" Lisa asked.

"Now by the time I got you out of Med yesterday you were both calling me Sharon, remember? Maybe not."

Lisa replied, "I know I don't remember."

Charles shrugged his shoulders and added, "Sorry, I don't either."

"Well you do remember the fifty dollars I loaned you, right?"

Lisa and Charles looked at each other and smiled as Lisa said, "Sorry Sharon, we'll remember you from now on though."

Sharon laughed and told Lisa, "Hold still for just a second, you have something on your collar." She pulled on something and then brushed Lisa's shirt and told her, "Something was stuck to your shirt, I think I got all of it off."

"Thanks. We were just getting ready to eat; would you like to join us?"

"Actually, Doc asked me to point you in her direction for one last inspection and to give you the meds she promised. I'll walk that way with you though."

"Thanks," Charles said. "Because I doubt if we remember where the Med Unit is." They continued making small talk until they arrived at a building marked Medical Center. "It's nice and cool in here," Charles noted as they walked in.

"Too cool for me," Sharon said. "But I don't spend a lot of time in here. This way to the Doc's office."

They walked down a hall and then through an unmarked door. Doctor Blacke looked up from her desk and said, "Sharon, I see you found them."

"I took care of everything," she replied.

"Great. Charles, Lisa, pull up a couple of chairs and I don't think this will take very long." As she examined them she asked, "Well, did you find the meeting exciting? I mean, a *billion* dollars. Wow."

"It is overwhelming," Charles replied. "I mean, it's unreal. I can't comprehend having a billion dollars. I might actually settle for less."

"Don't do that," Sharon said. "The Doc and I would be happy to help you spend it. Right Doc?"

Doctor Blacke smiled and said, "You need to take the money Charles. You lost everything, and they took everything you would have had. They owe it to you. Plus, I doubt if Sharon will be the last one to try and weasel money away from you."

"Weasel?" Sharon laughed. "They already owe me fifty dollars."

Doctor Blacke shook her head and told them, "You have to look out for Sharon." Then she asked them both, "How do you feel?"

"I feel fine," Charles replied.

"I do too," Lisa agreed.

"Great," Dr. Blacke said. "There are no problems with you. Well, other than you lied during the meeting today. And I guess since Charles did most of the talking he was the one that was lying, and you were just backing him up."

Lisa looked at Charles then asked, "What do you mean?"

"Have you ever been told you talk in your sleep?"

"Uh, yes."

"When you were under the anesthetic you talked. And you never mention Charles. It was always Ron or Ronnie. Never Charles."

"I'm sure she just - " Charles started.

Doctor Blacke held up her hand and said, "You don't have to explain. We just need to know what it is you are going to try to do."

"I don't know what you mean," Charles told her.

"Are you going back to rescue them?"

Charles shook his head and emphatically said, "No."

Sharon sat down and said quietly, "We thought you were."

Lisa looked at Charles for several seconds until he slowly nodded his head. Then she said, "We're going back to stop all time travel."

"How?" Doctor Blacke asked.

Charles paused then said, "I'm going to have a conversation with myself."

"We didn't see that coming," Sharon said.

Doctor Blacke smiled and told them, "Even better. Then you're going to need our help. Chief Richards didn't believe you today. He is making plans right now to stop your attempt."

"And I thought I did such a good job," Charles said.

"I did too," Sharon said. "But the Chief, well he is good at what he does. He's adamant that you're going to steal a time machine and go back."

"You'll need a diversion and help getting into buildings without setting off alarms," Dr. Blacke told them. "And as soon as you steal a time machine they'll know it and track you."

"We're not stealing a time machine," Charles said. "We have one waiting for us already."

Sharon smiled and said, "In the *Rex* pen. Of course, that's why you weren't detected getting into the pen. You were already inside of it."

'Okay," Doctor Blacke said. "That does change things but once they know you have traveled they will just wait for you somewhere. They'll know to watch the EXENCO site or...or your house. As soon as you are within scanner range they'll get you."

"Scanner range?"

Sharon walked over to Lisa and took some of her shirt material between her thumb and finger and said, "This is special. It's like time DNA fabric. When it goes to a different time period it can be tracked. It's just one of the ways that people are watched when they travel. There are a lot of others, too many to go over, but you'll need to change your clothes before you go."

"At the very least she'll need to leave the bug behind," Doctor Blacke said.

"Bug?" Lisa asked.

Sharon tapped Lisa's shirt collar and said, "I turned it off when we met. Remember?"

Charles shook his head and said, "We've been talking about things. If we've been listened to then there's already no way this will work."

"Don't worry," Sharon smiled. "I used a bug that speaks static and likes to shut off. Now when I turn it back on it will work fine for fifteen minutes and then it will malfunction again. Drives the Chief crazy."

Doctor Blacke looked at her watch and advised, "We can't be in here much longer. Tell us your basic plan and then we'll meet you for dinner in the main dining room. Sharon, keep the bug working until we meet in a few hours so there is nothing to bother the Chief and make him want to replace it."

"Got it."

"Well now that we have help, I do have a plan," Charles said. "Simply, it is this. Tonight, we need to go into the *Rex* pen. If the *Rex* is not there that would help the plan a lot. If there is something happening on the other side of this complex, say a fire or something like that, that would help too. Before we crawl under the fence the alarms need to be shut off. That's it. Sound simple?"

Sharon nodded her head and said, "Actually, it does. I'll tell you more at six, does that work for dinner?"

"It does," Charles said.

"Okay, Lisa hold still while I adjust this and then go along with what I'm saying," Sharon said. Then she laughed and said, "But it's a billion dollars Charles, I just need new shoes."

Lisa laughed too and Doctor Blacke said, "You need to be careful Charles, Sharon needs a lot of shoes."

Then Sharon asked, "Would all of you like to meet in the Dining Hall, say about six?"

As everyone agreed, Charles and Lisa walked outside and Charles asked, "Want to keep walking? I'd like to tour the facility some more and see if we can watch any of the animals."

"Okay," Lisa answered. "But I'm interested in where we'll live. I'd like to rebuild your old house. What do you think of that?"

He took her arm and said, "I'd like that."

Sharon called Chief Richards and said, "It should be coming in clear now."

"It is, good work. What did you think?"

"We didn't get to talk a lot, we walked over to the Doc's, so she could check them out before they left. We're supposed to meet them for dinner tonight and we'll talk some more. So far though I can't say I'm picking up anything."

"Did they ask about anything?"

"Charles asked what animals were here and where different things happened."

"Where we kept the time machines?"

"He asked about a few things and I guess…Chief you are smart. He could have figured things out by what I was telling him even if I didn't mention time machines."

"Don't beat yourself up Jenson, I've been doing this for a long time. I know where he'll be tonight. Call me after dinner."

"Will do," Sharon said as she left.

Richards leaned over and turned up the volume on Lisa's bug and listened to them talk about building a house for a few seconds then turned it off. Then he turned the volume back on for a station marked ED1 just in time to hear Sharon walk into Doctor Blacke's office and say, "He bought it."

Then he turned ED1 off and thought how smart he was to have bugged a lot of different places around Dino City. He knew a lot of things about people and after tonight he was going to cash everything in. And he knew where he wanted to live, and it wasn't around a bunch of dinosaurs. He got on his phone and said, "Cesar, get over to my office right now. No, I don't want you to get Jenson. I said get over here now, and don't tell anyone else. Got it? Now."

CHAPTER EIGHTEEN
THE END

Chief Richards stood in front of the room as the thirty security officers filed in and sat down. They were surprised by the sudden call-out and what it might mean. As soon as they were all in, Richards brought up a map of Dino City and began speaking.

"First, nothing that is discussed leaves this room until I say you can talk about it. Anyone who disobeys this order will be fired and you can bet you will never hold a job that's worth anything ever again. Is there anyone who doesn't understand what I just said?"

When no one answered he continued, "As you know, we have special guests in Dino City; Charles Dawson and Lisa Wells. They had some bad time travel experiences, Charles lost his wife and they both lost a lot of friends. Something like that will make you rethink what you could or should do with time travel.

"Tonight, at a time we do not know yet, we think Charles and Lisa plan on stealing a time machine. We believe they are going to go back and save at least a few people and maybe even everyone that was involved. Over two dozen people. It has to be tonight because they are scheduled to leave here tomorrow morning.

"You all know what that would do to the timeline. Irreparable changes of a global nature. The largest catastrophe in our time travel history. Who knows where any of us would end up and what we would be doing. That's if we were still alive. So, no matter how noble their thoughts and concerns are, we can't let this happen.

"Now we cannot just accuse them of something this big. We need proof, the overt act. So, we'll be disabling the time machines and waiting for them to get in one and attempt the theft. I don't know if they will attempt to shut off alarms, talk their way in because of who they are, stage a traffic accident, it could be anything. Whatever it is they try just let them succeed at it. Then we'll move in and take them into custody when they try and use a time machine.

"The public doesn't even know they have returned yet. I can guarantee the average person will sympathize with them. Their remorse about all the deaths, that somehow they survived, typical psychological trauma that led to the attempted theft. Others can judge them.

"We will be judged by how we handle this tonight so let's do it right. No one gets hurt. None of us, and especially neither of them."

"So, no one will have a live weapon. No one. If one of them gets antsy then we can stun them, but that's all. We do not want the public to learn that the person who invented time travel came back from the dead and we killed him."

Richards walked over and stood by Sharon and continued, "Officer Jenson has gained their trust and is getting ready to have dinner with them in just a few minutes. She'll bring back whatever intel she can get from that and we'll set up accordingly.

"Right now, Officer Cesar will brief everyone on where they will be stationed. We'll be heavy and hidden by the RABAR Travel building. Some of you will respond to all other types of calls just like usual."

Richards paused and then said, "I really hope nothing happens tonight. I hope they are not planning what I feel they are and if that's the case, well you earned some OT for just standing around. If it does happen though we will have stopped the biggest time travel problem ever. And that will be something for all of us to be proud of.

"Jenson, head out and report back as soon as you can. Officer Cesar, please begin your briefing."

Sharon stopped behind Lisa, turned the bug under her collar to static, then sat down next to Doctor Blacke. She smiled as she said, "They are sure you are going to steal a time machine. The Chief is moving everyone up to RABAR Travel, so they are ready to grab you as soon as you step inside one. I'm not sure you'll even need a distraction though he thinks it might be a car accident or something."

"That would work," Doctor Blacke said. "Maybe a car rolling out of a parking stall would make them think they were on the right track. They would really be watching for you at the Travel Building then."

Charles shook his head and said, "No, we need a distraction that helps Lisa and me and also creates as much confusion as possible."

"What were you thinking of?"

"Can we release all of the animals?"

Doctor Blacke sat back in her chair as if she had been slapped. "What?" she asked.

Charles leaned in and asked her, "Why do you want me to end time travel?"

"Because it's dangerous. Sooner or later something bad is going to happen. I know there are laws and restrictions, but mankind has been ignoring them for the last three years. I don't know what exactly, but at some point time travel will end up hurting all of us more than helping."

"And you?" he asked, turning to Sharon.

"We weren't meant to time travel. We should just live our lives and that's it. Learn from the past, but don't actually go and relive it."

"So, we are all agreed that time travel has to stop. Not because some vague *something* will happen, but because it already has. Many, many times. Time travel is more desirable than gold, it's an unbelievable treasure it seems. An invisible wealth that tears some of us apart and brings out the very worst in us.

"Think of Ray Taggit, Steve Weston and now Jack Barman and Rachel Sims. All of these people have connected death to time travel. It made them wealthy and made them feel powerful. They literally held the fate of mankind in their hands. And it will just keep going. There will always be another one of them. Always. And that means there will always be innocent people killed by greed."

"Or until one of them does something so stupid they tear the world apart," Dr. Blacke said.

Charles nodded, "You're right. So, I don't want a car accident or someone falling down some stairs for a distraction. I want the worst thing possible. Complete and utter confusion and disbelief. We need to release the '*saurs*."

"And, there is another reason," Lisa said.

"What's that?" Charles asked.

"We don't want the *Rex* in the pen when we go in."

Charles nodded as he said, "Yeah, that too."

Sharon was quiet then finally she said, "I can get all the gates open, but I'm not sure what team I'm on so I don't know where I'm being placed. Chief Richards, myself and Officer Cesar are the only ones who have the codes. If I can be in Command I can open the gates by entering the right codes and no one will notice. If I'm not, I'll have to enter them with my handheld and the Chief would see that." She paused then said, "If this doesn't go right, I'll go to prison."

"We all will," Lisa said.

"Chief doesn't think so," Sharon aid. "Too much public sympathy for you."

"That might be right," Charles said. "Still, we could - "

"No, you couldn't," Sharon stopped him. "If you spoke out for me it would turn everyone against you and who knows what would happen."

"Then I guess we can't fail," Lisa said.

"Be by the *Rex* pen no later than 2300, 11:00pm, tonight."

"I was thinking later," Charles said.

"How will you explain walking around at three in the morning? Do you know where the *Rex* pen is?"

"We found it earlier today."

"Then go for a walk and get as close to the runoff under the fence as you can. I'll be watching for you, so it won't matter when you go. When the front gate opens up and the *Rex* comes out, go and don't look back."

"What about other animals wandering into the *Rex* pen after its outside?"

"I've never seen anything just wander into the *Rex* pen whether it was there or not. And for your information you were right about the *Stegosaurus*. It was an accident. It got in with the *Rex* and three people died trying to get it out before they decided to just kill it."

"It's funny," Charles said. "Everyone at that meeting was lying."

"Some would say business as usual," Doctor Blacke said.

Sharon tapped the package she had brought and said, "Here are a few things I brought each of you. A night vision scope and some clothes that can't be time traced. If they set up on an area they expect you to be in, an old site or even your house, they won't know you are there by your clothing. You can sneak up on yourself and have your conversation. I have to say I'd like to be there for that."

"It will be interesting," Charles replied. "But I'm sure I can do it."

"Well, we've got about three and a half hours," Lisa announced. "Will the bug be working again?"

"No, I'm not going to fix it again. And…and hopefully I won't see you again. Good luck."

"Thank you," Charles and Lisa said, then they went back to their room.

As Sharon walked into the Security Building, Chief Richards called out, "Over here, Jenson. You're in Command tonight." She couldn't believe her luck as the Chief added, "We have all the security teams around the RABAR Building just like you suggested. Let's go over things in my office."

As she walked in and the door closed though the Chief suddenly spun her around and pinned her against the wall. "What are you doing?" she asked as he forced her hands behind her and handcuffed her.

"I know what you're up to. You and Charles and Lisa along with the doctor," he explained. "Take a look at the screens." She looked up and saw every security officer's electronic team I.D. was gathered around the RABAR Building. "Just like everyone knows you asked. All the teams are there.

"You see, I was listening to your earlier conversation with Charles, Lisa and the doctor. I bet that's a surprise isn't it? I'm going to be at the *Rex* pen waiting for them to show up. Once their time machine appears

I'm going to jam it, and what happens to it, will be my little secret. Then it's too bad."

"What do you mean?"

"Well whatever you and the doctor planned during dinner for the *Rex*, tranquilizer or something, well that's off already. The doctor is asleep in my vehicle. And of course, you'll be along for the ride too. Then what can I say? Apparently the four of you, in a very misguided attempt, tried to sneak into the *Rex* pen before Charles and Lisa stole a time machine. You were going to kill it for your time travel hating friends. Not a good idea though to try and sneak into the pen of a live *Tyrannosaurus Rex*.

"When it comes out that it was you who convinced me that Charles and Lisa were going to steal a time machine just to get me to move all my officers to the Travel Building, well, you aren't going to look too good in the media. Neither will the doctor. I'm sure there will be some sympathy for Charles and Lisa when it appears that you sunk your hooks into them as soon as they arrived and tricked them into helping you. Such is life."

He looked down at her and asked, "Nothing to say?" Then he roughly stood her up and said, "You know, I've wanted to do this all day." Then he punched her in the head and as she collapsed he caught her, threw her over his shoulder and carried her out the back door and down to his van. He opened up the back and tossed her in beside Doctor Blacke, then he laughed and went back inside.

"After you speak to yourself, what are we going to do?" Lisa asked.

"Well, as long as I do what I want me to do, and I don't have to kill me - "

"Please don't do that," Lisa asked.

"Just kidding," Charles said and then added, "I hope." He thought for a few seconds then continued, "Maybe we can stay in the house until I, meaning he, destroys the machine. We'll have to stay out of sight and not interact with anyone. We'll have to figure it out as we go. It won't be easy."

Lisa nodded and was quiet then she asked, "Can we go now?"

"It's still early."

"I know, but after tonight it's probable we'll just be inside of your house...his house. I know we won't be able to go anywhere or see anyone but...but right now that's too much to deal with."

"What do you think we should do?"

"I don't know. I want to have one last talk with Ron, but I know it can't really happen." As the room grew silent she smiled and said, "This isn't what I want to get into right now. Let's keep to the plan and be ready to go. We'll know what to do when the time comes."

They quickly changed clothes and Lisa asked, "I see you have your boots on and you are carrying Danny's. Do you expect a problem? Are we going to have to jump with them again?"

"I try to expect everything and yes there is a chance we'll have to use them again. Something could go wrong. But if everything goes right…well, I still think they might get used."

"How?"

"I'll tell you later," Charles said with a smile. Then they began walking around the courtyard and started toward the *Rex* pen.

Officer Cesar called Richards and said, "Chief, they are walking around right now and just headed west."

Richards smiled and replied, "Okay, they might be arranging a diversion in that area before starting toward you. I'm going to stay close to them and see if I can tell what they are planning. They will probably start your way soon so get everyone alerted and in place."

He cut Officer Cesar off before he answered and smiled, everything was going as planned. He walked to his van and as he started it up he heard a groan from behind him. "Are we starting to wake up?" he asked. A few minutes later he stopped the van near the *Rex* pen runoff and called back, "Don't worry, you'll have a front row seat soon enough. I'm going to see what our guests are up to."

Sharon was wide awake now and though her head was painful she remembered everything Richards had said. She elbowed Doctor Blacke and hissed, "Doc, Doc, wake up."

"What?"

"Wake up. The Chief is going to feed us to the *Rex*."

Doctor Blacke sat straight up and then almost fell over. "Feed us to…what?"

"He knows everything and he's going to get rid of me, you, Lisa and Charles."

"No."

"Yes. Are you handcuffed with your hands behind you?"

"Yes."

"Okay, roll over and spoon backwards up against me. You know the little pocket at the top of the right front pants pocket?"

"Yes, I know what you mean."

"Okay. That's where I keep one of my spare handcuff keys. Let me know when you have it and I will turn over and scoot up to you and take it from you. Don't try and hand it to me, okay? I'll roll over and take it from you."

"Okay," Doctor Blacke replied and after a few seconds of feeling in the pocket she said, "I have it." As Sharon rolled over and moved to take the key, the doctor asked, "Should I try and unlock your handcuffs?"

"No, just give me the key and I'll take care of it. I've practiced this many times."

As Doctor Blacke felt Sharon take the key, she said, "That's not something I ever would have thought of."

Sharon sat up with one cuff dangling from a wrist and quickly unlocked the other one. "Fortunately, I have," she said as she then took the handcuffs off of Doctor Blacke. Then she said, "He's back, be quiet."

Chief Richards watched as Charles and Lisa walked along the path that led to the *Rex* pen. Everything was looking good and since they were here early he might as well get it over with. As they stopped by the fence he pulled Sharon's scanner out of his pocket and using her code he turned off the *Rex* alarm and opened its gate.

Then he checked her scanner for the animal and saw it was still on the far side of the pen and not moving. As Charles and Lisa entered the runoff Richards smiled, things were going just like he thought they would. He turned and started back to the van.

As they ducked under the fence, Lisa whispered, "Where are the alarms?"

Charles thought for a moment and replied, "Maybe Sharon had to do things in a different order. Or maybe we're too early."

"Maybe, but it's too quiet."

The night vision scopes allowed them to move quickly through the ravine back to the point where they had first jumped into it. Charles slowly climbed to the top of the ravine and cautiously looked around, still nothing. Lisa climbed up beside him and they slowly moved out into the open area of the pen. They were within a few feet of where the time machine would appear when suddenly somewhere back behind them a car horn started honking.

"Let's go," Charles said as he took a few steps forward. Then they heard a 'whuff' and the heavy steps...and the *Rex* just appeared. They whirled around and ran back toward the ravine and the heavy steps followed.

Then Lisa shouted, "You have to live," and pushed Charles into the ravine as she turned to the right and ran toward the gate. The *Rex* paused, confused for a few seconds, then began moving after Lisa. She found it hard to run as she held the night vision scope in front of an eye, but she couldn't drop it without possibly missing a step and falling into the ravine. If that happened the *Rex* might still be able to stop Charles from getting to the time machine.

Then the alarms started blaring and the pen blazed with light. She threw down the night vision and ran as fast as she could. She remembered Ron telling her that a *Rex* ran at about twelve miles an hour and that a fast sprinting person could outrun one...over a short distance. She saw the gate ahead and ran even faster.

As Chief Richards opened the driver's side door of the van and leaned in he saw the movement and was just able to get his arm up in time to stop the boot to his head. The force of the kick still knocked him into the front door post and he fell back onto the ground. But he had been in fights before and he was back on his feet before Sharon was out the door. He pushed her back inside the van and tried to punch her again but there was not enough room to hit her very hard. He started slamming her into the steering wheel and then he laid her on it as he tried to strangle her. He could hear the horn honking and hoped everyone would think it was part of the planned diversion.

Then it felt like his head had exploded and he was flying back out of the van again. Sharon fell out too and landed on her knees. On the ground in front of her she recognized her scanner and as she picked it up Doctor Blacke jumped over her and began hitting Richards with a tire iron. Sharon punched in the code for the alarms and gates and suddenly everything was lit up and loud.

She turned just in time to see Richards roll away from the doctor and draw his semiautomatic, not the stun gun he said everyone was supposed to carry. Sharon tried to warn Doctor Blacke as she ran toward Richards, but he fired twice before she could say anything and Doctor Blacke dropped to the ground.

But Sharon didn't stop, she jumped straight into his right leg with both feet and hit his wrist with her arm. He dropped the gun as he yelled in pain and fell down. Sharon started to go in after him again when she saw Lisa run through the gate and when she saw what was behind her, she turned and ran with Lisa as she streaked past them.

"You can't outrun a bullet," Richards shouted as he stumbled toward his gun. Then a large shadow fell across him and he heard the heavy breathing. He turned slowly and instinctively brought up a hand to block the glare of the lights. He saw the teeth and turned to run. As they heard the screaming from behind them, Lisa and Sharon ran into the wooded area and knelt down and hid in the shadows.

Charles climbed out of the ravine and started after Lisa, then he stopped. She knew what she was doing, and he knew what he had to do. He checked his watch and it guided him to the time machine site. He activated the beacon and in a few seconds it arrived. He stepped in and paused for a moment as he looked in the direction Lisa had run. There was nothing there. He closed the door and pressed the button.

Charles was sure no one knew about the condos, so no one knew about the ranch house that the condos would replace in a few years. He was in it now. Still, he paused by the windows and watched for a few minutes. He checked his watch, it was about two in the morning. One day before it happened. Then he walked to the garage, lifted the keys off the hook, backed out and drove into the night. There was no one following him. He opened the sun roof and, using the night vision, checked overhead. No drones.

Charles took the long way around and stopped in a drive that ran into a field about a mile from his house. In the future it would be a fashionable gated community but now it was just waiting to be planted with crops. He stayed in the field and away from the road until he was about three hundred yards away from his house. Then he quietly walked through some thick brush he had planted to what looked like a drain pipe. He moved the pipe out of the way and exposed an opening that he quickly crawled into and then closed the pipe behind him. The small opening gave way to a large tunnel which lit up with a flick of a switch and Charles moved quickly along the passage to the entrance in the basement of his house.

He walked into his study and stayed there for a long while writing and then he went upstairs.

As he slowly woke up he had the feeling something wasn't right. In fact, something felt very wrong. He sat up in his bed and peered around the room. It was night or early morning, so it was still dark. It took him a few seconds to realize it was too dark, there was no light at all. He wondered if there had been a power outage as he tried to turn the lamp on. Nothing.

He had just decided there wasn't much he could do about it and he should just go back to sleep when a voice spoke out of the darkness, "I disabled the electrical system for this part of the house." He started and shrunk back against the bed's wooden headboard, staring in the direction the voice had come from. After a few seconds the voice asked, "Do you have any questions, Charles?"

"Who are you and how do you know my name?"

"That's two questions and they will be answered in a few minutes. Try again."

"How did you disable the electrical system for this part of the house? In fact, for any part of the house. I – "

"You," the voice cut in, "are the only one who can disable anything in this house, or control anything, period. Yes, I know. Again, you started to ask two questions. They will also be answered in a few minutes when I allow the lights to come back on. Try again."

"Okay, let me think for a second," he said as he slowly scooted to his left across the bed. "Let me see if – "

He was cut short again, this time by quiet laughter. Then the voice continued, "Do you think I can't see you?" There was a tapping sound and the voice continued, "I have the baseball bat and what were you going to swing it at?"

"Now you're asking two questions."

The voice laughed again and replied, "That's better. I'm not here to play twenty questions, I need to know if we can talk, if you are as smart as I remember. Ask me another question."

Charles was silent then asked, "Why are you here?"

"That's a good question. I'm here because of your work in – "

"I thought you were going to turn the lights on."

"Patience, Charles, patience. I need to explain a few things then I will turn on the lights. Okay?"

"Okay."

"Now then, you are working on a way to travel through time. You're close, you can feel it. Several things have gone right for you recently, but something is still missing. Something elusive, vague, but you know it's there. But that's okay because you only sleep for four or five hours each night and you *know* it's just a matter of time before you figure out what is wrong. You feel it in your bones."

"You're insane. No one can - "

"So, your every waking hour is consumed with searching, testing, thinking, cursing, throwing one idea out as another takes its place. There are sudden periods of elation when you think you have the answer followed by ever deepening periods of despair and frustration when you realize that once again you are wrong, and you are no closer to time travel now than you were when you first started. But no matter how many times you fail, there is still that spark, no a fire now, that burns within you driving you on. You don't know why, but it's there. You will keep searching until you find the answer."

Charles ran a hand through his hair and said, "Let's say you're right. That I am obsessed with time travel and I do think I am close to finding an answer. What does that have to do with you? Are you here to help?" A sudden thought came to Charles, "Do you time travel?"

"I do."

Charles tensed his fists tight with white knuckles. "Are you here to help?"

"No, I'm here to explain why you have to stop."

"Stop?" Charles asked angrily. "Am I stepping on your toes? Are you the only one who should be allowed to travel? Why should I stop?"

"Because you are going to succeed, Charles. Not through diligence and brilliance like you envision, but through the benevolence of chance. Tomorrow there will be an accident in your lab. At first it will seem like a complete catastrophe but then you will realize its significance. Within a week you will be sending items through time and then one day it will be you that steps through to the other side. Sounds exciting, doesn't it?"

"And yet you're telling me to stop?"

"Yes. Because with all of your success will come more pain and suffering than you can possibly know. Because of you, people will die in horrible ways that will keep you from sleeping at night. In the end, you will gain nothing and lose everything, including friends you don't know yet. You will be the catalyst for the greatest event in world history and you will pay for it dearly. You will wish you were dead until you realize you already are."

"How do you know these things? Are you one of these *new friends*?"

The voice said coldly, "No, Charles, because I'm you." Then the lights suddenly came back on and Charles stared in disbelief at the man sitting just a few feet from him.

"How – "

"I know, it seems impossible. But I'm only twenty years older than you, that is, we, are now. So, you can see that I am you. But I have to admit being reminded of how young I used to be made me pause. The joy of youth, I see it in your face."

"Just like I see there is no joy in yours. Tell me what happens."

"Do you really want to know?"

"Yes."

He told himself about the first three jumps. How he, Lauren, Ron, Lisa and Danny developed a complex relationship with Pete, Marilyn, Jimmy and Mitch. And Taggit. Couldn't forget him. "Wait, I've got a question," young Charles said.

Old Charles nodded and said, "I know. All of that doesn't seem too bad does it? The good guys won, and the bad guys lost. I married Lauren, Ron and Lisa ran all over the place having the time of their lives and Danny wrote a best-selling book. We stayed close, like family. But we always talked about the family that didn't make it back. That we were lucky. Because in the end, all of the bad guys weren't that bad and the things that happened to us, well, like I said, I just don't sleep that well." He paused for a moment then continued, "And then we had to do it again. All of us."

"What?"

"And this time we weren't so lucky."

"Tell me," young Charles said.

"I will, if I can finish before they get here."

"They?"

"Just listen." And old Charles told him about the second time. Tears were running down his face as he finished with, "And I'll never know what happened to Lisa. But I do know what happened to everyone else, and why. The only thing you want to do is jump. The adventure, the excitement will be your reward.

"But that's not what it will mean to everyone else. Riches beyond measure, infinite power to change the world to their own personal vision, that's what will drive everyone else. It can't be controlled or kept secret. Someone will learn about it and no matter who it is, eventually that other person, the bad one, will find out about it. That one person who will kill everyone without regard to satisfy their own perverse needs."

Old Charles stood up and continued, "Look at me. I created monsters but I'm actually the biggest monster of them all. I have betrayed the world and when I look at my hands I see there's blood on them."

He sat down on the bed and said, "In a minute I want you to call 911 and report that someone is outside of your house. I bet a squad car just happens to be in the area. I'll run, and I won't be caught, at least not by the officer who shows up. I'll be caught down the road by the people who want to control destiny.

"They'll talk to you. Tell them you couldn't sleep and that when you went downstairs for something to eat you saw the person outside trying to get in. You ran upstairs and called from here, so you don't know if he got in or not. They'll check, but not for me, they will just want to make sure I didn't interfere with your experiments.

"Then they will leave and seem to leave you alone. But they will be watching, making sure you are still going to the lab tomorrow, moving closer to your discovery. When it happens, you'll know it and you will be elated. You did it. You finally did it. Then destroy it."

"But now that you've told me _ "

"It still won't be safe. Remember what I told you. You'll be used by someone else and maybe you won't make it back from a jump next time. Remember, there will always be someone who will want to use your invention and will kill to do it."

Old Charles turned and then stopped and picked up the framed photo from the desk. "Mom and Dad…and me," he said. He took a deep breath as he set the picture down and then said, "Oh, I'm wearing a pair of your shoes. Now call 911. After you have talked with everyone and they are gone, look in the study. There's two pairs of boots downstairs and I've left you a note of some things you have to do, and also get ready to do, before and after you destroy your experiment. The after-part timing is crucial, you'll meet them all at just the right time I hope." Then old Charles left.

"Stop, don't move," the man shouted, and Charles did as he was told. Standing in the middle of the field there really wasn't anyplace else to go. He put his hands up and walked toward the group of people that were waiting for him.

Charles held out his hands and as Officer Cesar handcuffed him he was surprised when Jack Barman said, "Do you have to do that?"

"Yes, sir. Sorry, just standard procedure."

"Okay, but don't hurt him, we still can use him," Rachel Sims spoke up.

Charles was surprised, "How's that?" he asked.

"We'll talk when we get back," Barman said. "I have a feeling we can come to some sort of an agreement about things."

They walked him through the field to where he had parked his car. Now there was a small square building next to it. Barman said, "I have to hand it to you, we have no idea where your time machine is and if you hadn't alarmed your past self we still wouldn't know you were here."

Charles shook his head, "I used to sleep hard. Never woke up. What was the difference tonight?"

"You couldn't sleep, or you were hungry or something."

"Of all the nights."

They filed into a small square building and Officer Cesar said, "Let's go."

"On the way back?" Charles asked.

Barman answered, "Yes. By the way, what were you going to do?"

"At first I was just going to destroy all the work, all the notes, everything even remotely connected to time travel. Make me start all over. But then I realized I would just invent it again."

"So, what was the plan then?"

"I was going to kill me."

"I'm surprised," Barman said. "I didn't think you had it in you."

"That's because you don't know me, and you don't have a clue as to what the last week has done to me. You should have asked during our meeting."

"I don't need you to tell me - "

"You also needed to ask about this time machine. Not me, but someone. Do you know where it came from?"

"From the old EXENCO files," Barman replied. "Why?"

"From Steve Weston, right?"

"Yes."

"And you know where he got all of his information from?" Charles asked.

"Of course, you. We know he stole everything from you."

Charles looked down at his watch and asked, "Do you know what time it is?"

"Why?" Sims asked. "We can make it anytime we want."

"Because you control time, don't you?"

She laughed and said, "That's right."

Charles smiled and replied, "Not anymore."

Barman caught something in his voice and asked Charles, "What do you mean?"

"I mean I have become a very suspicious and cautious man because of people like you. And one day I understood that I might be standing inside my own creation watching something being done that I didn't agree with. And that I might have to shut it down. So deep in one of the programs I - "

"Grab him, stop him," Barman shouted.

As everyone rushed toward Charles, he crossed his arms in front his body and closed his eyes. Barman saw that his watch was counting down, and the number had already reached zero.

No one heard Charles say, "Lauren."

CHAPTER NINETEEN
QUE SERÁ, SERÁ

The man at the counter was very well dressed, too well for the neighborhood he was in. The man at the table was reading something and hadn't really noticed, but the woman had. She knew a score when she saw one. She leaned over and said quietly, "Pete, look at this guy drinking coffee. Look at that suit, he has money."

Pete glanced up and said, "Yeah, maybe. What of it?"

"Well, let's get it. We can shake him down as he leaves, and he won't know what hit him. He looks like he's loaded."

Pete looked up again as the man was saying something to Lucy, the old waitress behind the counter. Lucy was laughing and saying, "Now that was funny. Thanks."

Pete shook his head and said, "Let's leave him alone, Marilyn. We got other things to think about."

"What other things do we have to think about other than making money?" she asked. "There's absolutely nothing going on. Especially around here. Even Jimmy doesn't have anything going on."

"Just give it a rest," Pete told her.

Marilyn snorted but as the man stood up she smiled at him when he looked in their direction. He paused and walked over to them, but Marilyn was surprised when he spoke to Pete, "Excuse me, can I bother you for a moment?"

"No, we're busy," Marilyn jumped in. "Take a hike."

The man looked at her and said, "I was talking to him, not you." Then he looked back at Pete and asked, "What book are you looking at?"

As Marilyn stood up and balled her fists, Pete looked at the man for a few seconds then replied, "It's about hotel management."

"That's what I thought," the man said. "I wrote it. I've never actually seen one being read though. Can I sit down and talk to you for a few minutes?"

"No, you can't," Marilyn said angrily. "And in a minute I'm going to - "

"Can she wait outside?"

"What?" Marilyn spluttered.

Pete held up his hand and told Marilyn, "Stop." He thought for a moment then said, "Marilyn, wait outside."

"You can't mean you're going to talk to this clown can you? He's just - "

Pete gave her a look that made her immediately stop talking. "I said, wait outside. I'll call you back in when I need you."

She looked at the man then brushed against him as she stalked outside. She stood by the large plate glass window and kept looking in, waiting for Pete to signal her.

The man sat down and said, "I hope I'm not causing you any trouble with your girlfriend."

"She's not my girlfriend, she's a business associate is all. Now, why am I making her mad?"

As the man reached out a hand he said "First, my name is Charles Dawson."

Pete looked at it for a moment then sat up and as he shook hands he replied, "I'm Pete Reese."

"Pete, I have a question for you. Are you actually interested in hotel management?"

Pete paused again, then slowly he answered, "I do have some interest in it."

"Do you have any experience in it?"

Pete slumped back down and said, "No."

Charles sat back in his chair and said, "Okay. Now I have another question. When you look out the window, other than your extremely mad business associate, what do you see?"

"A run-down neighborhood that's getting worse every day."

"You're right, Pete. Now, what do you see with your heart?"

Pete blinked and looked out the window, back at Charles, and then out the window again. Slowly he answered, "I see a neighborhood that used to be a great place to live. My family lived two blocks from here and I don't remember any bad times until I became a teenager. Then it just went downhill. This place used to be one of our hangouts when I was a kid. Now it's just a dump."

"I see the same thing when I look out there," Charles agreed. "But I see something else, a way to make it a great neighborhood again. You see the building across the street?"

"The Lincoln Hotel? It's nothing but a flophouse. It's called the Stinken Hotel now."

"That's what it is now. But I just bought it, like I'm buying others just like it in neighborhoods just like this one. I'm also going to buy this café and a small movie theatre a block over. I'm going to remodel them and try to take this neighborhood back one building at a time. What do you think of that?"

Pete nodded his head and told Charles, "That would be good."

"I need someone to run the Lincoln for me. Someone like you."

Pete looked surprised and asked, "Don't you have people who can do that? I don't have any experience and I just started reading this book. I can't help you."

"You're right, I do have people who could run this hotel. But none of them will. Too bad of a neighborhood. I need someone who can provide me with ideas, fresh ideas, a list of things that need to be done to make the Lincoln respectable, and has the conviction to get it done. I like what I heard just now. What do you think? Do you have ideas?"

"Yeah, I have ideas, but I don't know how to run anything."

"We can teach you the basics, all you need to know. But there will be a lot of learning as you go, and it might be tough. You would need help."

"Marilyn would help."

Charles shook his head and said, "I don't know. She seems pretty volatile. You need someone who will do what you ask and do the right thing. I can't have this falling apart."

"She can do it."

"Call her back in."

Marilyn stormed in and as she sat down, Charles said, "Tell her."

"Tell me what?" she asked angrily.

"This man, Charles, is going to fix up the Lincoln across the street. He wants me to help him."

"What a - "

"Stop," Pete commanded. "What's the first thing you would suggest that needs to be done?"

"This is total - "

"Marilyn, you're smart. That's why we run together and why I thought of you for this. So be smart. Tell me, right now, what would you do?"

Marilyn smiled at Pete and asked, "Really?" Then she looked at Charles and told him, "You need to replace every ground level door and window with whatever will keep the wino's out. Make the lobby look nice to begin with then start on the top floor and work your way down. That way you can start booking some rooms and when the people walk out the front door they aren't walking through a bunch of trash and dead people."

Charles smiled and said, "Thanks Marilyn." Then he asked, "Is there anything I need to know about either one of you that will keep you from taking this job?"

"We've both been arrested," Pete admitted.

"Paid your dues?"

"Yes."

"Anything else?"

"No."

"Drugs?"

"Not really," Marilyn answered. "I mean a few here and there."

Charles looked at her for a moment and said, "What you mean is you used to use drugs, but you just gave them up."

Marilyn opened her mouth then closed it. She looked at Pete who was just starting to look through her, so she quickly said, "Yes, I just gave them up."

"Okay," Charles said. "But I do need to make something clear. I like what I've heard, but I've never been accused of being able to read people. I make mistakes just like anyone else and this deal in this café will cause a lot of people to question my sanity. You'll be handling money. You'll be in a position to take advantage of things if that is what you do. You'll have free time to do things you used to do. And then I'll probably get a call from Sharon Jenson, my Security Chief, and I don't want that."

As he handed them both a card he told them, "I'm going to put you in touch with my business director, Ben Weston. He probably won't like you at first, you're a little rough around the edges so to speak, but if you're honest with him you won't find anyone better to work for. He'll make sure you get all the training and backing you need. What do you say? Need to think on it?"

"No," they both said at once. "And you won't regret this," Pete added.

She was standing on the sidewalk in the rain, crying again, when the stranger came up and asked, "Do you know which one of these buildings is Terrace View." As she looked up to answer he continued, "I am so sorry. I didn't realize you were upset, I'll ask someone else."

As he turned to walk away she said, "It's okay. It's this building right here. Same one I live in, same as my ex-boyfriend."

"I am sorry to hear that," the man said, "but if I could bother you for one more second, do you know a Lisa Wells? She lives in this building."

"Well, that's me," Lisa said. "What do you want with me?"

"This is great. I'm Charles Dawson and Professor Welton told me you are the smartest person he has ever met."

"Yeah, so smart I don't know who to date or when to come in out of the rain."

"It is raining, isn't it?" Charles said. "Is that coffee shop across the street a good place to talk?"

"Yes," Lisa told him, and they quickly walked to it and sat in a booth. After she dried her hair with a napkin, Lisa asked, "Why do you want to talk to me?"

"I want to offer you a job, temporary to begin with, but possibly full time if you work out."

"What would I be doing? What do you do?"

"I own a multi-national conglomerate company that - "

"Of course, Dawson Enterprise. I thought I recognized you but why would you be in front of my apartment building? I like your diversification and - " she suddenly went red and stopped talking.

"What's wrong?"

"I...I was sounding too smart. I don't want you to think I'm a know it all. I'm sorry."

Charles leaned back and told her, "Lisa, I am surrounded by smart people. Men *and* women. I make it a point to hire the smartest people I can find. I think you would fit in with any group of people I asked you to meet after you accept a few things."

"What?"

"That you are smart, that you want to be smart, and you want to be accepted for being smart. And you won't listen to anyone who thinks you are *too* smart. In my business there is no such thing."

"I could try, I mean yes, sir."

"I'm Charles."

"Okay, Charles. What is it you would like me to do?"

"What do you know about dinosaurs?"

"I'm sorry, not much at all."

"If I give you a list of some books, could you learn a little something?"

"Of course."

"Great. I am meeting a well-known paleontologist, and his equally well-known paleontologist daughter, in a few days to discuss giving them a grant for a dig. I have had an interest in paleontology for quite some time, so I can talk the talk. But, I need someone who can understand some of what they are talking about and all about what they are spending. I know you are good with figures but if you can get up to speed with some dinosaur information, that will help. What do you think?"

Lisa smiled and said, "This sounds exciting, I'd love to help. What are the names of your paleontologists?"

"Ron and Lauren Fontana. Here is a list of their books and some others on paleontology that I have found quite interesting. Do what you can with them, we leave for New Mexico in three days. We'll be there at least a week meeting them and going to the dig site, so I can get a feel for things, or rather, so we can get a feel for things. I will want all the input you can give me." Charles paused and asked, "What's wrong? Can't get away from another job?"

"No, well, I mean I work part time at a nail salon, but I didn't realize we would be going someplace else and you know, spending the night."

Charles paused for a second then told her, "You don't know me, so I can understand any concern you might have about this sudden offer which includes sleeping arrangements. Let me tell you what I have planned. You and I will fly first class to New Mexico where hopefully we will be picked up and taken to our separate rooms. I have booked two rooms in what I have been told is an excellent hotel on the campus of Buckland University.

"We will attend a lot of meetings which will require us to look nice, listen attentively and probably eat some tasteless food at a diner or two. At the end of each day I will want you to tell me exactly what you think and why you think it. You will also need to write up reports that I can send to my board members.

"We will also need to dress down for the field and sleep in separate tents for at least one night and maybe more. I don't know if you like the outdoors but I'm sure there will be bugs of every description and a lot of sun.

"At no time will I hit on you or try and get you into my bed. I can only give you my word on that and tell you that you may carry a firearm with you at all times if you think it is necessary."

Lisa smiled and apologized, "I'm sorry. I didn't mean to imply that you are a bad man. It's just that I've - "

"You've had some problems with men who took advantage of you."

"Yes."

"Maybe one that made you cry recently?"

"Maybe."

"Is there anything else I need to know?"

"Well, I don't have very many nice things to wear. Can you give me an idea of what I need to buy, and I hate to ask, but can I get an advance on my salary?"

Charles took out his phone and as he sent a text he said, "You will need business casual clothing, but very nice." He wrote an address on the list of books he had given her and said, "You now have a thousand dollars of credit at this store. Tell them who you are, and they will provide you with everything you need. Is there anything else?"

"No, sir. Well, maybe, how much will I be making?"

"I am paying you $500 a day for your work. I hope that is satisfactory."

"But that's 3,500 dollars for the week. That's 182,000 dollars a year. It would take me over seven years to earn that much."

"Then you are seriously underpaid," Charles said. "I'll have a car waiting for you outside your building at 9am Friday morning. Does that work for you?"

"Yes, sir."

"Charles."

As they found their seats on the plane, Charles nodded and told Lisa, "I'm impressed, I can't believe you read all the books I suggested plus you found out all that extra information on the Fontanas. Did you find any of it interesting or was it just an assignment?"

"At first it was just reading but then I actually found it interesting. Not only the careers of the Fontanas but also paleontology in general. I'm not sure I could lay in the hot sun for hours brushing sand and dirt away from a fossil, but the results are fantastic. I also went over to the museum and checked out their dinosaur exhibit. They were much bigger than I imagined. I mean I expected big, but they were huge. I'm glad I never saw one."

"I'm glad you're taking an active interest in this," Charles told her. "Hold on for one second, I promised someone I would call them about now." He quickly made the call and said, "Good morning Major Donald, how is the camp? That's great, did you get the help I suggested? Are they working out like we hoped they would? Great. How about your people? Everything sounds great, I look forward to meeting with you sometime next week and we'll see about planning a schedule for the rest of the year. Well, you are welcome, but it was your idea. Thanks, and goodbye."

He looked at Lisa and told her, "I met Major Donald a couple of months ago at a retreat. She had recently retired and hadn't found a job she was really interested in, but she did have an idea. She wanted to build a campground that would focus on empowering women. There would be hiking, camping, zip lines, rock climbing, an obstacle course and well, a lot of other interesting things.

"She was wanting to work out a business deal with me and I just laughed and funded her for three years. She didn't realize I wasn't a business man."

"What do you see yourself as?" Lisa asked.

"A philanthropist, but one who will push you to do your best and expect nothing less."

"I better stay on my toes then."

"You're doing just fine. No, better than fine, you went way past that. Remember how smart you are and don't be afraid to show it." He paused for a second then added, "And be yourself."

"There they are," Danny said as he stopped the car near a sign that read Science Hall. Charles and Lisa got out of the car and the man walking toward them started smiling and said, "Mr. Dawson, how good it is to meet you."

"Please, I'm Charles and this is Lisa, my Executive Assistant. I have to tell you I have been looking forward to this meeting since you started corresponding with me. Well, you and Lauren of course."

"Of course, of course," Ron replied as he shook hands with Charles. "And this is my daughter, Lauren."

Charles shook her hand and said, "Hello," and Lauren nodded and quietly said "Hello."

As Ron shook Lisa's hand she exclaimed, "What an honor it is to meet you. I have read all of your work and you have gotten me very interested in fossils and dinosaurs."

Ron smiled again and said, "You know Lauren called me an old fossil and a dinosaur just this morning."

Lisa laughed and told him, "You are funny. I bet you are nothing but trouble."

Ron took her arm and replied, "You don't know how much. Come on in out of the heat and let me show you around the paleontology department."

Charles turned to Lauren and shrugged his shoulders as he said, "Sorry, I'm not that much fun."

"Is that what an Executive Assistant is for?" Lauren asked.

"Just a bonus," Charles replied. "I know thousands of people, and Lisa is the smartest person I have ever met. She knew nothing about paleontology three days ago and now she sounds like an encyclopedia. We talked about all kinds of fossils and dinosaurs on the flight."

"Do you like paleontology too?"

"Yes and, oh, just a minute." Charles turned back to Danny and asked, "Danny, would you like to go to lunch with us? I found what you were saying about your writing class very interesting."

"Uh, well, sure, I guess so."

"Great. Lauren, is there a dining hall here at Buckland or a restaurant close by we could all go to for lunch?"

"Sure, there's a nice little pizza place about a mile from here that we like."

"Sound good, Danny?"

"I'll drive and pick everyone up about noon."

"See you then," Charles said. Then he turned to Lauren and asked, "Do I get a tour of the paleontology department too?"

Lauren smiled and said, "Yes, but I don't think it will be as much fun as Dad's tour."

"This is very good pizza," Charles said.

"We like it," Lauren said. "At least usually. Dad why are you eating a salad?"

"You know I've been watching my weight recently."

"How recently?"

"Oh, about the last two hours."

Lauren shook her head and said, "Oh, brother."

"Not to change the subject," Charles started, "but tell me again about your book, Danny."

"You wrote a book?" Lauren asked.

"No, no, well, not yet. I'm just taking a writing class - "

"His second writing class," Lisa corrected.

"Yes, my second writing class and I'm…you know, I read a lot and these classes have started me thinking that I could write a book. That's all."

"What would it be about?" Lauren asked. "Police work?"

"Maybe, but I was hoping to write about something different. I don't know what yet."

"Well if it would help," Charles said, "I have an idea or two about a dinosaur time travel suspense type of book. I just don't have time to write anything but if you are interested I can send you my outline."

"But I don't really know anything about dinosaurs."

Charles pointed at Ron and Lauren and said, "But you know people who do."

Danny smiled and replied, "That is an idea. Sure, send me what you have and maybe we can write a book together. I'm taking a few days off and I'll put some thought into it"

"*You* are taking a vacation?" Ron asked.

"Okay, who are you and what did you do with the real Danny?" Lauren asked.

"I know, I don't usually take a real vacation," Danny said, "but the Chief would like to see me actually take some time off. Says I need it."

"Going anywhere?" Charles asked.

"When I take time off I like to fish and there are a lot of places around here to go for largemouth bass or pike."

"Ever go deep sea fishing?"

"No, it does look interesting though."

"You could catch a sea bass instead, or other interesting fish. When is your vacation?"

"Anytime I want it."

"Well, let me do this for you. Fly to Jacksonville and stay at my house. It's huge, lots of room. I can line you up with a deep-sea fishing charter and you'll have a great time."

"Well, I don't know. I - "

"Danny," Lisa interrupted, "Charles likes to do things for interesting people who do interesting things. Let him do this for you."

"I...well, okay."

"In fact," Lisa continued, "why don't both of you come out too after our field trip?"

"What a splendid idea," Ron immediately said.

"Well I don't know," Lauren said. "I don't know if I can get away."

"I understand," Charles told her. "In fact, Danny, that does remind me that I won't be at the house for a couple of days, I'll still be here. But just make yourself at home when you get there. I'll let Aria, she's my housekeeper, know that you'll be staying."

"That's great. I really appreciate this."

"Write us a good book and I'll appreciate that," Charles said.

"Uh-oh, writer's block," Danny laughed, and everyone laughed with him.

"What do you see when you look out there?" Charles asked Lauren.

"The setting sun, the land, a few clouds."

"Okay, I get that. But don't use your eyes, what does your heart see?"

Lauren squinted her eyes at Charles and then looked out again. "Okay, what I really see is a thick jungle with towering trees under a clear blue sky. It's a hot day, even hotter than it is now, and there are all types of animals out there. Most I recognize but some I don't, and I want to go and look at them close up, to touch them to know what they are like. To not have to guess. But that's only for an instant and then I'm happy just digging up their bones."

"I like that," Charles told her as they started walking into a deep ravine. "I may have Danny put that in his book."

Lauren looked up and Charles asked, "What is it?"

"Looks like a trackway," Lauren replied excitedly. She jumped up on a rock and as she pushed up on her tiptoes the rock moved, and Charles reached up quickly and put his hands on her waist to steady her. She turned to say something but instead she smiled and just relaxed as he held her there. After a few seconds she said, "It is a trackway. There are all types of tracks in it, we need to get back and tell Dad."

As they got closer to the camp they could hear Lisa and Ron laughing then Ron asking, "You do what?"

Lauren turned to Charles and said, "By the way, I took care of the business I had to finish, so I can come to Jacksonville with Dad if that's okay."

"That's fantastic," Charles told her.

"Good afternoon, sir, how can I help you?"

The man who had just walked into his office quickly shook his hand then sat down and said, "Mr. Young, you were expecting me I hope."

"Yes, sir."

"Please, it's Charles, and everything we say here is to be kept strictly confidential."

"Yes…Charles."

As Charles opened a briefcase he asked, "Mr. Young, I heard you like to read a lot of science fiction, is that right?"

Mr. Young nodded and said, "I do read a lot of science fiction. How did -"

"Ever write any of your own?"

"No, no. I'm not a writer."

"You also are a bird watcher and, what would I say…a part time ornithologist?"

"Yes, I am. I belong to…but how did -"

"Here, I brought you a present," Charles interrupted. As he set a two-inch thick, by one foot by two feet flat metal container on Mr. Young's desk, he continued, "Please, open it up."

Mr. Young did so then he paused and asked, "What do you have here? Are these birds stuffed?"

Charles shook his head and said, "No, they are not stuffed. In fact, I found their bodies just this morning. They were alive just a few hours ago."

Mr. Young looked up slowly with a puzzled look on his face and asked, "Why would you think I would be interested in these two dead birds?"

"Because in a few minutes you're going to take a closer look at them. And then you'll realize you need to have a detailed examination of them."

"What are they?"

"The light grey one with the dark grey wings that have black spots is a pigeon. Those bronze feathers on its neck are beautiful aren't they?"

"Well, yes they are, but a pigeon, I mean -"

"And the other one is obviously a parakeet. It's also beautifully colored, I mean look at how the red-orange face and yellow neck really contrast with the green body. Just fantastic."

"Yes, I agree it is a beautiful bird, but I have several parakeets at home and I -"

Charles leaned in close and whispered, "Not like this one you don't. Go home and check your books, all your bird books. And when you figure out why this pigeon and this parakeet are so special, think about your science fiction books.

"At first you won't believe what you are thinking but then you'll realize you have to. Nothing else will explain things. And then you'll know why I chose to speak with you, Mr. Young. A man with a passion for birds and science fiction and who works in a department of the United States Government that knows how to keep secrets."

Charles stood up and continued, "And this must be kept secret. Only you, and the very few people you have to tell, can ever know about this. If this information passes past a certain point of, let's say secretiveness, I can guarantee you an immediate prison sentence without due process."

As Mr. Young started to protest, Charles held up a hand and said, "Next, you will make sure this container is kept in a refrigerated area from now on and that it will only be looked at again under certain specific, and highly unlikely circumstances. In an envelope in the lid of the container is an explanation of those highly unlikely circumstances. Then make sure I am never contacted reference this item *unless* those highly unlikely circumstances occur."

Charles looked at Mr. Young for several seconds then asked, "Is there anything I have just said that you do not understand?"

Mr. Young blinked his eyes a couple of times and replied, "Well, yes, just about everything. But I will…" he trailed off as he looked at the pigeon again and then his head snapped up. "Is this a Passenger -"

Charles put a finger to his lips and then smiled as he said, "And Carolina was beautiful this morning. Thank you, Mr. Young," then he turned and walked out.

Charles sat in his bedroom and listened to the sound of voices and laughter coming from downstairs. For the millionth time it seemed he opened the packet of yellowing paper and took out his, well…*his*, notes. He crossed off the last item and as he stood up to go downstairs to his friends he picked up the picture by the door and said, "Charles, I started meeting these people when you said I should. I have done almost everything you asked. I hope everything turns out the way you hoped it would. Que será, será."

THE END

CHECK OUT OTHER GREAT DINOSAUR BOOKS

PRIMORDIA
by **Greig Beck**

Ben Cartwright, former soldier, home to mourn the loss of his father stumbles upon cryptic letters from the past between the author, Arthur Conan Doyle and his great, great grandfather who vanished while exploring the Amazon jungle in 1908.

Amazingly, these letters lead Ben to believe that his ancestor's expedition was the basis for Doyle's fantastical tale of a lost world inhabited by long extinct creatures. As Ben digs some more he finds clues to the whereabouts of a lost notebook that might contain a map to a place that is home to creatures that would rewrite everything known about history, biology and evolution.

But other parties now know about the notebook, and will do anything to obtain it. For Ben and his friends, it becomes a race against time and against ruthless rivals.

In the remotest corners of Venezuela, along winding river trails known only to lost tribes, and through near impenetrable jungle, Ben and his novice team find a forbidden place more terrifying and dangerous than anything they could ever have imagined.

PANGAEA EXILES
by **Jeff Brackett**

Tried and convicted for his crimes, Sean Barrow is sent into temporal exile—banished to a time so far before recorded history that there is no chance that he, or any other criminal sent back, has any chance of altering history.

Now Sean must find a way to survive more than 200 million years in the past, in a world populated by monstrous creatures that would rend him limb from limb if they got the chance. And that's just his fellow prisoners.

The dinosaurs are almost as bad.

CHECK OUT OTHER GREAT DINOSAUR BOOKS

FLIPSIDE
by JAKE BIBLE

The year is 2046 and dinosaurs are real.

Time bubbles across the world, many as large as one hundred square miles, turn like clockwork, revealing prehistoric landscapes from the Cretaceous Period.

They reveal the Flipside.

Now, thirty years after the first Turn, the clockwork is breaking down as one of the world's powers has decided to exploit the phenomenon for their own gain, possibly destroying everything then and now in the process.

A MAN OUT OF TIME
by Christopher Laflan

Five years after the Chinese Axis detonated an unknown weapon of mass destruction off the southern coast of the United States, Special Ops Sergeant John Crider and the members of Shadow Company have finally captured what they all hope will lead to the end of the war. Unfortunately, the population within the United States is no longer sustainable. In an effort to stabilize the economy, the government enacts the Cryonics Act. One hundred years in suspended animation, all debt forgiven, and a chance at a less crowded future are too good to pass up for John and his young daughter.

Except not everything always goes as planned as Sergeant John Crider finds himself pitted against a land of prehistoric monsters genetically resurrected from the fossil record, murderous inhabitants, and a future he never wanted.

CHECK OUT OTHER GREAT DINOSAUR BOOKS

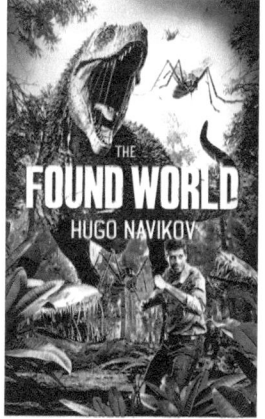

THE FOUND WORLD
by Hugo Navikov

A powerful global cabal wants adventurer Brett Russell to retrieve a superweapon stolen by the scientist who built it. To entice him to travel underneath one of the most dangerous volcanoes on Earth to find the scientist, this shadowy organization will pay him the only thing he cares about: information that will allow him to avenge his family's murder.

But before he can get paid, he and his team must enter an underground hellscape of killer plants, giant insects, terrifying dinosaurs, and an army of other predators never previously seen by man.

At the end of this journey awaits a revelation that could alter the fate of mankind ... if they can make it back from this horrifying found world.

HOUSE OF THE GODS
by Davide Mana

High above the steamy jungle of the Amazon basin, rise the flat plateaus known as the Tepui, the House of the Gods. Lost worlds of unknown beauty, a naturalistic wonder, each an ecology onto itself, shunned by the local tribes for centuries. The House of the Gods was not made for men.

But now, the crew and passengers of a small charter plane are about to find what was hidden for sixty million years.

Lost on an island in the clouds 10.000 feet above the jungle, surrounded by dinosaurs, hunted by mysterious mercenaries, the survivors of Sligo Air flight 001 will quickly learn the only rule of life on Earth: Extinction.

www.ingramcontent.com/pod-product-compliance
Lightning Source LLC
Chambersburg PA
CBHW022033240626
47154CB00007B/2390